FADE

**Center Point
Large Print**

**This Large Print Book carries the
Seal of Approval of N.A.V.H.**

FADE

KYLE MILLS

CENTER POINT PUBLISHING
THORNDIKE, MAINE

This Center Point Large Print edition
is published in the year 2005 by arrangement with
St. Martin's Press.

Copyright © 2005 by Kyle Mills.

All rights reserved.

The text of this Large Print edition is unabridged. In other
aspects, this book may vary from the original edition. Printed in
Thailand. Set in 16-point Times New Roman type.

ISBN 1-58547-675-7

Library of Congress Cataloging-in-Publication Data

Mills, Kyle, 1966-
    Fade / Kyle Mills.--Center Point large print ed.
        p. cm.
    ISBN 1-58547-675-7 (lib. bdg. : alk. paper)
    1. Undercover operations--Fiction. 2. Intelligence officers--Fiction. 3. Fugitives from
justice--Fiction. 4. Terrorism--Prevention--Fiction. 5. Wounds and injuries--Patients--Fiction.
6. Male friendship--Fiction. 7. Middle East--Fiction. 8. Large type books. I. Title.

PS3563.I42322F33 2005b
813'.54--dc22

                                                            2005014227

PROLOGUE

The few people visible in the street seemed to have no purpose other than to kick up dust that then hung in the air like smoke. They had no bags of groceries, no hangers draped with recently cleaned clothing, no impulsively purchased toys for their kids. They weren't exchanging gossip with friends or gazing into the village's nonexistent windows for interesting diversions. The overall impression was of rats temporarily flushed into the open and anxious to return to a dark, cramped space where the illusion of safety could conjure.

Salam al Fayed skirted along a broken rock wall, stopping before he reached a section that had been scattered by a mortar shell to squat down in the shade. The sun in that part of the world was strangely malignant. Unable to provide warmth in the thin, dry air, it just burned and sapped the strength of everything beneath it. Al Fayed pulled a goatskin water bladder from beneath his robes and watched the people in the street adjust their trajectory to give him as wide a berth as possible. They would see him as just another of the countless dangerous men who roamed the region promoting instability, starvation, and senseless violence. In a way, they were right.

He stared malevolently at anyone who didn't actively look away, dark eyes partially obscured by a tattered headdress. His Arabic was excellent, but it would instantly identify him as a foreigner if he were forced to open his mouth. Whether anyone would correctly place the accent as being from New York was hard to say. Best not to find out.

The water tasted of animal musk and mud, stinging his cracked lips and setting him to calculating exactly what he'd be willing to pay for some cherry-flavored SPF 30 Chapstick. And a shower. And a drink with ice in it. He managed to stop a thin smile from spreading far enough to start his lips bleeding again. At twenty-six, he was already getting downright delicate.

A rare combination of perfect weather, overly pessimistic intelligence, and sterling luck had allowed him to add four more corpses to the thousands already littering the countryside two hours ahead of schedule. Unfortunately, the Middle East was a bit short on Starbucks—a situation the U.S. was no doubt eager to remedy—so he couldn't go wash off the blood in a tidy little bathroom and then linger over a toffee nut latte. That left him nothing to do but squat there silently threatening the locals and picking goat hairs from his teeth.

JOIN THE NAVY, the recruiting poster had said. SEE THE WORLD. He'd thought they meant Hawaii.

A long semiretirement on a quiet island was starting to look better and better. Despite this operation going off perfectly, he'd felt something strange the minute his feet had hit the sand. Predictably, it was quickly lost in the unwavering focus his profession demanded, but now he had a few minutes to examine it. Doubt.

The truth was, this mission had the unmistakable feel of one too many. His luck had peaked and was now in the process of running out.

Or maybe that quiet sense of dread was just nature's way of gently hinting that he was moving into a stage of his life in which he wouldn't be quite as fast or strong as he once was. Perhaps it was a million-year-old survival reflex, speaking to him in a language his modern mind could understand. Or maybe it was simpler than that. Maybe it was just the hopelessness and futility of it all.

When he'd first started operating in the Middle East—four long years ago now—he'd been full of idealism. While his methods weren't exactly the most enlightened humanity had at its disposal, he'd thought he was making a difference. He could remember actually letting the words "make the world a better place" drool from his mouth, though he'd never admit it now.

The truth, it turned out, was a bit darker than his youthful fantasy. He was now fairly certain that he killed men for the sole purpose of making a bunch of master's degree–wielding men in Washington feel like they were doing something. Or worse, to allow them to wrap their soft, pale bodies in the lie that they were the courageous warriors their inflated egos told them they were.

Al Fayed was no longer naïve enough to believe that America was any safer because of the four men he'd left blackening beneath the powerful North African sun. They would have already been replaced. And one day their sons would rise up with revenge and hatred in their hearts to lead the fight against the country that had taken their fathers away from them.

It was clear to him now that the problems that plagued the world, and that were so glaring in this part of it, were ingrained to the point that there was really no solution—only pointless attempts to delay the inevitable. At the dawn of the twenty-first century, people were no different than they had been thousands of years ago, when humanity had been a twitchy and mean-spirited species barely enlightened enough to be trusted with swords and spears. How did anyone fool themselves into thinking that stability could be maintained in a time when individuals had the power to, in minutes, destroy what it took centuries to build?

Al Fayed took another sip of water and looked around him at the broken buildings lined up in front of him. Despite being built of hardened mud and stone, they had a strange aura of impermanence. Desperately inadequate bulwarks against the chaos that swirled around them. Whether they'd succumb to America's brilliant new bombs, a sudden flair of factional fighting, or just to decay and despair, was hard to predict. The only thing that was certain was that one day they would succumb.

The more time he spent in the Middle East, the more certain he became that the region was irreparably broken. How could these people learn to anchor themselves in a modern world never dreamed of by the ancient prophet they believed so deeply in? It was a psychological and moral conflict that left the people here both desiring and shunning the things progress could bring them.

In fairness, many Westerners really did want to help. They saw their culture as measurably superior—wealthier, less violent, healthier. They thought that if they could just persuade these barbarians to stop fighting and relax a little they, too, could be watching *Sex and the City* reruns on a big-screen TV and taking their kids to soccer practice in a brand-new sport utility vehicle. But it wasn't that simple.

Empathy, it turned out, was the only weapon worth wielding here and the only one the Americans simply didn't have the know-how to build. If you couldn't understand your enemy—if you couldn't get into their heads—you would never defeat them. Sending clueless general after clueless general to try to control situations and people they couldn't even talk to was absurd. Trying to solve Arab problems with American solutions had a long and illustrious history of failure that no one seemed to pay any attention to. And so the machine, no matter how broken, ground on.

Al Fayed leaned his head against the cool wall behind him and stared up at the uniform blue of the sky. For a man whose education had ended with a whimper in the twelfth grade, he was becoming quite the political philosopher. Not exactly a useful skill for someone with his vocation.

He tried to just let his mind go blank and when that failed he tried to tell himself a joke. Under the circumstances, though, he couldn't come up with one funny enough to do the job. Better to just move on and ponder a cushy job in security consulting. *Magnum, P.I.* seemed to make out like a bandit.

He pushed himself to his feet and started up the dirt road again but then ducked behind a burned-out half-track when he heard a high-pitched scream shake the air. He put a hand on the machine gun beneath his robe and looked back out into the suddenly empty street.

A few seconds later it came again, lasting long enough for him to identify its source as a young girl and to hypothesize that she was in an alley that started about fifty feet from where he was standing.

His planned route would take him right by that alley and he looked around him again, trying to find an alternate path to the other side of the village. What he didn't need was to get involved in some petty street violence and blow what had been, to this point, a dream mission. He'd been in the country for three days, killed four men, and covered sixty miles on foot without so much as a broken nail—a situation he wasn't looking to change.

He eased around the half-track and jogged twenty feet along the silent road, his eyes sweeping shadowy corners and rooftops as he turned left into a narrow pathway between two buildings. The third scream, combined with the fact that the passageway he found himself in was a little tight and blind to be strategic, stopped him. He was certain now that it was coming from a young girl. An odd acoustic trick made her voice clearly audible, pleading for help before suddenly going silent again.

Al Fayed looked behind him, cursing quietly in Arabic and trying to decide what to do. Continue down this cramped deathtrap or back toward something that had the clear potential to badly disrupt his plan of afternoon surfing and umbrella drinks.

He stood there for a few more seconds before turning around and running back onto the main street. As he approached the alleyway, he could hear voices of two men, sounding strangely distant as they bounced off the stone walls around them. Subtly repositioning his gun barrel to aim right, he continued to approach the alley.

The black scarf that should have covered the girl's face had been partially torn off, making it possible to estimate her age at around sixteen or seventeen. She was on her back in the thick dust, kicking and punching violently at the two men trying to hold her. One had a knee on her chest, making it more of a challenge for his compatriot to tear off the robe that covered her from neck to toe. The entire operation was a bit disorganized, but overwhelming force was on the men's side. With the aid of a knife, one of them exposed the girl's street clothes: a dirty T-shirt and the remnants of a gray wool skirt. By the time al Fayed realized that he was stopped in the middle of the street staring at them, the man on top had removed his knee from the girl's chest and was using it to pry her legs apart.

She managed to free a hand and was about to claw out at one of her attackers, but lost her focus when she spotted al Fayed standing in the mouth of the alley. She began pleading, fighting to maintain eye contact with the only hope she had.

Try as he might, a good joke still eluded him.

One of the men looked back and shouted at him to leave. When al Fayed remained frozen, the man just laughed and went back to the squirming child beneath him.

There was no reason to get involved in this. It was the reality of this particular girl's universe. Her parents were probably dead—victims of the violence that had swallowed this area long ago—leaving her to fend for herself. It was a precarious position that demanded a bit more caution than she had apparently shown.

Al Fayed had never been able to take religion all that seriously. The truth that he couldn't seem to let go of was that a person's God was nothing more than a function of their address. If you were born in North Carolina, you were absolutely certain that the Baptists were the only people on a first-name basis with God. In Afghanistan, you would sacrifice your life without a thought to defend Mohammed's vision. Thailand? Buddha was your man. There was just too much random chance involved for him to see any real mysticism in it.

Evolution, though . . . Now there was a philosophy that he could get behind. From what he'd been unfortunate enough to see, the fit survived and the meek weren't going to inherit shit. This girl had been stupid to let herself get pulled into that dirty little alley. The men he'd killed the day before hadn't been smart or strong enough to effectively defend themselves. And on a larger scale, North America thrived while much of the Middle East didn't. Life had a simple and oddly comforting symmetry once you exorcised all the mysterious deities.

The man temporarily gave up on the girl's skirt and was now holding her wrists above her head. With control reasserted, he looked up at al Fayed again. "What are you doing there?" he yelled in Arabic. "Go!"

It was good advice. This girl had no future. It wasn't anybody's fault and it wasn't worth crying or agonizing over. She was just born in the wrong place at the wrong time. Whether her life ended today or tomorrow or next week didn't matter. Not to him. Not to anyone.

"Go!" the man shouted again, offering the girl's wrists to his companion and standing. "Get out of here, now!"

The girl was getting tired and her pleas were coming between gasps as she continued to try to escape. Three more minutes and she wouldn't even be able to offer token resistance to whatever these men wanted to do to her. Which was probably a lot.

The face of the approaching man was almost invisible, covered by a thick beard that grew up his cheeks almost to his eyes. He continued to shout as he slipped a hand behind his back to retrieve what was

13

undoubtedly some kind of weapon.

Al Fayed took a step forward, putting a hand on the man's elbow and pinning his arm long enough to retrieve his own knife and shove it through the man's beard and into his throat.

Surprise was the only thing that registered on his face as his eyes angled downward to watch the knife slide back out and blood fan across his chest. Then a brief moment of confusion before he crumpled to the ground.

The girl's tired grunts turned into a piercing scream, tipping off the man holding her that al Fayed was running up behind. He was faster than he looked and managed to roll to the side and retrieve an archaic but undoubtedly effective pistol from his waistband.

Al Fayed threw his knife as he closed the distance between them, hoping to distract the man's aim. To his surprise—and in keeping with his stellar luck on this mission—it stuck in his chest. Not deep enough to seriously injure him, but plenty deep to cause the bullet that should have hit its target instead to smash into a building across the street.

The man was still on his knees when they collided and al Fayed jerked right as they fell to the ground, closing his eyes against the burn of gunpowder as a bullet screamed past his left temple. He ignored the flash of pain and the ringing in his ear, covering the man's face with his hand and shoving his head back into the unfortunately soft dirt. His own gun was trapped between them, so he was forced to begin the surprisingly difficult process of working the knife out of the man's breastbone.

It was almost free when an intense ache in his lower back suddenly robbed him of most of his strength. He fell to the left, throwing his body weight into one final yank. The knife came out with a wet crunching sound and al Fayed swung it behind him in a clumsy, blind arc. He caught the young girl across the throat, missing the critical arteries but creating a gash deep enough to make her drop the bloody shiv that she'd stuck him with in order to clamp her small hands over her own wound.

They hit the ground simultaneously and al Fayed used his momentum to roll onto his hands and knees. When he tried to stand, though, his body wouldn't do what it was told. He turned his head slowly toward the girl, watching her choke violently, spewing thick fountains of blood from her mouth that then fell back into her face. The entire scene had the feel of an out-of-focus and slightly overexposed movie.

He heard movement behind him and managed to crane his neck far enough to see the man rise unsteadily to his feet and aim his gun. The flash was surprisingly dim and was followed by an impact to al Fayed's back that was sufficient to cause him to collapse face-first into the dirt.

The girl was motionless now. Not dead but watching the sky, waiting for it to come. Strangely, the smile that stretched his chapped lips hurt more than anything else. He'd obviously been a little smug in assuming that the girl was so unfit. It had all been a setup—designed to draw him into the alley so that they could take what he had and use it to survive another few days. It had been stupid to allow himself to be lured so easily, and stupidity was not rewarded in this part of the world.

Charles Darwin would not be cheated.

1

"Roy Buckner."

"No."

Hillel Strand looked over the file in his hands as the distance between his eyebrows and the tops of his reading glasses increased. "Jesus Christ, Matt. What now? The man's former Army Delta with multiple successful missions in hostile territory. He has a reasonably clean service record. . . ."

"I know all about Roy," Matt Egan said. "We're looking for scalpels and this guy's a sledgehammer. A violent, arrogant, redneck sledgehammer."

"At this rate our team's going to consist of you and the secretarial pool, Matt. Is it possible that your standards are a bit high? These guys are Special Forces. I think we can expect them to be arrogant and a little violent."

"To a point," Egan agreed. "But Roy has a real problem with overestimating his abilities—which I'll admit are considerable—and he's a little too enamored with killing. A story about Roy: He was on a joint mission in Syria a few years back with a SEAL I worked with—the best operator I've ever known. Roy spent the entire mission grandstanding, trying to prove he was the best man, and damn near brought the entire thing down around their ears. He doesn't know it, but that SEAL was within about three seconds of putting a bullet in his back. And if he had, I'd have supported that decision."

Strand tossed the file onto his growing "maybe" stack and began digging through the ones they hadn't reviewed yet, finally pulling one from near the bottom.

"Your SEAL," he said, opening the manila folder. "Salam al Fayed. I assume there's no discussion necessary? We want him, right?"

Egan sighed quietly and leaned back in his chair, gazing at the photograph clipped to the file in Strand's hand. It had been a long time since he'd looked at that face. But nowhere near long enough.

Homeland Security had finally stabilized its organizational structure and Egan had been brought in to help create a division that would be involved in the more tangible side of ensuring the safety of America's citizens. The exact mission of the euphemistically named Office of Strategic Planning and Acquisition was still a bit hazy, but the bottom line was that the government was moving to what politicians politely called "a more surgical approach."

Apparently, they'd finally come to the rather

obvious conclusion that the U.S. couldn't go to war with every country that hated it or was starting a nuclear weapons program, and this was their solution.

Matt Egan had been recommended for the job as Hillel Strand's number two at OSPA and during his interview, Darren Crenshaw, the new director of Homeland Security, had described the program as being based on a Mossad-type model. Egan had assumed that his response to that characterization—essentially, "Yeah, and look how well it's worked out for the Israelis"—would quickly end his candidacy. It turned out that the opposite was true. General Crenshaw was looking for someone to be a voice of reason in what was becoming an increasingly paranoid and reactionary choir.

"I think it would be best if we stayed away from al Fayed."

Not surprisingly, Strand slammed the file down on his desk. "What are we getting paid for here, Matt? I'll tell you: To form a team that can get things done. Not to shitcan every possible candidate." He pointed to the folders stacked on his desk. "These are the men we have available. We need at least eight. So far we have zero."

OSPA had access to current and former Special Forces operatives from the various branches of the military but, even with that kind of talent available, it was a fairly delicate piece of staffing. This was made even more difficult by the fact that Strand was a political appointee with no field experience and an apparent inability to face the complexities of creating this team.

"A few years back he was on his way to his extraction point after completing—"

"I read the file, Matt. He let himself get involved in some street scuffle and got shot."

Egan nodded slowly. "He almost died, Hillel. Actually, it's a miracle he didn't. A radical Muslim man found him, took him home, and saved his life. It took us six months to find him and get him out."

"So you're saying, what? He's gone native? Some guy helps him out and now he's a terrorist sympathizer?"

Egan considered just saying yes and being done with it, but he didn't want to risk the possibility that something negative might then find its way into al Fayed's file. "Come on. You read what happened. When we got him back to the States we found out he had a bullet lodged next to his spine. There was a doctor in California who thought he could get it out but the procedure was expensive and experimental. Because the doctor was using a new technique, the surgery didn't fit onto any of the government's forms. So they just decided it wasn't covered. The bullet's going to paralyze him someday, Hillel, and we didn't lift a finger to help him. I think it's fair to say that when he walked away from us he didn't do it with a lot of warm feelings."

Strand sat thoughtfully for a moment, then opened the file and began paraphrasing from it. "Born to a first-generation Arab Christian family in New York. He looks Arab and his Arabic is near perfect—he has no problem passing. No siblings. Parents dead. Unmarried, no relatives in the U.S. He left the Navy to work for the CIA." Strand looked up for a moment. "Recruited by you personally."

"That might as well have been a thousand years ago," Egan responded.

"I did some checking into this one. Currently, he has no real job. No money. No friends. Things haven't been going so well for our Mr. al Fayed. Maybe he's ready to come back into the fold?"

"Look, Hillel . . . I knew this guy for years—actually, he was one of my best friends. Trust me when I tell you this is a dead end. Even before we screwed him over he was starting to put together this weird mishmash of history, politics, and Darwin in his head. . . . Let's just say that he was on his way out one way or another. Besides, he's injured to the point that he really isn't qualified anymore."

"I'm not sure I like the defeatist attitude you're adopting, Matt. You seem to be focused on 'why' instead of 'how.' If there's anything we're learning from this process it's that no candidate's perfect. But al Fayed is goddamn close. There are no other guys like this anywhere right now. We're looking at people with Arab backgrounds, but we're years from having anybody like this. Other than al Fayed, we don't have a single candidate who can move around unnoticed in an Arab country. This guy could walk in here and be operational in a week. Not to mention how useful he could be in a training capacity."

"Hillel—"

"What? You know the position I'm in. Those sons of bitches in Congress are coming down on the intelligence community for not taking chances but we know goddamn well that what they really mean is that they want us to take risks and win every time. If things get screwed up, then they're going to be falling all over themselves to be the ones who nail us to the cross. We need to have the best and as I see it, even with his drawbacks, al Fayed is head and shoulders above anyone else."

"But—"

Strand waved his hand for silence. "I don't want to hear the reasons we can't have him, Matt. What I want to hear is a way we *can* have him."

2

The house was warped and bowed enough that if it was painted in bright primary colors instead of peeling gray, it would look like a carnival funhouse. It was situated about two hours from Washington, D.C., in the center of a five-acre lot strewn with mature trees and jagged boulders. Al Fayed had apparently been renting the property for almost a year and was currently two months behind in his payments.

Egan eased off the dirt driveway about fifty yards

21

from the house and stepped from the car, looking out over the property. To the right of the house was a large metal building that leaned a bit less radically but that was rusted in a pattern that made it look like someone had dumped brown paint over the edges of the roof. In front, and only slightly less rusted, was an old car resting on blocks fashioned from rotting logs. A Thunderbird was Egan's best guess, though his knowledge of classic cars was spotty at best. The little he did know had come from al Fayed who, after a few beers, used to go on about them for hours.

"Are we just going to stand here?" Strand said, leaning over the roof of the car and slapping a palm down on it.

Not if running away is an option, Egan thought as he forced himself forward through the patchwork of dirt, gravel, and weeds that covered the ground. Strand came up alongside and frowned as he found himself forced to match Egan's unnaturally slow gait. On some level, he probably knew that this wasn't a great idea and he wasn't anxious to take point.

Egan slowed even more as they passed by the old car, examining the graceful lines barely visible beneath the toll time and weather had taken. It was hard not to see it as another one of al Fayed's dreams that hadn't quite worked out.

The man who stepped out onto the porch didn't seem familiar at first. His black hair was held back in a haphazard ponytail that hinted at going well down his broad back. His arms and shoulders were thick and powerful looking but lacked definition and gave him a beefy, almost clumsy, look. That slight softness continued in his face, rounding it out and smoothing the lines in the dark skin around his eyes.

Egan stopped a good fifteen feet from the house and Strand followed suit.

"Hello, Fade."

The nickname had been bestowed by his teammates years ago based, it was said, on his ability to disappear into the background and slit your throat. More likely it was because Salam al Fayed wasn't the name of someone your average SEAL wanted watching his back. Either way, it had stuck.

"What are you doing here, Matt?"

Strand found his voice, as he eventually always did, and answered. "We wanted to talk to you."

Fade walked down the steps and Egan fought an urge to back up.

"About what?"

"About getting you back into the game."

"The game?" Fade's gaze moved from Strand back to Egan. "Where'd you get this guy? Bureaucrats R Us? Get the hell off my property."

"It's not your property," Strand pointed out. He was controlling it, but there was a hint of anger audible in his voice. He wasn't accustomed to being insulted or spoken about like he wasn't there. "In fact, it seems that you're about a month away from being thrown off it."

"Hillel . . ." Egan cautioned, but Strand ignored him.

23

"Have you been watching the news, Mr. al Fayed? The world's changing and we have to control those changes. To do that, we need men like you."

Fade looked like he was about to walk away but then seemed to change his mind. "But you're doing such a great job on your own. We've got a big hole in the ground where the Trade Center used to be and every country in the world either hates us or is so afraid of us that they're spending every dime they have to build nuclear missiles to aim our way. If it weren't for dumbass politicians like you mucking around in things you don't understand, how would all those defense contractors keep themselves in Ferraris and trophy wives?"

This wasn't going quite as well as Egan had hoped. But at least no shots had been fired yet. "I think what—"

Strand cut him off. "I have a master's in public policy from Harvard and I'm doing graduate courses in Middle Eastern history. Now, remind me about your background? Did you ever graduate from high school?"

Fade's reply was undoubtedly less than civil but Egan couldn't be sure because it was in Arabic.

"What's the problem?" Fade asked, switching back to English. "Don't tell me you missed that. There are illiterate six-year-olds in Iraq who would have understood what I just said, so you'll excuse me if I'm not terribly impressed by your expertise. And by the way, who the fuck are you?"

"My name is Hillel Strand. I work for Homeland Security. I—"

"Ever read the Koran, Hillel Strand from Homeland Security? Ever even been to the Middle East? Or is your entire experience with the area from playing golf with one of those assholes you people keep sending over there to fuck things up?" He pointed at Egan. "At least Matt, the back-stabbing slug he is, was willing to go over there and get in front of a bullet. People like you make me—"

"Fade!" Egan shouted. "That's enough. You've got no beef with Hillel. He had nothing to do with what happened to you."

"Oh, right. That was you."

There it was again. That urge to back up.

Fade jerked forward, causing Strand to jump back, land on a rock, and almost fall over.

A smirk, a roll of the eyes, and then Fade turned his back and started toward his workshop.

"Why don't you two run on back to Homeland Security and tell them that this sand nigger is retired," he said as he disappeared into the building's bay doors.

Egan let out a long breath, relieved that Fade was gone. Strand, on the other hand, was standing there with his jaw set in a display of anger that was becoming all too familiar.

"Well, like you said," Egan began, trying to diffuse the situation. "It was worth a try. But the guy's obviously lost it. Look at him. He used to be chiseled out of stone. Now he's just some wacko hippie living in the woods." He turned back toward the car but stopped when Strand spoke.

"That's the difference between you and me, isn't it, Matt? I've never thought losing is acceptable."

Great.

"You're pushing your luck, Matt."

Egan stepped cautiously through the door and stood at the back, letting his eyes adjust to the lower light levels. The shop was packed with neatly arranged power tools and any number of other potentially deadly instruments.

"You could have handled that better, Fade. Hillel's a pretty powerful guy and he's not used to being talked to like that."

"So what happened, Matt? You get tired of kissing CIA ass and decided to go find some fresh cheeks at Homeland Security?"

The ironic truth was that he'd gone over his boss's head trying to get Fade his surgery and the director had slapped him down. After that, it had become pretty clear that his career at the CIA was dead-ended. Homeland Security was supposed to have been greener pastures.

Fade put on a pair of safety glasses and began cutting through a board with a radial arm saw. Egan walked to within a few feet of him and shouted over the scream of the blade. "I want to help you!"

Fade slammed a hand into the switch controlling the saw and threw the cut piece of wood to the ground as the motor died. "I haven't seen you in six years and suddenly you show up and you want to help me? What, like you did before?"

Egan walked over to the door he'd entered through, slid it closed, and turned back toward Fade. "Look, Hillel's just another asshole politician who thinks he's a tough guy. You know the type as well as I do. If you hadn't just stood there and insulted the man to his face, I'd have convinced him that you're crazy and you would have never heard from us again. But now his back's up and it's not going to be that easy. I can smooth this thing over, but you're going to have to come in and play the game a little bit."

"Or what?"

"You don't want to be—"

"What the hell happened to you, man? I can't believe I used to trust you with my life."

"Why do you have to make everything so hard?"

"Because it is hard!" Fade shouted, picking up a long screwdriver that was lying next to the saw. Egan kept his eyes glued to the instrument.

"I've given everything to this country! I've been shot, stabbed, poisoned. I've had malaria, dysentery, and dengue. I drowned once, for Christ's sake—they were barely able to bring me back. I was always there when my country needed me. But when I needed it, everybody just turned their backs and walked away. Do you know that after everything I've done, everything I've been through, I can't even get on a plane without someone trying to shove a camera up my ass first? Do you have any idea what my life is like now, Matt? What it's like to stand around waiting for this bullet in my back to move a millimeter in the wrong direction and paralyze me?"

Egan shook his head. "I don't."

"Well, let me tell you, then. I don't really sleep anymore because I'm afraid that if I do, I won't feel it coming and when I wake up, I won't be able to move. One day I realized that I'd found something I could kill myself with in every room of my house. Razors, knives, Drano, glass. An outlet and some water. It wasn't something I figured out on purpose. It just happened. But you know what the really sad thing is? I'm probably just fooling myself. The doctors tell me that there's a sixty percent chance that the paralysis will be from the neck down."

"Fade, I—"

"You know what my greatest fear is, Matt? That some UPS guy will find me before I die of thirst. That I'll end up lying in a nursing home wearing diapers and staring at the ceiling for the next thirty years."

What was the appropriate response to something like that? There was none. Egan pushed the door open and began backing out of it, holding his gaze on the screwdriver in Fade's hand.

"Hey, Matt . . ."

He glanced up long enough to see the dead expression on his old friend's face.

"If you ever come back here, I'll kill you."

"Yeah. I know."

"So what happened?" Strand said as he revved the car up the dirt road toward the highway.

"I told him he should show you more respect."

"Are we going to get him?"

"I tried, Hillel, but he said no and believe me, he meant it."

"You seem okay with failing here."

"We failed a long time ago. I'm on record saying that we fucked this guy. Maybe we should have been a little more forward thinking if there was a chance we were going to need him again."

"Mistakes were made," Strand admitted. "But maybe we can put them right. I'll talk to some people and we'll see what we can do about getting him the surgery he wants. When he's recovered, we'll talk again."

Egan shook his head. "The bullet shifted years ago and now it's surrounded by scar tissue. It's too late. There's nothing anyone can do."

Strand fell silent for long enough that Egan began to think the subject was closed. No such luck.

"Okay, then. What can we hold over him?"

"Excuse me?"

"You heard what I said."

"Nothing, Hillel. He did a great job. That's why you want him."

"Everybody's got something in their background that they're not proud of. Maybe we should take a look."

Egan didn't respond immediately; instead he just stared out the windshield into the bright blue sky. There was no way he was going to let this happen again. No way.

"Give me a couple of days, Hillel. I'll look into it."

A barely perceptible smile, completely devoid of humor, played at Strand's lips. "No, you've got plenty on your plate right now. We'll let Lauren run with this."

3

Matt Egan didn't bother to turn on any lights, instead making his way through the house by memory and partially blinding himself when he opened the refrigerator.

Maybe his luck was changing. There was still a single piece of browning banana cream pie perched on top of a container of cottage cheese. He shoved half of it in his mouth with one hand and used the other to fish out a carton of milk. Everything went black again when he closed the refrigerator and he felt around for an empty section of counter to sit on.

After leaving Fade's house, his day had actually managed to deteriorate—something he'd have bet good money wasn't possible. Strand's assistant had rebuffed his every offer to help her with her research into Fade and ignored every clever inquiry as to her progress. One way or another, this was going to end badly. Other than being a completely humorless ice princess, Lauren McCall had few other failings. She was smart, resourceful, and annoyingly tenacious. With no way to block her, it seemed likely that the rickety house of cards he'd built around his old friend was about to come tumbling down. A very bad thing for everyone involved.

He jammed the rest of the pie into his mouth and chewed violently, but it didn't make him feel any better. In fact, it combined with the hollow nervous sensation in his stomach to make him nauseous. A fitting end to a truly shitty day. Or more accurately, a fitting beginning to a situation that was almost certain to turn into a complete disaster.

He tossed the empty milk container in what he hoped was the sink, and began feeling his way toward the door to the basement.

The descent down the staircase was made easier by the glow of a single bare bulb at its base and he made his way through the piles of abandoned toys, laundry, and exercise equipment to a heavy door at the back. Turning the knob, he peeked inside.

"Anybody home?"

He'd built the room himself and it showed. It was a slightly crooked and windowless fifteen by fifteen, with thick walls covered in sound-absorbing empty egg cartons and a web of wires and cables. The thick carpet was stacked with amplifiers and musical instruments, some too obscure for him to identify. Along the far wall was an unfathomable electronic fire hazard that looked like a cross between an elaborate stereo system and NASA's Houston control center.

Through unwavering determination and considerable practice, his six-year-old daughter had carved out enough space from the chaos to set up an elaborate dollhouse, which she was in the process of redecorating.

"Where on earth did your mother get a banjo?" Egan said, leaning the instrument against a wall and lying down in the space it had inhabited. Kali shrugged and continued to experiment with the feng shui of her tiny living room. They'd adopted her as a toddler from Vietnam three years ago, but sometimes it was hard to believe that Elise wasn't her biological mother. They had the same thin, almost frail build, the same unconventionally brilliant minds, and the same almost autistic ability to concentrate. If one of the gadgets in this room ever really did catch on fire while the women of the house were thinking, it would undoubtedly burn down around them completely unnoticed.

"Here or here," she said, now working with a tiny armoire.

His influence wasn't as strong, but it had provided his daughter with an obsessive sense of organization completely lacking in her mother.

"I think next to the table. Then Barbie will be able to see the TV while she's arranging her china."

He glanced up at his wife, who was sitting motionless in a beanbag chair staring at a laptop through the long strands of hair hanging in her face. Even if she could hear him through the enormous headphones she was wearing, he knew better than to try to talk to her.

"What's your mom up to?"

"Dunno. Strawberry People, I think."

"Still?"

"Uh-huh."

"It's late. Have you had dinner?"

She pointed to a pizza box lying in the corner.

"More health food, huh. You're gonna waste away to nothing eating that stuff."

He leaned his head on a stuffed moose and focused on his wife again. She was still staring at the computer screen, bobbing her head a bit as she absorbed what was coming through her headphones.

Five years ago, in what could only be described as a wild contortion of fate, he'd married the woman *Spin* magazine had called America's most gifted song-writer. She'd been only twenty-five at the time, playing guitar in no less than three bands to make ends meet, and he'd been a thirty-three-year-old CIA operative.

Since then, there had never been a dull moment. She'd finally put a band together that had the right chemistry and their notoriety had begun to swell. Her last CD had been named to a number of alternative top ten lists and a few of her songs had recently been used in the sound track of a reasonably successful independent film about a homicidal bass player.

Of course, none of this really translated into money. Her career was break-even at best. Not that he really cared about that any more than he cared that every-thing she'd recorded sounded like cats fighting to him. She was the most amazing person he'd ever met and he still couldn't understand why she'd even lowered herself to talk to him.

He refocused on the ceiling, trying not to allow his mind to take the obvious path of comparing his life with Fade's—to see that warped, empty house and the car rusting away in the dirt out front. Their backgrounds really weren't all that different. Why had everything turned out so right for him and so wrong for Fade?

He reached out and tugged at his daughter's hair, trying to put Fade out of his mind.

"Quit being so immature!" she said, swatting at his hand. She'd just learned that word and it had quickly become her favorite.

His wife's eyes suddenly unglued themselves from the computer in her lap and a broad smile splashed across her face. They had been more than a year into their relationship before he'd gotten used to the almost schizophrenic way she could go from startling inten-sity to easygoing grins.

"Hard day?" she said, pushing off her headphones.

"What makes you say that?"

"Because it's nine o'clock and you're staring off into space with a milk mustache and a bunch of pie all over your face."

"That's gross, you know," Kali chimed in.

"I don't have to take that from someone whose dia-pers I changed."

"You did not!"

"I guess you're right. I've had better days."

"Ready to be cheered up?"

"Very."

She slid off her beanbag chair and lay down on the floor next to him. "The song I wrote for Madonna is going to make it. They're putting it on the record."

"You're joking."

"Swear to God. I got the call today."

Egan looked over at Kali. "Did you hear that, honey? Four years of male, white corporate indoctrination is all but paid for. If there's a dance mix, maybe even graduate school!"

That got him a hard poke in the ribs from his wife.

"Smart-ass. I wouldn't get your hopes up. There's no telling whether it'll ever get radio play."

"Still, though . . ." He almost said "congratulations," but stopped himself. The whole "selling out" thing was quite a stigma in the circles she ran in. But eventually you got to a point in life where there were certain realities.

"I know how hard it was for you to do that song, Elise."

"It's no big deal."

There was about thirty seconds of silence before he spoke again. "It's the best thing you ever wrote, you know."

She laughed, knowing full well he was completely serious. His proclivity for ABBA and KC and the Sunshine Band were well known to her, but she chose to ignore them. Among other things.

"How's Strawberry People coming?"

She had been bogged down for weeks in the last song for her upcoming CD, *A Long Night with the Strawberry People* (whatever the hell that meant). Deadlines were looming and things were starting to get desperate.

"Done."

"Is that a joke?"

"The answer was right in front of me."

"Really? What answer?"

"It's a country song."

"A country song?"

She nodded excitedly. "You wouldn't believe the sound you can get from a pedal steel guitar if you run it through a cheap distortion pedal and let it feed back. . . ."

Hank Williams was undoubtedly rolling over in his grave to retrieve his earplugs. "Well, this certainly calls for some serious celebration."

She rolled over and propped her head on his stomach. "Serious celebration."

Elise, full of cold pizza and warm beer, had fallen asleep more than an hour ago, but Matt Egan was still lying in bed wide awake. Finally, he slid his arm out from beneath her pillow and padded quietly out of the room.

The cramped den at the back of the house contained a small refrigerator and before sitting down behind his desk he pulled out a beer that was going to put him well into hangover territory. Determined to get crocked enough to drown the memories swimming around in his head, he opened the bottle and drank half of it, still clearly able to remember the first time he'd heard the name Salam al Fayed. He'd been working for Military Intelligence at the time and Fade was halfway through Hell Week—the brutal program used by the Navy to qualify SEAL candidates.

Fade's boat crew hadn't slept for more than two days and had endured countless miles of running, hours of live fire exercises, and an ocean swim in hypothermia-inducing temperatures. Two of his team had already quit and the others were so exhausted and cold that Fade was concerned they wouldn't make it through the upcoming obstacle course. He'd started telling jokes to try to boost their morale and, when that didn't work, he decided to perform an elaborate striptease right there on the beach. By the end of it, everyone, annoyed instructors excepted, was energetically humming along to his gyrations.

Not sure what else to do, the instructors had put him up against a wall and aimed a fire hose at him. Before they opened the hydrant, though, he yelled, "Wait!" and produced a pink bathing cap covered in bright yellow ducks from his fatigues. When, after fifteen minutes of being repeatedly knocked down by the icy flood, he went on to nearly set the record in the obstacle course, people began to speculate that he wasn't human.

Shortly thereafter, Egan had left the army and gone into the operational side of CIA, taking a position overseeing operations that weren't strictly legal but were seen as becoming increasingly necessary. There, he'd kept tabs on the young al Fayed with the idea that he was someone the CIA might be interested in after he'd proved himself under fire.

It hadn't taken long. Fade's first live mission had gone downhill fast. The helicopter his team had been in took a hit and one of his comrades had fallen out in hostile territory. Against orders, Fade had grabbed some weapons and jumped out into the dark after him. He lay there in the rocks with a broken leg and defended his unconscious friend for ten hours. By the time they were finally extracted, Fade had managed to completely demoralize a force estimated at over a hundred. A spy plane flying overhead had confirmed that Fade was hitting people as far out as nine hundred meters despite the darkness and wind.

Not surprisingly, Egan had recruited him right there in his hospital bed. After that, Fade had spent almost three years operating in the Middle East before being stabbed by that damn little girl. Then everything had gone in the toilet. In the end, all Egan had been able to do was offer his friend the pick of any instructor position he wanted. Not surprisingly, Fade had refused. As he saw it, he had been betrayed. And he was right.

4

The saw blade caught at the edge of the board and splintered it, sending a chunk of wood into Fade's bare shoulder.

"Damn it!"

He looked over at the half-finished set of kitchen cabinets he was working on and threw the board into one of the doors, leaving a deep vertical gouge. The only thing he'd managed to accomplish since Matt Egan and that other asshole had left that morning was to destroy more oak than he could afford. Everything he'd been so carefully masking with a combination of willpower, diversions, and drugs was now closing back in on him. He reached for a drill but the strength had gone out of him. Suddenly, it felt almost impossible even to put one foot in front of the other as he wandered out into the darkness and collapsed beneath a tree.

By then his breath was coming fast enough to make him dizzy and he put his head between his legs, concentrating on calming down.

It wasn't supposed to be this way. He'd been the best at what he did. And that was supposed to have translated into a great career. A wife. Kids . . .

None of that had materialized, though. Now at thirty-three he had next to nothing: some tools, a failing business, and a few deteriorating personal possessions. He'd given up on relationships years ago.

There was no way he was going to leave a family and friends tethered to him by guilt when the shrapnel in his back finally paralyzed him. The thought of lying there motionless watching the slowly shrinking procession of people from his former life drip pity on him drove him even more insane than he already was.

All he did now was survive. He'd tried going the self-help/psychologist route for a while but had given up when he'd come to the conclusion that it was just a bunch of bullshit for people who had problems that either existed only in their minds or were easily solved.

The only solution to his particular problem was death. But for some reason he hadn't been able to coax himself into suicide. So now he was a hypocrite. He'd never had a problem killing anyone else.

Maybe this was his punishment. The sentence: to be buried alive in his own body. But even that wasn't a fair analogy. People who were buried alive died in hours. With a little luck, the horrors of twenty-first century medicine might keep him alive for decades.

Now, to top it all off, there were a bunch of people at Homeland Security trying to figure out how to screw him over even worse. The American government could be infinitely vindictive when it didn't get what it wanted—a trait that would only get worse as the country felt increasingly threatened by uncontrollable outside forces. Strand would be back and that son of a bitch Matt Egan would be standing right there alongside him.

Fade pulled a wood-carving knife from the pocket of his overalls and held it up so he could see it in the dim light bleeding from the open door of his workshop. One last mission. When Strand and his goons came back determined not to take no for an answer, they'd find what was left of him rotting in the sun—the same way he'd left so many others.

He sat there for a long time, finally pressing the knife to his wrist hard enough to break the skin. The blood flowing down his arm looked black.

It was a beautiful night: warm, a sky full of stars, the sound of crickets hovering on the breeze. There would never be a better time. A little more pressure and the dark trail moving toward his elbow thickened.

He concentrated harder but it just caused his hand to shake. Finally, he just sunk to the ground, dry eyed, but with his chest heaving uncontrollably. He could no longer remember a time that he'd actually been able to cry, though there had been so many occasions he should have. People said that it helped and maybe it did. What other purpose could it have?

He didn't know how long he lay there like that—long enough for the stars to progress noticeably across the dark sky. Finally, he pushed himself to his feet and started toward his house, anger replacing the solitary hopelessness that normally swallowed any other emotion that dared try to surface. He washed the dried blood from his arm and wound a gauze bandage around his wrist before going into the living room and rummaging through a stack of woodworking books.

He finally found what he was looking for under the sofa: a catalog of small servos and motors used in the construction of entertainment centers.

He'd lost count of the brave and dedicated men who had died trying to kill him and there was no way he was going to roll over for that pissant Hillel Strand. It would be like spitting on the memory of all those men who'd fought so hard and lost.

The climb into the attic started his wrist bleeding again, but not badly enough to worry about. He threw open a battered footlocker, filling the air with ancient-smelling dust, and emptied it of the weapons it contained. He'd assumed he'd need them again one day, but hadn't guessed where the threat would come from.

At the bottom he found a handful of old pictures: him and his old teammates skulking around dive bars, photographic evidence of the elaborate practical jokes he used to put so much effort into. When he looked at himself in those old photos, it was like looking at a dead relative who you hadn't known all that well. Vague recognition colored with an even more vague sense of regret.

He let the photos fall from his hand and pulled out a tape measure, using it to determine the dimensions of the tiny attic. If Strand wanted a fight, he'd goddamn well get one.

5

Despite his third hangover in as many days, Matt Egan pushed through the door of OSPA's office suite at seven A.M. Kelly Braith, the office receptionist, was already talking on her headset but still managed to flash him a wide smile and a wave as he stalked toward the copy room for more coffee.

After topping off his go-cup, which some office smart-ass had covered in Elise Egan stickers, he wandered down an empty hallway only to find Hillel Strand already talking to his assistant behind the conference room's soundproof glass. He seemed pretty intent on what he was saying and Egan sped up, trying to get by without being seen. He was nowhere near caffeinated enough yet to face anything more serious than his mail.

He'd actually made it past the large window before the unmistakable sound of knuckles on glass stopped him. When he turned around, Strand was waving him back.

Fabulous.

"Morning," Egan said as he stepped through the door and closed it behind him.

Strand looked smug and Lauren wouldn't meet his eye. Not a good sign.

"We've come up with something on al Fayed that I think will interest you," Strand said, pointing to an empty chair and then motioning toward his assistant.

She started slowly, never taking her eyes from the stack of papers in her lap. "It wasn't easy, but I was finally able to connect everything. Al Fayed went to Bogota after he walked away from the CIA. When he was there—or possibly before—he went to work for the Vela cartel." Her mouth seemed to suddenly dry out and she took a sip from a glass of water in front of her.

"It seems that he killed off some of Vela's local competitors and scared the hell out of the others. It's likely that he, in combination with Castel Vela's head for business, is responsible for a lot of the cartel's success. Then, after about a year, it seems like al Fayed just walked away and came back to the States."

"It seems strange that someone like Castel Vela would just let him resign," Strand commented.

"I talked to a DEA guy who was down there at the time and he said that no one's really sure what happened. Half say that Vela was afraid of him and the other half say he loved him like a son. As you probably know, Vela died six months ago, so we'll never know for sure."

"Why didn't this come out in our initial background check on al Fayed?" Strand said in a tone that suggested he already knew the answer.

Lauren squirmed uncomfortably in her chair but didn't speak.

"You've got me on the edge of my seat," Egan said, finally. "Don't keep me waiting."

"Because the information was purposely obscured."

"Really. By whom?"

"By you."

"Very good, Lauren. In three days, you uncovered something I spent months burying. Gold star."

Strand pointed toward the door and she bolted before he could change his mind.

"You can imagine that I was a little surprised when I got that report, Matt."

"Fade was killing Colombian drug dealers on Colombian soil. As I see it, that's not an American problem. In fact, I know from personal experience that we're paying people down there to do the exact same thing."

"Those are official operations, Matt—planned and executed by the U.S. government to disrupt the drug trade. What al Fayed did was hardly the same thing. He was working to systematically eliminate weaker narcotics organizations so Castel Vela could more efficiently addict our kids."

Egan nodded in a way that indicated he'd heard, but not that he agreed. "There's enough cocaine coming into this country every week to sink a battleship, Hillel. Fade did this—"

"How much coke is coming in here or what al Fayed's motivations were aren't really relevant, are they? You don't have the authority to make these kinds of calls. And you damn well—"

"Fade did this," Egan repeated, deciding that he'd damn well be allowed to finish his thought, "to get the money to pay for the medical help that he should have

45

gotten from us. But when he got back to the States, the scar tissue had set and it was too late. *We're* the reason he was out there."

Strand frowned disinterestedly. "Fine. Thank you, Matt. That's all."

Egan stood and leaned forward across the table, looking directly into his boss's eyes. "That's not all, Hillel. I'm telling you to leave this alone. Nothing good can come of it."

Strand was silent for a moment as though he was trying to decide whether to respond or hold to his dismissal of Egan.

"I'm not sure how you come to that conclusion, Matt. We stand to gain a very talented, well-trained operative who speaks fluent Arabic. That's the good that can come of this."

Egan fell back into his chair, sliding his palms along the cold tabletop as he did. If he was ever going to figure out a way to make Hillel Strand see reason, this was the time. "Listen . . . The Fade you met yesterday isn't the man I knew. Trust me, he's on the verge of completely disintegrating. There's a lot more to know about him than you can read on a sheet of paper."

"Maybe the best thing for him would be to come back into a structured environment where he can be involved in something he's good at. Did you ever consider that?"

"He doesn't need a fucking structured environment!" Egan shouted before he could stop himself. He held up a hand, silencing Strand before he could yell back, and managed to bring his voice under control before he spoke again. "I'm sorry. I had a bad night. Let me try this from a different angle. You say he's good at what he does. But that's actually an understatement. Fade's one of those rare people who's just better than everybody else. Kind of like Michael Jordan, but with a rifle instead of a basketball. Right now, he's sitting around in his barn making quilting racks. And that's a good thing. There's no reason to go over there and start poking this guy with a stick. It's impossible to predict how he'll react."

An incredulous smile suddenly spread across Strand's face. "You're afraid of him, aren't you?"

"I'm terrified of him, Hillel."

6

Karen Manning tilted her head back and stared up at the dense web of tree limbs blocking the sun. It had rained the night before and the earth beneath her feet was still damp, intensifying the humidity and causing her blouse to stick to her back. It was a place that seemed to absorb everything—air, sound, light. Appropriate, she supposed.

The call, anticipated with such dread, had come in about an hour ago, a breathless stream of consciousness from a man whose dog had followed a faint odor that now seemed to permeate everything. The stench was fueling her rage and frustration to the very edge of her control. Just like it always did.

"Anything?" she said, finally looking down.

The young woman's naked body had turned a uniform yellowish-gray—except where the thin rope that ended her life had left a black ring. Karen had a damp photograph in her hand that depicted the corpse during happier times, waving and smiling energetically, clad in a yellow bikini.

"Nothing new," John Wakefield said, crouching with some difficulty next to the body and carefully moving one of its arms to examine the matted weeds growing beneath.

From looking at him, no one would ever guess that Wakefield had devoted his life to tracking down murderers. A more reasonable guess would be Mr. Rogers's stand-in. Or aging librarian.

He'd been only days from his retirement party when the bodies and letters started appearing. As the force's top investigator, he'd felt obligated to stay on and when he'd announced that decision everyone in Virginia had let out a sigh of relief.

"Very neat," he said, struggling to stand again. The arthritis in his knees caused him a lot of pain and Karen put a hand beneath his arm to help.

"Plenty of time to be methodical . . . All the time in the world."

It was always exactly the same. In fact, it was becoming almost monotonous. A young woman would disappear and shortly thereafter a letter would show up at both the department and the home of the woman's family spelling out in graphic detail what her kidnapper was going to do to her. Then, exactly sixteen days later, the body would be dumped in a semisecluded area in the Virginia countryside—always naked, strangled, and utterly sterile of clues.

Karen let out a frustrated growl and stalked deeper into the woods, snapping off any tree limbs that were unlucky enough to get in her way. She didn't stop until she was far enough to escape the smell of decay and the sounds of police cars running up and down the dirt road.

She had no idea how Wakefield could spend his days calmly pondering the few scraps of evidence they had and sipping those damn herbal teas of his. She wanted to do something. Anything. At the rate they were closing in on this asshole, he would die of old age before they caught him. And, in the meantime, a hundred more innocent women would spend the last few days of their lives praying for it to end.

She heard the erratic crunch of footsteps coming up behind her but didn't turn around.

"Are you all right, Karen?"

"No."

Wakefield came alongside her and followed her gaze through the trees stretching endlessly in front of them. "After a while you can start thinking it's your fault. It's not, you know. It's his fault." He leaned forward and tried to coax her into looking at him. "That's my speech. Did it help?"

"No."

"Is there anything I can say that will?"

She jerked around to face him, speaking in a voice that was too loud for their surroundings. "You can tell me why the hell you picked me for this assignment. I'm obviously not cut out for it and we both know it wasn't exactly the best political move you ever made."

Wakefield nodded thoughtfully, completely unfazed by her sudden display of anger. "It's a fair question. I picked you because I'm tired and you're not. You're strong and passionate and full of energy. I can't bring any of those things to this investigation. Not anymore. The only thing I come with is experience. As far as being political, the only benefit to being old enough to retire and taking on a job no one wants is that you don't have to be political. The truth is, if I wanted to, I could go over to the captain's house tonight and slap his wife. You know what the repercussions would be? Zip."

"Have you ever met her? You should do it."

He laughed in the host-of-a-children's-show way he always laughed.

"I've got to tell you, John. This is driving me crazy. Every time I try to think clearly, I end up fantasizing about getting my hands on this guy and twisting his head off."

"Maybe you should get a book on meditation?"

"Yeah, that's gonna happen."

"Did you ever think that maybe this guy's sick?"

She rolled her eyes. "Bullshit. He's just another geek

who can't get a date. You know who was sick? Jack the Ripper. Now there was a guy with a little get-up-and-go and some originality. Not some loser who didn't get enough attention from his mom and wants to see himself on TV."

That elicited a laugh that was a little more hearty and ironic than one you'd have gotten from Captain Kangaroo. "You know the other reason I picked you for this, Karen? 'Cause you're kinda fun and you don't think entirely inside the box. I'm going to go out on a limb and say that you're the first person in history to use the phrase 'get-up-and-go' to describe Jack the Ripper." He put a fatherly hand on her shoulder. "Look, can you remember one thing for me?"

"What?"

"I could have had the very best for this task force. And instead, I picked you."

"You're a funny guy, John." She tapped her chest. "Seriously. I'm laughing in here, where it counts."

"Detective Manning?"

They both turned toward the uniformed police officer running in their direction.

"The captain just pulled up. He wants to talk to you."

Wakefield winked at her. "Hopefully he didn't hear that comment you made about his wife."

When Karen broke from the trees, she saw Captain Pickering leaning against a squad car coolly surveying the chaos building around him. She slowed to a walk

51

and did the best she could to transform herself into the respectful and obedient subject he wanted her to be. Honestly, it was too little too late—he couldn't stand her and it was unlikely there was anything she could do to change that.

When she had been named the head of her precinct's SWAT team, he, as a former team leader himself, felt as though his accomplishments had suddenly been cheapened. And he wasn't alone. Cries of "feminist affirmative action" echoed throughout the state and the grapevine filled with enough blonde jokes to make her seriously consider dyeing her hair brown. The bottom line was that he and his boys' club let no opportunity to undermine her pass.

In the face of so much more resistance than she'd ever imagined, she'd decided to quit after only a few months. Before she did, though, she'd sat down with pen and paper to write a list of her qualifications versus the men she'd beat out for the position. What she managed to quantify was that she was clearly more qualified than all but one of them and, by most measures, edged out the one who was close. When she finally tossed the pen aside and stood up from her kitchen table, she was convinced that she deserved the position and was determined not to be so easily chased off.

"Did you want to talk to me, sir?"

He didn't answer; instead he reached through the open window of his car for a file that he handed to her. She flipped through it, pausing occasionally to dwell on the more interesting tidbits.

"Yes, sir?"

"I need your team to pick him up. Tonight."

"What's the charge?"

His mouth puckered a bit at the question. If he wasn't careful he was going to get those lines her mother feared so much.

"We got a tip that he's been working as some kind of half-assed enforcer for the Colombian drug cartels and that he's responsible for the deaths of the Ramirez brothers."

She nodded and resisted the urge to chew her lower lip as she leafed through a few more pages. The Ramirez brothers were a couple of mid-level drug pushers who had been found the month before with neat little holes in their skulls. There was no mention of them at all in the file, nor was there anything that suggested "half-assed" was a word anyone would use about the man it described. She stopped at a copy of a newspaper photo depicting a severely leaning house. "Not exactly living in the lap of luxury, is he? I wonder where all the money he's making is going."

"Well, maybe if you go out there and pick him up instead of standing around here, we could find out."

Karen managed to smile and ignore the sarcasm. In fact, she was on the verge of getting used to it. "Have we been watching this guy, sir? Do we know anything about his habits or—"

"Did you see it in the file?"

"No."

"Then it's a good bet that we haven't. Look, I'm not

asking for all that much here, Karen. We figure the guy's probably armed so we don't want to send a black and white. Just take your team over there and arrest the guy."

"Sir, he's a former Navy SEAL and now you're telling me he's a cartel enforcer. Are you sure this is the best way to get him? What about waiting for him to go into town and picking him up on a traffic violation? Something a little lower key and more on our turf."

Pickering looked over his sunglasses at her. "His military service is ancient history, Karen. Now he's a furniture builder or something. His property is well away from any civilians and I'm not about to start something with him on a crowded street if I don't have to. If you don't think you can handle this, I can find someone who can."

Another forced smile. "Yes, sir. I'll take care of it."

7

Fade had read a book once by a man who could manipulate his dreams. Just as the author entered that hypnotic state that bordered unconsciousness, he would concentrate and draw himself into whatever world he wanted. It was a trick Fade had been working on for years. He'd created the world. A pleasantly mundane one in which he was a healthy father and husband with a nine-to-five job, a few uncontrollable kids, and a car that got depressingly good gas mileage. But he'd never managed to inhabit it. That level of sleep hadn't come to him for years, replaced by a deep grogginess that never seemed to completely obscure the ceiling hovering above him or stop the endless procession of numbers on his clock.

Tonight, it was even worse. He rubbed his burning eyes and finally gave in, pressing his back against the bare wall behind his mattress and cursing himself for forgetting to buy cigarettes. Not that he actually smoked, but it was a habit he'd been meaning to take up.

At first, the sound didn't seem like much—a quiet crunching that barely managed to penetrate the heavy curtains flapping across his open window. Fade stopped breathing and turned his head in the darkness, listening intently. A raccoon? No, the sound, though quiet, had a certain weight to it. Another black bear looking to get at his garbage can? Maybe. Or maybe it was Hillel Strand, coming to make him an offer he couldn't refuse.

Fade pictured aiming a twelve-gauge at that closely shaved face and blowing the smug expression right off it. Of course Strand was unlikely ever to make a personal appearance. He'd undoubtedly send a team of former Special Forces guys more qualified to persuade Fade to see the error of his ways.

But he'd decided not to let that happen. Instead, he'd take out as many of Strand's men as he could before they finally put a bullet in him. A fittingly violent and futile end to a violent and futile life.

The sound didn't come again and Fade closed his eyes, concentrating on the image of Hillel Strand with a shotgun barrel a few inches from his nose. Maybe that was a dream world he could insert himself into. Something a little closer to reality.

He'd barely settled back on the mattress when he heard another quiet crunch, this time close enough to discern detail. The depth and length of it confirmed his suspicion that its source was heavy. The possibility of the soft pad of a bear's paw, though, was lost in the sound's crisp edge. Based on his considerable experience, that particular attack and decay was only caused by one thing: a boot.

Fade remained motionless on the bed, realizing suddenly that he wasn't in the mood for this tonight. He had undoubtedly just entered the last half hour of his life and all he could think about was how much trouble dying was going to be. A sure sign of having lived too long.

The man rather sloppily creeping up on him was getting close enough to force a decision. Fade had a pistol and the temptation to just shoot halfheartedly at whatever face appeared in his window was fairly strong. But then all that preparation and money would have been wasted. Seemed like a shame.

He quietly slid the blanket off his legs and crawled across the room. Keeping the fluttering curtains in his peripheral vision, he stood and stretched his arms overhead, unlatching a small door cut into the wall that led to his attic. It opened smoothly on brand new hinges and he swung himself up into it on a slightly creakier spine.

The "command center" he'd constructed didn't have the aesthetic grace he normally strived for, but time had been short and sacrifices had to be made. He lay down in something that looked disturbingly like a badly welded steel coffin with no lid and ran his finger along the edge of a bank of small monitors in front of him. Finally finding a switch, he flipped it and was immediately bathed in a dim green light that he'd made sure wouldn't be visible through the door.

He turned on the rest of the monitors, careful not to bump a series of switches he'd screwed to a piece of plywood or the heavily modified model airplane radio control lying next to him. After checking the neatly arranged M16, combat knife, and 9mm pistol, he refocused his attention on the small screens.

The images were surprisingly detailed. It was uncanny what you could get off the Internet these days. Most of the stuff was measurably better than the supposedly state-of-the-art stuff he'd worked with at the CIA only a few years before.

Honestly, he was surprised they worked at all. It had seemed likely that the team sent for him would be jamming the radio transmission from the cameras he'd set up. Using hardwired ones had just seemed like too much trouble. Stranger yet was that the generator he'd set up in the basement hadn't kicked on: His power hadn't been cut. Maybe he'd lost his touch. Maybe he was hiding from a squirrel.

The squirrel didn't materialize but a man in black fatigues holding a small assault rifle did, running up beneath the night vision–enabled camera hidden above Fade's front door.

A few moments later, there was motion on nearly every screen and he silently scanned them, watching men settling into the obvious positions that he'd created by digging a few natural-looking indentions in his yard and breaking off a number of strategic tree branches. Once they were settled in, two more men appeared at his back door, taking positions on either side of it. Fade eased his nose a little closer to the far right monitor, trying to see if anyone was covering his workshop, but lost interest when he realized that he'd forgotten one obvious item. Clothes. It looked like he was going to make his last stand in a pair of Bugs Bunny boxer shorts. At least they were reasonably new.

The monitor set up in the tree that would offer a sniper a perfect view of the front and sides of the house was still empty, which seemed kind of strange. Did they have some new techie gizmo that made that vantage point unnecessary? One of those unmanned things that hovered over the battlefield like a blimp over a football game? Were those things armed now? Something didn't feel right.

He propped himself up on his elbows and managed to shrug. Based on the ultimate objective of this operation, it wasn't really worth getting in a twist over the details. Besides, he'd never been one to worry about technology. Sure, it had its place in large theaters, but in situations like these it just tended to split people's focus. Assuming, of course, that whatever gadget you were relying on hadn't gotten a little dirt in it and stopped working.

Truthfully, he'd bought the monitors he was using based completely on their fun factor. If he'd known they were actually going to work, he'd have bought more and put a few farther afield. Was Strand out there somewhere within reach? Probably not. But Matt Egan would be. He'd be directing this little pageant, which pretty much guaranteed that Fade's time on this earth was coming to an end. Egan possessed an unusual combination of creativity and anal-retentiveness that had been truly confidence inspiring when Fade was working for him. But now, undoubtedly, it would prove deadly.

He tried to imagine lining up his sights on Egan and pulling the trigger but found it a much harder image to conjure than the one starring Hillel Strand. He tried again, but couldn't get past centering the crosshairs. Faced with it for real, though, he told himself, he'd goddamn well take the shot.

One man in the front and one in the back slipped through their respective unlocked doors simultaneously. Fade switched to interior cameras and watched them do an initial sweep of the living room and kitchen before being followed by their two comrades. The remainder of the team stayed outside, one in front

and the other in back, both lying in the comfy indentions provided for them.

Fade continued to toggle back and forth through his
interior cameras as the four men moved cautiously
through his house. After a complete sweep, they
relaxed a bit and began to turn on the lights. As
promised in the glossy brochure that had accompanied
them, the amazing little cameras adjusted automati-
cally to the new light levels. And they'd even been on
sale.

Two of the men had taken up positions in his living
room and the other two in his bedroom. They seemed
to be just standing at the foot of his bed while one of
them chatted into his throat mike.

Fade had access to both rooms—the bedroom
through the attic door and the living room through a
panel he'd cut in the ceiling. The question was what
should he do with that access. He assumed they'd
looked up the architectural details of the house, so it
seemed likely that they would suspect he was up
there. Were they trying to draw him out? Of course. It
was clearly a trap, but what kind of trap? They were
just standing there with their guns hanging at their
sides. What was that sneaky bastard Egan up to?

He watched one of the men in the living room walk
over and examine a heavy piece of steel plate with a
handle welded to it lying on the floor in front of a
large fireplace. He didn't seem to know what to make
of it. In the bedroom, one of the men had taken off his
gloves and was moving toward the bed, likely to see if

it was still warm. Another attempt to draw him out?

Fade smiled and shook his head. This was all ego— he just didn't want to be outsmarted. Best to keep in mind the end result he was after: essentially, lots of gunfire, a few cool explosions, and his own death. If he stayed up there much longer, the only thing he was going to die of was curiosity.

Grabbing the M16 next to him, he lifted himself out of his steel coffin and threw open the attic door.

The two men spun around at the sound of the door hitting the wall and one actually managed to get off a couple panicked shots at the wood floor before Fade's rounds hit them both in the face. He hung partially out of the attic and squinted at the pulverized flesh and bone beneath the men's helmets. What the hell was going on here? There was just no way he should have been able to take those guys out that easily. No way.

The sound of running and then sudden silence made him pull back just as a spray of bullets tore through the wall next to him.

"Attic! Attic!" he heard someone shout as he pulled the door shut with a piece of attached rope and fell back into his coffin, covering his ears.

As expected, bullets began tearing through the ceiling, shattering wood and plaster, and filling the air to the point that he had to touch his nose to the monitors to see them.

The man in the living room was in a half crouch, spraying bullets wildly upward while the other man moved into the bedroom, firing at what was left of the attic door. Their teammates outside were yelling on their throat mikes but seemed less than eager to get any more involved than that.

Fade watched as the man in the living room walked more or less directly beneath him, still firing upward. The sound of his rounds hitting the steel tub was deafening even through the fingers he had in his ears and he could feel the vibration as bullets struck. Then, suddenly the man was down. It took Fade a moment to figure out that he'd been hit by one of his own ricochets.

"You've got to be fucking kidding me," he said aloud, though he couldn't hear himself over the soldier still shooting from the bedroom. Despite the size of the monitor, Fade could see that the man's mouth was wide open and he seemed to be screaming as he fired. He'd know for sure before long, because at this rate, he had only a few more seconds of ammunition.

One of the monitors captured three men bursting from the trees and sprinting across his yard. When they came up alongside the house, one of them produced a set of bolt cutters and, predictably, cut power to the building. Fade hit a switch and started the generator in his basement, rerouting the power to his new toys. The screens restarted but after about five seconds they died again. He played with the toggle a few more times, but nothing happened. Hard to complain; it had held together a lot longer than he'd ever expected.

When the gun in the bedroom went silent, Fade slipped on a pair of night vision goggles he'd found at

Sharper Image, hung the model airplane controller across his bare chest, and dropped into the living room through the panel he'd cut.

The house was old, but surprisingly solid and that, combined with an old area rug, made his landing nearly silent. He held his knife in his teeth as he crawled up to the man lying on the floor, but it was clear he was dead. His own bullet had taken a downward trajectory and penetrated his neck just above his flak jacket. Bad piece of luck, that.

Fade continued to crawl forward, finally coming alongside the open door to his bedroom. A quick glance behind him and he rolled inside, sweeping his rifle across the room and finding the man who had been shooting at him standing in the exact same place he'd been before. He turned, a fresh magazine in his left hand, an expression of confusion on his face as Fade raised his rifle and avoided the man's body armor by putting a round into his face.

No wonder Strand wanted him so bad. Where had he found these guys? The local Quaker meeting?

When Fade crawled back out into the living room, the house seemed to be empty and he used the opportunity to take the radio off the body bleeding all over his genuine faux Oriental rug. He shoved the earpiece in his ear before sliding across the floor toward the fireplace.

"Entering through the kitchen!" the radio crackled.

That wasn't good.

He rolled right just in time to avoid the automatic

rifle fire that suddenly erupted and fired blindly back at the kitchen as he continued to slither toward the fireplace.

"We have a man down in the living room! I can see at least one man down in the bedroom!" he heard over the radio. "The suspect is moving toward the south corner of the living room!"

It seemed likely that the guys outside were moving around to the windows and if they made it before he could get to his enormous fireplace, he was going to find himself at the center of a nasty crossfire. Time to take a calculated risk. He jumped to his feet and dove over the sofa, hitting the floor on the back of his neck and rolling onto all fours. The sound of breaking glass behind him prompted another burst of speed that sent him sliding across a floor he now wished he'd spent more time polishing just as a volley began chipping away the brickwork in front of him. He felt a slight sting in his hip as he crammed himself into the fireplace and grabbed the handle on the back of the steel plate on the floor. Pulling it up, he covered the fireplace hole in time to hear the now unmistakable ring of bullets against metal instead of the equally familiar sound of bullets thudding into his flesh.

Reaching above him, he found the small penlight he'd taped to the flue damper handle and used it to illuminate the miraculously undamaged remote control hanging around his neck. He rubbed his fingers together for a moment and then ceremoniously pressed the buttons labeled KITCHEN and LIVING ROOM.

Nothing happened.

Frowning deeply, he looked around him in the darkness and then eased his grip on the chunk of steel blocking the fireplace opening. Sliding the remote's antenna through the narrow crack, he pressed the buttons again—this time with a more satisfying result. The plate was slammed back toward him hard enough to sever the antenna and slam him hard into the back of the fireplace.

He waited a few seconds, feeling the heat begin to creep into the handle he was gripping and listening to the ringing in his ears, then lowered the makeshift shield just long enough to take in the condition of the house.

The entire north wall was gone and he assumed most of the kitchen was, too, though he couldn't see it from his position. There were numerous small fires burning on the floor, and on what used to be his furniture. The smoke was on his side—thick enough to obscure movement but not thick enough to asphyxiate him. Yet.

"Report!" came a woman's voice over his commandeered radio. He eased his grip on the steel plate again to improve reception.

"Tom's down," a slightly shaky male voice responded. "I can see him from my position. I can't see Jim. He was in the kitchen and the kitchen's fucking gone."

"Maintain your position and stay cool! Any sign of the suspect?"

"No, but he's gotta be dead. Practically the whole house blew up."

"Craig! What have you got?"

"The south side of the house is pretty much intact, but the fire looks like it's getting worse. I have no movement, but there's a lot of smoke. If he is alive in there, he isn't going to last long."

Probably true, Fade knew. But, assuming that his remote would still carry with a broken antenna, he'd be around longer than they would.

Fade let the steel plate fall and laid himself out flat on the floor, holding the remote as high as he could to get maximum range.

"I think I've got movement!"

"Stay where—"

This time the explosions weren't as loud but the bright flashes briefly turned the smoke from black to gray as the model airplane servos pulled the pins from grenades he'd buried beneath the two men's exterior positions.

"Fuck!" he heard over the radio. "I'm hit. I'm hit!" The statement was followed by a less than encouraging fit of wet-sounding coughing. Obviously, the guy hadn't been where he was supposed to be. He should have been lying right on top of that grenade.

An unfortunate complication. Was it the guy on the north or the guy on the south? And was he still intact enough to shoot?

"Hold on, I'm coming." That woman's voice again. Where the hell was Matt in all this? Since when did he let other people direct operations? And since when did they put women in charge of things like this? You've come a long way, baby.

Fade ripped off his night vision goggles and jumped to his feet, dancing clumsily through the living room as small fires and hot debris burned his bare feet. North seemed the path of least resistance since there was no wall anymore, so he chose that direction, already starting to choke on the smoke as he ducked under the partially collapsed roof.

He ran half-crouched toward the low fire that was the last known position of the sniper who had been posted in his front yard. As it had been so many times before, luck was on his side and he could see the man's black-clad body parts strewn across the dirt.

He adjusted his trajectory and ran toward his shop as fast as his bare feet would carry him, but then spotted a set of headlights coming up the tree-lined road that served as his driveway.

"Craig! What's your situation?" the woman shouted over his earpiece.

No answer.

"Craig! Talk to me!"

It turned out that the headlights belonged to an enormous black van that was having a fairly hard time holding its speed on the unmaintained road surface. It bucked and crashed dramatically through the ruts, but probably wasn't going much faster than ten miles per hour.

Fade slid behind a tree and lined up his rifle sights

on the dark figure driving, but then changed his mind. His plan to die tonight seemed like it wasn't working out. Time for a little improvisation.

He crouched low and tried to arrange a few branches around him to obscure his white boxers from the truck's high beams as it continued to bounce up the road.

The driver's side window was open and he could clearly see an unhelmeted blonde head jerking back and forth inside. When she came up even with him, he leaped onto the running board and wrapped his hand around her soft ponytail and then slid back off onto the road.

He hadn't really considered what would have happened if she'd been wearing her seat belt—apparently an example of the toll his years as a reclusive furniture maker had taken on him. He guessed she would have ended up with either a broken neck or a very unattractive bald spot.

Fortunately, she wasn't all that safety conscious and instead was dragged through the window relatively unharmed. She clamped her hands around his forearm as he slammed her to the ground and the van veered into a tree.

Pulling sideways on her hair, he tried to roll her onto her stomach but when he did, she let go of his forearm and grabbed his elbow. He didn't really pay much attention until she used some tricky leverage to nearly dislocate his shoulder. Forced to release her, he found himself lying on his back in significant pain, reflecting on the fact that he probably should have learned about the dangers of women by now.

She managed to fight her way to her knees, then to her feet, and started to stumble toward her wrecked van. Fade pushed himself upright and rotated his arm experimentally. No serious damage done.

She made it about twenty feet before she dropped to her knees, fumbling at the leather strap holding her gun in its holster. He'd heard the wind go out of her when she'd come down on the surface of the road and there was just no way she could be getting much air. He jogged forward and grabbed her by the hair again and shoved her face-first to the ground, not bothering to dodge an elbow that looked like it was thrown in slow motion.

Conveniently, she had a pair of handcuffs on her belt and he used them to secure her hands behind her back while she concentrated on relearning how to breathe.

He shoved a hand beneath her waist and unbuckled her gun belt then pinned the handcuff chain to the small of her back while he performed a quick search that yielded nothing more than a small knife and her radio. By the time he'd tossed her gun into the woods and thrown her painfully over his shoulder, she was getting enough air in to make a feeble effort to kick him in the groin.

Fade walked back into the woods and grabbed his rifle with the hand he wasn't using to keep her from squirming off his shoulder. He was about to start off toward his car but instead he paused and used his toe to press the last button on his remote control. A moment later, the top of a tree about a hundred feet away exploded into flame. He ducked involuntarily and watched the burning shards of wood fly off into the night.

"I can't believe you didn't put someone up there," he said to the weakly struggling woman. "Do you have any idea what a pain in the ass it is to climb a tree with live explosives? I worked really hard on that."

"Let . . . Let me go," she managed to get out.

"Maybe later. We'll talk."

8

It was hard for Fade to shake off the persistent sense of disorientation buzzing at the back of his mind. It was kind of what he imagined he'd feel like if someone aimed a gun at his head, pulled the trigger, and discovered it wasn't loaded. When he'd gone up into his attic, he'd been comfortable in the certainty that he wouldn't survive the night. Now here he was, cruising up the highway in his underwear with a woman who wanted to kill him in the passenger seat. Or more precisely, kneeling on the floor with her face in the seat and her bound hands jammed up under the dash.

He slowed and squinted at the exit, searching his memory for a moment, then swerving onto it. The darkness deepened on the narrow rural highway, broken only occasionally by lonely gas stations and nearly nonexistent towns. After no less than three wrong turns, he found the ancient industrial park he'd been searching for and eased along the dirty, intermittently occupied façades.

The woman tensed visibly when he stopped the car and reached over her back to pull the glove compartment open and fish out a garage door opener. He hadn't used it in almost five years and didn't really expect it to work but when he pressed the button the rusted metal door in front of him began to grind its way open. His lucky day.

He pulled inside and pushed the button again, closing the door behind them. It was the only entrance to his section of the building—a long, low warehouse partitioned into a number of separate bays with the same crumbling brick that made up its exterior. This particular unit, which he'd purchased with cash when he'd come back from Colombia, consisted of three windowless rooms: the concrete pad he was parked on, a small living area, and a bedroom furnished only with a large safe and a mattress. Other than that, there wasn't much more than a tiny bathroom and a closet that he'd never bothered to clear of debris.

"We're home," he said, grabbing the woman's ponytail again and using it to drag her out through the driver's side door. She didn't bother to resist but even in the dim light being thrown off by the door opener, she looked pretty pissed off.

He stayed close behind her as they walked, holding

71

her own knife to her throat with one hand and using the other to open the metal door that led to his makeshift living room.

When they stepped through, there was a loud click in the darkness to their right. He jerked her around to use as a shield, reaching for the gunbelt slung across his shoulder. Before he could get the gun free, though, a tinny version of the song "Don't Worry, Be Happy" filled the room.

Fade let out a long breath and snapped on an overhead light. The plastic fish that he'd purchased as a joke on himself was wriggling joyfully as it sang. The idea was that if he ever came back there, it probably meant that his life was completely fucked. A pretty accurate prediction, as it turned out.

"Would you excuse me a second?" he said as he came around the woman and pulled the fish off the wall. He dropped it and began jumping up and down on it, listening to the final gurgling strains of the song as shards of plastic went skittering across the concrete floor. Despite the superficial cuts and scrapes the plastic had inflicted on his bare feet, he actually felt a little better.

When he looked up again, the woman was staring at him with a guarded, but still wide-eyed, expression. She was actually kind of striking, now that he took the time to notice. Probably about the same height as he was if it weren't for the combat boots that had elevated her to at least six feet. The black fatigues she wore were a bit formless, but the occasional points of contact hinted at the athleticism she'd used to nearly tear his arm off earlier. Her longish blonde hair was a little out of place on a woman of her profession, but complemented her slightly angular features and mildly sunburned nose. Overall impression? Professional beach volleyball player. Or surfer. Or maybe—

"What now?" she said.

Fade considered that for a moment and then began digging through a cardboard box sitting next to the sink. Finally he came up with a roll of duct tape.

"A thousand and one uses," he said, pointing to the only chair in the room.

She looked down at it but didn't move.

"For now at least, I seem to have the advantage," he reminded her, swinging the tape on his index finger. She sat hesitantly and he secured the chain of her handcuffs to the back of the chair and her ankles to the legs—being careful never to put his skull in range of one of those boots.

Satisfied that she was sufficiently stuck, he strolled into the bedroom and ripped open a garbage bag lying in the corner. Fortunately, he'd had the presence of mind to put a few changes of clothes and a couple of pairs of shoes in it next to some now rock-hard Power Bars, a few boxes of Kraft mac and cheese, and some toiletries. It could be surprisingly hard to buy clothes when you didn't have any. NO SHIRT, NO SHOES, NO SERVICE.

"Better," he said, walking back out fully clothed and scooting a plywood table in front of the woman. For

73

being in such a nasty predicament, she was holding together pretty well. She seemed to be furiously calculating behind those blue eyes, but truthfully she didn't have a whole lot of options to work with.

"Nice place," she said when the silence finally became too uncomfortable for her.

He hopped up on the table. "You like it? I got it when I came back to the States. I figured the Colombians might change their minds about me at some point and I'd have to run. They can be kind of fickle, you know? In the end, though, Castel retired and I hadn't really left anyone alive who'd want to mess with me, so I was starting to think this place was a waste of money. Then you came along."

"You . . . You should turn yourself in."

She sounded a little less sure than last time she'd spoken. The night's events and her current situation were obviously starting to sink in. It probably made sense to let that work for him for a bit. He tore a six-inch strip of tape from the roll and slapped it over her mouth before heading back into the bedroom. The safe wasn't anything fancy—he'd gotten it from Sam's Club—but it was anchored solidly to the brick wall behind it and was sturdy enough to discourage anyone but the most industrious of thieves. Judging from the thick layer of dust on it, there hadn't been any.

Fade rubbed his hands together vigorously and attacked the combination dial. On the fourth try he got it and pulled back the heavy door, exposing neatly organized racks of weapons, cash, disguises, and other accessories for the fugitive who had everything.

First, he pulled down a shoe box full of documents held together with rubber bands. Each grouping had a passport, driver's license, and at least two credit cards. The first one he pulled out had a picture of him with a long beard and the name Mohammed Fasal. Clever before 9/11 but probably no longer ideal for deflecting suspicion. The second one seemed a little more appropriate and he dropped it in a duffel along with the disguise he'd been wearing when the passport photo had been taken.

The woman in the other room seemed to be getting a bit impatient—he could hear the chair rocking back and forth as she struggled to free herself from it. When he peeked around the doorway she stopped.

Another ten minutes and he'd taken inventory of everything in the safe and filled his duffel with what he'd need that day. After closing the door and spinning the dial, he walked back out and ripped the tape off the woman's mouth.

"Goddamnit!"

"Has anyone ever told you that you exude a lot of negative energy?"

She obviously wasn't sure how to respond to that so she just watched silently as he hopped up on the table again.

"Let's talk."

"Why don't you take the rest of the tape off and we will."

He smirked and shook his head.

"Tough guy like you afraid of a woman?"

"I've been given good reason to be afraid of women. Besides, I've heard about you."

"You don't know anything about me."

"Not you specifically," Fade said, casually crossing his legs. "But I'd heard that the military was training female Special Forces to deploy in the Middle East. I figured it wasn't true because it's actually a good idea. A bunch of Christian army guys frisking women in Afghanistan just doesn't make us many friends. I guess the program's a little further along than I thought."

"What the hell are you talking about?"

"Uh, Special Forces, the Middle East, religious dif—"

"I'm a cop!"

"Uh huh."

"Look, why don't you just tell me what you want? Then I can help you, okay? I want to keep this from getting any worse than it is."

"How could it get any worse?"

Her brow actually knitted for a moment as she considered the question. "You could kill me."

Fade shrugged. "Worse for you, but not really either here or there to me."

"You don't want to get in any dee—"

"What's your name?"

"What?"

"You heard me."

"Karen."

"Okay, Karen. Let's cut to the chase. You want to survive and I want to know all about Strand. Why don't we make a trade?"

"What? I don't know any Strand."

Fade frowned deeply. "Have you not looked around? If there was any time to start running on at the mouth this would be it."

"Look, I don't know what you think is going on—"

"You don't seem stupid to me, Karen, so don't act stupid. Do you think Strand would risk his life to protect you?"

She fidgeted in her chair to the degree the tape would allow and stared down at the floor, obviously unsure how to proceed. It was probably a full thirty seconds before she looked up at him again.

"Maybe you have some problems . . . Maybe some stuff you saw when you were in the navy messed you up. The courts take that kind of stuff into consideration. I really *can* help you."

Fade couldn't help laughing. "The courts, huh?" He slid off the table and grabbed her hair again, yanking her head back. "Listen to me. I don't want to hurt you but I do want Strand and I'll do to you whatever I have to to get him. Did I mention that I was trained in interrogation techniques by the Israelis? So why don't you just tell me where he works, where he lives, and how much juice he's got. Then we'll go from there."

"I don't—"

He wrenched her head back far enough to cut off her air and noticed that her eyes weren't really blue. One was but the other was more green.

"No one's going to find you here, Karen. I can do anything I want to you for as long as it takes. Why don't we just bypass all that unpleasantness and go straight to the information part."

He released her and she damn near managed to take a bite out of his hand as he was withdrawing it. Credit where credit was due—she had guts.

"I don't know who you're talking about, you paranoid son of a bitch! So why don't you just shut up and kill me like you did my men? We both know you're going to anyway."

He leaned back against the table and crossed his arms over his chest. "You should learn to control that temper, Karen. It'll get you in trouble some day."

This was getting more complicated than he'd anticipated. The smart move was to torture her for information, kill her, and then go cut Hillel Strand's heart out with a spoon. But, while it really was true that he'd been trained by those scumbag Israelis, he'd never actually used any of that training. And he sure as hell wasn't going to start now. If she called his bluff, he was more or less out of luck.

"So you're a cop?"

"Yes! I don't know who you think I am, but I swear to God I'm just a cop. We weren't looking to hurt you. Just to arrest you and give you your day in court."

Fade nodded thoughtfully. "I would think that a bunch of cops getting shot up in the Virginia countryside would be big news."

She didn't respond and he thumbed behind him at a small black and white TV on the floor.

"So, it stands to reason that if you're telling the truth and I turn on my TV here, I'll be on damn near every channel."

He had to admit that she was pretty good. Her slightly perplexed shrug was perfect. No doubt her excuse when he flipped on an old episode of *Jeopardy* would be equally practiced.

It took a few moments for the old television to warm up, but when it did, Fade found himself looking at his front yard and what was left of his house. A reporter stood in front of a barrier of police tape speaking into a microphone.

". . . appear to have walked into an ambush led by Salam al Fayed. We don't have any information on the warrant for al Fayed, however, there is speculation that he is wanted on suspicion of terrorist activities . . ."

Fade fell over backward from his crouched position, landing on his ass as he remained glued to the screen. He'd heard sirens closing in as he'd been driving away, but he'd just assumed that one of his neighbors had called about the explosions.

"We do have confirmation that a number of police officers were injured in this attack, though we don't have any particulars at this point. What we do know, though, is that the SWAT team leader, Karen Manning, has disappeared." A photo of the woman taped to the chair behind him flashed on the screen. "If anyone has any information regarding her whereabouts, the police are asking you to call immediately—"

Fade snapped off the television and then withdrew his hand as though he'd been burned.

"No way," he said, standing and backing up until he bumped the wall behind him. "There's just no way . . ."

He suddenly remembered feeling a wallet in the back pocket of the woman's fatigues and he reached through the slats of the chair for it as she tried to squirm away.

Her driver's license was encased in plastic on one side and the name matched. Karen Manning. A little more digging and he came up with a business card and ID identifying her as Detective Karen Manning, a Virginia cop.

"Jesus Christ!" he shouted. "What were you doing out there, Karen? What on earth would make you do something like that? Are you nuts? What did you think would happen?"

"I told you," she said in a tone obviously calculated to calm him. "We weren't there to hurt you. We were just there to arrest you and give you your day in court."

"Arrest me? For what? I didn't do anything. I don't do anything. I mean nothing at all. I sit around by myself and build mediocre furniture." He thumbed back toward the television. "And don't even say you think I'm a terrorist, because that's just bullshit racial profiling."

She watched him carefully, but didn't answer.

"For the time being, at least, this is still America,

right? Don't I have a right to know what I'm being arrested for?"

"I wasn't the investigating officer, Mr. al Fayed, but my understanding is that you're suspected of working for the Colombian cartels and of involvement in the deaths of the Ramirez brothers."

"The Ramirez brothers?" he shouted. "Who the fuck are the Ramirez brothers?"

"Mr. al Fayed . . . Maybe you should just try to take a few deep breaths and relax."

Instead he picked up one of the larger pieces of his singing fish and smashed it repeatedly into the wall. Defending himself against a bunch of Homeland Security assassins was one thing—they would have known who they were up against and that they probably weren't all going home. But a police SWAT team sent in blind? That was a whole other thing . . .

"Mr. al Fayed! Calm down! Please."

"You calm down! I just killed a bunch of cops."

"And kidnapped another."

"Seems kind of irrelevant at this point," he said, dropping what was left of the fish and taking a position directly in front of her. "Who told you I killed the Fernandez brothers?"

"Ramirez. And I don't know. Apparently we got a tip."

"From who?"

"I think it was anonymous, but I'm not sure . . ."

"Bullshit! You don't send a SWAT team out to a person's house because someone called 911 and said I was a bad person."

"Like I said, I'm not the investigating officer."

"Shit!" Fade yelled and began pacing back and forth across the tiny room. What had happened was pretty clear. Strand somehow found out about the Colombians and figured he'd use it. Then, after Fade had cooled his heels in the clink for a few weeks, Strand would come and offer to spring him. For a price.

Unfortunately, things hadn't worked out quite that smoothly.

He finally stopped pacing, positioning himself behind Karen and pulling her knife from his pocket. She tried to crane her head around to see him but her bonds wouldn't allow it.

"I guess you wouldn't believe me if I told you I was sorry, would you, Karen?"

9

The dust blowing off the deserted dirt road was almost enough to blind him, but Fade left the window down anyway. From a weather perspective at least, the morning had turned out beautifully—still air almost completely lacking in humidity beneath a cloudless sky. He leaned forward and turned the car's underpowered CD player up another notch. In his experience, it was almost impossible to be depressed when listening to the Go-Gos. The Ramones and The Monkees were a close second and third, but he was convinced that a giant loudspeaker playing "Beauty and the Beat" could bring peace to Congo.

The trip odometer turned over twenty miles and Fade skidded the car to a stop in the quickly diminishing shade of a tree.

"End of the line."

Karen Manning lifted her face from the car seat and looked up at him, eyes registering the fear that she wouldn't let her face show.

"Oh. Sorry, bad choice of words." Fade leaned over her and threw the passenger door open. A solid shove sent her rolling into a dense patch of weeds next to the car.

He stepped on the gas, accelerating quickly enough for the door to slam itself shut and did a one-eighty in the road, leaving a cloud of dust that almost completely obscured the woman struggling to her feet with her hands cuffed behind her.

As he passed, she tripped on something and rolled down into a dry creek bed. It was kind of a pathetic scene and, as he watched her in the rearview mirror, he started to think maybe he was being overly harsh. Jamming his foot down on the brake pedal, he slammed the car into reverse and pulled up even with her, once again creating a nearly opaque cloud of dust.

She was letting out an impressive stream of obscenities as she tried to extract herself from the creek bed without the use of her hands and Fade jumped out of the car to help.

"Mouth like that, you should have been in the navy," he said, grabbing her under one arm and hauling her to her feet. "Do you have a key for the handcuffs?"

Her eyes shifted almost imperceptibly toward the breast pocket of her shirt and he reached for it, but she jerked back.

"You sure? It's gonna be hard to get those things over your boots and even harder to take the boots off. How about if I promise that under no circumstances will I enjoy a single moment of feeling you up?"

"You just stay away from me."

"Your call."

He reached through his car's back window and pulled out a liter bottle of water, which he dropped on the ground. "It's twenty miles straight back up this road to the main highway. You look pretty fast, but it's gonna get hot today and that's not a lot of water. Watch your pace and try to stay in the shade where you can." He turned and started to climb back into the car.

"Wait. You've got to give yourself up. You've got no chance."

Fade smiled and looked back at her. "I don't get your logic."

"You just killed a bunch of cops and they're going to pull out the stops to get you. Give yourself up now and let me take you in. I'm willing to personally guarantee your safety. Then you'll have a chance to get a lawyer and tell your side of the story. If you honestly thought you were being attacked and were in danger, a jury will listen to that."

"I don't think so. Thanks for the offer, though."

"Where are you going to go? What are you going to do? By now, there are pictures of you all over the TV. The police will be in the process of contacting everyone you ever knew and looking into everywhere you've ever been. That's no way to live."

"As sad as it sounds, it's a step up for me." He tried to get back in the car again but she actually moved to block him.

"More people could get hurt."

"I can almost guarantee it."

He grabbed her shoulders to move her aside, but as he did, his cell phone started to ring. Sighing quietly, he pulled it from his pocket. "Probably Mrs. Melman wondering why I haven't delivered her daughter's hope chest. Woman's driving me nuts . . ."

The number registering on caller ID didn't look familiar, and the fact that he didn't have any friends, combined with the fact that his number was unlisted, suggested that the call related in some way to last night.

"Look familiar?" he said, holding the phone up in front of Karen.

"My boss's direct line."

"What's his name?"

"Seymore Pickering."

"You made that up."

"Why would I lie? That's really his name."

Fade shrugged and pressed the phone to his ear. "Good morning, Seymore."

The silence on the other end suggested that this

85

man's mother indeed had named him Seymore Pickering.

"Am I speaking to Salam al Fayed?"

"Yup."

"I want to know where Karen Manning is. Has she been harmed?"

"I wouldn't really say harmed. A little dented . . ."

"I want to talk to her."

"Relax, Seymore. She's fine. You have my word."

"Then you won't mind putting her on. As a gesture of good will."

Fade rolled his eyes and held the phone up to Karen's ear. She glanced at his car, probably considering blurting out a description, but then wisely thought better of it. It seemed likely the cops had the description already anyway.

"Captain? I'm fine."

Fade pulled the phone back. "See? You should try to be more trusting."

"You have no reason to keep her or hurt her, Mr. al Fayed. She was just doing her job. As a former soldier, you should understand that."

"Whatever."

"I want you to let her go."

"Okay."

Another confused silence. "Uh, what do you want in return?"

"Nothing that I can think of."

A third silence. This guy wasn't exactly a riveting conversationalist.

"I want you to turn yourself in, Mr. Fayed. I can guarantee your safety—"

"It's *al* Fayed and let me stop you there. I've already been through this with Officer Manning. So why don't we just cut through the crap. Here's the situation, Seymore: I've got a couple of things I need to do and they don't include getting a lethal injection. You've got some freak running around Virginia killing young women and making you look like a jerk. So why don't you focus on that for a while and stay the hell away from me. In return for that small favor, I can pretty much guarantee you I'll be dead in a month."

"You know as well as I do that I can't just ignore this. Even if I wanted to."

"Yeah, I guess not . . ." When Fade spoke again, his voice had softened slightly. "Look, I'm sorry about your men. Tell their families that. Tell them that they fought really well and showed a lot of courage. I don't know if they're going to want to hear that. Probably not. What I'm trying to say here is that I don't want to get into it with any more of your guys. But if they start shooting at me, I'm going to shoot back. And I almost never come up on the short end of those kinds of exchanges."

"Mr. Fayed—"

Fade hung up and threw the phone back through the car window. "It's *al* Fayed, you dick," he mumbled to no one in particular and then slapped Karen on the shoulder. "Catch you later."

Her eyes widened again in that nearly imperceptible

way that was kind of endearing.

"It's just a figure of speech," he said as he slid behind the wheel. "You need to lighten up."

Fade couldn't help laughing at his reflection in the rearview mirror that was now wedged in the trunk of a tree. His long black hair was gone, replaced by a blond crewcut that had an unnatural red hue in the sun. There was a tiny drop of blood around the post of the gold earring he'd shoved through his left lobe, and a pair of blue-tinted, wire-rimmed glasses finished things off. The overall effect wasn't as startling as he had expected—he'd managed only to transform himself from a hippie Arab assassin into a gay Arab assassin. It seemed almost certain now that he was going to meet his maker looking like Saddam Hussein's hairdresser.

Stranger still was the fact that while he was chopping his hair off, he'd noticed his hands were rock steady. They'd been shaking incessantly for years—not enough to be generally noticeable, but enough to be a pain in the ass during fine cabinet work. The slight tightness in his chest that had become so ubiquitous was gone too, leaving him feeling . . . good. Really good.

He flashed a wide smile at the mirror and tried to decide if he looked insane. More or less. But was it just the hair and the glasses or something deeper? A little bit of both, he supposed. Having half the cops in America wanting to put a bullet in his skull shouldn't be an occasion for celebration, but with his history it also couldn't be dismissed as all bad either. Killing Hillel Strand and Matt Egan gave him a purpose—something he'd been lacking for too long. The cops just added an extra dash of excitement.

The worst case scenario for him was that he failed to get those two assholes before they got him. Not the worst thing in the world—it certainly put an end to the loneliness, boredom, and low-grade panic he'd been living with since his injury. So a few weeks of heat and flash and then it would be all over. Not exactly a lottery win, but it beat the hell out of what had come before it.

Fade tore the bandage from the self-inflicted wound on his wrist, loaded his wallet with the documents that matched the disguise he'd chosen, and then glanced at his watch. He'd stopped about fifteen miles from where he'd left Karen Manning and had probably already been there too long. The cops would have gotten his general location from his cell phone and if he read Karen right, she was running.

10

She was pushing too hard—running at close to the speed she would have in college when she'd been nationally ranked in the ten thousand meters. Slowing down, though, meant taking the advice of the man who had butchered her entire team so instead she sped up, intensifying the burning in her lungs and the draw of the bottle of water sloshing seductively in her hand. Anger and frustration managed to overpower her lack of fitness and combat boots, allowing her to maintain that pace for more than ten minutes before she began to stumble uncontrollably. Finally, she stopped and sagged against a tree, bending at the waist and coughing violently as she tried to hide from the sun.

She'd always used running to shut out the rest of the world. The worse things were, the harder she went, ratcheting up her suffering until everything just drowned in it. But she'd never had to face anything like this before. There was just no pace hard enough to silence the panicked voices of her men right before they went irretrievably silent.

"Pull it together, Karen," she said between gasps.

This wasn't about her. She had to get to the highway as fast as she could and doing twenty miles in a series of two-mile sprints wasn't going to get that done. She started running again, with a more reasonable gait, but began to falter almost immediately.

What was the hurry, really? Al Fayed, while very possibly completely out of his mind, didn't strike her as stupid. He'd have dropped her off far enough out that he'd be long gone before she could contact the office and tell them . . . what? In the end, she'd wind up sitting in the interrogation room answering questions that would become increasingly accusatory and probably wouldn't contribute at all to catching him. Or bring her men back from the dead.

She tried to run again, but made it only a few steps before slowing to a walk.

The tension since she'd taken the job as SWAT team leader had been almost unbearable—between her and management, between her and her men. Between her and just about everyone. Was that an excuse? No. The bottom line was that she had been in charge. She had planned the assault; she'd given the order to go in. And now they all were dead.

What she didn't completely understand was how. She'd done everything she'd been trained to do—based on al Fayed's military history, she'd been absolutely fanatic about playing everything by the numbers. She'd been prepared for a violent, paranoid asshole with a stack of automatic rifles and a deep-seated hatred for authority. SEAL or no SEAL, this guy had walked through her and her men like they weren't there.

Based on the elaborate booby traps and the fact that he was hiding in the attic armed to the teeth, it seemed almost certain that he'd been ready for them. Or was he just a complete paranoid and had been waiting every night for the last five years to be attacked?

Karen considered herself a fairly good judge of people and based on that, she more or less believed everything al Fayed had told her. Or at least she believed that he believed what he'd said. Clearly, he had been expecting someone named Strand. Maybe someone attached to the Colombian cartels he'd worked for? Kind of a long time ago, but it wasn't out of the question that those types of people might hold a grudge. Another interesting point was that he seemed genuinely not to have a clue who the Ramirez brothers were. And then there was the odd fact that she was still alive. After killing that many cops, she seemed like kind of a glaring loose end.

Karen took a measured sip of her water and started out again, this time at a pace that she could maintain to the highway and that would allow her to think—to try to recall every detail of her conversation with al Fayed. While she hadn't panicked, she had been scared half to death. Being taped to a chair by a psycho who had taken out an entire SWAT team single-handedly wasn't a situation she'd ever thought to prepare herself for.

11

Matt Egan threw open the door to Strand's office and pointed at Lauren, who was scribbling on a notepad as her boss spoke.

"Out!"

She looked up at him then at Strand before deciding that a quick exit was probably in her best interest. Egan stepped aside and held the door open as she hustled, head down, through it.

"What the hell do you think—" Strand started.

"Are you crazy?" Egan shouted, slamming the door hard enough to rattle the framed photos on the wall.

"You sent the cops over there? *The cops?* That was a fucking stroke of genius, wasn't it?"

"I think maybe you should keep in mind who you're talking to and the position you're in," Strand said with calm that looked a little practiced.

"The position *I'm* in?"

"What exactly did you say to him when you two were alone, Matt? Did you warn him?"

"Is that a joke?"

Strand was leaning back in his chair, hands folded across his stomach. "I'm not sure what choice I had here, Matt. Al Fayed—a former American soldier—was working for the drug cartels. The police should have been called in a long time ago. But his involvement was covered up. By you. And now, perhaps also because of you, he was expecting something. The police should have been able to just walk in there and catch him sleeping."

One of the many sad ironies in all this was that Egan actually *had* considered calling Fade and telling him that Strand knew about his connection to the cartels. He'd quickly abandoned the idea, though. It would have been impossible to predict how he'd react. Better to just let Strand play his hand and deal with it then. The new director of Homeland Security was a former Marine general and an honorable man. Egan could go to him and tell him everything—a move that would probably end his career and maybe land him in jail, but would hopefully leave Fade to live out what was left of his life in peace.

How the hell could he have anticipated that Strand would do something this stupid?

"Nice speech, Hillel. Are there hidden mikes in here or are you just trying to convince yourself? You set Fade up so you could swoop in and save him later—in return for him kissing your ass and going to work for you. How much did the cops know? How much did you tell them?"

"They had full access to his military record and any other information they wanted to dig up. That's their job."

"But his military record doesn't really tell the whole story, does it? You sent a bunch of cops up against one of the most efficient killers this country ever produced and now they're dead. Strange, though, that I haven't seen your name on the TV—you being the law-abiding hero of this story and all."

"The police knew he was a former SEAL," Strand said, the volume of his voice rising a bit. "And an enforcer for the Colombian cartels. I don't think they needed me to tell them he was dangerous."

He had to hand it to Strand. The man was the master of his arena. Unfortunately, that arena was political and he seemed completely incapable of seeing beyond it. The time might be coming that he'd have to learn, though. Fade had never been all that interested in working through bureaucratic channels.

"Why don't you just calm down and sit, Matt."

Egan didn't move.

"I'm just trying to be a little bit practical here," he

continued. "If al Fayed is captured and goes to trial, this is all going to come out. That could be very damaging—to the country, to our relationship with the Arabs, and frankly to you personally."

Matt shook his head slowly. It wasn't hard to picture Strand speaking earnestly to a group of enraged congressmen, carefully shifting blame. It would go something like, "I first came into contact with al Fayed in order to interview him for a position at Homeland Security. Obviously, we're looking to get the best people possible to protect this great country against the ever-present threat of terrorism. Unfortunately, we discovered that he'd been involved in the drug trade and had no choice but to call the police with that information. Of course, we did this anonymously to protect our intelligence sources. Only later did it come to my attention that my deputy, Matt Egan—that's E-G-A-N—had been involved in this illegal and irresponsible cover-up."

"If it was anyone but you, Hillel, I'd think they were just playing dumb. But you really are this stupid, aren't you? You have no idea what you've done. Not a fucking clue . . ."

"Stand down!" Strand shouted from behind his desk. He was famous for his extensive knowledge of military jargon, though it was widely known that he had transferred from the Naval Academy to Harvard after a whopping three weeks.

"Do you just want to ignore this situation?" Strand continued, the anger still audible in his voice. "Or do you want to sit your ass down and talk rationally about what needs to be done? I assume that you agree that it isn't exactly in your best interest *or* the police's for them to find al Fayed before we do . . ."

The sentence seemed to hang in the air, purposely unfinished. Egan decided to finish it.

"And get rid of him."

Strand frowned slightly in an expression that clearly signaled his agreement. No matter how slick he was, Strand figured that there was no way al Fayed could be run through the legal system without getting everyone involved dirty. A situation made even more complicated by the fact that if Egan went down over this, he'd do everything in his power to make sure he took his boss with him.

"Where would he go, Matt? Friends? Family? Would he leave the country? Maybe go back to Colombia? Or maybe somewhere like Syria where he could blend in and we'd have a hard time tracking him?"

Egan stared down at his boss for a few more seconds, shook his head in disbelief, and then walked out.

12

"Is your mind closed, or is it just your ears?"

Matt turned away from a sink full of dishes and looked at his wife, but didn't say anything. She was leaning over Kali's shoulder, silently supervising the crayon selection being used in the creation of tonight's portrait. It was the rule of the house—Kali had to produce something artistic before she got her daily hour of television. Elise tended to lump TVs in with handguns and household poisons on the danger scale, and he'd had to fight tooth and nail just to get her to agree to have one in the house. The hour-for-a-portrait exchange was just another of the many bizarre compromises that made their marriage work.

"Matt?" she said, finally looking up at him. "Are you in there?"

"I was listening."

He'd first seen Elise at a party his former neighbor, a reasonably successful sculptor, had asked him to. It was obvious that the invitation had been semirhetorical and offered mostly because the guy was afraid of him, but Egan had gone anyway. Mostly just to get a glimpse at a world he'd never had an opportunity to see. At the time, he was still adjusting to his move from the army to the CIA and was in the process of trying to expand his horizons a bit. Having said that, he remembered he'd still had the buzz cut and walked into the party like he had a broom handle up his ass.

Predictably, the other guests had given him a wide berth. After about a half an hour, he'd taken to pinning people in corners, trying out increasingly friendly and innocuous opening lines, only to have his quarry squirm back and forth for a few seconds before breaking free.

Eventually, he'd resigned himself to stuffing tasteless vegetarian hors d'oeuvres in his mouth and watching from the sidelines. Elise was hard to miss. The combination of her striking physical appearance and the completely unself-conscious theatrical quality of her movements created a weird charisma. Even from a distance.

Not surprisingly, he wasn't the only person who noticed—she was constantly surrounded by people who looked and acted more like admirers than friends. He abandoned the bowl of tabbouleh and found some lonely wall space close enough to her to eavesdrop. After ten minutes or so, he managed to piece together a few things. First, that she was some kind of musician. Second, that she took the praise being heaped on her with considerable discomfort—constantly trying to change the subject from her to the people around her.

He'd considered trying to talk to her, sensing that she might be relieved to have a conversation with someone who had no clue who she was, but the crowd around her never diminished. Besides, what would he have to say that could possibly interest a woman like that?

Eventually, he wandered back to the food table and by the time he raised his head from the sushi rolls, she'd disappeared. With her gone and his stomach uncomfortably full, there didn't seem to be much holding him there. After embarrassing the hell out of his neighbor by profusely thanking him for the invitation in front of all his friends, Egan had grabbed a fresh beer and headed out into the night.

He wandered toward his house, reading the socially conscious bumper stickers on the cars lined up along the curb and ignoring the sound of someone in a rusted panel van trying to start a very sick-sounding motor. He knew a fair amount about engines, but didn't stop. Hell if he was going to get all greasy for some person who wouldn't lower himself to say three words to him. And why weren't they on a bicycle anyway? Wouldn't that be more environmentally friendly?

The would-be driver kept trying and the engine kept refusing. After another fifty feet, Egan, starting to feel guilty, sighed quietly and turned around.

"You wouldn't happen to be a brilliant mechanic who works on a completely philanthropic basis, would you?"

He froze as the young woman stepped from the van and stared sadly at the hood without bothering to open it. It was her.

Fortunately, it only took a few seconds for him to realize he was standing motionless on the sidewalk for no apparent reason. A quick recovery sent him strolling casually up next to her.

"I'm a marginal mechanic with an occasional charitable streak."

"Beggars can't be choosers. My name's Elise." She looked straight into his eyes when she offered her hand, giving the impression that she didn't see his dopey clothes and nearly nonexistent hair. "You were at the party, right? Holding up the wall?"

"That was me." For some reason he'd expected her skin to be cold but it wasn't. "Why don't you pop the hood and I'll take a look."

A three-minute examination with a penlight she'd dug from a pile of junk on her floorboard was all he needed.

"When you use the word 'hopeless,' " she said, "do you mean a bit forlorn or truly despondent?"

"Probably somewhere in between. You're looking at about two hundred and fifty bucks."

"No way to just give it a few good kicks so I can get home?"

" 'Fraid not. Do you have Triple-A?"

She shook her head.

He'd offered to give her a ride home and, surprisingly, she'd taken him up on it despite the fact that the party was lousy with people who would have given their eyeteeth to do it.

He couldn't remember how the conversation had come around to politics, but it had and she'd displayed a not too surprising activist liberal streak. He, on the other hand, had been smack in the middle of his brief "humanity is doomed" period and thrown every plot she had to help the downtrodden back in her face. He'd seen a lot in his short life and had come to the conclusion that the downtrodden were downtrodden because they deserved to be. It wasn't about poor soil and drought. It was about culture and politics.

Now, why he'd not just agreed with everything this

unbelievable creature sitting in his passenger seat had said, he still wasn't sure. Some unhealthy combination of nervousness and self-doubt, probably.

By the time she stepped out into her driveway, she was pretty angry. Which made it all the more strange when she'd called him the next day and told him she was doing some reading to prepare for continuing their discussion at the Italian restaurant around the corner from her house.

"Matt?" Elise sang. "Oh, Matt, darling."

He blinked. "Yeah?"

"What's wrong with you tonight? You look like you're auditioning for a zombie movie."

"Uh, I've got a business trip."

"A what?"

"It just came up today."

"What are you talking about? When?"

"I have to leave tonight."

"Tonight?"

"It just came up."

"You said that already."

He nodded dumbly. Fade was probably still in the process of working through his new reality, but pretty soon he'd get his shit together and then there was no telling what he'd do. Actually, that wasn't true. It wasn't hard to predict at all.

"How long are you going to be gone?"

"I'm not exactly sure."

"A day? A month? A year?"

"Maybe a week?"

"Where are you going?"

"Kind of around . . ."

Elise's mouth hung open for a moment and then she patted Kali on her head and told her to go watch TV.

"But I'm not finished."

"You can let your audience finish it in their minds, honey. It could be a catalyst for their own imagination."

Kali had no idea what that meant, but a moment later it sunk in that her TV time was going to be extended and she ran off before her mother could change her mind.

"Have a seat, Matt."

"The dishes aren't done."

She pointed to a chair and he did as he was told.

"What's going on?"

"Nothing."

"Tell me this isn't an operational job. We talked about this before we adopted Kali. You're too old and you have a family now. You're a paper pusher."

"I am a paper pusher. I'm—"

"You agreed to this, Matt." She waved her hand around the kitchen. "You wanted all this. I didn't stand here and dictate your life to you."

He was not in the habit of lying to her and it was making him uncomfortable enough to turn him defensive. "I don't know what you want me to say, Elise. When you and Madonna are like sisters, maybe I can quit. But for now, a job is a job."

"Don't even go there, Matt. If you're walking out of here tomorrow to go shoot Afghans, I can damn well get a nine-to-five job in sound production or something. I—"

The ringing of his cell phone interrupted her train of thought. "For God's sake, Matt! That's the fifth time tonight. Pick it up or turn it off!"

The previous five times it had been Hillel Strand, who was obviously a bit concerned about him disappearing from the office after their meeting. He was undoubtedly wondering if his deputy had found an angle he hadn't covered.

Egan pulled the phone from his pocket and was about to shut it off, but then realized it wasn't Strand's number appearing in the window. He couldn't remember ever seeing it before.

"Matt?"

He felt an uncomfortable jolt of adrenaline and held a hand up, silencing her and hoping the blood hadn't drained visibly from his face. She was looking right at him.

"Hello," he said, pressing the phone to his ear.

"Hello, Matt."

"Could you hold on for a second?"

"Sure. Why not."

Egan pressed the mute button and walked around the table. "I'm sorry," he said, kissing her on top of the head. "I don't want you to get a nine-to-five job and I'm not going to shoot any Afghans. It's just a training thing. That's all."

She didn't seem convinced, but there wasn't anything that he could do about that now. He clicked the mute off and started for his den.

"Hello, Fade."

"Cops. That wasn't nice."

"I don't suppose you'd believe me if I told you that I had nothing to do with that."

"I don't suppose I would. You've been spying on me, man. Who else would have known about the Colombians? Who else would have cared what I did after I left?"

Egan closed the door and sat down behind his desk, not bothering to turn on a light. The moon glowing outside the window was enough to see by and he couldn't shake the feeling that Fade might be across the street with a rifle.

"There were . . ." Egan let his voice trail off. What was the point? "What's done is done, Fade."

No response.

"So where do we stand?"

"You fucked me, man. Again."

"You know, I'm getting a little tired of hearing this shit. I went to the very top to get you that surgery. And when you went to Colombia to get the money yourself, I covered it up—"

"Thank God you've got my back, huh? Without you, my life might be screwed up."

"What did you want me to do? Put a gun to the president's head and get him to write your doctor a check? This is Washington, Fade. Not Rwanda. If I'd had the fucking money, I'd have given it to you myself. You know that."

Silence.

"So where are we, Fade? How do we get out of this?"

"There is no way out."

"Bullshit. What if I help you leave the country? How much money do you have? Enough to live on?"

"You're remembering me stupider than I am, Matt. You and Strand got a bunch of cops killed to make a point. I doubt you're going to take the chance that information—or anything else I might have to say—could come out in court. I imagine it'd be a little tough on your careers."

"Fade, we can—"

"You can what? Just let this go? What about the cops? Are they just going to forget about me? Are you going to give me a few million and set me up in a beachfront place in Brazil? Or maybe you think I ought to just slink off there myself and hide in a sewer until my legs don't work anymore. Come on, Matt. Say it. I want to hear you say it, you son of a bitch. Say, 'Come in, Fade. We'll fix this. We'll put it all right again.'"

"I can't make guarantees—not about things I don't have control over. All I can tell you is that I'll do my best."

"Your best isn't good enough, though, is it? I've never gotten anything but fucked by your best."

"Fade—"

"I let it slide the first time, man. But not again. I'm not looking forward to it, but I'm going to kill you."

Egan had known where this conversation was going from the beginning but actually hearing the words hit him hard. Suddenly, breathing didn't seem to come naturally and he had to concentrate on not stopping. Nothing had ever felt like this before—not even when he'd worked in the field. The difference, of course, was simple. Back then, he hadn't had all that much to lose. So what now? Argue? Beg? Reason? Too little too late. Always too little too late.

"I . . . I assume it goes without saying that Elise and Kali are out of this, right? Nothing happens in front of them."

"And I assume it goes without saying that you're still man enough not to hide behind them?"

Matt nodded into the phone. "See you soon, Fade."

13

"All I'm saying, Karen, is it's kind of strange that he drilled your entire team and left you without a goddamn scratch."

The interrogation room was what anyone who watched television would expect: gray walls, a single table surrounded with uncomfortable chairs, a small window covered in chicken wire. The fact that she was there and not in a slightly more cheerful conference room probably wasn't good news. On the other hand, maybe it was a blessing in disguise—at least it blocked out the rest of the precinct. When she'd walked through it that morning, she'd been preceded by dead silence and followed by quiet whispers. No one bothered to hide the fact that they were staring and very few bothered to hide their animosity.

"Your team's dead. And you're sitting here sipping tea."

Not an entirely accurate statement. All reports suggested that Erin was going to pull through. And she was drinking a Coke. Karen leaned back in her chair and looked up at Captain Pickering, who seemed content to stand against the wall and let Ken, the department's top interrogator, do the heavy lifting.

"I just want you to tell me why you think that is, Karen."

It was the fifth time this particular question had come up. The first time it was delivered in a friendly, offhand way. Now, though, Ken was leaning over the table, supporting himself with his knuckles, face turning a light shade of pink. The fact that this puffy jerk thought he could intimidate her was just more proof that no one in this organization had a clue who she was. They were still locked onto what they needed her to be.

"He was kind of cute so I fucked his brains out. After that, I guess he thought it would be rude to kill me."

Ken's jaw tightened. "Maybe he wants something from you going forward?"

"What would that be exactly?"

"I don't know. Maybe you made a deal with him,

107

He lets you go and you give him information about our investigation." He softened so suddenly and perceptibly that there was little doubt it was affected. "I sure as hell might have if I'd been in your situation. Tied to a chair by some psycho . . ."

The general theme taking shape was that her guys had fought valiantly and died heroically while she cowered and bargained to save her neck. No big surprise. Many of the men she worked with had turned searching for her weaknesses into a full-time job. Whenever she failed at anything, they were there with yet another blonde joke. And more often than not, they weren't even funny.

"Taped actually—I was taped to the chair. And I have no doubt you'd have made a deal. But I'm not you, am I?"

Ken backed away from the table for a moment, shoving his hands in his pockets and trying to calculate a new angle. She sipped her Coke and stared directly at him.

The truth was, she deserved at least part of the anger some of her colleagues directed at her. When she'd gotten the job, the combination of her own self-doubt and all the affirmative action talk had caused her to react in a way typical for her but not exactly productive. She should have been in the bars after hours drinking beers with the guys, but instead she'd let that spark of insecurity focus her solely on making sure she did everything just a little better than everyone else. She'd told herself that she was doing it to gain her team's respect, but that wasn't really the whole truth.

Worse, she'd refused to allow herself to be politicized and walked away from the feminist contingent who were her only supporters. They'd quickly labeled her as a traitor and now probably wanted to see her fail as much as anyone. The lesson to be learned? The end result of mixing slightly tarnished intentions with defensiveness and ego could be kind of explosive.

"You said he was expecting you," Ken said, spitting the words out with disgust that she figured he really felt. "Are you suggesting he has a source in the police department?"

Again, the implication was clear: that she was trying to divert blame from herself. To make excuses.

"I said he was waiting for *someone*. Not us. I honestly don't believe that he knew we were cops until he saw it on TV. If he had known, I'd be dead now."

"The mysterious Strand . . ."

She shrugged. "That's who he wanted information on."

"We've run the name through every database in the country and come up with nothing. No one in the drug trade, no one involved in terrorism, no one he was involved with in the military . . ."

"Maybe it's someone the DEA doesn't know about. Maybe it's an alias. Where did you get the tip? Are you talking to your informant?"

Ken just frowned and looked away.

"I'm serious," she said, leaning across the desk and

trying to get him to look at her. "When you start putting all this together, it gets a hell of a lot more complicated than some paranoid ex-soldier blowing a—"

"Oh, so you've—"

"I hate being interrupted, Ken!"

He actually stopped talking, more out of surprise than anything else.

"First, I don't think he had anything to do with killing the Ramirez brothers."

"So we're going to just take his word for that?" Ken managed to get in.

"After wiping out a bunch of cops, why would he bother to lie about killing a couple of drug dealers?" She paused for a moment to take a breath. "Second, I believe that al Fayed was expecting someone named Strand to attack him. If he knew that we were cops from the beginning, why let me go?"

"Because you're going to help him keep ahead of our investigation?"

She leaned back in her chair. "Come on, Ken . . . Are we going to talk seriously or not? Where did we get our information on this guy? Some kind of tip, right? From who?"

He ignored the question as he had every other time she'd posed it. Clearly it was something that either he didn't know or didn't want to tell her.

"That's where I'd be looking, if I was you," she continued. "What if this informant knew al Fayed was ready for him and decided to call us and let us do his dirty work for him?"

"Shut the hell up!" Captain Pickering shouted, finally unsticking himself from the wall. "Just shut your mouth. You completely fuck up this operation and get your entire team killed and now what? It's my fault? Based on a bunch of half-assed theories, you've got the force being manipulated into doing the cartel's wet work? All I asked you to do was go in and arrest this son of a bitch so we could talk to him. But you couldn't handle it. You can sit there and try to deflect the blame all you want but it just looks pathetic."

"Pathetic?" she shouted back. "Who told you that it wasn't exactly a stroke of genius to go in there with guns blazing and no intelligence? Who told you that we should just pick him up on a traffic violation? And who told you that it seemed a little strange that some big shot cartel enforcer was living in a falling-down house building furniture? Maybe you ought to focus a little less on making sure none of this sticks to you and a little more on trying to find this guy! Because I'll tell you that standing around here waiting for me to remember that he gave me his address and phone number isn't going to get us anywhere."

Pickering just stood there for a moment and then motioned for Ken to follow him outside. When the door closed, Karen slammed a fist down on the table and jumped up from her chair. She walked over to the window, curling her fingers through the chicken wire and leaning her forehead on the sill.

Stupid. Why the hell couldn't she learn to keep her goddamn mouth shut? What was it al Fayed had said to her? That her temper would get her in trouble someday? That psycho was just full of astute observations.

Nothing good was going to come of any of this. Her men were dead and there was nothing that could be done about that. The best Pickering could hope for was to assign blame and exact revenge. On the first count, they had a pretty strong hand. Pickering would stay away from the question of who had provided the tip and why, concentrating instead on the indisputable fact that al Fayed had killed a bunch of cops. Then he'd imply that he'd been under political pressure to put her in charge of the SWAT team and that she had always been a disaster waiting to happen. The fact that she'd done everything by the book would be carefully obscured. No one wanted to hear it anyway. They just wanted someone to blame.

Hell, maybe they were right. The book notwithstanding, it had been her plan, her team. She could have done more than make a few weak protests and then allow herself to be bullied into charging in like an idiot. She could have demanded more intelligence or insisted on waiting until he was isolated and unarmed. But she hadn't.

Even worse was the manhunt that was gearing up. There was little doubt that given enough time, they would turn up al Fayed—the police had a way of raising the level of their game when it came to dealing with people who killed their own. And that meant another showdown. The problem was that she wasn't sure if they'd do any better in round two.

14

The dress shirt Matt Egan was carefully folding into his suitcase was purely for the benefit of his wife in case she walked in. The only realistic use for it he could think of was making his body presentable at the funeral home. Now that was cheerful, wasn't it?

He carried the half-full suitcase into the bathroom and swept his things into it, turning away before he could catch his reflection in the mirror. No point in reminding himself of his slightly shaggy hair or the wire-rimmed glasses or the inevitable reproportioning of his thirty-eight-year-old body into something a little narrower at the shoulder and wider at the waist. Not that he was what most people would call soft. He ran five miles at a reasonable clip three days a week and spent an hour in the weight room on the other four days. Sometimes, though, it seemed like a losing battle. He latched the top of his suitcase and walked down the hall toward his den, reminding himself that his slow physical decline wasn't all that relevant. Seven years ago, Fade had singlehandedly taken out him and his entire team in a training exercise in the North Carolina back country.

Elise was nowhere to be seen as he padded through the kitchen; probably entangled in the ever-lengthening process of putting Kali to bed. He stopped in the hallway, considering going to help, but for some reason he suddenly felt like an outsider—like he didn't belong with them anymore. It was more than just the lies, it was the fact that he shouldn't have allowed himself to be put in this situation. It wasn't his right anymore.

Egan closed the door behind him and sat at his desk, dropping the suitcase on top. It took almost a minute of flipping through his overstuffed key ring in the semidarkness to find the one that fit to his lower right drawer. If Elise had ever noticed the drawer being locked—and she almost certainly had—she'd never mentioned it. It seemed likely that she didn't want to know what was inside.

The pistol that he extracted seemed kind of pathetic compared to the arsenal he imagined Fade had amassed. It was more a memento than a weapon, really. In fact, it was the only reminder of his military career that hadn't made its way to the attic. His den had evolved into more of a shrine to his wife's accomplishments than his own: framed CDs, concert posters, magazine articles, reviews. She'd protested, of course, but the truth was he didn't really want to dwell on his past. While it was true that the army had done a lot for him, he couldn't exactly say he had fond memories of it.

The Egans could only be described as coming from solid poor white trash stock. The family tradition was to barely graduate from high school, enlist in the Marines, spend a few years getting harassed by the military police, then get a job as a mechanic or factory worker. Bowling every Wednesday night, a drunken brawl every other Saturday. Once a month, slap the wife around.

And for a long time he managed to convince himself that he would follow that same path. He'd thrown classes on purpose, only to sneak off and bury himself in books when his father thought he was practicing sports. Despite his best effort to the contrary, he'd actually graduated high school with a B average. Of course, no one—not even he himself—saw that achievement as anything other than a mildly amusing fluke and it had certainly never occurred to him that there were directions in life that had never been taken by his relatives before him.

Despite his admitted lack of imagination, he'd shown a small glimmer of independent thought when, much to the disappointment of his father, he'd joined the Army instead of the Marines after graduation. He'd really wanted to go for the even more cushy Air Force, but had figured the ensuing family scandal would be too much to bear.

After showing up for basic training, it had taken only about thirty seconds for him to begin to loathe the restrictions and relentless structure of military life. And after a few months of it, he'd been almost ready to shoot himself. Then, one day, he'd been drowning his sorrows at a local bar and gotten to talking to a Green Beret who painted a fairly attractive picture of the Special Forces—intelligence gathering, the encouragement of intellectual pursuits, and most of all, the fact that they were left alone as much as an enlisted man could hope.

Egan made it through the rigorous training program by sheer force of will. After that, it had turned out to be a pretty good gig all around—his success had closed the rift between him and his father to the degree it could be closed, and the learning opportunities were incredible. While he was never going to be the strongest or fastest on the team, he'd shown a real aptitude for foreign cultures, languages, and analysis.

Everything was going along just fine when the Army suddenly decided to ask him to actually do something for his paycheck. They'd sent him to Jordan and he'd been forced to kill a man. Six, actually. And that marked the end of his love affair with the Special Forces. As soon as he landed back in the States, he'd typed up a resignation letter. His commanding officer promptly tore it up and told him to come back in two days. When he'd returned, exactly forty-eight hours later, there was a guy from West Point waiting for him. Suddenly, he was in college.

Not having much of a work ethic when it came to things he wasn't interested in, he hadn't much cared for the university atmosphere. He'd quickly developed a bad habit of looking at issues from too many angles and then arguing vehemently with his professors—something that hadn't exactly endeared him to the faculty. The whole idea of having someone stand at the head of a class and tell him what to think just never sat well with him.

The bottom line was that he had a problem with authority figures and that wasn't a great trait in a soldier. So he was floored when Military Intelligence had come sniffing around at the recommendation of a number of his instructors.

Suddenly, he was a spook. And a pretty good one. Still, though, his personal life had remained kind of a mess. His wife probably would have called it an identity crisis. A little touchy-feely, but more or less accurate. There had been so much cultural baggage to unload before he could see the possibilities that his West Point friends took for granted.

It had all come together when he'd finally gone over to the more liberal CIA and then met Elise. It wasn't until then that he figured out that he was being driven slowly crazy by a life of trying to stuff his square peg into other people's round hole.

And now here he was, a thirty-eight-year-old man finally at peace with himself. He had everything he'd grown up not even knowing that he wanted. And now he was going to lose it all.

15

The car was a little beat up and pulled hard to the left, but in so many other ways it was perfect. How far wrong could you go with a sky-blue '65 Cadillac Deville convertible? It was spacious, had snappy acceleration, and offered almost infinite opportunities to let the wind blow through his newly sheared hair. Fade pulled the beer from a drink holder hanging on the door and checked the speedometer to make sure he was hovering just below the speed limit as he aimed the car north on I-95.

For a reason that he couldn't seem to put his finger on, he was feeling a bit down. The sky was cloudless, the trunk of his sweet new ride was full of cash, guns, and liquor, and his problems were so insurmountable that there was no point in even worrying about them. So what was the rub? A little more consideration and the answer came to him: Matt Egan.

Even after everything that had happened, there was no way he could completely turn his back on their history. Egan had saved his ass on more than one occasion—not by doing anything as showy as dragging his injured body through a minefield, but his efforts were just as real. Matt always put the safety of his men at the top of the list and his intelligence almost never failed to be impeccable. When things got hairy, there was nothing like hearing his voice come over the radio. You knew if you did exactly what he said, you were going to make it.

And then there was Mary Jane.

Fade had been working with Egan for about a year when word got around that his father was dying. The other rumor was that he wasn't going to see him because of some bad blood. By then, Fade and he had gotten pretty close and it seemed obvious that this was going to be a decision that his friend would regret. So, one morning Fade had stacked the back seat of his piece of shit Corvette with four cases of beer, driven to Matt Egan's house, and under serious protest taken him to Kentucky.

It had been a bizarre trip for a twenty-five-year-old Arab-American kid from Brooklyn. To him, the Egan family seemed like a bunch of toothless, possum gumming freakazoids from the planet Hillbilly. One notable exception was Matt's sister Mary Jane, who he was putting through nursing school. Fade and she hit it off and made a pact to stay in touch. By the time she graduated a year later, they were meeting halfway between their homes every other weekend.

Not knowing how Matt would react, they kept it quiet, but it was inevitable that he'd eventually find out. When he did, he was actually happy about it and couldn't understand why they hadn't told him. It had occurred to Fade at the time that you could be fairly certain a guy wasn't just pretending to be your friend when he found out you were sleeping with his sister and he seemed psyched about it.

Who knows what would have happened if he hadn't gotten shot and fucked over? Matt would probably be his brother-in-law and his kids would be getting guitar lessons from Elise Egan.

But it hadn't worked out that way. When he'd returned, MJ tried to call him and see him a thousand times and a thousand times he'd turned away. Eventually the phone just stopped ringing.

Fade drained the rest of his beer and tossed the bottle in the back seat, trying to shake off the memory. Deep thinking about the Egan family was in no way part of his brilliant three-step plan to cheer himself up. With the car purchased, it was time to move on to phase two. He dialed a number written on the back of his hand into his fancy new phone and pressed it hard to his ear, trying to block out the rush of the wind.

"Homeland Security, how can I direct your call?"

"Hillel Strand's office, please," he shouted.

There was a brief pause and then a woman's voice. "Yes, can I help you?"

"Put Hillel on, please."

"May I ask who's calling?"

"Salam al Fayed."

Obviously the woman either knew what was going on or was following the news, because there was an uncomfortably long pause before she spoke again. "Could you hold for a moment?"

He fished another beer off the floorboard.

"Mr. al Fayed? Are you all right?"

"I'm great, Hillel. Thanks for asking. How about you?"

"Where are you? Can you get to us?"

"Oh, I'm counting on it. Sending the police to my house wasn't very sporting."

"I didn't know anything about that. How would I?"

"No one seems to want to take the rap for this. But that's what sucks about being in charge, isn't it, Hillel? The buck has to stop somewhere."

"Look, Mr. al Fayed . . . I'm sorry about all this— I'm trying to find out exactly what happened, but I don't know anything yet. It's true that I wanted you to work for us. You're the best and we want the best, but we heard you loud and clear. I certainly understand the genesis of your feelings about the government and frankly I don't blame you. It was the government's responsibility to stand behind you and it didn't. Maybe we can make up for that now."

He had to admit that Strand was a good talker. Very soothing. Very earnest. Quite a change from the man he'd met in his front yard.

"And how would you do that?"

"We have fairly substantial resources and a certain amount of freedom to make decisions. Not enough to get you off the hook for this—no one's got that kind of juice. What we can do, though, is get you another identity and get you out of the country. We might also be able to convince the police that you're dead. I can't guarantee that last thing, though."

"You're quite the little politician aren't you, Hillel? Big future. But I'm guessing that a meeting between you and me could only end with a bullet in my back, and I've already got one of those. No. No politics, no legal maneuvering, no mind fucking. Just you and me."

"Mr. al Fayed—" Strand said, the pitch of his voice going up a bit.

"Remember the game you were talking about at my house, Hillel? Welcome to it."

Fade pressed the phone's OFF button and tossed it into the passenger seat. Getting to Strand was going to be a fairly tall order. Unlike Matt, the son of a bitch would probably crawl under his desk behind a billion dollar's worth of security until he could be certain Fade was dead. Even if he failed, though, he'd give that bastard a taste of what it was like to spend every minute waiting helplessly for something to end your life.

16

"Matt! Is your phone working? I was starting to think you'd dropped off the face of the earth."

As the office receptionist, Kelly Braith wouldn't know anything about what was going on but undoubtedly had been hounded all day by an increasingly anxious Hillel Strand. Egan had quietly unplugged his home phones the afternoon before and hadn't plugged them back in again until nine A.M. when he left the house that morning.

Based on the messages on his cell phone, Strand had been fairly agitated by his disappearance yesterday, but hadn't become really panicked until a few hours ago. It was impossible to be certain what had caused the sudden escalation, but it wasn't hard to guess.

Egan glanced at his watch. One P.M. He'd spent the morning relocating to a hotel just outside of D.C. and renting a car, the windows of which he'd immediately had tinted. Despite confirming that it was impossible to see through them in the afternoon sun, his heart rate had risen about ten beats per minute when he'd pulled into the building's underground parking. If he could help it, this would be the last time he'd get within ten miles of Homeland Security until either he or Fade put an end to this. No point in making things too easy for his old friend.

"Sorry, Kel. There was some stuff I had to do this morning. Hope it didn't cause you too much hassle."

By way of answer, she rolled her eyes and flicked them in the general direction of Strand's office.

He forced a knowing smile on his face and kept walking.

"Matt!"

He didn't turn around, instead stepping through the door to his office and starting to rifle through a file cabinet.

"Matt!" Strand repeated, coming inside and slamming the door behind him. "Why the hell aren't you returning my calls?"

Egan bent down and emptied a box of printer paper to use to pack his things in, but didn't answer.

"Al Fayed called me," Strand said. "He threatened me."

"Uh huh," Egan answered, trying to determine if his coffee mug was clean before tossing it in the box.

"Did you hear me?"

"Yeah, Hillel. I heard you."

Strand grabbed him by the shoulder and spun him around, looking carefully into his face. "He's threatened you, too, hasn't he?"

Egan just frowned and went back to digging through

his file cabinet while Strand sat down on the edge of the desk, suddenly seeming a bit more relaxed. Misery loved company.

"Then why the hell aren't you calling me back? We need to deal with this. We need to talk."

"About what?" Egan replied, mentally adding, *You stupid prick.*

"About al Fayed and what we're going to do about him. Like it or not, Matt, we're in this together."

Egan finally slammed the file drawer shut and turned around. Strand didn't look quite as crisp as he normally did, suggesting he'd spent the night at the office. Lucky. There was a fair chance that Fade had found his house by now.

"Actually, Hillel, you're just another problem to me—buzzing around trying to figure out a way to make me the scapegoat for your fuck-up. It really wouldn't be accurate for me to say that I don't care one way or another if Fade kills you because at this point it'd work better for me if he does. I don't want you to take this the wrong way, but your survival isn't really in my best interest."

Strand opened his mouth, but no sound came out. The concept of death was so far outside the world he lived in that there was some question as to whether he could even process the possibility. Did he really understand that the downside to this situation was a little steeper than failing to secure some clever political alliance or getting a bump in his pay grade? It was hard to say.

"I . . . I spoke out of turn when we talked last," he said. "I was upset and I wasn't thinking. Look, what I'm trying to say is that I was wrong . . ."

Egan stared silently at him for a few moments, trying to decide what to do. Clearly, this was a completely opportunistic change of heart—Strand was out of his depth and starting to face the fact that he needed help. Having said that, Egan knew what he had to do would be easier with access to Homeland Security resources.

"Who are the Ramirez brothers?"

Strand's impenetrable poker face failed him and the surprise on it was unmistakable. There had been nothing in the press about the Ramirezes. Not yet anyway.

"I have my sources too, Hillel."

Strand glanced back at the door to make sure it was closed and then sat quietly for a few seconds, probably trying to calculate just how much Egan knew and how much he had to admit to.

"The Ramirez brothers were a convenience," he said finally. "It was going to be hard to get the police motivated with stories about al Fayed killing drug dealers in Colombia years ago . . ."

"So you manufactured something."

Strand nodded hesitantly. "I had Lauren collect information on both the Ramirezes and al Fayed that no crank would have access to and then called in a very convincing anonymous tip."

And there it was. Strand had, for his own gain, given the police a false tip that had left a number of cops in the morgue. If his involvement was discovered, he'd have to be able to provide an airtight connection between Fade and the Ramirezes in the face of what would undoubtedly be a major FBI investigation. Otherwise the pseudo-patriotic excuses he'd made yesterday wouldn't mean shit.

"I made a bad call," Strand continued calmly. "I expected the police to just go in there and arrest al Fayed and then we'd come to his rescue with information exonerating him . . ."

"If he agreed to work for us," Egan added.

"I have a lot of responsibility here, Matt. We both do. We're a big piece of the security of this country going forward and you know as well as I do that al Fayed is a unique resource. I had no choice but to pull out all the stops to try to get him. It should have been a win-win for everybody involved. It never occurred to me that something like this could happen . . ."

That was probably true, but kind of irrelevant at this point.

"As I see it, Matt, we both have our backs against the wall here. I sent a bunch of cops to Fade's door under false pretenses and he killed them. But don't forget that you covered up his activities in Colombia. There's no way people are going to buy that you weren't involved in this."

"And if it comes to that, I imagine that I can count on you to do everything in your power to heap the blame on me."

"Let's not turn this into a war we'll both lose, Matt.

You know as well as I do that I won't have to say a word. You know how the government works. Guilt by association." Strand paused for a moment. "The bottom line is that we need to get together on this and make it go away. That's what's good for everybody."

"Everybody," Egan repeated quietly and then turned to look out a small window that opened onto D.C. He wondered if Fade would agree with that—lying in a grave somewhere remembered by history as nothing more than a psychotic cop killer and drug dealer.

What was the right thing to do?

He could go to the director and spill his guts. How would he react? Not well. General Crenshaw was a surprisingly moderate man and a very nervous student of history. For every hour he spent talking about security, he spent probably a half an hour talking about the Constitution. To the degree he could be, he was an opponent of the powers the government was quietly consolidating. The suspending of people's right to due process, the government's ability to take away people's right to fly with no reason, the holding of terrorist suspects in indefinite limbo—he saw it all as a dangerous path that historically had never led to anything but disaster. The slightest indication that men under his command were abusing the authority he wasn't completely convinced they should have would be dealt with in the harshest way possible. And that would almost certainly leave Egan in prison until his daughter was retired.

And what about Fade? The government couldn't

afford to have a pissed-off Salam al Fayed running around the country, or even worse, the court system. They would assemble a team to track down and exterminate him or throw him in Guantanamo Bay for the rest of his life. The cost there wouldn't just be to Fade, either. If there was one thing that was absolutely certain, Salam al Fayed wasn't going to go quietly. More people would die.

"We have an enormous advantage here, Matt. You know al Fayed better than anyone, I can get us real-time access to reports on the police investigation, we have background files on him that aren't going to be available to anyone else, and we have a hell of a team right here in this office . . ."

"You're suggesting we handle this ourselves," Egan said.

"I don't see how bringing in anyone else would improve our capacity to find him."

Egan didn't answer for a long time, though he knew there was only one path available to him. The more he thought about it, the more certain he became that if this went public, he'd end up in prison and Fade would end up dead—but only after taking more good men with him.

"I run the operation," Egan said finally. "I'm in charge."

Strand looked down at the floor and folded his hands on his lap. "I know you were friends—that you feel partially responsible for what's happened to him. But the fact is, there is no pleasant way out of this."

What Strand was getting at was clear but he obviously wanted it said out loud so that he could be certain that they were both on the same page. He needed Fade killed and he expected Egan to do the honors.

"He called me, too, Hillel. We were friends once but now I have a family to think about. He's too dangerous to play around with."

All the more convincing, because it was true. If he got the opportunity, Egan knew that it would be insane not to take the shot. And maybe he would. But until he was faced with that situation, it was impossible to say. To actually kill Fade. To pull the trigger. How could it have come to this?

Of course, all this soul-searching, plotting, and negotiating was probably moot. It was hard not to dwell on the fact that no one had ever survived being targeted by Salam al Fayed. It didn't seem likely that he and Strand would be the first.

17

Fade eased the Cadillac through a set of large metal doors and then followed the direction of a Latino with heavy, tattooed arms to the center of the cavernous shop. Part three of his plan to cheer himself up was now in motion.

"What a piece of shit."

Fade climbed over the driver's side door, which he'd discovered stuck pretty badly, and dropped onto the black-and-white-checked floor. Turning in a slow circle, he took in the state-of-the-art machinery, signed photos of famous athletes, and inevitable posters of half-naked women. The contrast between the spotless building and the grubby, dangerous-looking men crawling all over his car was even more startling in person than on TV.

"I appreciate you taking me so fast, Isidro."

"Ain't no problem. We been trying to get you movie guys to wake up for years. You got all those famous actors driving around in cars that any asshole can buy down the street. We did a hot rod for Tom Hanks and he told me some bullshit about product placement . . ."

"Tom Hanks has a hot rod?"

"*The* hot rod, man. The hot rod."

Fade had first seen Isidro on a Discovery Channel game show where a team of gifted mechanics could win a bunch of tools by modifying a car to the pro-ducer's liking. In five days, Isidro and his guys had transformed a Porsche into an amphibious landing craft that could do forty knots on water and still cornered like a dream. In light of that, what he had in mind for the Caddy should be a piece of cake.

"So James Bond's going to drive this old junk?" said a man standing on the Caddy's trunk. "What's up with that?"

When Fade had called, he'd told Isidro that he was with MGM and that he was working on the new Bond flick. It would go a long way to explaining what he wanted done.

"That's the idea. They've decided to do kind of a period film. Take it back to the early seventies, when the Bond movies were still really cool. He's on a mission in the U.S. so he has to blend in. And what car's more American than a convertible Caddy?"

The man adjusted the red bandanna on his head and began bouncing up and down on the back of the vehicle, obviously disappointed in the condition of the suspension.

Fade looked back at Isidro. "I figured with all the work you guys were going to do, there was no point in buying something mint."

He shrugged and Fade followed him on a quick circuit of the car. "Quit jumping on the fucking trunk, man. The thing's gonna fall apart."

Fade couldn't help feeling a little starstruck as he stood next to the man. While they looked like a bunch of gangbangers from east L.A., Isidro and his guys were probably the best in the world at what they did. In fact, they were so precise, rumor had it that a few parts on the space shuttle bore the Death Valley Hot Rod symbol.

Isidro went into motion again and Fade followed, this time to an artfully airbrushed refrigerator full of nothing but beer.

"So what are we talking about, man?" Isidro said, popping the top off a bottle and offering it to Fade.

"I'm glad you asked. Two machine guns in front, one over each headlight. One machine gun in the back, firing out of the center of the trunk. I'd like the

131

back seat to flip up and expose a rifle and a couple other things set into foam. The armrest between the front seats should have a pistol, also custom cut into foam. A police scanner . . . Oh, and an ejector seat. We'll definitely need one of those."

"The seat assembly's one piece," the man on the trunk said.

"We could cut 'em," someone else offered. "But you're going to lose your back to front adjustment."

"No problem," Fade said.

"What do you think?" Isidro said to the only Caucasian in the room. He had an enormous white ass, the crack of which was almost completely on display as he got on all fours and shoved his head beneath the seat.

"Does it actually have to work?"

Fade shrugged. "You mean does it really have to be able to throw a guy out of the car? Nah. Just make it cool, you know?"

"Springs aren't going to cut it. It'd be too hard to operate the latching system . . ."

"It'd be hard to reset, too," Isidro added, then turned back to Fade. "Anything else?"

"Nothing major. I need a kick-ass motor and suspension good enough so we can use it in the chase scenes. And a really elegant paint job—I'm thinking black. And, of course, a really sweet sound system. Pierce Brosnan's gonna end up spending a lot of time sitting around in it and he's a classical music fan, you know?"

Isidro nodded slowly and chewed his bottom lip for a few seconds. "Not gonna be cheap."

"I know."

"When do you need it?"

"I hate to do this to you, but I need it fast. Like, middle of next week."

That got a chorus of laughter and Spanish expletives loud enough to echo off the high walls.

"I know, I know," Fade said, spreading his hands wide in a gesture of helplessness. "I just got hit with this. Pierce is coming to the States and they want to unveil the project at a big thing in L.A. He's going to drive up in it and park it on the lawn—it'll be the centerpiece of the party. Also we're talking about a TV show on the making of the movie that you guys would be included in. I know it's a pain in the ass, but it could be some great publicity for you."

Isidro took a long pull on his beer bottle and circled the car one last time. "Shit, the body will have to go out to paint and chrome, like today. Did I mention this isn't gonna be cheap?"

Fade grinned and took the knapsack off his shoulder, tossing it to the man. "There's fifty thousand in cash to get you started."

This time, the reaction wasn't quite as loud, but it was a hell of a lot more positive.

"Guns," Isidro said. "What are we talking about there?"

Fade grinned and opened the trunk.

"*Maldición!* Are those real?"

133

"Actually, they are. It's a lot cheaper to just get permitted for the real thing and shoot blanks than to try to build something. Will they work?"

Isidro grabbed one of the machine guns, striking a pose with it and bobbing his head approvingly. "Bad ass, man."

"So they're okay?"

He sighted along it, aiming at a candy apple red Harley parked on the other side of the building. "Probably have to chop 'em up to make 'em fit."

"Do what you got to do. You've got carte blanche."

Isidro walked back around to the front of the car and tossed the gun onto the hood, apparently not at all concerned by the large dent it left. "You're my kind of client, man."

18

Matt Egan had positioned himself against the back wall of the conference room, reluctant for some reason to sit at the table Strand was now standing in front of.

The Office of Strategic Planning and Acquisition consisted of only eight core employees—the idea being that the smaller it was, the easier it would be to keep quiet. Of those eight, only four knew what had happened with Fade: Strand, himself, and their respective assistants William Fraiser and Lauren McCall. Both were young, ambitious, well educated, and utterly inexperienced in the workings of the real world. In fact, to his knowledge, he was the only person in Homeland Security's new clandestine operational wing who had ever fired a gun or visited the Middle East. No, that wasn't entirely true. Their lawyer, hired to interpret the Constitution and the Patriot Act's occasional circumvention of it, had once gone on a church trip to Jerusalem.

Fraiser, who Egan called Billy just to annoy him, had only been out of grad school for five years and had been assigned to Egan with no input at all from him. Of course, he had all the credentials: a former Ivy League athlete with great grades, a clean background, and a solid east coast pedigree. Despite all that—or maybe because of it—Egan had never been able to warm up to him. Fraiser was a former president of his class and just came off as a little too slick and political for Egan's taste. Honestly, though, the bias was based more on impression than action—Billy hadn't done anything that wasn't damn near perfect since he'd started. Clearly a young man with the tools to carve out a serious future for himself.

Lauren, on the other hand, was a perfect match for Strand: a beautiful blonde who didn't seem interested in her job beyond how she could use it as a springboard to greater things, but who was so close to being brilliant that it didn't matter. Not that Strand had probably given her abilities all that much thought when he'd hired her. It seemed more likely that he'd based his decision more on her appearance (Scandinavian ice princess) and the way she carried herself (aristocratic dominatrix) than her abilities. It wasn't sexual, though—nothing so pure as that. He just thought she was a classy ornament for his office.

He knew the other two men in the room only from their files. They'd been the two front-runners for populating OSPA's operational arm.

"I'd like to introduce Doug Banes and Steve Despain," Strand said when everyone was settled. "They've both come over from Marine Special Forces and are the first operatives to be recruited by us."

Egan reluctantly joined the brief interlude of hand shaking and small talk, but then immediately returned to his wall. Banes and Despain were both good men but for some reason they made him uncomfortable. Probably something to do with the fact that Strand hadn't said a word about their hiring and that they had undoubtedly been told that they answered only to him. In the end, they would almost certainly turn out to be just another thing to worry about.

"Al Fayed contacted me yesterday," Strand said, plummeting the room into complete silence. Interestingly, Billy and Lauren looked more nervous than anyone. They were more or less aware of what had happened and undoubtedly had been watching OSPA's clandestine attempt to persuade Fade to join up get splashed all over the TV. They were probably thinking that it was often the people at their level who ended up doing jail time while the higher-ups just rode the old-boy network into a lucrative private industry job.

"He's lost it," Strand continued. "He was ranting. I tried to calm him down, to bring him in, but there was no way . . ." He paused dramatically. "I don't want anyone to panic, but I don't think I have the right to keep this from you. He's threatened us. All of us. He says he intends to kill me and my entire team."

Egan frowned as Billy and Lauren's eyes turned completely round. Funny how Fade hadn't mentioned any grudge against the team to him. Come to think of it, he hadn't done a lot of ranting, either. But Strand needed everyone motivated and he probably figured there was nothing that lit a fire under people like a glimpse of their own violent deaths. In Egan's experience, though, that strategy wasn't always as effective as one would expect. Motivated and panicked were two very different things. This kind of situation always had the potential to degenerate into an anarchic game of every-man-for-himself.

"Obviously, we need to find him and neutralize the situation as quickly and quietly as possible."

There was a short silence and then Billy cleared his throat. For a moment, Egan thought he was going to ask what "neutralize the situation" meant, but he didn't.

"Matt's going to take the lead in this," Strand continued. "While it's true that he doesn't have the pure investigative experience of a twenty-year FBI veteran, I believe he's the most qualified man for the job. He has an intimate knowledge of al Fayed's history, his tendencies, and his training. And he has you—the best team in the business. I don't think there's any question that if we stay focused, we've got a winning hand."

Strand's meeting had gone on for another hour, finally descending into a jittery, and ultimately pointless, flood of questions for which he had no answers.

The knock at his door was timid enough that Egan decided to ignore it and hope whoever it was would go away. It was already over two hours past the absolute outside time he'd targeted for being the hell out of there. It was not his plan to get shot driving out of the most obvious place he could possibly be. If he was going to lose this thing, he'd like to do it with a little more dignity than that.

The knocking started again just as he was closing the flaps of the box on his desk. This time a bit more assertive.

"What?"

The door opened slowly, revealing Billy and Lauren. They just stood there on the threshold, making no move to enter.

"What?" Egan repeated as he used his fingernail to try to lift the edge of a roll of packing tape.

"Can we talk to you a second?" Billy looked like he'd had better days, but the change in Lauren was downright startling. She actually had a few hairs out of place and the collar of her blouse was crooked. It didn't sound like much, but in a woman who arranged her sushi by size before eating it, those subtle signals were nearly the equivalent of a nervous breakdown.

"Talk fast," Egan said.

They stepped inside, closing the door quietly behind them and ignoring his request by just standing there silently.

"For God's sake, what?" Egan said, his frustration increasing as he wrestled with the tape roll.

Lauren took an uncharacteristically hesitant step forward. "We're wondering what we should do, Matt. I mean, I live alone in a ground floor apartment. How am I supposed to protect myself? Should I be buying a gun?"

Egan let out a long breath and tossed the tape on his desk. "All right. I want you both to listen to me very carefully. Fade wants Hillel and he wants me, though I'm not sure in what order. He has no interest in you—he's not going to run the risk of exposing himself and missing his chance at me and Hillel. Don't buy guns, don't buy pit bulls, and don't buy security systems. None of them would do a thing to deter Fade if he was interested. But he's not, okay? Hell, he would have no way of even knowing who you are. He has absolutely no investigative background and from what I remember, he can barely even turn on a computer."

"If he's not interested in us, then why did he threaten us?" Lauren said. Billy seemed content to let her lead.

The short answer, of course, was that he hadn't. But Egan wasn't prepared to call his boss a liar. Not yet anyway.

"He wants to rattle you, Lauren. He doesn't want you thinking straight."

"But if we *do* think straight and we start getting too close, what's to keep him from coming after us to slow us down?"

It was a good question, but impossible to answer in a way that would sound even remotely convincing. What would stop him is that, despite current evidence to the contrary, he wasn't a murderer. He didn't purposely kill women, children, innocent bystanders, or office staff. How could Egan sum up in two minutes a person that he'd spent years with?

"Look, you can either listen to what I'm telling you or not," Egan said, hefting the box and starting toward the door. "Do whatever makes you sleep better at night."

Billy stepped out of the way, but Lauren didn't.

"That's it, Matt? Our lives are on the line and that's all you have to say? I'm sorry. Are we delaying your escape?"

"Lauren—" Billy cautioned.

"What the fuck do you want from me?" Egan said, cutting him off. "You want me to tell you that if you put a pistol under your pillow you'll be safe? Maybe you should go over to intensive care and ask that SWAT guy if he thinks that'll work out for you. Now if you'll get out of my way, I'm going to go out there and try to find him and when I do, I'll mention to him that he's stressing you out right before he kills me."

Egan swung the box, catching her in the shoulder hard enough to shove her out of the doorway, and started for the elevators.

19

"My husband never thought she was ready. She was just promoted because of feminist politics, you know. And now . . ." The woman's voice faltered and she dabbed at her eyes without disturbing the meticulously applied mascara. "And now he's dead."

Her name was Brandy Slater, though rumor had it she was considering changing the spelling to end with an *i*. She was actually quite a beautiful woman in a porn star kind of way and the camera clearly loved her as much as she loved it. Karen Manning reached for the television remote, put her thumb against the OFF button, but couldn't quite bring herself to press it.

"You shouldn't be able to play politics with things like this," Brandy continued earnestly. "People's lives are at stake."

Her husband, Hal, had been one of the men killed by al Fayed and Brandy seemed to have found solace in the act of offering her expert criticism of Karen on every station in the western hemisphere. Ironically, Hal had been a pretty good guy. While he understandably hadn't gone out on any social or political limbs to defend his team leader, he'd always been pretty fair. And even more ironically, Karen suspected that Hal's death wasn't what had poisoned Brandy against her. They'd met five or six times at parties and the bottom line was that she was one of those women who saw Karen's ilk as endangering the pampered life women with her physical attributes so deserved to lead. Every effort Karen had made to create some kind of connection with Brandy had been met with nothing but anger and paranoia. What was she worried about? There would always be a place in this world for big-haired bimbos.

"None of the guys thought she was qualified—they were always talking about how she could get them killed . . ."

Karen grimaced and wondered if ol' Brandy would have anticipated radio-controlled bombs in the goddamn trees. At the pre-op briefing, she didn't remember Hal bringing up that particular possibility. Or anyone else, for that matter.

She fell over sideways on the sofa, still staring at the screen and reminding herself that it hadn't been Brandy or Hal's job to anticipate anything. It had been hers.

The camera moved off Brandy and the interviewer started into a now familiar monologue about possible peculiarities in her promotion and errors of judgment, but carefully avoided giving examples.

Of course, there was no mention that she was the fastest member of the team—able to fly by the runner-up without even breaking a sweat. And there would be no comment on the fact that she was the best educated—a 3.4 undergrad average and some postgraduate work in criminology. Pound for pound, she was also the strongest physically. Shooting had been her biggest weakness but she'd hired a coach and devoted months to it, ending up third best on the team. It wasn't like any of these qualities were subjective—they had all been tested, recorded, and apparently completely forgotten.

The screen flickered and then joined a press conference already in the question and answer session.

"What is Officer Manning's status now?"

Captain Pickering frowned disapprovingly from behind his lectern. "She is currently on administrative leave pending the completion of an investigation into this incident."

"Do you have any leads as to al Fayed's whereabouts?" another off-screen reporter asked.

"I can't comment directly, but I will tell you that I'm very happy with the progress of the investigation thus far." He pointed to a raised hand at the bottom of the screen.

"Captain, based on Mr. al Fayed's military history, were any special precautions taken in trying to capture him?"

Karen sat up straight again and propped her feet against the coffee table. "Why don't you tell them that I wanted to pick him up for speeding, you asshole?"

"That's something we're looking into. Next question?"

The same reporter yelled out a follow-up. "Captain, a single man, with rather old military experience, nearly killed an entire SWAT team. How does this reflect on the training your men receive?"

Karen leaned into the television, interested to hear

how Pickering would spin the answer to that. It would be hard to blame her, since she didn't really have anything to do with setting training policy, but it was going to be even harder for him to admit that his beloved elite warriors had suddenly been transformed into cannon fodder when faced with a competent opponent.

"These were top men!" he nearly shouted. "And they gave their lives in the performance of their duty. I will not have their bravery and dedication questioned." A rather obvious nonanswer, but emphatic enough not to get a challenge.

"Captain, a two-part question if I may," came a woman's voice. "You mentioned that Karen Manning has been put on administrative leave pending an investigation. Isn't this standard procedure in this type of situation? And second, based on your preliminary findings, is there any reason to believe that Officer Manning did not follow department procedures in trying to apprehend the suspect?"

Karen tried to will the camera to shift to the reporter who had asked the question. It paid to keep track of news people who weren't carrying torches and pitchforks.

"Our investigation into this can be measured in hours, ma'am. I have no idea at this point of what happened and what didn't and even if I did know, I couldn't comment on it at this juncture. Next ques—"

"And the first part of my question? The administrative leave?"

"You go, girl," Karen muttered.

"Yes . . ." Pickering was forced to concede. "Yes, it's standard procedure."

Karen clicked off the television and flopped back onto the sofa that had been beneath her all day. This wasn't healthy. She should just leave the television off and go for a run. Or clean the dishes stacked in the sink. Or . . .

Instead she turned the TV back on and began another slow scan of the channels.

For what reason, she wasn't sure. It seemed almost certain now that her side of the story would never be told. Pickering had sent her up against al Fayed despite her protests and it had turned into a disaster. Now he was going to say as little as possible and let anonymous sources and widows do their work.

The phone rang and she craned her neck around to look at it. No fewer than five reporters had already called that day, but it had been made very clear to her that she wasn't to speak to them while the investigation was in process. And while she might be forced eventually to disobey that order, it wasn't time to go to war on this yet.

When the machine picked up, she heard John Wakefield's voice.

"Get off the sofa and answer the phone, Karen."

She reached for the handset. "Hello, John."

"So how are things?"

"Have you been watching the news?"

He didn't answer.

"Then you know how things are going."

"I've had a couple of calls from reporters, but I haven't taken them. I'm not sure what to say."

Karen pulled a pillow over her head and stared into the darkness. Not him, too. If there was one thing she knew she couldn't take, it was Wakefield turning away from her.

"Karen? Are you there?"

"John, I . . ." She heard her voice break and wiped away a tear by pressing the pillow harder into her face. "I know I'm responsible. But was it my fault? Tell me the truth."

"That's not what I meant, Karen. If I didn't believe in you one hundred percent, I wouldn't have walked through the fire to bring you in on the Collector case. I am more than willing to call these reporters back when we hang up, but I wanted to talk to you first."

Karen let the pillow slide to the floor and reemerged into the light. "Thanks, John. That means a lot."

"So? Do you want me involved?"

"No. Thanks, but not yet. I'm going to let it run its course for a little while and see what happens."

"You know that Pickering is going to do everything he can to save his ass."

"Yeah. I know. What's up with the Collector?"

"The letters came in. He's got his new girl."

Karen let out a long breath. "Stephany Narwal?"

"Yeah."

Narwal had been reported missing four days ago—a beautiful young woman who fit the victim profile perfectly.

"I wish you could have been there to help me talk to her family. I tried to get you off leave and back in the office, but there's no way. Policy. If I come up with anything, though, I'll figure out a way to get you in on it. I miss having your eyes on this thing."

"Thanks. I appreciate that."

"Keep your chin up."

She hung up and for the first time that day didn't feel an urge to stare at the news. Thank God for John Wakefield.

The phone rang again just as she was starting into the kitchen and she grabbed it and took it along with her.

"Hello?" she said, pulling open the door to the dishwasher and beginning to dig silverware out of the sink.

"How are you holding up, honey?"

"Hi, Mom. I'm fine."

"You don't sound fine. Have you been watching TV? It's horrible. When are you going to get in there and straighten things out?"

"I can't, Mom. We talked about this already."

"I mean, of course, this incident is unfortunate, but that's no reason for people to get on TV and say these things about you."

Her mother was nothing if not incredibly civil. Her most powerful admonishment was "just plain rude." Adolph Hitler? Just plain rude. Anything less got "unfortunate." Your entire team gunned down, leaving their children fatherless? Unfortunate. She and Dad were both sweethearts and had done what they could to understand and support their black sheep daughter, though it hadn't always made her life easier.

When Karen's already reticent colleagues had discovered that her parents were not only multi-millionaires but stalwart members of the country club set, things had gotten even more complicated. There hadn't been much she could do but take the snide comments with rolled eyes and smirks. It was a little hard to protest too much—the house she was standing in was a graduation present and the car she'd insisted on buying herself had one day been miraculously paid off.

More complicated still was the fact that her folks didn't think much more of cops than cops thought of them. Neither her mother nor father had thought this "police thing" would last more than a year or two. By then they assumed she would have sowed her wild oats, quit, found a nice man, and settled down. Some-times she thought she was in danger of being crushed by the weight of all the clichés.

"The TV says you're on administrative leave. Does that mean you're off?"

"In a way, I guess," Karen said, trying to pry some old pasta off a pan.

"Why don't we go to our place in Hawaii? Your father has some time. You and he should sit down and talk."

"Don't start, Mom."

"Start what? He's your father and he wants to help

you. But you know he won't do anything without you asking."

Her father had started life delivering cigarettes from the back of a pickup truck and built that into a megamillion-dollar shipping company using nothing but his incredible intelligence, borderline ruthlessness, and innate political savvy. During his rise, he'd made sure that his money and other resources were always available to the Republican Party, and to date he'd never backed a loser. That had left him extremely powerful and well connected, something she'd soundly criticized him for during that idealistic phase everyone went through in college.

"I really can't, Mom."

"You can't go to Hawaii or you can't ask for his help?"

"Neither. I don't think I'd feel right lying on a beach while my men are being buried and I can't ask for Dad's help because I was a complete bitch to him about this kind of stuff during school."

"Oh, he didn't take any of that seriously, honey. If you won't do it for yourself, do it for him. It's killing him to just sit on his hands. All he does when he's not at the office is storm around the house and mumble about coming down on people like the wrath of God. Actually, you should do it for me. He's driving me crazy."

"I'll think about it."

"That's all I can ask."

Her call waiting beeped and while she wasn't sure

she wanted to talk to the person on the other line, it was a good excuse. Guilt about her parents' position in all this was starting to set in and if there was one thing she didn't need, it was more guilt. It seemed certain that they were taking a serious social thrashing. It was bad enough to have a daughter who was an unmarried cop (with all the lesbian innuendo that inevitably followed) but having a daughter who was an incompetent unmarried cop had to really suck.

"Look, Mom, I gotta run. I'll talk to you tomorrow, okay?"

"Okay. But think about Hawaii. You sound like you could use some time away."

"I will," Karen said and then switched lines. "Hello?"

"Hi, Karen. What's going on?"

It took her a moment to process the voice and when she did, she froze.

"Man, you're getting your ass kicked in the press. Have you ever considered a good PR firm? And what about a makeover? With enough hairspray, I'll bet you could have almost as good a bouffant as that bitch who's been dissing you."

"What do you want?"

The silence over the line lasted probably ten seconds. "I want to say I'm sorry about this . . ."

"About what, exactly? About killing my friends? Or about turning me into the poster girl for government incompetence?"

It had never really occurred to her that Salam al

Fayed would call her at home and she was completely unprepared. How many times was this guy going to catch her flat-footed?

"Both, I guess. But you're going to have a hard time convincing me that all those guys were your friends. I thought being an Arab SEAL was tough, but I'll bet being a woman SWAT team leader really blows. At least I didn't have people constantly questioning my ability and my right to be where I was—they were too busy wondering if I was going to suddenly start screaming 'Allah Akbar!' and shoot them in the back."

"You don't know a goddamn thing about me and you sure as hell don't know anything about my men. I have nothing in common with you, Mr. al Fayed. Do you understand me? Nothing."

"Jesus. You're the worst interrogator I've ever met. Aren't you supposed to be nice to me, gain my trust, and get me to slip up and tell you something I shouldn't?"

Now that he mentioned it, that probably was what she was supposed to be doing. "I wasn't trained by the Israelis, Mr. al Fayed."

"Yeah . . . I'm sorry about that, too. You must have been pretty scared."

She opened her mouth to shout something back at him but then stopped herself when she realized there wasn't even a hint of condescension in the statement. His apologies had a strangely sincere ring to them.

"I swear to you that if I had even an inkling that you guys were cops, I would have never fired a shot."

"If not the police, then who? This Strand person?"

He laughed quietly over the phone. "You remember that, huh. I guess I mustn't be as scary as I thought."

"I guess not."

"So who told the police about me, Karen?"

"I'm not at liberty to say."

"'I'm not at liberty to say,'" he mocked and then laughed again. "I love the way cops talk. Do they teach you that stuff at the academy? Come on, I have the right to face my accuser. All you patriots haven't carved that out of the Constitution yet, have you?"

She didn't respond.

"You don't know, do you, Karen? You have no idea why you were even there."

"We've already been through this, haven't we? You're involved with the Colombian drug cartels and you killed the Ramirez brothers."

"*Was* involved with the Colombian cartels. Was. But that was years ago."

"And the Ramirezes?"

"Look, I've killed a lot of people in my life, but not so many that I forget them."

"So you're saying you're innocent."

"Innocent . . . Your word, not mine. But I *am* saying that I didn't kill these Ramirez guys. And I'm guessing that you believe me because after wiping out an entire SWAT team, there's not much of a reason for me to split hairs on the subject."

Karen dried her hands on a towel and sat down behind a small dining table. He was right. She did believe him.

"A very unfortunate mistake," she said, grimacing at her use of her mother's favorite word. Then, suddenly, she stood again, trying to shake off the confused haze she was in. She needed to pull herself together and stop letting him control the conversation. "But you did work for the cartels. Isn't that right? What did you do for them?"

"I, uh, thinned out Castel Vela's competition. But only in Colombia. Never in the States. Now I build furniture. You wouldn't happen to need a nice hope chest, would you? I doubt the woman I built it for is going to want it now that I'm public enemy number one."

"My marriage prospects aren't at the point that I would have a whole hell of a lot of use for a hope chest."

"Keep your newspaper clippings in it."

"Screw you."

"Right."

"So who is Strand?"

"A little obvious, but I guess you are new at this . . ."

"Is he an enemy you made when you were working in Colombia?"

"No, they're pretty much all dead. He's a more recent addition to my list."

"Come on, Mr. al Fayed. Why on earth wouldn't you want to tell me this? If you had reason to believe that someone was trying to kill you, that might mitigate the charges against you. Hell, maybe this Strand person called us on purpose to set you up. That kind of information could give your lawyer a lot to work with . . ."

"I don't think that I really need to worry about my case ever going to trial. But I appreciate the thought."

His tone suggested that the conversation was over, leaving Karen scrambling to come up with a way to keep him on the line.

"Why don't we meet? Talk more about this . . ." She smacked herself silently in the forehead before the statement was even fully out of her mouth. Smooth. Very smooth.

He was polite enough to ignore the statement entirely. "So, anyway, the real reason I called was to tell you something . . ."

"Yes?"

"I know what it's like to lose men and I know what it's like to be abandoned by the people who should be standing behind you. But this wasn't your fault. You were put in an impossible situation. Just try to remember that while you can't always control what other people think of you, you can control what you think of yourself."

She wasn't sure how to respond. After thirty seconds of silence she could still hear him breathing.

"Mr. al Fayed?"

"Call me Fade."

"Why did you *really* call me?"

Another one of those easygoing laughs. "I guess because I don't have anyone else to talk to."

The line went dead and she stared at the handset for a few seconds before dialing the police.

20

The large rolling chalkboard he'd bought took up almost all the available floor space and forced Egan to lie sideways on the hotel bed in order to read what he'd written on it. Heavy curtains were pulled against the cloudless day outside, adding to the claustrophobia and giving the worn-out room the feel and smell of a damp cave.

He'd read through all the files on Fade as well as the ones on the men Fade had fought with—essentially, everything the government had that even remotely related to Salam al Fayed. The results had been less than overwhelming. About half the chalkboard was still completely blank and the other half was covered with ideas that seemed shaky at best. He tried to focus on them, but instead found himself staring blankly at the beer bottle balanced on his chest.

It didn't take long for thoughts of Elise and Kali to start to crowd his mind. He tried to push them away, but they weren't easily defeated. After about half an hour of getting nothing done, he pulled out his cell and dialed his home number.

"Hello?"

"What are you doing?"

"Hey, Matt. I just hung up with Charlie. We were talking about the release."

Charlie was the head of Elise's record label, a pretty good guy who was inexplicably devoted to her less-than-profitable career.

"Are you still going to be able to make the date?"

"Shouldn't be a problem. We're going to have to start rehearsing hard and get into the studio pretty quick, though. I'm hoping we can get a few songs together for the show in D.C. next week. Try 'em out in front of real people."

"Sorry I can't be there to help with Kali."

"It's not a big deal. I'll manage. When are you coming home?"

"It's turned out to be a lot more than I expected. It'll probably be a while."

"Oppressing the masses is a demanding profession."

"I knew you'd understand."

"Well, I'm going to get my revenge. It looks like Charlie wants me to expand my tour schedule. Maybe as many as thirty cities."

"I guess that's good, though," Egan mumbled. "He must recognize that the songs are strong."

"You seem kind of down, Matt. Are you all right?"

"Just sitting in a hotel, looking forward to endless, boring meetings, you know?"

"Are you sure that's all it is?"

The purpose of this call wasn't to practice his dismal ability to deceive his wife. Actually, what was the purpose? To remind himself that he was probably never going to see her again?

"Hey, there's someone at my door," he lied. "I've got to run."

"Kali's jumping up and down trying to grab the

phone. Say hello to her."

"Elise, I—"

"Hi, Daddy! Daddy?"

Her voice was full of trust and excitement, and for some reason that made it hard for him to breathe.

"Hi, honey. How was school?"

"I'm going to be a gymnast."

"Well, that's sort of sudden. What kind of gymnast are you going to be?"

"We had a class and I did a flip and it was the best one in class and Ms. Reynolds said I could be a gymnast. There are things you walk along and bars you swing from and—"

He heard Elise's distant voice. "Daddy can't talk long, Kali, he has to work. Maybe you should tell him all about your class later."

"Okay. Are you coming home tomorrow? I can show you . . ."

"Not tomorrow," Egan said quietly. "But soon, okay? So practice up. I want that flip perfect . . ."

When he hung up, he squeezed his eyes shut, blocking out everything around him. A poor idea poorly executed. It was time to lock Elise and Kali in a part of his mind he never traveled. They were nothing but a liability to him now.

He removed the beer bottle from his chest and forced himself to focus on the chalkboard again.

It seemed most productive to work this problem based on the assumption that Fade would kill him in a stand-up fight. And if Strand's new enforcers were unfortunate enough to be there at the time, they'd probably end up dead, too. And if cops showed up, then the body count would just keep on going. That meant that Egan had to be smarter. To find a way to slink up behind him . . .

And then what?

Egan shook his head violently, trying again to discipline his mind. Concentrate on finding him first, then worry about the rest of it.

The first column of writing on the board covered the path the cops were taking—essentially the most obvious lines of investigation based on the information they had available to them. According to the reports that he'd seen so far, though, their enthusiasm wasn't what he'd expected. The Collector case was sucking up enormous resources and Pickering seemed more interested in making sure his own ass was covered than actually finding the man responsible for wiping out his SWAT team.

So far, the police had examined Fade's phone records and found that he didn't really talk to anyone—the most notable recent calls being to Sharper Image and a model airplane supplier who sold him the things he needed to turn his house into a giant booby trap. Interviews with his neighbors, customers, and colleagues completed a picture of a man without a friend in the world.

Egan pulled another beer from the tiny refrigerator behind him, trying not to think about what it had taken to turn Fade into the angry, violent, and depressed man he'd become. People used to reschedule parties if he couldn't attend.

The remaining space on the right side of the board described the rest of the dead ends the police were pursuing. Fade's parents were deceased and he and his one sister had never gotten along.

Of course, there was an APB on the car Karen saw him drive away in, but he would have dumped it by now. Searches of airports, bus terminals, rental car agencies, and cab records had yielded exactly zip, as had their half-hearted examination of local car and motorcycle purchases.

One of the police's fundamental problems was that they assumed Fade was running, whereas Egan could pretty much guarantee that he was going nowhere until he did what he'd set out to do. Initially, Pickering's people had tried to track Fade with his cell phone, using real-time information on which repeater was picking up his signal. Unfortunately, though, Fade seemed to have become a bit more technologically savvy in the past few years and had used cash to purchase a satellite phone with a thousand prepaid hours. According to Billy, the best they could hope for is that he'd be on the phone when the satellite he was linked to went over the horizon, giving them his longitude and narrowing his location down to a not so helpful few thousand square miles.

The car was an opportunity. Fade loved old cars—particularly convertibles. Egan remembered his encyclopedic knowledge and the long sermons on the subject that Fade had used to fill the inevitable downtime people in his profession suffered. Based on the car Egan had seen up on blocks in his yard, that fascination was one of the few things he hadn't abandoned.

Fade would see this as his last hurrah and, as such, it seemed like he'd want to go out driving something fitting. Money was an issue, of course, but based on his lifestyle and the fact that the money he'd made from the Colombians was never used for his back operation, it seemed reasonable to assume he was cash rich.

Beyond that, Egan didn't have much. The safe house he'd taken Karen Manning to proved that he'd been ready for somebody from his past to come after him eventually—though he probably hadn't expected it to be the U.S. government. That meant he probably had a number of disguises and identities set up, as well as an appropriate weapons collection.

Strand's name had been mentioned in Manning's debriefing, but there had been no mention of a first name or Homeland Security. The police had cross-referenced the thousands of Strands in America with people who had done prison time or were suspected of being involved in the drug trade and come up empty. At this point, it wasn't a line of investigation they were willing to devote much manpower to. Likewise Fade's history in Colombia. The buried DEA reports and the CIA stuff were unavailable to them, so they really had no way even to start down that road.

Pickering's people had pulled rental and purchase

records of the type of real estate Karen had described being taken to, but there wasn't much to go on. She had seen only the inside and could only tell them approximately how long it took to get there from his house. It would be found eventually, but it was going to take a while.

The police had a copy of his brief military record, but would run into a dead end when they tried to look into the now-defunct CIA front company he'd worked for after being discharged. Any attempt to track down the former employees of Ramsey Security Systems would lead them into a maze with no outlet.

So Egan was left with something of an advantage over Fade's other pursuers. He not only had intimate knowledge of Ramsey Security—which he'd worked for—but access to the CIA background check done on Fade, including detailed information that went back to his early childhood.

Unfortunately, it was a street that went both ways. After years of friendship, Fade knew Egan's entire life story, too. And what little he didn't know wouldn't be terribly hard to find out.

Strand, though, was a different story. Fade knew only his name and that he worked at Homeland Security. In addition, Strand's phone number and address were unlisted, making finding him even harder. Of course, Fade could try to acquire him at the office, but that was kind of risky and obvious.

Would it be possible to use Strand to draw Fade in? Maybe place some false information in the public record? Honestly, the idea of using Strand as bait was pretty attractive—essentially, a no-lose situation. If it helped him find Fade, great. On the other hand, if Strand ended up stopping a bullet, oh well.

Unfortunately, he seemed a little reluctant to leave his office these days.

Egan laid his head back on the mattress and stared up at the ceiling. Finally, he took a deep breath and spoke aloud to the empty room. "How the hell did we get here, Fade?"

21

"Close the door and grab a chair, Bill," Strand said, moving his own out from behind his desk and into a position that would make the meeting feel less autocratic. Fraiser did as he was told, sitting next to Lauren and running a hand through his hair. It was ten o'clock at night and the three of them were the only people left in the office. No one had said anything out loud, but none of them were going home. Strand had sent for his clothes and other supplies, and he knew that both Lauren and Fraiser were quietly making similar arrangements.

Having his team scared and sleeping on the floor wasn't ideal, but it was the price he had to pay for their unwavering focus and round-the-clock vigilance. He was convinced that telling them al Fayed had threatened them was the right decision.

"I just wanted to talk a little—to get a feel for how things are going, how you're holding up, and maybe to bounce around some ideas." Strand kept his tone as relaxed as he could manage, though under the circumstances it took a fair amount of concentration just to keep his voice even. "Why don't you start by giving me a run-down on where we stand right now."

Lauren looked over at Fraiser, but neither spoke.

"Is there a problem?"

"We don't really stand anywhere," Lauren said finally. "We gathered up the initial information that you and Matt asked for and he just walked out of here with it. When we tried to talk to him, he basically told me to shut up and shoved me out of the way . . ."

Fraiser stared uncomfortably at the floor. He undoubtedly wanted to defend his boss, but was smart enough to know that, in the end, he worked for Strand.

"I see. Bill? Do you know what Matt's up to?"

"He's not at home—he's afraid al Fayed could acquire him there. He's at a hotel going through the information we gave him and figuring out the best way to track him."

"Do we know what hotel?"

Fraiser shook his head. "I never asked. I could find out."

"Do it. Have you talked to him since he left?"

Another shake of the head. "But he'll call. He just needs some time."

Strand leaned back in his chair, fighting to keep his expression completely passive. How in the fuck had this happened? The plan he'd devised couldn't have been more simple or foolproof. Who could have anticipated that the police were too stupid and incompetent to arrest a single man? And now that incompetence had left him almost completely reliant on Matt Egan—a man with questionable loyalties and the political instincts of a head of cabbage.

"I think we need to give him a chance, Lauren. Matt's a good man . . ." Strand let his voice trail off, leaving an obvious "but" at the end of his sentence. He put a finger to his lips and pretended to be mulling over what to say next. Finally, "That brings me to a difficult point. Matt's had a long friendship with al Fayed and while that has positive aspects for us, it could also have some drawbacks."

The trick here was to create just enough suspicion to ensure that Fraiser and Lauren's loyalties stayed with him, but not so much that they might undermine Egan's efforts. It seemed likely that he was harboring some half-assed idea about trying to extricate al Fayed from the position he was in and that it would likely blow up in their faces. Over the years, Strand had learned to tolerate all the Neanderthal military brotherhood crap that swirled around this part of the government, but hell if he was going to let it get him killed.

"Obviously, Matt is a very loyal and honorable man and, because of that, he must be struggling with this situation. If he comes face to face with al Fayed, will he hesitate? And if he does, will al Fayed escape? Or worse, kill him? What I'm saying here is that Matt's judgment might be a bit clouded and that we need to be thinking and questioning all the time. If you have any problems—ideas that we should be looking at, or if you feel like Matt may not be giving you the whole story, I want you to come straight to me. If we work as a team, I have no doubt that we're going to get through this. Al Fayed has virtually no resources and ours are pretty much unlimited."

Lauren and Fraiser nodded weakly.

"Look, we don't want Matt taking this thing on by himself—or, for that matter, anyone doing anything on their own. We may have only one chance at al Fayed and we need to make sure that we don't blow that chance."

In truth, his objective was to remove Egan from everything his involvement wasn't critical to. Strand already had Lauren quietly sanitizing the police reports of any mention that al Fayed had contacted Karen Manning. The cops continued to display their idiocy by assuming that al Fayed had fled and weren't even bothering to watch Manning. He wouldn't make the same mistake.

"So, in order to be sure we have a grasp of what's going on, I want everything you get to come straight to me for approval before it goes out to Matt. Is that understood?"

More nods.

"Finally, we need to start tracking the news agencies. Al Fayed might try to go to someone to get his story out. Bill, why don't you take the lead on that."

"Yes, sir."

"Okay. Are we all on the same page? Again, I'm not trying to single Matt out here, I'm just saying that we need to have multiple eyes on everything that comes through—we can't afford to miss anything. Does everyone understand? Bill?"

"I understand."

"But do you agree? Because if you don't or you have some other ideas on the subject, I want to hear them. That's why we're here."

"No, sir, I don't. I think you're right—we can't afford to miss anything."

22

Fade put on his headset and began playing the twelve messages on his cell phone. The fact that his number wasn't listed had done little to discourage his more resourceful admirers.

He slurped the last of his coffee, smiling as a man with a shaking voice recounted an elaborate theory regarding the police department's infiltration by space aliens and asking what color the men he'd killed bled. The second message had a more typical "fuck the fuzz" theme and he deleted it after listening to only a few seconds. Number three was a reporter: "Mr. al Fayed, my name is Kevin Swale and I'm with *The Washington Post*. I'd really like to talk to you. I know you're probably reluctant, but if you look at my stuff I think you'll find it pretty even-handed. It wouldn't hurt for you to get your side of the story—"

Fade deleted the message and skipped through a few others until stopping on the soothing voice of a police negotiator who didn't really have much to say. Then a few more cop haters and that was it.

Earlier that day he'd gotten a message suggesting he was one of the four horsemen of the Apocalypse and that the whole episode had been foretold by Revelations. Or was it Nostradamus? One of those.

"Can I get you anything else?"

Fade removed his earpiece and glanced up at the waitress. It was Saturday and they were the only two people in the small Internet café he'd found near the Columbia University campus, which worked well for him. His disguise was pretty thorough, if somewhat dopey looking, but you never knew when some art student with a photographic memory for faces would point a finger and start screaming.

"This wasn't bad," he said, pointing to his empty coffee mug. "But I'm thinking something more festive. One of those coffee mocha chai latte things."

She looked a little perplexed.

"Just bring me something really elaborate and expensive."

She shrugged and started for the counter, allowing him to return his attention to the computer screen in front of him. The whole Internet thing had turned out to be a bit of a letdown. After all the hype, he'd assumed that he could just type Strand's name into a search engine and come away with pretty much his whole life story. The sad truth was that the only thing he'd turned up was a brief bio on a site devoted to a conference where he'd spoken.

So now he knew that Strand was forty-nine years old, unmarried, went to Harvard for his undergrad, and was now taking classes at Georgetown. He'd been with the NSA before taking a job at Homeland Security where he worked on "classified projects." He was a native of the Chicago area, where there were countless Strands who may or may not have been related to him. The D.C. area had even more Strands but not a single Hillel. Not that it really mattered. It seemed unlikely that he was hanging out at home waiting to be shot.

In retrospect, calling him had been stupid. It had put him on guard. Fade didn't really regret it, though. He wanted him to be afraid. He wanted him to be consumed by it.

The waitress slid a tall glass mug containing an artistically swirled drink onto the table next to him. An energetic slurp left him with nothing much more than a whipped cream mustache and a burned tongue, prompting him to set the mug back down and return his attention to the computer.

The likely scenario was that Strand had picked up a few Special Ops guys as protection and that he was either living at his office or had retreated to an "undisclosed location." That didn't leave a lot of options. He could stake out Homeland Security headquarters in the hope that he was still there and would eventually leave, but that seemed a little obvious and a lot dangerous.

The bottom line was that this investigative crap sucked. Tedious, time consuming, and complicated. He'd always had Matt to take care of this stuff for him. Good thing, too. If it had been left to him, he and his team would have probably ended up in the middle of Syria asking the local farmers how to get to Iraq. It was hard not to wonder what exactly Egan was doing at that moment. Not hiding out at his office. Not his style. No, he was out there devising some sneaky and underhanded way to track him down and shoot him in the back. Not that he didn't respect that approach. It was smart and added a much-needed element of excitement to the whole operation. . . .

He took another, slightly more cautious sip of his drink and reminded himself that Matt wasn't the priority. Hillel Strand was at the top of the list and he needed to focus if he was going to get him.

So where did he go from here? No doubt there were people who could use the Internet and public records to track down everything including Strand's favorite color, but he wasn't one of them. Maybe he should be calling back some of those wackos who'd figured out his unlisted number and asking them for advice.

Or better yet, maybe he should call about the Caddy. See how Isidro was doing . . .

No. No more excuses. As hard as this was now, it'd

only get harder when Egan and the cops started to close in. And, of course, there was his back to think about. His scuffle with SWAT hadn't helped a whole hell of a lot and he was still waiting to get full feeling back into his right foot. Chasing people around was going to get kind of complicated if his legs stopped working.

Someone—probably Egan—had once told him that Domino's gathered up unlisted numbers and sold them to private intelligence companies. Maybe there was something there. He grinned and tried to picture himself putting a gun to some pimply kid's head and demanding access to the company's national database. Oh, and a pie with pepperoni and black olives.

Amazon listed a bunch of books about finding people that covered things like land records, credit reports, and high school reunion lists, but who wanted to get involved in that nonsense? What was he, a librarian?

Karen Manning. That's who he needed. According to the news, she was not only a kind of hot looking badass, she was smart enough to be one of the people trying to find that loser who was running around Virginia killing girls.

Fade glanced over at a very unfair and unflattering article about her in the newspaper lying next to him and shook his head. The woman took a job that demanded she put her life on the line to help others and now she was getting completely screwed. He wondered how many reporters out there would have driven blindly into the war zone he'd created to try to save their guys.

He started to reach for his drink but then forgot about it as he lost himself in wondering how many twists of fate it would have taken to put them together. He could have decided to ignore the attack on that little Arab girl and instead gone straight to the extraction site. Karen could have blown off the cops and joined the military where a woman like her would have been encouraged to go out for the new female Special Ops program. And if those two things had been the case, it seems certain that they would have eventually run into each other. Maybe they'd have hit it off. Maybe even gotten married. After a while, they would have taken training or administrative jobs and started a family . . .

"Do you like the latte?"

Fade blinked hard and looked up at the waitress. "It's great. Thanks."

"Anything else?"

He shook his head and watched her weave through the empty café toward the bar. Enough daydreaming. It was time to either move forward on this thing or walk away from it.

He glanced down at a legal pad sitting next to the keyboard and dialed the number he'd written there into his cell phone.

"Homeland Security. How can I direct your call?"

"Hillel Strand's office, please."

There was a brief delay and then a woman's voice.

"Office of Strategic Planning and Acquisition. How can I help you?"

"Hi. Hillel asked me to send him some documents and he neglected to give me his floor, which I assume I need to include in the address."

"Go ahead and send it to the sixth. That'll get it there."

"Great. And who am I speaking to? Is this his assistant?"

"No, this is Kelly Braith. I'm the receptionist."

"Oh, okay. Thanks, Kelly. I'll get this right to him."

Fade clicked off the phone and pulled up Big-Book.com. Maybe Ms. Braith wasn't as secretive as her boss.

23

Perhaps if he'd written bigger or added some graphs, the chalkboard wouldn't look so empty. But he hadn't and it was time to face the fact that not only were there very few potential paths to Fade, the ones that did exist were more than a little bit overgrown.

"Okay, we're all here," came Strand's distant-sounding voice over the phone.

Egan adjusted his earpiece and began pacing back and forth to the degree that the cramped hotel room would allow. "The first thing we need to look at is cars. Fade is a nut for classic cars—and he particularly likes convertibles. Billy, I want you to go through the local papers and call the used dealers. Find out if any-thing old and sexy has been sold to anyone even close to Fade's description."

"What about rental places, Matt? They've got these dream car rental places now," Billy replied.

"News to me. Give it a shot."

"I'm on it."

"Okay. Next. When we did the background check on Fade at the CIA we had some problems with a friend of his from high school. He'd never spent a day in jail but we concluded that he was a fairly well-placed drug dealer in New York."

"Javan Franklin," Lauren said.

"That's him. It seems likely that he's the one who put Fade in touch with the Colombians. I'd like to talk to him."

"We'll find him," Strand said.

"I assume there's no activity on his credit cards or ATM?"

"Nothing," Lauren said. "And even if there is, remember that the police are watching, too."

"What else are they doing?"

"Their most recent report is on your e-mail," Fraiser said. "Basically they're doing exactly what we expected. No surprises. Not yet."

"Good. Keep me up on that. I don't need to run into any cops."

"Don't worry," Strand said. "We're staying on top of it. Where do you stand? Any movement?"

"I'm working on contacting some of the men he

served with in the navy and at Ramsey Security—people who he might have stayed in touch with. Maybe they'll have some ideas about where he'd go."

"Who exactly? Do we need to get you current addresses and background?"

Egan didn't answer immediately. It was certain that Strand would want to keep as close an eye on him as possible and was anxious to get a tail on him. While Egan hadn't really done anything to actively keep his location secret, he also hadn't volunteered it. At some point it was a fence he'd be forced to stop straddling, but for now he felt better on his own.

"Thanks, but I think I can handle it. Is there anything else?"

Silence.

"Okay, then. You can get me on my cell."

24

Karen Manning had never been to this part of southeast D.C. and, judging by the stares she was getting from the people on the street, not many other young blonde women in Hondas ever had either. The route hadn't looked particularly easy to follow on the map and the reality turned out to be even worse—a maze of poorly paved, garbage-strewn roads bordered by crumbling old homes and boxlike apartment buildings.

She stopped at an intersection with no sign, took a

wild guess, and turned right. Not exactly the most scientific navigation method available, but it worked. After about two miles she found a street blocked by police cars and pedestrians. She eased forward, slowing enough to allow time for parents to shoo their children back onto the sidewalks and to hear the occasional obscene suggestion from a laughing teenaged boy.

She made it to within twenty feet of a yellow barricade and stepped from the car, digging her badge from her pocket as she approached a young cop working crowd control. It turned out not to be necessary and he waved her through, not bothering to hide a mildly disgusted expression that she was quickly growing accustomed to.

Most of the activity seemed to be centered around something that at one time had been a car but was now just a few parts clinging precariously to a wheelless chassis. There were two fingerprint guys going over the dented remains of the body and someone else beneath what was left of the dashboard, apparently looking for fibers. The rest of the cops on duty were fanning out, questioning the people in the street, and knocking on doors.

She spotted John Wakefield leaning against one of the barricades and started toward him.

"Karen! What are you doing here?" he said, pushing himself to a full upright position and giving her a brief hug.

"I was going to ask you the same thing. If some

reporter sees you and thinks you're looking into this, they're going to come after us for putting the deaths of our guys over the deaths of all those women . . ."

He shrugged disinterestedly. "I miss my sidekick and I was curious. Besides, I'm dead-ended on the Collector until . . . Well, you know."

Unfortunately, she did. Until another woman disappeared and Stephany Narwal's body showed up.

"Well, I can't say I'm not glad to see you. You're probably the only person on the force who's still willing to talk to me." She motioned toward the steel skeleton parked against the curb. "What's the story?"

"Not much so far. Obviously, the car's seen better days."

"But it's definitely Fade's?"

"Fade?"

"Apparently that's what he calls himself."

"I heard that you'd talked to him, but I thought it was just another rumor."

"No, it's true, but I didn't do a very good job. I couldn't get anything out of him that we could use."

He nodded thoughtfully, looking down and picking imaginary lint from his slacks, a mannerism she'd seen a thousand times but still didn't know how to read.

"Well, to answer your question, yes. It is definitely al Fayed's—we managed to get a serial number off one of the pieces that's left. It looks like he dropped it off late last night but there are no security cameras in the area and, of course, no one saw a thing."

Karen motioned behind him and they retreated back to the barricades where he could take some of the weight off his arthritic knees. "I doubt anyone is going to be very anxious to talk to us. I'm guessing they don't love cops around here and everyone will think we're trying to finger them for stripping the car or to get them to inform on whoever did it."

"That's about the size of it," Wakefield agreed. "We're checking cab companies to see if anyone was picked up here, but cabbies aren't fond of coming into this area at night, so I'm guessing he hoofed it to the closest metro or to another car he had stashed . . ."

"That seems a little risky in this neighborhood."

Wakefield smiled. "I'm going to go out on a limb and say that this guy walks pretty much wherever he wants."

"So another dead end," she said, the frustration creeping into her voice despite her effort to stay in control. "That's turning into the story of our lives, John."

"It kind of is, isn't it . . . Uh-oh."

"What?" Karen said, noticing that he was staring over her left shoulder.

"Our fearless leader."

"Great."

"What the hell are you doing here?" she heard Captain Pickering say. When she turned to respond it became clear that he wasn't talking to her. In fact, he didn't even seem to be aware of her existence.

"I was in the neighborhood," Wakefield said.

"Well, get the hell out of the neighborhood. The goddamn press is going to show up any minute."

Wakefield pushed himself off the barricade again and patted Karen on the arm before wandering off. "Call me if you need anything. And keep your chin up."

She watched him as he started to push his way through the people surrounding the crime scene, feeling a slight pang of jealousy mixed with her gratitude. It must be nice to be bulletproof.

"These people are trying to work," Pickering said. "I don't need you disrupting them."

A number of responses came to mind but she kept them to herself, instead brushing by him without a word. She'd only made it about ten feet before he called after her.

"Wait for me in my car, Karen."

His tone was both commanding and dismissive. Why wouldn't it be? She just kept going along, not uttering a single meaningful protest while he twisted the knife he'd put in her back. Always the loyal scapegoat.

He was parked right next to her and she considered just getting in her car and driving away, but immediately dismissed the idea. As satisfying as it would be, it was time for them to have this thing out.

When she walked by the young cop watching the perimeter again, his expression had evolved into a superior smirk that she actually wasn't accustomed to.

"You have a problem?" she said before she could stop herself.

He apparently hadn't expected to be challenged and took a step back. "No."

With that cleared up, Karen covered the rest of the distance to Pickering's car and sat down on the immaculate hood, feeling the rivets in her jeans subtly scrape the paint. Childish? Of course. But oddly satisfying.

From her slightly elevated position, she could see him speaking to the men dusting the car, arms crossed regally over his decorated chest. What they were saying was impossible to know, but judging from his body language, it wasn't what he wanted to hear.

He circled the remains of the vehicle a few times, crouching occasionally to get a closer look, and then started back toward his car and her.

"Our psychologist thinks al Fayed might be developing a connection to you," he said, when he came within earshot. "Ken thinks you should call him. Try to build a rapport."

She remained silent, deducing that he must be fairly desperate to forego ordering her the hell off his hood.

"I want you to follow me to the precinct and we're going to set up a call."

She looked past him at the faces of a group of small children playing on the sidewalk. If Pickering managed to get Fade through using her, it seemed likely that he'd do everything he could to minimize her role and take all the credit.

"What's in it for me, Captain?"

"What?"

"You heard me."

"You get to help us find the person who killed your men."

"My men are dead and catching al Fayed isn't going to change that."

"What the hell are you talking about, Karen? You're a cop. This is what you get paid for."

"What I'm talking about is the fact that I'm being crucified in the press and you won't let me defend myself."

"I can't control what they're saying about you."

"No, but you could get on TV and make some supportive comments instead of letting a couple of wives and anonymous sources do all the talking. How would you have done things different, Captain? I haven't heard a lot about that. I also haven't heard that I recommended against going in like that. All anyone's talking about is how bad I screwed up and how I'm not qualified to lead a SWAT team."

Pickering shrugged noncommittally. "I can't comment about an ongoing investigation."

"I'm not asking you to. I'm asking you to show the same support for me as you do the men on the force. Or to ungag me and let me tell my side of the story."

"You know I can't let you—"

"I don't know anything about the investigation into al Fayed or, for that matter, the investigation into my conduct. So I really have no way of saying anything except my version of what happened."

"Jesus Christ, Karen! We've got a heavily armed

lunatic running around the streets and you're worried about some bad PR? You know what you're going to do? You're going to do exactly what I tell you. And that's get in your car and follow me back to the precinct where you're going to get on the phone and help us catch this asshole. Do you understand?"

He started around to the driver's side door but then stopped when she didn't move. "That's an order, Karen."

"And one I'm more than willing to follow. I just want a little something in return."

"You're determined to play politics with this, aren't you? You're willing to just let the psychopath who killed your men walk around free . . ."

"It might be better than helping you find him so you can throw another SWAT team at him."

"Still trying to make this all my fault?" he shouted. "Let me tell you what the difference will be. This time we'll have someone competent in command."

She slid off the hood, scraping paint as she went, and spun toward him ready to shout back, but managed to stop herself. If there was any time to keep her infamous temper in check, this was it.

"Look, Captain . . . You don't like me and I'm sorry for that. The truth is, though, I was and am a qualified SWAT leader and I followed procedure to a T on this operation. The whole department is being made to look bad by all this—I look like an idiot, our guys look poorly trained, and you look like you can't run an effective organization. No matter how often you imply that I was forced down your throat by the feminists, eventually the press is going to get bored hearing it and they're going to turn on you."

He managed to unset his jaw and opened his mouth to say something but she cut him off.

"I'm not trying to portray myself as a hero here. Our guys died and I was in charge. But the treatment I'm getting isn't fair. All I'm asking is for you to tell the whole story of what happened. I'm willing to take my lumps where I deserve them, but I won't stand silent anymore while my name is dragged through the mud."

He opened his mouth again but no sound came out until he'd thoroughly scanned the area to see if anyone was close enough to hear. "Call Fayed and I'll think about it."

"I'd also like to be taken off administrative leave and put back on the Collector case. John needs me and it'll help show that I have the department's confidence."

"But you don't have the department's confidence, Karen. Jesus, what are you going to ask for next? A fucking promotion? A raise? What kind of other rewards do you feel you deserve for getting an entire SWAT team wiped out? People are calling you the Widowmaker for Christ's sake. How would it look to the men if I start making excuses for you?"

"I'm not asking for excuses," she said, still controlling her anger. Her mother would be so proud. "I just want *all* the facts out there and I want to be allowed to go back to working on catching a man who is, right now, torturing a woman to death."

He didn't answer for almost a minute. "We'll see how you do with Fayed."

Karen shook her head. "You first."

"You're overplaying your hand, Karen. How about instead I get on TV and tell the press you're not cooperating with our investigation into the deaths of your men?"

"Or you could just get on TV and tell the press that, based on the facts you've gathered so far, I acted within department policy and therefore you're reinstating me to active duty."

"I'm not prepared to do that. I don't know what the facts are."

"Come on, Captain!" she said, finally losing her meticulously constructed calm. "You know exactly what happened out there. You have a recording of everything that was said during the assault! You have craters from bomb blasts. You have a burned-out house. You have bodies. You have al Fayed's remote control and night vision cameras. This isn't rocket science!"

Her outburst caused a barely perceptible smile to stretch his lips. "Is this an ultimatum?"

"I'm sorry. I thought I was being clear. Yes, it is."

"Then, no. I won't be dictated to."

She pulled her badge from her pocket again and this time threw it, hitting him hard in the chest. "Then let the games begin."

25

Matt Egan squinted against the sun glaring off the cars lined up in front of him and walked quickly across the lot to a freshly painted trailer on the other side.

Billy and Lauren had done an inhuman amount of work over the last forty-eight hours, helped along by the fact that they had decided to relocate permanently to OSPA's office suite. Both were absolutely convinced that Fade was hiding in their bushes with a piano wire in just their neck size. Maybe Strand had been right—so far their boundless motivation and long hours had been a serious plus.

Based on an exhaustive review of regional classified ads and a poll of every used car dealer within five hundred miles, they'd determined that twenty-eight classic cars had changed hands in the relevant time frame. Based on Fade's historical love of convertibles, as well as the rather noisy call he'd made to Strand, Egan had decided to focus first on the three ragtops. It turned out that one didn't run and was towed away by its sixty-year-old purchaser. The second was in mint condition, but was purchased by a woman as a gift for her husband. The third, though, had been sold by this small Baltimore dealership to a male in his early thirties.

The man who stepped from the trailer and closed the distance to Egan with his hand outstretched didn't fit the stereotype of a used car salesman. Barely forty, he had a relaxed smile and gait that fit perfectly with his unpressed cotton dress shirt and khakis.

"Hi, my name's Troy Powell," he said. "Can I help you with something or are you just browsing?"

Egan had run through a number of ways to introduce himself, but none had been completely free of drawbacks. Normally, he'd just whip out his Homeland Security credentials and get whatever information he wanted. Not his best option under the circumstances.

"I'm Matt. Nice to meet you. Actually, I wanted to talk to you about a guy who bought an old Caddy from you a couple of days ago."

The man withdrew his hand with a little more force than was necessary. "Look, that car had a lot of potential, but I told the guy it wasn't all that sound. He told me he was a mechanic and was looking to make a project out of it. Just because I sell used cars doesn't make me—"

Egan grinned as disarmingly as he could and held his hands out in a gesture for peace. "Take it easy. I don't care about the car. I'm looking for the man."

"Are you a cop?"

He shook his head.

"Then I really can't help you—I can't just hand out personal information on my customers. I've got some nice cars on the lot, though, if you're in the market . . ."

"Could we talk inside for a moment?"

Powell shrugged and Egan followed him up the stairs, closing the door behind them.

"The thing is, I'm a private investigator specializing

185

in tracking down deadbeat dads. The guy I'm looking for disappeared about a year ago and left his wife high and dry with two little boys. She's trying to go to school and work full time to put food on the table while this jerk-off collects classic cars. I just want to find him and get him to comply with a court order to help support his kids."

Powell fell into a chair behind his cluttered desk and folded his arms across his chest. "I'm not sure what I can do to help you, even if I wanted to. People aren't obligated to provide information when they buy a car unless they're looking for a loan and this guy paid cash. Basically, all he told me was his name."

"And that was?"

Powell didn't answer, prompting Egan to dig into his wallet and produce three one-hundred-dollar bills. "This probably doesn't seem like much to you," he said, pushing the money across the desk toward the man. "But it's a fortune to the woman who gave it to me."

Powell stared at the money for a good thirty seconds and then said, "I've got two kids of my own. Girls. You?"

It was a simple question. Why was the answer so hard? "I'm not married," Egan said finally.

"Did you get that, Billy?" Egan said into his cell phone as he took a left that he hoped would lead him to the highway. Powell had finally agreed to tell him what he knew. It wasn't much, but it was enough. His description of the Cadillac's buyer had hit all the right buttons—a fit looking man of about thirty-five, five foot ten, dark complexion. More interesting was the bleached blond hair, earring, and blue tinted rectangular glasses. A maximally effective disguise for a man who couldn't go the fake beard route without looking like he was going to blow something up.

"Got it," Fraiser said. "Do you think it's him?"

"I think it's him."

"Yes!" Fraiser shouted. "I knew you'd get him, Matt."

"I haven't gotten anything—it's just a start. Run down the name he gave, but I'm guessing he just made it up on the spot."

"And the car?"

"I don't know. The guy said it wasn't all that sound mechanically, so he might be taking it in to get some work done. Call around and see what you can find. Do the quickie paint places first, okay?"

"No problem. But even if we know the color and have the temporary tag number, what're the chances you're going to just drive by him?"

"We're going to have to call the police and get an APB put out. Tell them it's a terrorism suspect and that under no circumstances are they to stop or approach the vehicle. Tell them we need him to lead us to his cell, or something."

"Uh, okay," he replied, sounding a bit uncertain. It seemed likely that he would run off to report all this to Strand right after he hung up and there would be some subsequent hand wringing about involving the police. But what choice did they have? They needed the manpower.

"If Hillel has a problem with the APB have him call me."

"Right. Anything else?"

"Unfortunately, that's it."

"Are you getting anywhere with his old friends? Have you talked to them yet?"

"Most of them, but I've come up empty. None of them have seen or heard from Fade in years."

"Would they tell you if they had?"

It was a good question. Egan was playing it like he was trying to quietly track him down before the cops cornered him and more people died, but Fade's old teammates would still be reluctant to give him up—both because they liked and respected him and because nobody wanted to take the chance of crossing him. In their minds, the smart move was not to get involved one way or another and let Fade take care of himself.

"I honestly don't know, Billy. I've got one more name on my list. If I get anything, I'll call you."

He hung up and immediately dialed the number of Roy Buckner, the former Delta operative and major redneck asshole that Strand had wanted to hire. Unlike the people Egan had talked to so far, Buckner hated Fade. After the mission they had completed together, Fade had made it clear he'd never work with the man again. And when Salam al Fayed said something like that, it tended to ring in the ears of the people who ran things. It didn't take long for Buckner to find himself removed from the operational side and eventually forced out. Typically, he blamed Fade instead of his own piss-poor performance.

Egan would use a slightly different backstory with Buckner: that Fade had lost it and he was helping the cops track him down. It seemed unlikely that Buckner would know anything useful, but if he did he'd almost certainly be happy to do anything he could to contribute to Fade's destruction.

"Hello?"

"Hi. This is Matt Egan again. I'm still trying to track down Roy."

"Look," Buckner's wife said over the sound of a screaming child. "He's not here, just like he wasn't here the last two times you called. What do you want me to do?"

"Maybe you could give me his cell number and then I wouldn't have to keep bothering you."

"He doesn't have it on. Like I told you, I left him a message that you called—"

"Is there an office, or a place he eats, or anywhere else I might be able to reach him?"

"He's on a job and I don't know where the hell he is. He's been up in D.C. and Virginia and he called me a few hours ago from Baltimore. Come to think of it, he didn't mention you at all. So maybe that means he doesn't want to talk to you."

Egan accelerated up the on ramp to I-95, feeling his

189

jaw tighten as he replayed the woman's words over in his head. *He's been up in D.C. and Virginia and he called me a few hours ago from Baltimore.*

"Thank you," he said finally. "You've been very helpful."

Egan wrote the things he'd learned from the used car dealer on his chalkboard and fell back onto the empty bed, covering the neck of his beer with his thumb to keep it from sloshing. The board was almost two-thirds full now—providing at least the illusion of progress. He lay there and contemplated it uselessly until his cell phone began ringing.

"Hello?"

"Matt. I hear you're already on your way to cracking this thing. Excellent work." Hillel Strand's voice. "I've got Lauren and Bill here, let me put you on the speaker."

"Matt? Can you hear me?" Lauren said.

"Yeah."

"We've been working on the car, but we can't find anyone who's painted it. We'll call around again in a couple of days. Also, there's nothing under the name he gave. We've checked for bank accounts, driver's licenses, credit cards. You name it. Your instinct was probably right on this—he just made it up as he was walking onto the lot."

"And the place he took Karen Manning?"

"We're working through real estate rentals and purchases of those types of properties over the past few years, but there's a huge number and no efficient way to search it."

"What about the APB?"

Strand's voice came back on. "That's a pretty risky strategy, Matt . . . But I agree. We need to take the chance. The police have the description of the car, the tag, and al Fayed. We've told them not to approach him and to contact us immediately if they spot him."

"Fine. Anything else?"

"I'm closing in on al Fayed's drug dealer friend," Fraiser said. "But these kinds of people don't exactly put their names in the phone book."

"When?"

"Tomorrow, hopefully. The next day at the latest."

"Faster is better, Billy. Anything else?"

"Not really. You probably saw on the news that the police found al Fayed's car in a shitty area of D.C. but there wasn't much left of it. The police reports are on your e-mail if you want to take a look at them, but I wouldn't bother. There's nothing there."

26

"It's green."

Isidro chewed his lip and danced uncomfortably from foot to foot—an incredibly odd mannerism for a two-hundred-and-fifty-pound mound of tattoo-covered muscle.

"We did the first coat of black and the painter called.

191

. . . It, uh, looked more like something Batman would drive than James Bond. Our paint guy came up with this. It's British Racing Green over a pearl base coat. It's not stock, but you gotta admit, it's fucking stunning."

Fade nodded but didn't say anything, instead continuing his circumnavigation of the Cadillac. When he made it to the gleaming front bumper, he motioned toward a subtle bulge in the hood.

"What's up with that?"

"We had to fabricate an entirely new hood, but it doesn't really change the car's lines. We needed to be able to fit this . . ." He popped the latch and exposed an entirely new motor. Fade leaned inside, actually feeling a little giddy as he examined the massive red, black, and chrome power plant, then turned his attention to the matte black machine guns running alongside it. The barrels lined up with two cleverly camouflaged holes just above the headlights. When he stood up straight again, he was struggling to appear unimpressed.

"Zero to sixty so fast you'll need a neck brace," Isidro continued. "Full racing tuned suspension. You can leave a half a mile of rubber in this bitch and it corners like a Porsche."

Fade nodded and walked the length of it again, running a hand over the elegant tan interior and neatly retracted hand-sewn top.

"All European leather, man. They don't use barbed wire over there, so it's flawless."

Fade pointed to the fuzzy dice hanging from the rear view mirror. "Nice touch."

"No extra charge," Isidro said and then stuck a key in the trunk, stepping back as it rose slowly on its own. "We had to reinforce the back end and it made the thing real heavy to open, so we put in hydraulics."

Fade pointed to a metal tank that took up most of the right side of the trunk. "What the hell's that?"

"The ejector seat, man."

"You're kidding. You got it to work?"

"Fuck, yeah, we got it to work. But it wasn't easy. Springs were a complete bust. We went with compressed air."

Fade pointed to the machine gun, secured by heavy steel brackets, aiming out another cleverly camouflaged hole, this time over the license plate. It had a long belt of ammunition that he'd never seen before feeding into it from an artistically crafted spool. "Where'd you get the ammo?"

"Got a friend who builds custom guns and he got us a bunch of blanks. We were afraid that firing the guns with the car moving was gonna throw off the handling. Turns out that the front ones ain't a problem but the back gun lifts the rear a little bit . . . Hey, check this shit out." Isidro took his shoes off and stood on the passenger seat as his men gathered near the passenger door.

"Get in the driver's seat," he said and Fade climbed in, sinking luxuriously into the new upholstery.

"The switch is on the floor above the accelerator.

You've got to really stomp on it."

Fade ran a hand over the burled wood of the steering wheel. "Now?"

"Go for it."

He looked up into Isidro's slightly nervous face and slammed his foot onto the switch.

There was a brief whoosh and suddenly the man was in flight, gaining a good five feet before starting to descend. Obviously, this wasn't the first time they'd tested the seat, because his men were in exactly the right place to catch him.

Fade realized his mouth was hanging open as he watched the seat slowly settle back into its original position. There was no more containing himself. He yanked his shoes off and jumped into the passenger seat. "The car is fucking *perfect!* Incredible!" He pointed toward the switch on the floor. "Come on, Isidro, do me."

The enormous Latino grinned and leaned into the car, careful not to let his dirty shirt touch the interior, and slammed a hand down on the switch.

The amount of thrust surprised him, almost buckling his knees and sending him in an uncontrolled arc that quickly reversed itself and sent him into an even more uncontrolled descent toward the edge of the door. Isidro's men were quicker than they looked, though, and managed to catch him before he damaged either himself or the paint.

"Unbelievable!" Fade said, helping a man he knocked over to his feet. "It's a car you could die in."

"So you like it?"

"Like it? I love it. You've really outdone yourself, Isidro."

The Latino bowed theatrically. "You're going to tell people about us, then? We could use the publicity. I've been dyin' to get into the movie business . . ."

"Don't even worry about it. If things go the way I think they will, you're going to get more publicity than you can handle."

Fade had been parked in the lot of a seemingly endless shopping mall for almost an hour, watching cars slowly cruise by and listening to the police scanner playing over the Caddy's ten thousand-dollar sound system. He grabbed a beer from a cooler on the floor and held it out the door to open it, directing the spray at an old Subaru parked next to him. Satisfied that it was no longer dripping, he took a few sips and then went back to scanning the lot with a small pair of binoculars. Still nothing.

Another fifteen minutes and boredom started to set in. He turned off the scanner and slipped in a rap CD thoughtfully provided by Isidro, but that only managed to hold his interest for another five minutes or so. Finally, he reached for his phone and dialed a number from memory.

"Hello?"

"Why don't you quit that stupid job and come on the road with me? We'll hit a few nice restaurants, go dancing, kill a few people . . . It'll be good fun."

"Sounds great," Karen Manning responded. "Why don't you drop by my house and pick me up?"

Fade laughed and grabbed for his binoculars again. A Lexus sedan with temporary tags was cruising for a space three rows down. When it turned, he saw the ASK ME ABOUT MY GRANDCHILDREN bumper sticker on the back. Nice.

"You reminded me of a joke," he said, picking up the tags he'd just removed from his car and making sure the electric screwdriver he'd bought was charged. "How do porcupines mate?"

"I don't know, how?"

"Very carefully."

He put the phone in his shirt pocket and stuck the earpiece in his ear, then jumped out and started walking casually toward the gray-haired woman easing herself from her Lexus. He slowed slightly and let her get most of the way to the mall entrance before crouching down between her front bumper and the bumper of the car in front of her. "So how's the five-oh doing finding me? I heard they tracked down my car. Can you believe that? I thought for sure that thing would have been stolen, painted, and sold to some guy in Nebraska by now. You just can't count on people anymore."

"Well, there wasn't much left of it."

"Get anything?"

"I don't know. I assume they're following up with the residents, but it's not a neighborhood known for cooperating with the police, and now that it's come

196

out that it's your car, I'm guessing it's gotten even harder. Cop killers are popular in that part of D.C."

Fade frowned slightly as he pulled off the car's tag and began screwing his own on in its place. "Cop killer" was a label he could have happily lived his whole life without.

"You know what, Fade? You've caught me at a good time. I'm sitting in my house all alone with nothing to do. Why don't you tell me your story?"

"Oh, you don't want to hear me drone on about myself," Fade said, going around to the back of the car and trying to act natural as he began removing the rear tag. He doubted the cops would ever come up with the fact that he'd bought the Caddy, but you could never be too careful.

"Actually, I do."

"Same old story, really. Poor Arab trash from New York joins the navy because he's too dumb and lazy to go to college. Ends up a SEAL because of an uncontrollable rubber fetish. Runs around the world killing people who never did anything to him. . . . What about you?"

"If you have a TV, you already know everything there is to know about me. Everyone does." He was surprised that she didn't bother to hide the bitterness in her voice.

"You're getting so much better at this, Karen. I feel almost compelled to give you my address and an inventory of my weapons. So I've got to know, were you really a debutante?"

There was a short pause, as one might expect. "Yes."

"I love that," he said, finishing with the back tag and then leaning against the car trying to give the impression that he'd finished his chores and was now waiting for his mom to return from her errands. "Who picked the dress?"

This time she sounded a little irritated. "My mother."

"Nice."

"You know what they say. Once you've seen a girl in a hoop skirt, there isn't much more to—"

"But what's the story behind the story, Karen? What's beneath that nice tan, the crushing incompetence, and the uncooperative attitude?"

"A lot of unresolved anger. Who's Strand?"

"Long story."

"I told you, I have time."

"Nah. Let's not talk about him. It kind of brings me down."

"Why don't you let me help you, Fade?"

"Help me how?"

She didn't immediately answer and he looked around him before walking back to attach the old lady's tags to his car.

"Look, Fade . . . The police are running this investigation with blinders on. They want to get you and they don't want to hear anything that doesn't relate to getting you."

"But don't you want exactly the same thing? Hell, if you could shoot me personally, all your problems would be solved."

"I don't want to shoot you, Fade."

"Of course you do. Admit it. Why wouldn't you?"

"Because I don't want to shoot anyone. And even more, I don't want you to shoot any more of our people—which is what might happen if we end up in some kind of macho showdown. I believe you when you say you never meant to kill a bunch of cops and I assume you don't want to kill any more. So why not just defuse the situation? Come in. Get a good lawyer. Survive this."

"Somehow I don't think anyone is going to be interested in me getting my story out and I imagine that giving myself up is going to get me nothing but executed. I don't picture myself dying strapped to a table with my victims' families watching. Hell, if you invited everybody, you'd have to rent a stadium . . ."

"But if—"

"Look, Karen. My situation has certain . . . complications. But I appreciate your concern. I really do."

He finished with the tags and stood, trying to stretch the knot that had tied itself in his lower back and wondering if the Kmart across the street sold BB guns.

"Fade—"

"Thanks for the chat, Karen. But I gotta run."

27

It took Egan six hours to get to the outskirts of New York and then another two to wade through the vehicular anarchy that led to the dangerous-looking neighborhood he'd been directed to.

It seemed to have become hotter since the sun went down and he stepped out of the car into damp air that smelled of concrete and exhaust. The street was empty but there were a few people scattered along the sidewalk and more sitting on steps leading to the dilapidated brownstones that crowded the narrow avenue. All were engaged in the same activity: staring directly at him. He made a move to cross the road but first turned and ducked back into his car, locking his gun into the glove compartment. Whether that was smart or suicidal would be determined later.

"Watch your car for you, mister?"

Egan slammed his door shut and turned toward the voice. The kid was probably thirteen, dressed in a pair of jeans and a clean white T-shirt oddly devoid of logos.

"You don't look that tough."

"Tougher'n you."

Egan laughed and looked around him again, confirming that everyone was still staring. He wondered if Fade had gotten the same reaction when he'd abandoned his car in D.C. With one significant difference, of course. Anyone who hadn't been kicked in the head by a horse knew instinctively that Fade was not to be fucked with. He, on the other hand, had settled into the look of exactly what he was—a man who lived in the suburbs with a crazy wife and a daughter who was bearing down on adolescence at the speed of light.

"Good investment, man. Guaranteed."

"Guaranteed, huh. How much?" The darkness and deep brown of the boy's eyes didn't hide the intelligence there. Either the car would be completely safe or it would be long gone when he returned.

"Twenty bucks."

Egan pulled out his wallet and gave him a fifty.

"Do I look like I carry change, man?"

"Why don't you tell me where Javan Franklin lives and we'll call it even."

An exasperated lungful of air escaped the boy. "Man, see how my mother makes me dress? My life's hard enough without running my mouth."

"I see your point," Egan said, starting toward a wide building at the end of the block. "If the car's the way I left it when I get back, there's another fifty in it for you."

The young men crowded onto the steps in front of him were all standing by the time he made it to within twenty feet, and no fewer than three were talking urgently into cell phones. At ten feet, about half flowed down onto the sidewalk and surrounded him.

"What the fuck you doing here, boy? You lost or are you a cop?" one of them said.

"Neither."

"Then you're one crazy bitch, aren't you?"

"I'm looking for Javan Franklin."

"Who?"

Egan turned toward the young man who was emerging as the mob's spokesman and pointed to the cell phone on his hip. "Why don't you give Javan a call and tell him a friend of Salam al Fayed is here to see him."

The group fell silent, but kept inching toward him, closing to the point where he wouldn't be able to do much but fall on the ground and be beaten to death if they decided to attack. No, that wasn't entirely true. He could probably get a hold of the one in front of him before he went down. Of course, there was no real point other than the fact that he'd die a little happier with one of their broken necks in his hands.

Maybe the guy perceived what he was thinking, or maybe he knew something about Fade, but after a moment, he retreated and was replaced by a wall of flesh barely contained by a Chicago Bulls T-shirt.

Egan couldn't hear what the kid was saying into his phone but when he hung up he gave a short nod of his head and Egan felt himself being slammed facedown onto the sidewalk. He tried to get a grip on one of the countless arms holding him, almost managing to grab a heavily ringed finger tangled in his shirt before the fat guy who'd been in front of him landed both knees in his back.

So that was it, he thought as he struggled to keep breathing beneath the man's weight. The survivor of numerous missions behind enemy lines and the coordinator of many more was going to die in the Big Apple at the hands of a bunch of teenagers. The thought of Elise and Kali gave him a brief burst of strength that he used to get an arm free. Raising his

202

head as far as he could off the sidewalk, he scanned the waistbands in front of him. One of these assholes had to have a gun. If he could just get to it . . .

He still hadn't spotted anything more deadly than a belt buckle when it occurred to him that he was more or less intact. He'd absorbed no punches, kicks, blades, or bullets. The hands on him were just sliding up and down, looking for weapons and wires.

"Believe me. We've been through this."

"And we'll go through it again."

Egan was pushed into the wall and frisked again, this time with the barrel of a .45 pressed behind his ear. "You just stay cool, huh?" the man searching him suggested.

Finally, the man stepped back, grabbed him by the collar and shoved him through a kitchen that looked like it hadn't been used since the fifties. The back bedroom of the large apartment turned out to be set up with sofas and leather easy chairs in an arrangement that recalled a royal court. The apparent king, nestled in a red La-Z-Boy, was flanked by two young men with shoulder holsters.

"I know a cop when I see one and that's a fucking cop," one of them said.

The man in the chair appeared to be unarmed and was dressed in a white linen shirt, cream colored slacks, and bare feet. He nodded and one of the men standing behind Egan grabbed his wallet and walked it over.

"Cute," the man in the chair said, holding up a picture of Kali. "Yours?"

Egan nodded.

"So what is it I can do for you, Matt?" the man said, tossing the wallet back to him.

"Are you Javan Franklin?"

His expression suggested that he wasn't inclined to answer that question.

"I want to talk to you about Salam al Fayed."

"Yeah? I'm hearing good things about Sal these days."

The other men in the room, seven in all now, snickered in unison.

"Have you talked to him recently?"

"What the fuck do you care? You said you're not a cop, right?"

Egan shook his head, deciding that the truth was the only thing that had even the slightest chance of getting him what he wanted. Franklin had the look of a serious skeptic.

"I used to work with him. He thinks I set him up and he told me he's going to kill me. I want to find him before he can accomplish that."

Franklin seemed to have been expecting a more complex line of bullshit and it took a moment for Egan's explanation to process.

"Did you?"

"What?"

"Set him up."

"That's a complicated question."

"Is it?"

"Let's just say that I didn't have his back like I should have."

Franklin nodded silently and looked around the room at his people. "Well, Matt, it sounds like you've landed yourself in some deep shit. But I'm not sure why I care if Sal kills you or not."

"Because we have the same interests on this."

"How you figure?"

"We're both friends of his who, unfortunately, need him dead. Me, because he wants to kill me, and you, because you hooked him up with the Colombians and I'm guessing with a stack of fake IDs. The longer this thing drags out, the better the chance the cops are going to get around to you. I don't have to tell you that they're not all that happy about the deaths of their men. They're looking for somebody to take the blame."

Franklin chewed his lip for a moment and then waved a hand in the air. For a moment Egan thought he'd been dismissed, but then the other people in the room began filing out. He caught the man who had frisked him by the arm as he went by. "Hey, could you do me a favor? I think I've got a shadow. White guy about my age—a real dangerous redneck son of a bitch. Could you take a look around and if you see him, maybe ask him to wait for me? I'd like to talk with him."

Franklin nodded his assent and Egan released the man's arm. When the door clicked shut and they were alone, he motioned for Egan to sit.

"I've known Sal since we were kids. I wanted him to come work for me but for some reason, he ran off and joined the navy. Why the fuck anyone would want to wake up every morning at five A.M. with some asshole white guy screaming at him is beyond me. But then, he was always kinda weird. He never seemed that interested in what was going on in the neighborhood. So I was pretty surprised when he showed up on my doorstep after I haven't seen him for years and asked me for work."

"Did you give it to him?"

"Fuck no. I'm not tall enough to ride that ride, man. You go hiring some badass Navy SEAL and people start getting nervous, you know? They think maybe you're looking to upset the balance of things."

"But the Colombians aren't as concerned about balance."

"Bunch of fucking freaks. They got more money than they could spend in ten lifetimes and it's not enough. I mean, what the fuck do you buy in Colombia? They don't even have paved roads. But, yeah. I put Sal in touch with them. I understand he did a good job and made some bank. But as far as I know he walked away from that a long time ago."

Egan nodded but didn't say anything.

"So what do you want from me, man?"

"He was prepared for something like this to happen, Javan. He had a safe house set up, he has money, he has disguises, and so it stands to reason that he'd have some aliases. It occurs to me that you'd be the go-to guy on something like that."

Franklin leaned back in his chair, apparently not happy with where the conversation was going.

"Look, Javan, Salam did this to himself. It's not your fault. You helped him the best you could and that's left you involved with a man of Arab extraction running around killing cops. I mean, the press is already spouting a bunch of bullshit about possible ties to al Qaeda. How long before Homeland Security gets involved? I'm willing to bet you have a hell of a lawyer, but he isn't going to do you much good if you're stuck in a five-by-five cage on the beach in Guantanamo."

Franklin drummed his fingers on the arm of his chair for a few moments, eyes locked on Egan, and then pulled a small pad from his shirt pocket. After scribbling something on it, he tore the page off, folded it, and held it out. "I gave him this name, but I don't know what he did with it. Seriously."

Egan took it and started for the door.

"Hey, Matt?"

He stopped with his hand on the knob. "Yeah?"

"You better think hard about whether you really want to find Sal. Because if you do, that little girl's not gonna have a father no more."

"Over there," his escort said, stopping on the sidewalk and pointing. "Behind the Dumpster."

Egan hesitated for a moment and then stepped into

the garbage-strewn alley, wishing he'd retrieved his gun when he'd passed by his car. On the bright side, though, the kid he'd paid to watch it was still sitting patiently on the hood waiting for his other fifty.

He continued forward, moving as far left as the narrow alley would allow and focusing on the area behind a large Dumpster that was becoming visible as he approached.

Roy Buckner was pretty much like he remembered. His retirement from the military hadn't altered his choice of haircuts, but it had put a little weight on him. His slightly hooked nose looked a little less severe with the extra flesh around it, but his eyes had sunken a bit to compensate. There was a trickle of blood running from the side of his mouth and, judging by his expression, he was more than a little put out by the fact that he was being held at bay by four black high school kids with automatic pistols.

"How you doing, Roy?"

He pursed his swelling lips in a way that was meant to suggest that he was in complete control of the situation. "I'm doing okay, Matt. How about you?"

"Can't complain."

Egan slipped by one of the kids and wrapped an arm around Buckner's shoulders, leading him back down the alley followed closely by his new team. "This is the thing, Roy. I don't want you following me. The thought that I could get between you and Fade, frankly, scares the shit out of me."

"Not really my problem, is it, Matt?"

"Well, it is kind of. Because if I ever see you again, I'm going to shoot you."

28

Hillel Strand's receptionist seemed to be doing pretty well for herself. Even in the dark, the neighborhood had a brand new feel to it—unmarked pavement, fledgling trees held to stakes by pieces of green hose, and empty cul de sacs. The houses that had been completed were homogenous and sprawling, nearly overwhelming the narrow lots that contained them.

Fade strode down the sidewalk, navigating by the light of widely spaced streetlamps, and tried to remember the word he'd heard for houses like these.

McMansions. That was it. As flawlessly conceived a word as he'd ever heard.

Predictably, the numbers descended in perfect order and were uniformly lit. When he arrived at six-nineteen he turned up the right side of the driveway and slipped through an unlocked gate that led to the backyard.

From his position in an unfinished home a few doors down, Fade had watched Kelly Braith and her husband pack two teenaged boys into a minivan and drive off a few hours ago. He hadn't moved until it was dark enough to give him cover and to allow him to confirm that no one was still home to turn on lights.

The backyard was completely encircled by a

wooden fence built more for privacy than security. Fade listened for activity in the adjoining yards, and hearing none, used his elbow to knock through one of the glass panels in the back door. After reaching through and flipping the lock, he took a step back and waited for the beeping of an alarm system. Nothing. The Braiths must have blown the whole wad on upgrading to the genuine faux-cherry kitchen cabinets.

Fade removed a dead bird from the plastic grocery bag he was carrying and carefully arranged it on the ground to look like it had broken its neck flying into the glass, then padded quietly inside. His time exploring the similar floor plan of the house down the street paid off and he was able to make his way to a small den behind the living room without turning on any lights.

Slipping into the chair behind a cluttered desk, he reached for a keyboard and watched a flat panel display come to life in an exuberant family portrait. After a few moments, he found the My Documents folder and began going through the files contained in it.

Most of them related to Braith's husband's electronics store but there were occasional interesting tidbits. The address book contained a fair amount of personal information on Strand and Egan—including birth dates, addresses, and phone numbers. In fact, Strand was turning fifty in only a few days. Unless, of course, things went in Fade's direction.

While a lot easier than going through land records

and a lot more sanitary than sifting through garbage, no groundbreaking piece of information jumped to the screen. Neither man would be out mowing his lawn this weekend and he doubted Strand would be throwing himself a big birthday bash in a venue with lots of unprotected angles of attack. What about appointments that might force them out of hiding? He pulled up the computer's calendar program and did a quick search but, not surprisingly, Kelly didn't keep her boss's schedule on it. He was about to close it when an entry two days in the future caught his eye.

Pick up cake.

He froze for a moment and then went back to the address book, confirming Strand's birth date. Two days from now.

A smile spread across his face as a plan began to form in his mind. Not just any plan either. An Albert Einstein of a plan. A Leonardo da Vinci of a plan. A plan so sublime and elegant that if Mozart were still alive, he'd write a symphony to honor it.

The rumble of a garage door opener drifted in from the other side of the house and Fade started back toward the kitchen, his grin continuing to widen. As was almost always the case, the logistical details would cause all kinds of complications but if he could just focus and think them through, it could actually work. What he really needed was Matt Egan to help him create an airtight plan. But, in the absence of that, he'd count on the luck he always seemed to have when it came to killing people.

29

Hillel Strand flipped a page in the police report and used a Magic Marker to blacken out a paragraph at the top. That fucking moron Pickering had been so obvious and unbending in his efforts to use Karen Manning to cover his ass that she'd quit—introducing yet another unpredictable element into an already nearly uncontrollable situation. He grabbed a pen and wrote a note in the margin of the report. *Lauren: What's she going to do now? The press? MONITOR!!*

Strand flipped another page and put an X through the remainder of Manning's written report on the call she'd received from al Fayed, making certain that all mention of their contact would be removed before the file was scanned and e-mailed to Matt Egan. Al Fayed's apparent interest in Manning was the best lead they had that Egan wasn't involved in. Doug Banes was watching her and if al Fayed ever decided to try to make physical contact he'd disappear forever with no concerns about hand-wringing and old loyalties.

It was an avenue the police, in their questionable wisdom, had chosen to more or less ignore. Manning had agreed to a tap on her phone but beyond that, they were just trusting her to report anything of interest that didn't show up on that tap. They continued to rely on the assumption that al Fayed was on the run and were giving little thought to the possibility that he was lurking around D.C. playing a fucking game.

Strand shoved the file aside and looked down at the pile of clothes folded neatly on the floor. He hadn't left the office in nearly a week and it seemed that with every passing hour, his anger and frustration were doubling. That this uneducated former enlisted man could affect his life at all was enough to infuriate him, but the fact that he was now imprisoned on this floor, sharing a bathroom with his assistants, living on cold takeout, made him want to kill someone.

He sat quietly, eyes closed, forcing himself to believe that all this was going to go away when his private line rang. He snatched up the phone and pressed it to his ear.

"What?"

"He made me."

Strand remained motionless for a moment and then grabbed the electric pencil sharpener on his desk and threw it into a wall, sending a cloud of wood dust and shattered plastic across his folded clothes.

"What the fuck are you talking about, Roy? You told me there was no chance of that! You told me that this was not a problem!"

"Don't know what happened, man. He didn't see me, I guarantee it. Hell, he's been calling my house leaving messages for me. There must be a leak on your end."

Strand jumped up from behind his desk but didn't have anywhere to go. Egan had been right about Roy Buckner—he was an arrogant asshole who overestimated his own abilities. But he had a background in the Special Forces and he hated al Fayed with irrational passion. That gave him certain unique qualifications that had forced Strand to ignore his drawbacks.

"It was just you and me, Roy. No one else here knows I have you following Matt. This was your fuck-up."

"Whatever. No use crying over it. Point is, he's gone."

"You lost him, too?"

"He had a bunch of niggers pull guns on me and then told me if he saw me again, he'd kill me. Fucker's lucky I didn't drop him right there."

"Jesus Christ," Strand said, collapsing back into his chair and trying to think. There weren't a lot of options.

"I want you to take over for Doug Banes covering Karen Manning."

"The bitch from SWAT?"

"We have reason to believe al Fayed might try to contact her face to face."

"I'd like to contact her face to face myself. Have you seen that ass?"

"Shut up. Just shut up and get over there. And do you think you could manage not to get spotted this time?"

There was a rap on his door and a moment later Lauren poked her head in. He waved violently at her to get out, but she stood her ground, jabbing a finger toward his phone.

"What?" he mouthed silently, covering the handset's mouthpiece.

"Matt's on three."

Another violent wave and she retreated through the door, slamming it behind her.

"Are we done?" he heard Buckner say.

"Get on Karen Manning. Now," Strand replied and switched lines, cutting Buckner off.

"Matt? Are you there?"

"Talked to Roy yet?"

"I just got off the phone with him. He said you threatened him. What's going on?"

"What's going on? You told that psycho to tail me."

"I put a qualified operator on you as backup, Matt . . ."

"Backup. Right. Don't ever do that again, Hillel."

"This isn't just about you, Matt," Strand said, forcing himself to remain calm. "We're not going to have a lot of chances at this thing."

There was a short silence over the phone before Egan spoke again. "I figure Fade's not going to worry too much about me until you're dead, Hillel. I guess I could just take a leave of absence until then . . ."

"Is that some kind of threat?"

"Take it any way you want."

Strand's jaw tightened, but he knew there was nothing he could do. For now, Egan had him by the balls.

"Matt, I—"

There was a quiet click and the line went dead.

"Fuck!" He pressed a button on his phone, opening

the intercom to Lauren's office. "Get in here and bring Bill with you."

By the time they settled into the chairs in front of his desk, Strand had regained enough of his composure to force his voice into a monotone that was a reasonable facsimile of calm.

"I just spoke with Matt and I'm not quite sure what's happening with him. I don't think he's coming in anymore and I have a feeling he's not going back to the hotel. It seems like the further we get into this, the more Matt wants to go it on his own. There's no reason for him to avoid us unless he's starting to have second thoughts about what needs to be done. And if that's the case, I think we have to consider the possibility that he's going to get himself killed out of some misguided sense of loyalty to al Fayed. Or he's going to cause us to miss an opportunity to neutralize a very dangerous man whose only goal in life is to kill us . . ." He let his voice trail off for a moment. "Thoughts?"

"I talked to him just last night," Fraiser said. "He sounded fine."

Fraiser didn't know anything about Roy Buckner and he was getting the same sanitized files as Egan. At this point, there was no reason for him to know that Egan wasn't being given the whole story.

"What did he get from the drug dealer, Bill?"

"He said not much, but he didn't give any details. He said he was still working on it."

"Can we get to him?"

"Javan Franklin? I don't know. He's basically living in a fortress and unless we want to get the police involved, I'm not sure what we can do to strong-arm him . . ."

Strand turned and stared out the window at the blanket of lights that D.C. became at night. "How are we going to find Matt?"

There was a long silence, eventually broken by Lauren. "We should send someone to the hotel to make sure it's clean and see if he left anything pointing to what he was going to do."

Strand nodded, but didn't look back. "Get Steve Despain on it."

"Beyond that, I'm not sure. Track his ATM and credit cards? He'll have anticipated that."

"What about his wife?"

"They're really close," Fraiser said. "But I doubt that's going to do much good. He's staying away from her because he thinks al Fayed would try to acquire him there."

Strand took a deep breath and let it out slowly. "We need to think harder."

"He'll have to come back to us eventually," Lauren said. "If we stop talking to him he's going to have a hard time analyzing intelligence and he isn't going to have any idea what the police are doing."

Strand didn't respond. It was a difficult question. Without Egan, the entire machine ground to a halt.

"We're not going to cut him off," Strand said, turning back toward them. "But I'm going to tell you this again. He gets absolutely nothing that doesn't go through me first. Do you understand?"

30

It was definitely the address Franklin had given him, but it didn't look right—an aging rancher in a middle-class neighborhood filled with sensible cars and golf carts.

Egan slowed and turned into the driveway, admiring a large family of lawn gnomes guarding a shrub by the door. He sat there for a few seconds, seriously considering backing up and driving out of there. Franklin had obviously fucked him. No big surprise—it had never been anything more than a long shot.

Finally, he made a deal with himself. He'd look over the yard one more time and if there was even a hint of a plastic pink flamingo, he'd get the hell out of there. If not, he'd knock on the door.

It wasn't exactly a thorough search, but there seemed to be no representations of birds of any color at all so Egan climbed from the car and walked along a gravel path to the front door.

The man who answered his knock made Egan even more certain that he'd been screwed. He was about fifty, with a ponytail made up of what few strands of hair he had left and a Hawaiian shirt that arced gracefully over the gut hiding the top of his cutoff khakis. All that was missing was an umbrella drink in a pineapple husk and the cheerful strains of Jimmy Buffett.

"I'm looking for an ID," Egan said with a complete lack of enthusiasm.

To his surprise, there was a flash of understanding in the man's eyes before he managed to cloak his expression.

"I think you got the wrong place. Who are you looking for?"

Egan glanced over his shoulder, and seeing no one on the street, shoved the man back before slipping inside.

"Hey! What the hell do you think you're doing? Get out of here before I call the cops!"

"I need information on Salam al Fayed," Egan said, closing the door behind him. There were no lights on in the house, leaving it in a deep gloom that smelled of cigarettes and pot.

"Never heard of him," the man said reflexively.

"Seems kind of unlikely since he's been on about every news program in the country."

The man, whose name he hadn't been given, took a step backward. "I mean, I don't know anything about him . . . You know what I meant! Who are you? A cop? Do you have a warrant?"

"I don't work for the police. And I could care less about you or what you do for money. But you made some IDs for al Fayed a while back and I need copies of them. So why don't you get on your computer and print them out for me. Then I'll leave and you'll never have to think about me again."

"I don't know what you're talking about with all this ID shit, man. You got the wrong guy. Now get out of here before I call the police." He made a move toward a phone sitting on a shelf next to an expensive-looking stereo system but Egan cut him off.

"Look . . . What's your name?"

"Syd."

"Syd. I'm not a bad guy but I really need this information and I'm going to do what I have to to get it. So why don't we skip the unpleasant part and get to the payoff?"

"My neighbors are only about ten feet away," the man warned. "If I start yelling, they'll be on to 911 in half a second."

"Come on, Syd. Be reasonable here."

"On the count of three, I'm gonna yell. I swear I am. One . . . two . . ."

Egan swung his foot up between the man's legs hard enough that for a moment he actually thought he might have hurt his ankle. Pulling his foot back, he rolled it in circles, testing it as the man grabbed his crotch and let out a low squeal that his neighbors wouldn't hear no matter how close they were. Egan gave him a little shove, tipping him over onto the carpet, and then pulled a full rack of CDs down on top of him. With his ankle feeling more or less normal again, he swung his foot back to deliver a moderately hard kick to the man's ribs when he saw his wife staring up at him. Her second record was lying on the carpet.

"Hey," Egan said, leaning over and slapping the man across the face. "Syd! You all right? Can you hear me?"

He couldn't talk yet, but managed to nod.

"I hate this kind of thing. Really. And it makes it that much worse when it's completely unnecessary. All I'm asking for is copies of the stuff you did for al Fayed. I swear to you that the cops will never hear about any of this from me . . ."

"I don't have it," the man managed to get out. He rolled on his back, still desperately clutching at his crotch. The color of his face made Egan wonder if he was about to have a stroke. That's all he needed.

"Why would I keep records? They'd . . . they'd just incriminate me."

"Oh, please . . . I'm not an idiot, Syd. You can buy damn near unbreakable encryption for less than a cup of coffee and save things anonymously on servers all over the world. No, I'm guessing you've got all kinds of records. I mean, you never know when the cops are going to show up and you're going to need to deal, right?"

"You don't know what you're talking about!"

Egan grabbed a sofa pillow that looked like a skinned poodle and laid it on the man's knee, then pulled out his pistol and pressed the barrel against it.

"Fuck! Are you crazy?"

"No," Egan said. "I'm desperate."

31

Fade was quickly gaining a grudging respect for those millions of people who made their living working with computers. He'd once spent two completely motionless days nose-deep in a muddy river waiting for a particular Cambodian gentleman to make the mistake of walking too close. At the time, he'd considered it tough duty, but compared to the physical and mental torture of hunching over his new laptop hour after hour, it had been nothing. He felt like he had a knife between his shoulder blades and the inactivity was driving him insane. Or, in the eyes of the press and police, more insane than he already was.

Worse, the increasingly familiar deadened tingling in his foot was more acute than it had ever been before. The cramping in his lower back seemed to be pressing his pet bullet deeper into his spine. What he needed was an assistant. Maybe he should take out a want ad in the *Post*. Something like "Exciting entry level position in the growing field of assassination. Almost certain potential for advancement."

Fade grinned as he stood unsteadily and went to check the pot of Lipton's noodles boiling over a hot plate next to the sink. Floating on top was a gray layer of lead paint and asbestos that was constantly drizzling from the ancient ceiling. In hindsight, he probably should have sprung for a slightly nicer safe house, but who knew he'd really need it? The plan was to give him a place to pick up his IDs, cash, and weapons, and then get the hell out of Dodge. Long-term comfort hadn't been on his mind.

He switched on the tiny black and white television sitting next to him and flipped through the channels, relieved to find that the soaps had returned and that for the time being at least, there was no mention of him at all. The last story he'd seen, on the eleven o'clock news the night before, reported that Karen had quit the force and that the police were pursuing "significant leads" in their search for him. He was tempted to call her and find out what was going on, but instead skimmed the poisonous muck off his pasta and carried the pan over to his makeshift workstation.

It took another two hours of hard work, but he finally finished plotting phonebook addresses against his computer's mapping software, identifying every bakery between Kelly Braith's house and Homeland Security's headquarters. The hope here was that Braith liked her boss enough not to just pick him up a grocery store cake but not so much that she'd use some boutique bakery miles out of her way. If that assumption was wrong, it was going to be a very long day.

He picked up the new satellite phone he'd bought that morning and started dialing.

By the time he was onto his twentieth bakery, he had his headset on and was doing pull-ups from a doorjamb that looked like it was going to separate from the wall any moment. The activity was bringing the feeling back into his right foot, as it always did, but not as quickly as it had in the past. Apparently, all this excitement wasn't good for his delicate constitution.

"Wild Flour, can I help you?"

"Yeah. A friend of mine, Kelly Braith, asked me to pick up a cake there for her tomorrow and I was wondering if I could come by a little early."

"What's the name again?"

"B-R-A-I-T-H." He dropped off the doorjamb and began jogging around the Cadillac.

"Uh, right. Here it is . . ."

He stopped short, barely avoiding ramming his shin into the back bumper. "What did you say?"

"I've got it right here. Carrot cake. Happy Birthday Hillel, right?"

"That's the one."

"I've got this down for a seven thirty pickup. We open at seven, so you could come in then."

"Great, thanks. And what time do you close tonight?"

"Five thirty, but it won't be ready then. I'll make it fresh in the morning."

Fade pumped a fist in the air and danced as much of a solo tango as space would allow. "Of course you will. Thanks. I'll see you soon."

The role luck played in killing people couldn't be overestimated—probably contributing about the same as talent and training when the moment came. Fade, while not exactly on speaking terms with Fate lately, had always been Death's favorite son. Apparently, their long separation hadn't changed that. The bakery was perfect. A tiny storefront on a quiet street, surrounded by other small shops that didn't start opening until ten.

He'd arrived at three A.M., peeking in the dark windows at the front and then pulling around to the empty parking lot in back. Still cramped from sitting for so long, he ended up lying across the back seat of the Caddy watching what stars could defeat the weak security light at the far end of the lot. He gauged time by their movement across the sky, occasionally looking at his watch to check his accuracy.

At four A.M. it was still dead quiet, despite what those Dunkin' Donuts commercials said. He pulled his jacket over him and closed his eyes, allowing himself to drift a bit.

The sound of a motor and the flash of headlights sweeping over the car jerked him awake and he slid to the floor, enveloping himself in the deep shadow cast by the front seats. The motor and lights died and he heard a car door open and then close. Footsteps started, paused, and then began coming his way. He held his breath and watched as a woman stopped a few feet away, moving her gaze slowly over the car.

"Nice," she said aloud and then turned and disappeared from sight.

Clearly a woman of breeding and taste.

He waited to hear the jingling of keys before easing

himself into a sitting position and peering through the front windshield. The woman seemed absorbed by the lock on the bakery's rear door, so he slid silently to the pavement and padded up behind her.

He was only a few feet away when the door opened. Rushing forward, he clamped a hand over her mouth and dragged her inside before kicking the door shut behind them.

She struggled admirably, but then froze when he pressed the barrel of his pistol against her cheek.

"If you scream, I'm going to shoot you."

Her back was pushed against his chest and he could feel her trembling as he eased his hand off her mouth. The fact that she was young and reasonably fit was kind of a relief. He'd been afraid she was going to be some seventy-year-old woman with arteries clogged by years of pastry sampling. Giving somebody's grandmother a heart attack wasn't in his plan.

"I . . . I take the money to the bank after we close at night. I've only got . . ."

"I'm not here for money."

That had been the wrong thing to say. A nearly inaudible squeak came from her throat and her trembling turned to outright shaking.

"No, no. Relax. I'm not here for that either. Start breathing again, please."

She did and he backed away, keeping his gun pointed at her face. She was actually kind of cute. Dark, shoulder-length hair and big, beautiful eyes that were almost black. Maybe she had a thing for murderous sociopaths? Hell, he was nearly famous.

"What do you want then?" she managed to get out, glancing over at a magnetic strip containing a few rather nasty looking knives. Fade couldn't help smiling.

"I just want you to bake me a cake. Carrot, if it's not too much trouble."

"You could have just called."

"Well, I have some special ingredients that I want you to work with." He pulled a couple of glass vials from his pocket and put them on the counter.

"What . . . what are they?"

It was a good question. He honestly didn't know exactly. His shopping spree earlier that night predictably had begun in the rat poison aisle. He'd been in a fairly dark mood at the time. After fondling the box for a few minutes, reading the wonderfully sadistic sounding list of ingredients on the back, he'd finally been forced to return it to its shelf. Simple and effective, yes. But impossible. There was just no way to control who was going to sample Strand's birthday cake.

So, what then? There was always LSD, which definitely blew the top off the fun meter. Unfortunately, he had no idea where to get it, beyond a Grateful Dead concert, and Jerry Garcia was dead.

The possibility of Ex-Lax was hard to ignore and had a really appealing "fuck you" quality to it. But it didn't really get him anywhere.

A few hours later, in an all-night drug store devoid

of customers, a young pharmacist had become very helpful when Fade had put a gun in his ear, suggesting a concoction that was guaranteed to create a truly obscene combination of explosive diarrhea and projectile vomiting. After that, a new and improved plan had begun to evolve.

"What are they?" the woman repeated, examining the vials in her peripheral vision but never taking her eyes off Fade.

"What's the difference?"

"You want me to poison someone. I won't do it."

Fade frowned deeply and folded his arms across his chest, tapping the trigger of his pistol impatiently. Ninety-nine percent of humanity was a complete waste of skin and he gets a woman with principles.

"Look," he said finally. "I don't mean to nitpick here, but I have a gun and you don't."

Karen Manning forced herself to stop pacing and instead stood in the middle of the room taking slow, deep breaths and staring at the door only a few feet away. If she dove for it now, she could sprint down the hall, knock over a security guard or two, and be free in less than ten seconds.

She'd finally swallowed what little pride she had left and called her father on the way home from throwing her badge at Pickering. He'd told her to turn around and come directly to his office. By the time she arrived, there were three people from one of the world's top public relations firms sitting in a conference and he was on the phone with the governor of Virginia. Apparently, he'd already spent over a hundred thousand dollars laying the groundwork for the day she came crawling back to Daddy. How embarrassing.

And now, here she was in the green room of *The O'Reilly Factor*, waiting to be interviewed by one of the country's most vicious and highest rated talk show hosts. Despite hours of intensive coaching by her new PR team and a warm-up interview on a local news show that had been thoroughly analyzed by a twenty-person focus group, she didn't feel ready.

But ready or not, here she was. And when it was over, the family Learjet would immediately whisk her to a meeting with a top New York law firm to see if a defamation suit against the department was feasible. Her father promised her that it was only a threat, but she knew that she was going to have to keep a close eye on him. He had a way of getting carried away when there was blood in the water.

Her cell phone rang and she pulled it from her pocket, hoping it was someone with a few last-minute words of wisdom. When she saw the incoming number, she froze. This wasn't what she needed right now. She needed to focus on what was ahead of her, not what was behind her. Right?

"Hello, Fade," she said, putting the phone to her ear.

"I saw you on TV. Why didn't you tell me you'd quit? The dress was a little weird, though. You let your mom pick that one out, too?"

"The focus group loved it. Apparently it exuded competence without being overbearing."

"Focus group? Very smart, Karen. The media can hurt you, but it can also help you if you play your cards right."

"You know what would really help me?"

"Wait, don't tell me . . ."

"If you turned yourself in."

"I'm a little busy right now. Actually, I got a job."

"A job?"

"Yeah. I'm working in a bakery. Though, to be honest, I don't think it's going to be a long-term thing. Tell you what, give me a little more time and if you want, I'll let you kill me."

"How many times do I have to tell you—" Karen got out before she realized she was shouting. "How many times do I have to tell you that I don't want to kill you."

"I know. You—"

Fade suddenly went silent and she heard a quiet jingle over the phone. Like the bell stores hung on their doors.

"Oops. It looks like I've got a customer . . ."

"A customer? Fade, what are you—"

"Sorry. Gotta run."

The line went dead and she found herself staring dumbly down at the phone. Why did she actually believe he was working in a bakery? And why was he calling her? And who the hell was he? She shoved the phone back in her pocket and started her deep breathing exercises again, trying unsuccessfully to put him out of her mind.

Who was he? The strangest mass murderer she'd ever met—that's who.

32

While Egan's prior hotel room had been no prize, this one gave the impression that it wasn't meant to be used for more than an hour at a time. In light of the fact that Strand was almost certainly pulling out the stops to find him, he'd bypassed the hotel chains and settled in an independent that happily accepted cash and false names, and that had no computer link to the outside world. Egan pulled a beer from a trash can full of ice, and flopped down on the bed. He'd considered buying a new chalkboard, but what was the point? He'd already exhausted most of the possibilities for finding Fade. At this point a sticky note would probably do.

On the brighter side, Syd had become much more cooperative with a gun barrel pressed against his knee, and Egan now had a manila envelope filled with color copies of all Fade's phony driver's licenses and passports. Thank God Syd was a complete coward—Egan doubted he would have been able to pull the trigger. He wasn't sure, though. And that uncertainty bothered him.

He twisted the top off his beer and took a long pull.

No point dwelling on obscure moral conundrums when he hadn't yet been able to answer the obvious ones. Getting the IDs was a major step in the right direction and brought the prospect of actually finding Fade into sharper focus. What was he going to do if he did? Would Fade be ready to talk or would he just start shooting? And, in the unlikely event that he missed, would Egan shoot back?

The sad truth was that that was the easy scenario. A more likely one would be that he'd figure out a way to creep up behind Fade and give himself the chance to safely shoot his old friend in the back. That left him with two choices: yell something stupid like "Freeze!" and give Fade a chance or just pull the trigger and take that chance away.

After fifteen minutes of concentrating on the problem, he'd gotten nowhere. Maybe it was better that way. Worry about it when—and if—the time came.

He picked up his new phone and dialed, letting him-self sink farther into the formless pillows propped beneath his head.

"Hello?"

"I heard a thing on the radio today about the new Madonna record and they didn't even mention you."

Elise laughed. "Thank God."

"When are the people who actually write the songs going to get a little respect?"

"Just not the way of the world, honey. Actually, I spoke to her, uh, people yesterday and they're already

232

talking about me doing another one for her next record. Apparently she really likes it."

Normally, he would have told her only to do it if she wanted—but under the circumstances . . .

"It's probably not a bad little side business to get into, Elise."

"Yeah, but you know how I like to play the artistic martyr. Honestly, though, it's pretty easy money. I mean, you loop a beat that makes people want to shake their butts around, throw in a catchy hook, layer on an ethereal, sexy vocal to give it that Euro feel she's going for, and then repeat for five minutes."

"And deposit the check," he reminded her.

"Of course. How could I forget the best part?"

He took another sip from his beer and wondered how long they'd have to be together for him to actually believe that she'd married him. Sometimes the entire idea that she was his wife terrified him. When she went drinking with the guys from Pearl Jam, or R.E.M., or whoever, he just sent her off with a stomach full of pasta and the admonition to call him if she drank too much to drive. What a load of crap. Those guys were rich and famous and talented, and actually understood her music. If she ever found out he felt that way, she'd undoubtedly laugh for days. But how could he help it?

"You're not unhappy, are you?" he heard himself say.

"What do you mean? About the Madonna thing?"

"No. I mean in general. About living in the suburbs.

233

About owning a minivan."

"What's going on with you lately, Matt? Of course not. I wouldn't change anything. Not a single thing. Though you've got to admit that it's kind of funny that I drive a minivan."

"You said you could fit Kali's car seat and a full set of drums," he reminded her.

"I know what I said. Are you sure you're all right?"

"Yeah. Fine."

There was a short silence and when she spoke again she sounded a little hesitant. "What about you? You're not unhappy, are you?"

"Me? Why would I be?"

"I don't know. Because everybody you work with thinks your wife's a nut? You never mentioned it, but I'm guessing that you didn't miss the fact that my songs have been specifically mentioned in government hearings on rock lyrics. I bet that's a hot topic of conversation around the Homeland Security water cooler."

Egan examined a stain on the ceiling that looked like an elephant. "That's just politicians trying to keep their jobs. The more afraid they can make people, the easier it is for them to get re-elected."

He heard her let out a long breath. "They're doing a good job."

"What do you mean?"

"I don't know. When I was young, everything was so black and white. I felt so comfortable in my . . . would you call it morality? Philosophy? I was so confident that I was different. But maybe I was just young. And now I'm not anymore."

"You just turned thirty-one, Elise. It's not time for the nursing home yet."

"You know what I mean. I was watching the news yesterday and it was so horrible. What if that maniac running around killing women got Kali? Or what if some Arab who thinks God speaks only to him blew her up? Or what if some kid who isn't getting enough attention at home comes into her school someday and shoots her for no reason?"

"The media's no different than the government, Elise. Everyone has the impression that America is becoming the most dangerous place in the world, but it isn't. In some ways, it's actually getting safer. But those twenty-four-hour news stations have to keep people glued to their sets so they can sell Pampers or SUVs or whatever. People who think they're in danger don't channel surf."

"I know. It's just getting to me lately . . ."

Egan nodded as best the pillow half wrapped around his head would allow. "Parenthood tends to make you think in a whole other way."

"I guess. Have you been watching that story about the guy who killed all those policemen?"

Egan tensed. Fade was gone from his life before he'd met Elise and for obvious reasons, Egan had never spoken of him.

"They say he was a Navy SEAL," she continued. "Did you know him?"

"I was in the army, Elise. How's Kali?"

Surprisingly, she let him get away with evading the question.

"She's got a cold and she's convinced that I don't care but if Daddy were here he'd make it all better. I finally got her to sleep a half an hour ago. She's going to be disappointed she missed you."

"Tell her I promise I'll catch her next time. I just haven't had a minute, you know? In fact, I've got to run . . ."

"Wait! You didn't tell me how you're doing. Or when you're going to be home."

"Okay, and I don't know. Soon."

"Have you been getting out at all? New York's a great town."

"Not really."

"Ow!"

"What?"

"Oh, nothing. I'm trying to solder this stupid effects board back together again. I've got a show in D.C. in a few days."

"Right. I totally forgot. Good luck if I don't talk to you . . ."

Egan polished off his beer while he went through the identities that had been created for Fade and poked around the Internet searching for the various names. In total there were six, with each including a driver's license, a birth certificate, a social security card, and a passport. Two looked just like him and therefore wouldn't be terribly practical with his face all over the TV. The third showed him with a long, shaggy beard looking a little too Arab to be practical in a post-9/11 world. Number four was the bespectacled preppy persona the guy who'd sold him the Cadillac had described. And the last two had kind of a blond gay intellectual feel. Egan was prepared to bet good money that he was using one of those—his own mother wouldn't have recognized him.

The phone line he had his laptop plugged into wasn't exactly fast, but it had been adequate to pull credit reports on the various identities and do a brief background check on each. Not surprisingly, there wasn't much there. The addresses were all the same P.O. box in Manassas—a place he doubted Fade would visit again—and there were no entries from power or mortgage companies that might hint at the location of the place he'd taken Karen Manning.

Each persona had two credit cards, but none seemed to have ever been used. Egan pulled up each issuer's Web site and found that Fade never signed up for Internet access to his accounts, making it possible for him to put in his own passwords so he could monitor credit card usage in close to real time. Beyond that, there wasn't much he could do with the information.

He grabbed his phone and dialed Billy Fraiser's cell number, listening to it ring as he twisted the top off another beer.

"Hi, honey. Hang on and let me go into my office."

Egan's eyebrows rose. "No problem, sweetie."

He heard a door close and then. "Matt! What the hell's going on?"

"What do you mean?"

"Hillel's saying that you've pretty much lost it—that you're ducking us and going it on your own."

"What's he doing about it?"

No answer.

"Listen to my voice, Billy. Do I sound like I've come unglued? But I'll tell you that there's shit going on behind my back and I'm not happy about it. In the position I'm in, things I don't know damn well can kill me."

No answer again, but Egan decided not to fill the silence. After another ten seconds Fraiser spoke again.

"I know what you think of me, Matt. You think I'm just another government slicky-boy. A young Hillel Strand."

"No, I don—"

"Sure you do. And hey, I'm not bitching. I play the game, and I'm pretty good at it. But there's one big difference between me and Hillel: I know the game's a load of crap."

"I'm not sure what that means," Egan said.

"It means that when the shit hits the fan I'm smart enough to know that I want you watching my back. Not Hillel."

Egan propped himself up against the long mirror that passed for a headboard, unsure whether or not to believe what he was hearing.

"If that's true, then start talking."

Egan imagined Fraiser pacing back and forth

through his office, twirling that chewed-up pen he liked to play with when he was nervous. What he couldn't conjure an image of, though, was Strand. Was he sitting in his office, blissfully ignorant, or was he sitting on Fraiser's desk, listening?

"Hillel's got Lauren looking for you, but she's pretty much just going through the motions. She figures if you don't want to be found, she's not going to find you. The cops are spinning their wheels—still assuming Fade's trying to get out of the country. Which brings us to the question of whether we're doing ourselves any favors by holding out on them."

"I don't know," Egan said. "But the truth is that beyond the APB that we've already got out, they can't really do anything we're not doing already. Besides, if they do manage to corner Fade, they're going to lose more guys. As things are now, he isn't a danger to anyone but me and Hillel. Though I know you don't believe that. What else?"

"Everything that's come to you is going through Strand first."

"What's he keeping from me?"

"I don't know. Maybe nothing. If he is censoring your information, I'd be the last person he'd tell."

"You're probably right. Is that it?"

" 'Fraid so."

"Okay. Call me if you get anything else. Let me give you a new number you can reach me on . . ."

"Satellite phone," Fraiser said. "Lauren showed me the charge on your Visa."

239

"I assumed Strand was watching my cell."

"You assumed right."

He read off the number and was about to hang up, but then changed his mind. "Oh, and Billy?"

"Yeah?"

"Try to relax, okay? I don't believe for a second that Fade is going to try to hurt you or Lauren, but if he does, it'll be over my dead body. I mean that."

"I know. That's why we're talking."

33

Hillel Strand forced himself to smile as an off-key rendition of "Happy Birthday" filled the OSPA reception area. Other than Bill and Lauren, no one else in the office knew what was going on—though certainly they knew something was happening. With Egan nowhere to be found and Strand sleeping in the office with the assistants, it was reasonable to expect that there would be a fair amount of speculation. Just as a reminder, he'd made a brief speech that morning about the importance of discretion at Homeland Security and the rather draconian penalties that would be suffered by anyone who let something slip.

Threats could only go so far, though. It was critical to maintain as much of an illusion of normalcy as possible. He joined in the applause as Kelly Braith marched out of the copy room holding a large cake covered in candles.

Karen Manning had been on *The O'Reilly Factor* the night before and the memory of her very convincing performance was causing a tightness in his chest that actually made it difficult for him to take a breath deep enough to blow out the candles. While she had focused on the details of her encounter with al Fayed and the circumstances of her resignation, there was no denying that this story's foothold in the national media had become just a bit more solid. Until last night, al Fayed's complete disappearance and the lack of progress in the police investigation had left the press treating the issue as more a dramatic one-off event than an ongoing story. Combine that with the existence of the infinitely more lurid Collector case and coverage was beginning to dissipate. Manning had the power to reverse that critical trend, though. An attractive woman in a bitter fight to clear her name, a hint of sexual politics, and a heavily connected father who was apparently willing to spend any amount necessary to make sure his daughter's face was everywhere. It would only take one goddamn reporter looking for a new angle to cause this thing to implode. A little too much digging into al Fayed's past, a lucky inquiry into the source of the police's suspicions . . . The only thing that could ensure his safety was a satisfying and final end to the story. And the only thing that could do that was al Fayed's corpse.

To his surprise, he managed to get all the candles out. He put one hand up to silence the muted cheering and accepted a large slice of cake with the other. "I'm really feeling it this year. I'm now officially too old for the workload that's been dumped on us in the past couple of weeks. I want to say that I appreciate everybody's support, particularly the hard work Lauren and Bill have done helping me dig myself out, and Matt, who couldn't be here, for all the footwork he's been doing. Hopefully, we'll get it all wrapped up before I lose my golf swing."

Polite laughter filled the room as he walked over to Kelly's desk and picked up a fork. "Now, everybody grab some cake. It looks great."

"Matt?" Strand said as Lauren closed the door to his office behind her.

"Nothing. He made a large withdrawal from his savings account before you talked to him and I'm guessing he's using that money—"

"I'm not asking you to guess!" he shouted.

She blinked hard and pushed away the damp hair that was stuck to her cheek. Strand jerked a finger toward the chair in front of his desk, swallowing hard. Stress had been taking its toll on his stomach for days but over the last hour it had taken a serious turn for the worse. The constant burning had been replaced by a weak, quivering sensation occasionally broken by increasingly severe cramps.

Lauren sat, a little unsteadily, and continued. "We assume he's staying in an independent hotel somewhere in the area, but with our limited resources and the fact that we have to keep a low profile, our ability . . ." Her voice trailed off for a moment. "Our ability to look into them is limited. We could put an APB out on his car, like we did with al Fayed, but then we might end up having to explain why a high level employee of Ho—"

She suddenly jumped from her chair, holding a hand tightly over her mouth and ran for the door. Strand watched her claw at the knob for a moment and then disappear in the direction of the bathroom as his own stomach reacted to the excitement by rolling danger-ously. He took a few breaths and pressed his forehead against the cool wood of his desk. A bead of sweat gathered on his nose and then fell, leaving a dark spot on the carpet.

"Hillel?"

His damp forehead made a sucking sound as he peeled it from the desk and tried to focus on the sag-ging outline of Kelly Braith propped against his door-jamb. The motion, slow as it was, prompted another cramp and he clenched his teeth tightly waiting for it to pass.

"There's a . . . a call for you on two," she managed to get out.

He wanted to tell her to take a message but found he couldn't speak. He shook his head instead.

"It's Salam al Fayed," she said as though the name meant nothing to her. "He said you'd want—"

And then she was gone. Running, like Lauren had, toward the bathroom.

What the hell was going on? Was the cake bad?

What in a cake could go bad? He glanced over at the phone and saw the red light on it flashing. His cramp had subsided enough that he thought he could speak, but he wasn't sure he wanted to.

Why was al Fayed calling? What did he want? To make more threats? Had he finally figured out that Strand wasn't going to expose himself and wanted to talk deal? Finally, he picked up the phone.

"Yes?"

"Hillel! How you feeling?"

"What?"

"I poisoned your cake, dumbass. You're just too easy. I mean, this wasn't even a challenge. Anyway, I guess this is the last time we'll be talking. Happy birthday."

"Billy, calm down! I can't understand a word you're saying. Hold on." Matt Egan eased the car over to the curb and turned off the motor. "Now what the hell are you going on about?"

"The son of a bitch poisoned it! We're completely screwed! Everyone in the office but me. I didn't eat any. Fuck! You said he wouldn't touch us!"

"Billy? Listen to me. Calm down. Now let's pretend for a second that I don't know what the hell you're talking about. Start from the beginning."

"Hillel's cake," Billy said, managing to speak a little more slowly this time. "It was his birthday and the office had a party for him. I blew it off, 'cause I'm with you, you know? I figured fuck him."

244

"The point," Egan said. "Get to the point."

"Kelly got him a cake. Everyone ate some but me and they all started getting really sick. Then al Fayed called and told Hillel he'd poisoned it. Shit. You can't believe what it was like! They're all dead, man. They're all dead."

Egan sat motionless, looking through his windshield at people in business suits hurrying along the sidewalk to escape the soft rain that had begun to fall. This didn't make sense.

"Back up for a second, Billy. You're telling me everyone's dead? Right now, you're standing knee deep in corpses."

"No, the paramedics took them away. They were throwing up all over the place, convulsing . . . By now, they've gotta be dead. Al Fayed said they would be."

Egan sat silently for a few seconds and then a smile began to spread across his face. Fade was still quite the little prankster. Then his smile disappeared.

"Shit! Billy, listen to me very carefully. Call the ambulances that picked them up and tell them to divert to another ho—" He fell silent.

"What? Matt? Are you still there?"

He didn't answer immediately. Maybe he'd reacted a little too hastily. This could be the opportunity he'd been waiting for.

"What hospital?"

"Huh?"

"What hospital, Billy? What hospital are they being taken to?"

245

34

"Three tens," Fade said, laying his cards down on the small table. The man next to him chewed on the unlit cigarette in his mouth and stared at his hand with an intensity that suggested he was trying to will it to change. His wife and son had been in a car accident less than an hour ago and while it looked like they were both going to survive, there was some question as to whether the boy would keep his pitching arm.

He'd agreed to a nickel and dime game of poker to try to keep the man's mind occupied, though it didn't seem to be working. His lack of concentration had left Fade five dollars richer.

"Looks like you're taking me to the cleaners," the man said as he shuffled and dealt.

Fade examined his hand halfheartedly, focusing most of his attention on the doctors and nurses moving around behind the long counter to his left. "I'll take—"

"Those poisoning victims are two minutes out," he heard one of the nurses say.

"How many?" someone else asked.

"Seven. All from the same source."

The man waved a hand in front of Fade's face. "You all right? Do you need cards?"

"Yeah. Give me three. And this is going to have to be my last hand, so I think I'll just bet everything."

Fade pushed his pile of change to the center of the

table and then slapped down a pair of deuces. Pre-dictably, he lost.

"Looks like your luck might be changing," he said, standing and shaking the man's hand. "I hope things work out."

By the time Fade came around the corner and started down the hallway, the large double doors at the end were propped open, displaying a group of men pulling a gurney from an ambulance. He watched as they passed it off to a couple of orderlies and ducked back into the vehicle for victim number two.

Doctors and nurses had already surrounded the first gurney by the time it passed through the doors and Fade listened to the paramedics give their report while the patient, partially obscured by a vomit-soaked sheet, writhed weakly.

Being an emergency room doctor wouldn't have been a bad gig, Fade mused. It had both intellectual and physical components, and it seemed like it would provide the same mind-clearing intensity as combat. Maybe he should have studied a little harder in school and gone this route. How hard could it be? No one was shooting at you and you sure wouldn't have to work with the same precision as you would, say, putting together a nice dovetailed joint.

Fade stopped when he was only a few feet from the first patient who had come through the door and stood on his tiptoes to try to get a glimpse of a face. One of the nurses leaned over to set up an IV, exposing a woman in her early thirties with dark hair and a thin face that, after a moment, he recognized as Kelly Braith. The green complexion had thrown him.

The gurneys continued to roll through the doors and Fade moved to a position by the wall where he could watch them pass by.

An attractive, if somewhat severe-looking, young woman with eyes that didn't seem quite able to fix on anything. A man in his forties who looked like an overdosing accountant . . .

Fade covered his nose with his hand and took a hesitant step forward as a gurney with just the right sized lump came rolling toward him. It wasn't the worst smell he'd ever experienced, but it wasn't exactly pleasant either. Somewhere on the gross-out scale between dirty diapers and mass cremation.

A nurse rushed past him and pulled the sheet back, exposing Hillel Strand just in time for him to vomit all over the floor. Fade reached for the gun in his waistband as he tried to devise a safe path around the contents of Strand's stomach.

"Sir!" a nurse shouted at him. "You're going to have to step back!"

Fade ignored her, refusing to let her dampen his mood. A perfect end to a perfect ass. It was almost a shame to shoot him when he was suffering in such a completely undignified way. But, what the hell.

"Sir!"

She saw his gun at the same time Fade spotted Matt Egan sprinting past the ambulance outside and barreling through the doors. Sometimes that guy could be a real killjoy.

The nurse dove to the ground, landing partially in Strand's expelled carrot cake and shouting, "Gun! Gun!" Everyone scattered, but before they did, one of the paramedics gave the gurney containing Strand a hard shove, sending it rolling down the hall and leaving Fade with no cover. He crouched and ran toward Kelly Braith, ducking behind her and aiming over her heaving chest.

Egan had missed his opportunity to end things quickly and had been forced to take cover behind a soda machine.

"Drop your gun! Now!"

Fade could see the side of his face peeking around the machine but Kelly was convulsing to the point that she was screwing up his aim. "Oh, come on, man. The guy's a complete asshole. Let me shoot him. Just once, I swear."

"If it was up to me, I'd say go ahead," Egan said. "But I've got kind of an obligation here."

"What if I promise to just wing him?"

"Tick tock," Egan said.

Kelly suddenly seemed to become aware of what was happening and began to try to fight, her barely clenched fist banging uselessly against him and a weak squeal starting at the back of her throat. Fade sighed quietly. As usual, Egan was right. This was a classic example of a Mexican standoff. Matt wasn't going to want to shoot and risk the possibility of hitting his receptionist or having his bullet go through a wall and hit some pregnant lady. Having said that, he was a pretty good shot and if Fade adjusted his aim toward Strand, it would give Egan the opportunity to get a bead that he might be comfortable enough with to use. And just about as bad, hospital security was probably waddling this way right now. Tick tock.

"You're a real thorn in my side," Fade said, backing away slowly, rolling Kelly Braith along with him. "We'll finish this later."

35

"You've got to be fucking kidding me," Matt Egan said under his breath as the elevator opened onto his floor at Homeland Security. There was a heavy curtain of clear plastic blocking the hallway, behind which everyone was wearing full biohazard suits. As he stepped out of the elevator, one of the spacemen held a hand out in a gesture reminiscent of a grade school crossing guard.

"Sir," the man shouted, though it sounded more like a whisper after making its way through his face plate and the curtain. "This is a restricted area! Didn't you see the—"

"Shut up," Egan said, tearing through the plastic and starting toward his office. When the man tried to block his path, Egan stuck a hand in his chest and shoved him back. He lost his footing in all the biohazard gear and went crashing to the floor, taking the rest of the curtain with him.

"Out!" Egan shouted as he entered OSPA's reception area. "Everyone out." Three men, similarly clad in orange suits and respirators, interrupted their sample taking and turned awkwardly.

"Sir! This is a bio—"

"Where's Billy?" Egan said, cutting the man off.

"But you can't be—"

"Where is he?"

"He's . . . in his office. It's possible that he's been cont—"

"Do you have people at the hospital?"

The man didn't seem to know what to say and looked to his companions for support. Neither spoke.

"Hey! Focus! Do you have people at the hospital?"

"They're on their way, but I don't think they've arrived ye—"

"Shit!" Egan shouted and started jogging toward Billy's office.

"Sir! You can't go back there. There's a possible—"

But he was already through Fraiser's door and in the process of slamming it behind him.

"Matt! What are you doing here? Why aren't you wearing any protection? They think we might have been exposed to a biological agent. They say we might all be infected!"

"It wasn't a biological agent, for Christ's sake. It was probably Ex-Lax." He thumbed back toward the door.

"Do you know who's in charge of this cluster fuck?"

"Yeah, it's—"

"Get him on the phone right now and tell him to stop his men from going to the hospital. Tell him that we have confirmation that this was a simple chemical agent and that he'll blow a top secret terrorism investigation if they show up. Tell him that you've spoken to Hillel and this is coming directly from him."

"I don't think Hillel can—"

"Do it!"

Billy stared at him for a moment and then dropped behind his desk and began dialing his phone. Egan took the opportunity to go back out into the hallway in search of some water. His confrontation with Fade had left his mouth completely devoid of moisture. As he passed the reception area on the way to the cooler, he found the haz-mat team still standing around, looking confused.

"Why the hell are you still here? I thought I told you to get out. And take all your crap with you."

He went through three little paper cones, throwing each violently into the trash can when he had drained it. He should have just taken the shot. He'd told himself that Kelly was too close, but the chance of him hitting her at that range wasn't much higher than zero. If he'd have lined up on him, Fade would have gone for Strand and taken the bullet—Egan had seen it in his eyes. And now this would all be over instead of getting ready to blow up in his face. He would have killed Salam al Fayed.

"Well?" Egan said as he slammed Fraiser's door behind him again.

"I did it. They're turning around. I hope to hell you're sure—"

Egan's cell phone rang and when he saw the incoming number he fell into a chair and pressed it to his ear.

"Hello, Fade."

Fraiser's eyes widened a bit and he stared at the phone.

"What kind of person misses their own boss's birthday party? How are you ever going to get ahead with that attitude?"

"Look, I've got a guy here who thinks you've given him Ebola and an office full of people in space suits. Can I call you right back?"

"No problema."

The line went dead and he stuffed the phone back in his pocket.

"That was him? That was al Fayed?"

"Priority one," Egan said, ignoring the question. "Find out what the media knows. If there's any security video of me and Fade from the hospital we need to get hold of it. And none of the hospital staff talks to anyone about this. Tell them whatever you have to—that it's part of a confidential terrorism investigation. I don't want to see or hear about anyone I know on TV. Especially Fade. With his disguise, I doubt anyone would have recognized him, but if it goes out over the air . . ."

"Uh, okay. I—"

"Priority two: Get Banes and Despain on Hillel at the hospital. Fade might get the idea to go back."

"They're already there. I've got them covering everyone, but with just two of them, it's pretty thin."

"Just worry about Hillel. Put one of them in the room with him and get the other one after those security tapes."

"But—"

Egan pointed at the phone on Fraiser's desk and went back out into the reception area for another drink. The haz-mat people were actually gone, though most of their equipment was still strewn around what was left of the office suite. A good half of the furniture was either out of place or overturned, and no less than three still-wet puddles of vomit stained the carpet, filling the air with a sour, acidic odor. He retreated into his office and closed the door, wishing there was a way to open the windows.

Fade picked up almost immediately when Egan called him back.

"Matt, you scumbag! You knew I was waiting at that hospital. You had plenty of time to divert those ambulances. You were using your own boss as bait."

"Worst case, I figured I'd miss and you'd shoot him. Not the end of the world."

"I've been saying it for years: With a friend like you, a guy doesn't need enemies."

"Fuck you, too."

"Oh, that reminds me, man. There are a couple of

gals handcuffed to a toilet at the Wild Flour Bakery. Could you send someone over there to let them go?"

Egan wrote the name down on a piece of paper. "I'll take care of it."

"That's about it then. I guess I'll be seeing you."

"Wait! Come on, Fade. This is starting to get stupid. You've got no chance now. I've got Hillel covered at the hospital by good men—guys whose names you'd recognize. And when he gets out, he's going to come straight back to Homeland Security, where he's going to stay until he sees your body. And I can tell you that he's not going to be eating any takeout from now on. So, you're screwed. You can't get in here without killing a bunch of people, which we both know you aren't going to do—"

"Well, what about you? Why don't we get together and finish what's between us?"

"Not likely. I've got too much to lose now and I'm smart enough to know that getting involved in a stand-up fight with you would be suicide. If you and I can't work this thing out, I'm going to fall back on what I do best. I'm going to figure out where you are and shoot you from a safe distance."

"Or maybe I'll find you first."

"Maybe."

"No way to live, is it, Matt? Waiting for that other shoe to drop."

"No. I guess it isn't."

The line went dead and Egan leaned back against his desk, standing there silently for a few minutes before going back to Fraiser's office.

"I've got to go, Billy. Fade probably figures I'm here and I don't want him picking me up."

Fraiser nodded. "I talked to the hospital and the docs say all our people are going to be fine. You were right. But no one I talked to could give me an idea when they'd be released, so for now I'm all you've got. What do you want me to do?"

Egan leaned his shoulder against the doorjamb and crossed his arms in front of him. "I need everything, Billy. If Hillel's holding anything back on us, you've got to find it. Fast."

"I'm on it."

He turned to leave, but then stopped. "Oh yeah. Fade said we need to get someone down to the Wild Flour Bakery to let the people who made the cake go."

"Haz-mat's already there."

"Christ . . ."

36

"You're going to have to speak up!" Egan shouted into his phone.

Fraiser repeated himself, but was still unintelligible.

"Yell!"

A disorderly line of people had completely covered the sidewalk and was starting to spill out into the road, eliciting irritated honks from cars trying to get by. Egan moved right, sliding his shoulder along the worn brick of the building next to him as he pushed his way through the impatient crush of people. After about twenty feet, he was forced out into the street by a particularly dense knot of revelers splashing each other with beer. The club's door was almost within striking distance.

"We got the report from the hospital," Billy shouted. "The stuff that was in the cake is all easily available prescription stuff—nothing that could kill anyone. But the way it was mixed would apparently make you wish you were dead. Anyway, the haz-mat people are finally completely out of it."

"What about Hillel's files?" Egan said, continuing his slow progress.

"I managed to get into his cabinet but there wasn't anything there. I'm having a harder time with his computer. I'm not a hacker, you know? I don't think I'm going to be able to get access."

"Shit," Egan said quietly, nodding at two enormous bouncers who stepped aside and let him through. He had to wait for the frustrated shouts from the people in line behind him to subside before he could speak again.

"Okay. Keep on it."

Even empty, the corridor was surprisingly cramped and dark, lit only with ultraviolet, which caused the graffiti scrawled on the walls to fluoresce garishly. A moment later, he broke out into a cavernous concert hall ringed with a wide balcony. At the far end he could see a dimly lit, empty stage squeezed between walls of speakers. Egan made his way directly to the closest of four strategically positioned bars.

Even with the crowd still being held at bay outside, the coveted bar stools were already full. He vaguely recognized most of the people on them—employees of the venue, promoters, roadies, friends of the band members. And they recognized him. The stool he'd locked onto was quickly abandoned and by the time he'd settled in, so were the ones surrounding it.

He waved at the bartender for a beer and watched the crowd begin spilling in, fanning out at a half run, seeking to stake out the best real estate for the show. In less than a minute the empty stools around him had filled with people who weren't aware of the alternative music industry's widely held belief that he was a government constructed killing machine ready to snap at any moment.

As always, he was amazed at the sheer size and broad diversity of the crowd: everything from dreadlocks and tie-dye to shaved heads and leather jackets. Elise had a strangely universal appeal—meaning that weirdos of all types loved her. She rarely played live locally anymore and when she did, the shows sold out within a few hours. He reached for his wallet but the bartender just shook his head and slid the beer across the bar to him. The free drink seemed to increase the interest his khakis and polo shirt were getting from the two typically dangerous looking skinheads sitting next to him.

They were right, of course. He shouldn't have been

there, but his confrontation with Fade and the chaos that was sure to ensue had left him feeling completely unanchored. It was almost like he was going back-ward in time—rewinding himself into the ball of nerves and violence that the Special Forces had tem-porarily transformed him into. He needed something to remind himself that he wasn't that person anymore and frankly had never aspired to be that person in the first place.

Besides, the risk was almost nonexistent. There was no way that Fade would think he'd be stupid enough to show up at one of his own wife's concerts. Too obvious.

He was on his second beer when a general roar from the crowd prompted him to spin around on his stool, just in time to see a young woman with shockingly green hair and a matching bass guitar stride out onto the stage. She was undeniably his least favorite person in the band—an evil bitch who had gone out of her way to make sure he was aware that she had an insane crush on his wife, while carefully keeping it com-pletely hidden from everyone else. Even Elise was completely oblivious. Next out was the violin player, an incredibly gifted and impossibly thin guy with an uncontrollable passion for heroin and an even more uncontrollable paranoia that Egan was a DEA snitch. Finally, Erik, a genuinely good guy, stepped into the lights. He was the only person in the band other than Elise who didn't refer to him as "The Baby Killer" behind his back. Thank God for drummers.

The roar turned to screams when Elise stepped out, wearing a black miniskirt and a rather Puritan white blouse that had been her mother's. She plugged in a glittery silver guitar that he'd gone into hock to buy her a few Christmases ago, sang a few a cappella lines into her microphone and then slammed a hand into the strings, producing a wall of sound that seemed like it should have shattered the mirror behind him. Predictably, people near the stage went nuts—gyrating wildly and bouncing off one another in a display of childlike enthusiasm that he'd once mistaken for a riot.

He inserted a pair of custom made earplugs and watched his wife put a foot up on a monitor, flinging her black hair back and forth against her face. It was hard to imagine what he'd have said if, ten years ago, a fortune-teller had told him that one day he would be sitting in a concert hall with nine hundred people looking up his wife's skirt while she tried to destroy a guitar he still had seven payments to go on. And that he'd be happier than he'd ever imagined he could be.

What would that fortune-teller have to say to him today? Would she tell him that he was going to lose everything just when he'd finally gotten it?

Someone tapped him on the shoulder and he glanced up. The light had turned a bit chaotic and for a moment he could only see a six-foot-tall outline wearing a white, vaguely Asian-looking shirt tucked into a pair of jeans. When one of the wandering spotlights hit the mirror behind the bar, there was a sudden flash that revealed the man's tan skin, short brown hair, and a pair of blue tinted glasses perched on an elegant, Mesopotamian nose.

Egan half jumped, half fell, off his stool, landing both himself and his beer in the lap of the person next to him. That person, understandably upset, shoved him hard from behind and Egan ended up on all fours on the floor. By the time he'd made it to his feet, the skinhead wearing his beer was off his stool and coming at him. He looked to weigh about two hundred and fifty pounds and wasn't a distraction that Egan needed at that moment.

He braced himself for the inevitable impact but, before it could happen, Fade swung an arm into the man's throat, clotheslining him and sending him crashing to the floor. He followed up with a bored-looking kick, connecting the silver tip of his cowboy boot with the man's temple.

In his peripheral vision, Egan saw two bouncers running as fast as they could in their direction and tried to watch both them and Fade, who was now seated and waving a ten dollar bill at the frozen bartender.

"Stop!" Egan shouted loud enough to be heard over the feedback emanating from his wife's guitar. The bouncers both knew him and did as they were told, eyeing Fade but, fortunately, not making a move toward him. Egan pointed at the man lying motionless on the floor and then toward the door. The bouncers grabbed him by the jacket and began dragging him out, never taking their eyes off Fade, who was now perched cross-legged on his stool, sipping at a Budweiser.

Egan looked around him, making sure that everything was as under control as could be expected during one of his wife's shows and pulled his earplugs out.

"I underestimated you," he shouted, sitting down again and waving for a fresh beer. "Good guess."

"I'd love to take credit," Fade said, leaning in close enough to be heard, but still keeping some distance between them. "But I bought my ticket weeks ago. Your wife's a genius. Honestly, I remember you as more of a Village People kind of guy."

Egan gave the bartender a twenty and indicated that he should keep the change.

"Who's the bass player, Matt? She's cute in kind of a character-from-a-Japanese-cartoon sort of way."

"I'd be happy to introduce you."

"Nah. Not a great time for me to be starting relationships . . . How's your sister?"

"She's okay. Married a lawyer and has three kids. Plays golf."

Fade smiled and turned so he could better see the show. "Good. That's good."

Egan wasn't sure what else they had to say to each other, so they ended up just sitting there pretending to watch Elise but really watching each other.

Egan had a pistol in the small of his back—he'd known the bouncers wouldn't frisk him. Had Fade gotten a weapon in? Did it matter? There were people everywhere—jammed in so tight that even sitting at the bar they were being bumped when the crowd surged. The gun would have to stay where it was.

"Do you think we did any good?" Fade said finally.

"What do you mean?"

"I mean what was the point of us going out there and risking our asses and then coming home to the funerals of our friends? The Africans are still butchering and starving each other. The Arabs are still running around with bombs stuffed down their pants. The North Koreans and Iranians are still trying to figure out a way to nuke us. What was the point?"

"Fighting for truth, justice, and the American way?"

Fade laughed. "But what is truth? Or justice? Or, for that matter, the American way? It changes every day. Remember when cheese was a healthy snack, Saddam Hussein was defending the Middle East against extremism, and Milli Vanilli were brilliant musicians? What ideals are guys younger than us dying for that will be completely out of style in five years? I mean, we clearly don't know what the fuck to do with the world, so why don't we just leave it alone?"

Egan shrugged and took a pull from his beer bottle. "Sometimes it's hard to stand by and watch without trying to do something. And sometimes it's not that noble. Sometimes it's just fear, or politics, or a hangover from the Cold War. Hell, I don't know."

Fade fell silent again and watched a man in a flannel shirt jump onto the stage and then dive off into the crowd as Elise continued to shorten the life expectancy of her guitar.

Sitting so close made it almost impossible not to let memories of their past partially blot out the realities of their present. Egan had always been the boss and, in his own right, had been extremely successful. But somewhere in the back of every man's mind, there was that spark that made you want to be Salam al Fayed. Sure, it was great to be a respected businessman or actor or whatever, but there was something a million years old that made you yearn to be the strongest, the bravest, the fastest. To be the great warrior whose name was spoken in whispers.

"I admired the cake thing," Egan said as Elise's song degenerated into random noise and then went silent. She put her guitar in a metal stand and the band abandoned the stage.

Fade grinned. "I'm not sure if I'm pissed about you stopping me from killing Strand or not. Giving the guy explosive diarrhea was almost as good."

"Then why not call it a win and skip the country?"

"Watch this." He kicked his heel into the brass rail at the bottom of the bar with enough force to shake the bottles on top. "Didn't feel a thing."

"Fade, I—"

He put a finger to his lips and then pointed over Egan's shoulder.

"I heard you were here," Elise said, wrapping her arms around his neck and kissing him. Fade watched the scene intently for a moment and then redirected his gaze to the floor when Elise jumped up on her husband's lap and waved at the bartender.

"What are you doing here?" she said, turning so that she was as invisible to the crowd as possible. Despite that, she was attracting a fair amount of attention. For the moment, though, people seemed to be keeping their distance.

"My meeting let out early, so I drove down for the show."

She accepted a tall glass of ice water from the bartender and downed almost all of it in a single effort. Egan maneuvered her into a more comfortable position in his lap and pushed some of the sweaty hair from her face.

"So when do you have to go back?"

"Tonight. Right after the show."

She rolled her eyes. "You've got to be kidding me. How many meetings can one person have?"

"I—"

"You've got to at least come by and see Kali."

He glanced up and caught Fade studying them again. Having Elise pressed up against him was exactly what he'd come there for, so why did he suddenly want to push her away? The answer wasn't hard to come up with. How would he feel if his life and Fade's were reversed? What would it be like to watch this?

"I really don't think I can. I—"

"Aren't you going to introduce us?"

Elise looked over at Fade and then back at him.

"Uh, yeah," Egan said quietly. "Sorry. Elise, this is

. . . John. He's an old friend of mine. We just bumped into each other."

"An old friend?" Elise said, shaking Fade's hand. "What would an old friend of Matt's be doing at one of my shows? Shouldn't you be at the ABBA reunion?"

Nothing at all registered on Fade's face and for some reason that complete lack of emotion made Egan even more tense than he already was.

"I don't share your husband's atrocious taste in music."

She smiled. "Until now, all of Matt's old friends have either looked like G.I. Joe or extras from *The Dukes of Hazzard*. How do you know each other?"

"Long, boring story," Egan cut in.

"Yeah, I guess it is." Fade stood. "Actually, I've got to hit the road."

"You're not going to watch the last set?" Elise said.

He shook his head and offered her his hand again. "It's been a real honor meeting you." Then he stepped around and leaned in close enough that his lips brushed Egan's ear. "You should go see your daughter, Matt. We'll continue this tomorrow night."

He nodded toward Elise and then began to back cautiously away. Once he had a few people between them, he turned and disappeared.

"Interesting guy," Elise said, finishing her glass of water. "You'll have to tell me that long, boring story some day."

Egan forced a smile. "Sure. Whatever."

She twisted around and pulled away a bit, examining his face. "Are you all right, Matt?"

"Why wouldn't I be?"

"I don't know. You look weird. Like the Grim Reaper just walked by or something."

As long as he lived he would never get used to Elise's occasional bursts of extremely disturbing clairvoyance.

"I'm just kind of tired. Maybe you're right. Maybe I should spend the night and go back in the morning."

She jumped off the stool and leaned against his knees. "Are you serious?"

"Yeah."

"Meet me backstage after the show and maybe, if you play your cards right, I'll let you give me a lift home."

37

"Talk to me, Bill."

Hillel Strand managed to walk across the office with a reasonable amount of dignity, but the facial contortions he made when he bent to sit behind his desk made Fraiser wonder if this meeting wouldn't be better conducted in the bathroom. Lauren probably felt about the same but managed to keep the wrinkle-free mask she showed the world intact as she propped herself against the wall.

Other than the three of them, OSPA's office suite

was completely empty. Lauren and Strand had ignored their doctor's advice and left the hospital early but everyone else would probably be there for a few more days of observation.

"From a media standpoint, everything is surprisingly under control," Fraiser started. "We've changed all your names in the hospital record to be thorough, but they wouldn't be released anyway because of confidentiality. We have the only copy of the security tape and the hospital administration is saying that the camera was defective. The press is running the story, but they don't have anything but eyewitness accounts to go by. There's a vague description that no one seems to completely agree on beyond the fact that he was blond, tan, and male."

"The police?"

"We're watching their progress, but they seem to just think that it was some wacko. They're more confused about who Matt was, but they're thinking he was just some bystander with a gun."

"How did Matt end up being there?" Lauren said.

An obvious question, but a complicated one to answer. Fraiser had been angry and confused when he realized that Egan had used his own innocent coworkers as bait, but then after watching the security tape, he'd understood.

"I finally managed to get in touch with Matt when you were already on your way to the hospital. He figured that al Fayed would be waiting for you there and wanted me to divert the ambulances, but it was too

268

late. Luckily he was in the car and he wasn't far from the hospital they were taking you to . . ."

Both Strand and Lauren seemed to buy the completely plausible lie. Not too surprising since they both looked like it was taking all their concentration just not to fall over.

"Is there any movement on finding al Fayed?"

Fraiser shook his head. "We're still pursuing the leads we've got but they aren't getting us anywhere."

"Goddamnit!" The outburst seemed to temporarily rob Strand of his balance and he was forced to grip his desk. "Get Matt on the phone. I want to talk to him. Now."

"I'll do what I can, but—"

"I don't want to hear that you'll do what you can! Our entire team was nearly killed yesterday and I goddamn well want to find out how this half-educated son of a bitch is keeping one step ahead of us."

"Yes, sir."

Strand waved his hand at them. "Get out."

Fraiser followed Lauren down the hall in silence but when she began to turn into her office, he grabbed her by the arm and pulled her along behind him.

"What are you doing?"

"I want to talk to you."

"Shouldn't you be trying to get in touch with Matt?" she said, struggling to escape his grip but not having the strength to make a real effort.

"Fuck Hillel."

"Bill, are you—"

He dragged her through his door and closed it behind them. "I want to know what you have that you're not telling us."

"I don't know what you're talking about."

"Bullshit. Look, Lauren, while Hillel's in here hiding in his office, Matt's out there putting himself on the line. He deserves to know everything."

"I don't know what to tell you, Bill. I—"

"He could have killed you. All of you. Why didn't al Fayed just put cyanide in that cake?"

"Because he's a sadistic nut and likes to do his killing face to face?"

Obviously, Strand had been working to prop up the illusion he'd created.

"Come on, Lauren. Would you—"

"I've got work to do," she said, turning to leave. He caught her by the arm again and, again, she tried to pull away.

"Watch the security tape," he said. "Then, if you want to, you can just go back to your office and do whatever."

"Jesus, Bill . . . Okay. Fine. Put on the tape."

He released her and took a remote off his desk, aiming it at a small television stuffed into his book-case. The video was black and white and the angle wasn't perfect, but overall it was pretty clear.

"That's al Fayed," he said pointing to a man coming on screen from the left. "And here you all come."

The doors at the end of the hospital corridor were open and the sunlight flooding through them caused a bit of overexposure, giving gurneys and the convulsing patients they contained a ghostly quality. Lauren wrapped her arms around herself as she watched the nurses and paramedics running back and forth, shouting silently.

"Okay, now watch him," Fraiser said as Fade stepped forward and examined Lauren's face. It wasn't possible to read his expression, but his disinterest was obvious.

It wasn't until he locked onto Strand that he began to pull a gun from his waistband. A nurse motioned him back but then saw the gun. Everyone scattered and a moment later, Matt Egan ran through the door.

"Well?" Fraiser said, pausing the tape.

"I don't know what you want from me, Bill. I don't work for Matt. I work for Hillel."

"It doesn't matter who you work for. This isn't politics. This is real."

"Don't you think I know that? Do you have any idea what I just went through? What it's like to be lying there thinking you're dying while some guy gets off on it?"

"But you didn't die. Al Fayed had two opportunities to kill you and he didn't take either one. Matt was telling us the truth when he said al Fayed isn't after us. Hillel just said that because he wanted us motivated."

"Maybe he just wants Hillel most and wanted to get him first in case security showed up before he could kill all of us."

Fraiser shrugged. "Maybe you're right. But if you

are there's a question you need to ask yourself." He tapped the frozen image of Egan on the small screen. "If al Fayed's really after you, who do you want watching your back? Hillel or Matt?"

38

It was a beautiful spot—a little more than an hour outside of D.C. and not all that far from where he used to live. On the downside, because of the dense foliage lining both sides of the narrow dirt road, it was impossible to avoid the deep ruts crisscrossing it. Isidro hadn't anticipated the Caddy ever leaving the asphalt and the finely tuned racing suspension was protesting loudly. Fade turned the police scanner off in favor of the intermittent drone of mosquitoes buzzing around the open car and slid a little farther down in his seat, focusing more on the clear sky above him than the deserted road in front of him.

Over the last twenty-four hours it seemed like everything had changed. He wasn't ready to fully admit it yet, but Matt Egan was right. He'd blown what was probably going to be his only chance at Hillel Strand. Why hadn't he just aimed and taken the shot? Fifty-fifty chance that he'd have gotten a round off before Egan killed him. Then it would have all been over. Too many years of training for survival, he supposed. It was turning out to be harder to overcome than he'd expected.

Despite hours of driving around thinking, he didn't even know where to start again with Strand. He was either at the hospital under heavy guard or he was at his office sitting behind half a billion dollars' worth of concrete, Plexiglas, and state-of-the-art security systems.

Which left only Matt. Fade could still picture him sitting there with Elise on his lap, but he couldn't decipher how he felt about that image. He was trying hard for outrage and jealousy but he couldn't seem to get it to burn. The more he thought about how much they looked like they loved each other and their lives, the more tired and disconnected he felt.

He shook his head violently and turned on the stereo, trying to drive away the depression that was starting to grip him. He'd thrown out the interminably cheerful Go-Gos CD in favor of the more appropriate Ministry. In his experience, it was impossible not to be angry when listening to Ministry.

He slid still farther down in the seat, trying to relieve the sickening ache in his back. Deciding it was hopeless, he straightened and instead concentrated on the pain, the music, and the memory of Hillel Strand lying there helpless only a few feet away.

The road dead-ended in a small clearing that contained a single empty car—Karen Manning's. If there was a second drawback to the Caddy, it was that it was a little too flashy to effectively tail someone in. He'd had to hang way back and had almost missed her turning off the highway. Based on the tank top and shorts she was wearing, he assumed she was going for a run, but had expected her to head for a town park or school track—not to drive fifty miles to the middle of nowhere.

He eased to a stop and stepped out of the car, going around to the front and leaning backward across the hood as far as he could. The quiet crunching sound coming from his spine was mildly alarming, but the muscles around it reacted to the position and warmth of the engine, relaxing a bit.

When he was satisfied that he was as loose as he was going to get, he crossed the clearing to an obvious trailhead and began jogging up the narrow path. He started slowly, increasing his speed every minute or so until his lungs began to burn and the sweat stung his eyes.

It took almost half an hour for him to catch his first glimpse of Karen Manning, cresting a depressingly distant hill. There had been a time when he'd known exactly how hard he could push himself and exactly how the effort would affect him. Now, though, he had no idea. Despite the fact that he was holding a pace that was probably only half of what he'd been able to sustain before, his heart felt like it was going to burst through his chest. And worse, he was losing coordination in his right leg.

When he saw her next, it was only for a moment—a brief flash of pink and yellow that was clearly starting to pull away.

Karen Manning glanced behind her when she came

briefly out of the trees and saw that the runner behind her had lost some time. Based on his stumbling gait, though, he was doing everything he could to gain it back.

She shook her head and jumped over a tree that had fallen across the trail, dodging through the limbs scattered on the other side. Sometimes she was more than happy to hook up with somebody on the trail—a little interesting conversation could help pass the miles. But not here. When she drove all the way out to this trail, it was for solitude. Besides, anyone trying that hard to catch her was doing it for a reason. She'd end up spending the next hour listening to choked-off pick up lines and watching the guy drool on himself.

"See ya," she said out loud and lengthened her stride, starting up a steep incline at a pace almost no one in Virginia could match. Ten minutes later, when she reached the top of a ridge and looked back, her pursuer was nowhere in sight.

It felt good to run hard, to block everything out. But that wasn't why she'd come there. She needed some time to think. Satisfied that she wasn't going to be caught, she slowed to a pace that would allow her to concentrate on more complex issues than where her feet were falling.

According to John Wakefield, the investigation into Fade was more or less stalled. They were reasonably certain that he was still in the country but couldn't narrow it down much more than that. Inquiries into his background had ended in the conclusion that he'd left his past almost completely behind.

As the fortunes of her former colleagues waned, though, her situation just kept getting better. She'd aced the Bill O'Reilly interview and Pickering had gone into hiding after his meeting with her father's legal team—a group of men and women who considered Genghis Khan soft. And, on an even brighter note, the media had become bored with interviewing her men's widows and were looking for a new angle. Her PR people were busy making certain that angle would be her own saintly and tireless devotion to protecting the American people, helping her church, and baking cookies for the local orphanage.

Her dad, who loved nothing more than manipulating the media and crushing people he perceived to be his enemies, had informed her that he wouldn't be satisfied until everyone in the U.S. saw her as a cross between Joan of Arc and Mother Teresa. There was little doubt that he would succeed—he'd never failed at anything in his life. But even with her reputation reconstructed, it seemed unlikely that she would ever be a cop again. Or that she would ever want to be. No matter what way public opinion swung, her men were dead and she bore a lot of the responsibility for that. She doubted a week would go by for the rest of her life that she didn't wake up seeing their faces.

So what now? If she bought into her mother's recent "you can do anything you put your mind to" speech, things looked pretty wide open. Movie star? President? Brain surgeon? Not likely.

The idea of becoming a prosecuting attorney had crossed her mind, but the mere thought of law school made her want to shoot herself. College track coach? Maybe . . .

She sped up again, not yet ready to make any decisions about the rest of her life. It was only another ten minutes to her turnaround point and then it was downhill the rest of the way.

Karen was about two miles from her car when she came around a sharp bend and saw a man lying on a boulder next to the trail. Her pace faltered as she got closer and recognized his clothes as the ones worn by the man who had been running behind her.

He looked dead.

She finally stopped a few feet away and stared down at him. Could he have had a heart attack trying to catch her? No way. Her luck just couldn't be that bad.

"Sir? Excuse me. Sir?" she said, taking a hesitant step toward him. "Are you all right?"

She let out the breath she hadn't been aware she was holding when his head lolled over in her direction and he opened his eyes. "You're either really fast or I've gotten really slow."

"I'm pretty fast."

He smiled and looked back up at the sky muttering something under his breath. She couldn't be sure, but she thought it was "How the mighty have fallen."

"So you're okay?"

"I can see why you run here," he said. "It feels like

you're a million miles away from everything."

She leaned forward a bit, squinting at what was visible of his face behind the sunglasses he wore. There was something familiar there.

"Have a nice afternoon," she said finally and stepped back onto the trail. "Enjoy the view."

"Hold on. I have something for you."

"Excuse me?"

He reached for something beside him on the rock and tossed it to her. She caught it and immediately recognized her wallet. When she raised her head again, the man had pushed his sunglasses up on his head and was looking right at her. With his eyes exposed, there was little question as to where she'd seen him before.

The jolt of adrenaline hit her hard and she bolted down the trail, getting a good fifteen feet before looking back. He hadn't moved. She eased off, letting her momentum carry her another five feet before she stopped and turned back toward him. He was just lying there, staring at the sky.

Under normal circumstances, when faced with a cop killer, she'd be trying to devise a way to capture him. Even unarmed, her one hundred and forty-five pounds of muscle and her brown belt in jujitsu made her fairly confident against men much larger than she was. These weren't normal circumstances, though. Last time they'd met, he'd gone through her like she wasn't even there. Besides, he probably had a gun and she was armed with nothing but nylon shorts, a tank top, and a pair of Adidas.

That left plan B, which was to run and call the police when she got back to her car. There was no way he was going to catch her on foot. No way.

When he pushed himself to a sitting position, she backed away another five feet and watched him light a cigarette.

"You should quit," she said when he began coughing violently.

"Quit? I just started."

She remained planted when he swung his legs off the boulder and stood.

"What are you doing here, Mr. al Fayed? What do you want?"

He pointed to the wallet in her hand.

"You could have mailed it."

He shrugged. "My killing spree isn't turning out to be as fun as I'd hoped. Every morning lately I get up more tired than I was when I went to bed. I'm having a hard time remembering things that last week were really important to me . . ."

Her first impression of him had been badly tainted by fear, she realized. Certainly he was well above average looking—even with the Billy Idol hair—but that wasn't what struck her. It was his sadness. When he started toward her, she realized that she wasn't afraid of him. Though she knew that she probably should be.

"You're finally going to tell me your story," she said, as he passed by and continued down the trail.

"Am I?"

"I figure it's that or you're here to turn yourself in," she said, catching up and walking alongside him.

"I might be here to kill you," he suggested.

"You might . . ."

They'd been walking in silence for what seemed like a long time when they finally reached the clearing where she'd parked. Her head had been spinning the entire time.

She'd known about his military background, but the fact that the company he'd left the navy to join was a CIA front was definitely news. And based on the amount of trouble that the police were having getting information on that now defunct company, it was probably true. The fact that he'd been a highly successful assassin working primarily in the Middle East also jibed nicely with his ethnic background and the fact that he'd singlehandedly wiped out an entire SWAT team. The details of his back injury and subsequent work with the Colombians rang depressingly true, too.

Even more startling, though, was the involvement of Homeland Security and Hillel Strand—the man who had stupidly caused all this and was undoubtedly working very hard to keep his role hidden.

When they reached the middle of the clearing, she stopped and grabbed his shoulder. "Why tell me this, Fade? Do you want me to go to the police with it? The press?"

He shook his head and for a moment she thought

that was the only answer she was going to get.

"It's hard . . ." he started, speaking slowly and seeming to concentrate on every word. "It's hard to do everything I've done, to give everything I've given, and to know you're going to be remembered as nothing more than some pathetic psychopath. I mean, I don't want a medal or anything—I don't deserve one. But for some reason I wanted at least one person to know the truth after I'm gone."

"Gone where?"

He smiled and started toward an immaculate old convertible.

"Why me?" she called after him.

"Oh, come on, sweetie!"

Karen spun toward the voice and watched a man with a .45 step from behind her car.

"Obviously, Fade thinks if he blubbers enough, you're going to let him get in your pants."

Karen glanced over at Fade, who was standing completely motionless, watching the man with an almost perplexed expression.

"Look, I don't know who you are but I'm a cop—"

"I know who the fuck you are, Karen," the man said, moving cautiously toward her, but keeping his gun trained on Fade. "And I believe it's more accurate to say that you're a former cop."

He stopped about ten feet away and tossed her a couple of zip ties. "I think you know how to use those. Down on your face, Fade."

He didn't move until the man swung his gun level

with Karen's head. "Hillel doesn't want you killed until he talks to you, but I don't have orders one way or another about the bitch."

Fade sunk to his knees and then lay facedown on the ground. The man waved his gun, prompting Karen to walk over and kneel beside Fade.

"A friend of yours?"

"Roy Buckner. Army Delta."

"Shut up!"

Karen tightened a zip tie around Fade's wrists and then looped the other around his ankles. He didn't react at all to being bound, he just lay there with his cheek pressed into the dirt and his eyes fixed on nothing.

"Why don't you give that one around his hands another tug," Buckner said.

She glared at him for a moment, but in light of the gun aimed at her, did as he asked.

Buckner stepped a little closer. "One more."

"It'll cut off his circulation."

"He's not going to need his hands anymore."

"Fuck you."

He was pretty fast, but she still saw the kick coming and managed to get an arm up, partially blocking it. Still, the force sent her sprawling to the ground. She heard a quiet ratcheting as Buckner gave the zip tie one last pull and then felt him grab the back of her neck and shove her face into the dirt. She was in the process of using his momentum to roll him off her when the unmistakable coldness of a gun barrel pressed against the back of her head.

"Now you wouldn't be armed, would you?" he said, not letting the fact that she wasn't wearing enough to conceal a weapon keep him from entertaining himself by searching her thoroughly. After about a minute of having his knee in her back and his hands all over her, he slapped her on the butt.

"Looks like she's clean, Fade. But she could just be tricky, huh? What do you think? Maybe I missed a spot."

Fade remained silent, eyes still focused on nothing but the air. He didn't react at all when Buckner knelt beside him and conducted an only slightly less thorough search. He seemed a little worried that he didn't find anything.

"You look like a strong little thing," he said, stepping back and pointing the gun at Karen again. "Tell you what I want you to do. I want you to pick up our friend here and throw him in the back seat of his car."

She did as she was told, rolling Fade onto his back and dragging him across the clearing. He didn't seem interested in being helpful and it was clear that Buckner didn't want to get within ten feet of his prisoner, so Karen found herself having to use a combination of brute strength and leverage to get Fade's dead weight off the ground.

When she started tipping him forward over the side of the convertible, Buckner ran up behind them and threw a vicious kick to his lower back. Karen got partially in the way of it and took some of the blow with her own back, but Fade still absorbed enough force to flip him over the side of the car and into the back seat.

"How's the ol' spine?" Buckner said, looking down at Fade's motionless body. "Still bothering you?"

"You son of a bitch!" Karen shouted, taking a step toward him but then stopping when he aimed his gun between her eyes.

"Get his keys."

She didn't move immediately, instead standing there grinding her teeth. Finally, she crawled into the back seat and began fishing around in Fade's pockets. "Are you all right?"

His eyes were closed now and his muscles seemed completely slack.

"Get behind the wheel and put your seat belt on," Buckner ordered.

When she'd complied, he slid into the passenger seat and slammed the door shut.

"Pretty stupid to set me up like this, Fade," he said, turning in the seat so he could watch both of them at the same time. "I mean if you had a hard-on for this bitch, why didn't you do something about it when you had the chance? You can be a sneaky bastard and you're a pretty good shot—I'll give you that. But I swear you were always a little soft in the head."

39

It had been a classic no-win situation. Strand could have stayed at the hospital but Banes and Despain had made it clear that they couldn't guarantee his safety there. The only other option was to return to the office, ensuring his physical survival but also guaranteeing a political showdown that he wasn't prepared for.

He sat quietly as Darren Crenshaw, the recently appointed director of Homeland Security, put a foot up on one of the drawers in his desk and tapped out a monotonous rhythm with a pencil.

Crenshaw was a former Marine general and Rhodes Scholar who saw no reason to evolve personally to better fit his new political role. His spacious office was sparsely decorated with government-issue furniture, his hair was chopped in a ruler-straight flattop, and his dark suit had the look of a dress uniform stripped of its emblems and medals. He had been a surprise appointee considering the fact that he didn't bother to hide his distaste for political reality and his bias toward people who had, in his words, "been in the trenches."

To make matters even worse, Crenshaw was strangely unpredictable. Many of the men who had enjoyed success in the military were quite brilliant, but most could be counted on to have a somewhat plodding and easily anticipated thought process.

"I'm not sure I completely understand this cake

thing," Crenshaw said finally.

Obviously, there had been no way to keep that incident quiet. The best Strand could hope to do was massage the truth in a way that would keep him out of harm's way until al Fayed could be dealt with.

"We believe now that the perpetrator broke into my assistant's house and found a note she'd written to remind herself to pick up a cake for my birthday. He held the baker hostage and forced her to poison that cake."

"The word 'poison' might be a little strong," Crenshaw pointed out. "Best guess is that this guy just wanted to make you real sick."

"Yes, sir. He obviously wanted to get us to the hospital where he could kill us face to face . . ."

The timing of this meeting couldn't have been worse. Strand's head was pounding mercilessly and his stomach felt like it was twisted in a vise. In a conversation that demanded complete mental agility, it was taking everything he had to just track on what was being said.

"I wonder. Why deal with all that uncertainty when you could just dump a bunch of shoe polish or something in there and get you all for sure."

"This way was more public. The description of the perpetrator suggests that he could have been Arab."

"But with blond hair and no accent."

"Yes, sir."

The only path Strand could take was to suggest that he and his people were attacked by an unknown terrorist who had discovered the existence of their unit. Reasonably plausible and difficult to disprove.

"And Matt somehow figured out the hospital was the place to be and intercepted the guy there."

"Yes, sir. He talked to—"

"How did he know this wasn't a biological attack?"

"Excuse me?" Strand said, trying to give himself time to adjust to the sudden change in subject.

"From what I hear, he walked into the office after you were hauled off and not too gently threw our haz-mat people out. Now, I don't know Matt well, but I know him well enough to say he's not careless or stupid."

Strand kept his expression passive, but felt the anger building inside him. Egan had fucked up badly bursting in like that.

"I'm sorry, I can't answer that. He's out chasing leads and I've not talked to him. My assumption is that he spoke with one of the doctors and they told him what we'd ingested, but I just had the strength to follow up on—"

"So would it be fair to say that, in your delicate condition, you've put Matt in charge of this investigation?"

"I'm in the process of getting back up to speed, sir. I—"

"But you're not yet."

"Obviously, I'm still feeling the effects of—"

"I don't want to hear it, Hillel. We've got an attack on a Homeland Security division that no one's supposed to know about—and for good goddamn reason—by a guy who may or may not be of Arab extraction. I want to know who this guy is, where he is, and how the hell he found out about you. But you don't seem to be able to tell me any of those things."

Strand felt his phone begin to vibrate. "Excuse me, sir." He pulled the phone from his pocket and looked down at the incoming number. Roy Buckner. "This could be an update on the situation, sir. Do you mind if I take it?"

Crenshaw waved a hand dismissively and began flipping through a file on the desk.

"Hello?" Strand said, pressing the phone to his ear hard enough to ensure that Crenshaw wouldn't be able to hear the other side of the conversation.

"I got him."

Strand let out a long, quiet breath and slumped slightly in his chair. Thank God. This was finally going to be over.

"I also got the lady cop."

Crenshaw glanced up at him when he suddenly snapped straight in his chair.

"What?" Strand said, keeping his tone even. "You were breaking up."

"I got Manning. There was no avoiding it—they were talking about you when I found them. Sounds like she's heard his whole life story."

Strand felt the beads of sweat begin on his forehead and resisted the urge to wipe them away. Why in the fuck couldn't anything just be simple? Why couldn't things just work out the way they were supposed to?

"Easiest way," Buckner continued, "is if I do her here and then he can either, uh, commit suicide or I can bring him in so you can talk to him first."

"Was there any communication with anyone else?"

"Nah. She was jogging in the woods. No cell phone."

"You're sure."

"Believe me. I checked."

Strand slowly turned Buckner's report over in his mind. There was no way to know how much al Fayed had told her and no way to guarantee she would remain silent. Particularly when his body turned up.

Unable to stay in his chair any longer, he stood and turned toward the wall, running a hand through his hair.

The risk of killing the woman seemed minimal. Al Fayed had murdered nearly her entire team and it didn't stretch credibility that he might try to finish the job and then kill himself. It seemed almost certain that no one would pursue the issue any further than his dead body. In fact, the police hierarchy would be ecstatic to see Manning silenced. Of course, Egan would have his suspicions but what could he do with them?

When he turned back around, Crenshaw had abandoned the pretense of reading the file in front of him and was staring impatiently in his direction.

"I'm going to have to call you back on this," Strand said. "I'm in a meeting." He couldn't let himself be rushed into this kind of a decision without time to think it through.

"What the fuck are you talking about, a meeting? Jesus Christ, I'm sitting out here in the goddamn woods . . ."

Strand hung up the phone and sat down again. "I'm sorry, sir. Nothing conclusive yet."

40

"Can you believe that asshole?" Buckner said, leaning against the car door and snapping off a branch that was hanging next to him. "He wants to think about it. No wonder you want to kill him."

At Buckner's orders, Karen Manning had eased the Cadillac into the woods, scraping along the trees and rocks for twenty yards until the forest became an impassable barrier. It was far enough, though—they would be completely invisible to anyone who might show up in the clearing her car was still parked in.

Fade was lying motionless on his stomach in the back seat trying to concentrate, but there wasn't really that much to think about. Buckner was a sadistic asshole, but he was well trained and clearly had the upper hand.

Apparently his life as a clinically depressed cabinetmaker had left him stupid, careless, and slow. After everything he'd been through, he was going to be shot like a dog by one of the biggest losers the Special

Forces had ever produced. The really strange thing, though, was that he couldn't bring himself to care.

Fade tried to move his completely numb right leg, but the blow he'd taken to his back had pretty much paralyzed it. His left still worked okay, but there was a pins and needles sensation in it that he'd never felt before. He tried his fingers next, but couldn't be certain whether or not they functioned. The zip ties around his wrists had turned them into what felt like lumps of dead flesh.

He was so tired. Just a little catnap. He closed his eyes and had almost drifted off when Buckner spoke again.

"You're driving me crazy in that tank top, honey. Hopefully I'll be able to do Fade first so we can spend some time together."

"What's the difference?" he heard Karen reply. "He's all tied up. You're not afraid of him, are you?"

Good try, Fade thought, but unfortunately Buckner was nowhere near as dumb as he looked.

"All that jujitsu shit, right?" he said, laughing. "You're thinking you can get one of those arms around my neck, aren't you? It'd be fun to let you try, but the truth is that everyone who's ever turned their back on Fade is dead now. I think I'm going to try to learn from their mistakes."

Karen's voice cleared his mind enough for him to remember that she probably wasn't as ready as he was to be dead. She still had a life, a family, a future. He managed to focus for almost a minute but no brilliant escape plans came to mind. Despite the fact that he was sitting on a virtual arsenal—Isidro had put the back seat on a hinge and it flipped up to reveal a sniper rifle and compact submachine gun cradled in custom foam—he had no way of getting to it. And perhaps even more frustrating, he had no way of telling Karen that the flip-down armrest between her and Buckner contained a similarly stored .45 and combat knife. James Bond would be so disappointed.

The ring of a cell phone interrupted his train of thought and Fade craned his neck to watch Buckner put it to his ear.

"Yeah."

There was a long pause before he spoke again. "I understand, but how the hell would I know who else he might have talked to? Yeah. Okay. But I'll need someone to drive my car outta here. Uh-huh. Tell them they'll see it parked in the trees about a mile off the main highway. They should just pull up behind it and call me on my cell."

"Bad news, sweetie," he said, stuffing the phone back into his pocket. "Looks like Fade is going to kill you and then commit suicide. Tragic story."

Fade closed his eyes, wishing he could drift off into the darkness again. This was his fault. Karen was going to die because of him. He jerked pointlessly against the zip ties holding his wrists, knowing that he was cutting through his skin but unable to feel it. How could he have been so stupid?

"Do you have this bitch brainwashed or what?" he

heard Buckner say. "She looks like she thinks you're going to jump up and save her any minute now. Are you her knight in shining armor, Fade?" The scrunching of leather suggested that he was turning back toward Karen. "So is that what you think? That he's a hero? Well, let me tell you a story about that. We're in Syria to take out some guy—I can't even remember his name anymore. Anyway, the guy comes out of his house with his family—his wife, their baby, and his son who was probably ten or something. So Fade takes the shot and hits the guy dead center. The bullet goes through him, through the baby who the mother is holding, through her, then deflects like ninety degrees and takes the son's head off." Buckner laughed hard enough to almost start coughing and Fade opened his eyes, watching him rock back and forth gleefully. "You know what your hero said? Do you remember, Fade? No? He said 'oops.' That's it. 'Oops.'"

Karen didn't respond.

"You don't believe me, do you? Come on, Fade, tell her. She wasn't ever gonna fuck you anyway. Talk about going for the unobtainable. You should see a shrink."

"You talk a lot, don't you?" Karen said finally, eliciting a quiet snicker from Fade.

"Oh, so you are alive back there," Buckner snapped. "I guarantee you I'm going to make you wish you weren't."

"Look, if you're going to kill me," Karen said, "why

don't we just get it over with?"

"We got a little while before my guys show up. You in a hurry to be dead?"

"It's got to be better than sitting here listening to you run on at the mouth."

Fade snickered again and Buckner twisted around, glaring down at him. The sun had gone behind the mountains and, combined with the dense foliage overhead, there was no way to see his expression. He could imagine it, though.

"If it was anyone but Fade back there, I'd be doing a lot more than running on at the mouth. Nah, I think I'll wait on killing you. I don't want to put a hole in those museum class tits until I absolutely have to."

He pulled a pack of cigarettes from his pocket and tried to tap one out while still keeping an eye on his two prisoners. It fell to the floorboard and he leaned sideways, feeling around for it with his free hand. The combination of the deep shadow on the floor and the fact that he would only allow himself brief glances down made the search less than successful. Finally, he motioned toward Karen with his gun. "Hit the lights a second, would you, honey?"

A surge of adrenaline suddenly brought Fade fully alert.

"Fuck you," Karen said.

Buckner's only response was to swing the butt of his pistol into her face. Belted into the seat and with no room to maneuver, she took a pretty hard shot across her cheek. Over the seats, Fade could see her trying to shake off the effects of the blow. It didn't take long. "Am I supposed to start crying now and do exactly what you say? Turn on your own goddamn lights."

"For God's sake, Karen, just do it!" Fade said. "He'll kill you."

She twisted around and looked down at him for a moment and then faced forward again, searching the dark console in front of her. "Fine. How?"

"It's on the floor," Fade said, trying to keep his voice a quiet monotone. "About one o'clock from the accelerator. It tends to stick so you have to stomp on it."

Buckner leaned right again, obviously wanting to be ready so that the lights remained on as briefly as possible. A moment later, Karen found the switch.

There was an explosion of compressed air and Fade watched the passenger seat shoot violently upward, followed by the sound of crunching glass, bending metal, and a short, surprised squeal from Karen. He was about to shout "Go! Go!" when he realized that he hadn't seen Buckner fly from the car as expected.

It was a bit of an effort, but he managed to roll on his back and get his foot under the seat, which seemed to be jammed about a foot up on the telescoping rail beneath it. A little pulling with his good leg and he was sitting upright.

Karen had her back pressed against the door and there was blood splashed artistically across her face. Buckner hadn't fared quite as well. Apparently, his knee had caught under the dash when the ejector seat activated and the force had snapped his leg; but not before it had acted as a fulcrum and swung his head—which was now kind of flat on one side—into the spiderwebbed windshield.

"It worked better in *Dr. No* . . ." Fade said, leaning forward.

The sound of his voice snapped Karen out of her catatonia. She yanked off her seat belt and jumped to her feet in the driver's seat. "What the hell was that?"

"It's supposed to be an ejector seat, but it seems to have a few bugs."

"An ejector seat? Your car has an ejector seat?"

"What, are you complaining?"

When she finally looked down in his direction he turned so she could see his hands, which were dripping blood around the zip ties and leaving large smears on his leather upholstery.

"Jesus," she said, dropping to her knees in the seat. "Is there a knife in the glove box? I don't—"

"The top of the armrest flips up."

She played with it for a few seconds, finally getting it open and staring at the neatly arranged weapons inside.

"Have you ever considered seeking professional help?" she said, cutting the zip tie from his wrists and then handing him the knife. The combination of the blood coating his palms and the complete numbness in his hands made it impossible to hold. She picked it up off the seat and cut his ankles free, then helped him out of the car.

He limped in circles, trying to get his right leg working, while she leaned into the passenger seat and checked Buckner for a pulse.

"Dead," she said.

"Finally. I should have killed that asshole years ago."

After he'd circled the car a few times, the pins and needles were completely gone from his left leg and he had about 50 percent mobility in the right. Suddenly, he felt good. In fact, he felt downright giddy.

He grabbed an overhead tree branch, ignoring the pain in his hands as the blood flowed back into them, and did a few sloppy pull-ups.

"Uh, Fade? Now might not be the time for a workout. This guy called someone and they're going to be here any minute." Her tone was reminiscent of a kindergarten teacher talking to a slow student. Obviously, she thought he'd lost it. Maybe she was right.

Fade let go of the tree branch and limped back to the car. "Give me a hand," he said, dragging Buckner's body out and dropping it unceremoniously on the ground. "Get in the back seat and push down. I think it's bent."

She jumped in and they both put their full weight on the passenger seat, managing to return it to almost its normal position. When it was clear it wouldn't go any farther, Fade leaned in and retrieved Buckner's gun.

"What are you doing?"

"Getting ready."

"For what?"

"For Roy's guys to show up."

"Why?"

"Uh, because I'm going to kill them?"

"Or better yet, we could just drive the hell out of here."

Fade frowned as he examined a deep scratch in his front fender. "Think about it, Karen. Hillel's got to keep this as quiet as he can and that means he has to limit the size of his team. If I take out three of them, I've got to think he's going to be temporarily crippled. That gives me more time to track him down."

"You can't kill them, Fade."

He glanced up at her and then went back to surveying the damage to his car. "Well, the leg's not ideal, I guess. But I've got surprise on my side . . ."

"You know what I meant!"

"I'm sorry about getting you involved in this, Karen. It was my fault and it was stupid. But you are involved and that means that if I don't get these guys today, there's a good chance they'll be showing up on your doorstep tomorrow."

"I'm not going to let you just go out there and murder them. That's not who I am."

Fade looked up at her. "Okay. You're right. Relationships are about compromise. What if I just shoot them in the kneecaps?"

She shook her head angrily, muttering something he didn't catch and climbed back into the driver's seat. "We're going to get the hell out of here and think this thing through." She twisted the key in the ignition and began slowly backing, steering carefully around Roy Buckner's broken body. "I just need a few goddamn minutes to think, okay?"

The trip out was faster than the one in, since Karen was showing no regard at all for the Caddy's delicately tuned suspension. Fade decided to let it go, though, figuring that he'd rather she took out her frustrations on the car than on him.

They came onto the two-lane rural highway without so much as a tap on the brake and he watched one of his custom hubcaps go spinning off into a ditch. Even worse, though, was the fact that a set of headlights visible about two hundred yards back suddenly seemed to be closing.

"Is that car chasing us?" Karen said, glancing calmly in the rearview mirror.

"Looks like it."

"Damn it!" she shouted, hammering her hand on the steering wheel. "If you hadn't been screwing around climbing trees we'd be ten miles down the road by now."

"Oh, so now it's my fault. The way I remember it is that if it weren't for me, you'd be dead right now."

"If it weren't for you, I'd be sitting in my office drinking coffee." She slammed her foot to the floor and Isidro's engine shoved them back into their seats. "But instead I'm driving around with the guy who killed my men while we get chased by government assassins."

"I said I was sorry."

The headlights behind them receded steadily, but then the road turned winding and the bulk of the Cadillac became a disadvantage.

"Shit," she yelped, ducking at the sound of a gunshot behind them. "They're shooting at us!"

Fade looked back at the car bearing down on them and saw the dark outline of a man aiming a rifle out the passenger window.

"Yup."

"Well, do something!" she shouted over the wind whipping through the car's open interior. "Aren't you supposed to be good at this kind of thing?"

"Hey, I wouldn't want to hurt anybody."

The next shot put a neat hole in the windshield between them. No big deal, Buckner's head had already trashed it.

"Fade!"

He shrugged and lay down across the seats, resting his cheek on her bare left thigh. It was kind of comfortable—firm, almost hard, muscles covered in smooth, dry skin . . .

"What the hell are you doing?"

He found the trunk release and pulled it, then rolled on his back so he was looking directly up at her. "Did the trunk open?"

"Yeah."

"It should be pretty much bulletproof. They had to reinforce it 'cause of the air compressor."

As if to prove his point, a bullet collided with the

thick metal, creating an ear-splitting clang as it ricocheted off.

"Can it do any other tricks?"

"Yeah, but it's kind of a good news, bad news thing. The good news is that there's a machine gun mounted in the trunk that shoots out over the license plate."

"You're kidding."

"This surprises you?"

"I guess not," she said, over the sound of squealing tires and another bullet impacting the trunk. "What's the bad news?"

"It's got blanks in it."

"Blanks! What kind of person would go through the trouble of mounting a machine gun in his trunk and then not load it?"

"You know, I only did it because it was cool. I never thought I'd actually use any of this stuff."

"Jesus Christ!"

"Here's an idea, though. When we get to a straight section, let them close in a little. Then, when we're just about to go into a corner, tell me."

"I don't know, Fade. If I let them get any closer, they could hit a tire."

"Come on, it'll be fun. I've got a rifle with real bullets under the back seat. If they shoot out a tire, we'll just stop and I'll kill them while you put on the spare."

She glanced down at him and then focused again on the road. "Fine. Why not?"

He smiled and wrapped his hand around the cable connected to the trigger of the rear gun. "The back might lift a little when the gun goes off."

"Here comes a corner, get ready," she said easing off on the accelerator and watching the rearview mirror. "Now!"

He yanked on the cable and the satisfying sound of machine gun fire was followed by the even more satisfying sound of screeching tires preceding a loud crash.

He pulled himself into a sitting position and then stood in the seat, trying to see over the trunk. The car chasing them had gone off the road and slid sideways into a tree. The man with the rifle was already out in the street but he looked a little dazed. The driver must have still been inside the car.

They rounded another corner and Fade stepped into the back seat to push the trunk closed.

"It wasn't cheap," he said as he slid back down next to Karen and flipped on the police scanner. "But it was worth it."

Not surprisingly, no call to the police had been made and there was no mention of a Cadillac armed with machine guns roaming the streets of Virginia. Karen had taken the first exit off the highway and since then she'd been driving exactly the speed limit, taking occasional random turns and generally trying to throw off the government agents, who were most likely still waiting for AAA.

Fade was dying to call Hillel Strand and gloat a bit, but Karen would probably look down on that kind of childish behavior. She was already pretty pissed off and didn't seem that impressed with their incredibly stylish escape from the clutches of evil.

"So what now?" he said, pretending to examine the scabs forming on his wrists. "We can't just drive around forever."

She cut through a McDonald's parking lot and reversed their direction. "I don't know."

"I can drop you off wherever you want," he said tentatively. "The cops. The FBI. Your house. It's up to you."

She didn't answer.

"Karen?"

"I'm thinking!"

"About what?"

"About the fact that someone high up in the government just ordered my death and I have no idea how well connected he is to the police or the FBI or whoever. That suddenly, the only person I know who seems even slightly trustworthy is a James Bond wannabe who just happens to have murdered six of my men."

"Uh-huh. You wanna know what always helps me think?"

"Not really."

"Mexican. A couple of tacos, a few margaritas . . . There's a great place right up the—"

"You just killed a man and now you want to go out for Mexican?"

"Strictly speaking, you killed him. But maybe

you're right. Italian?"

She looked over at him, her mouth hanging partially open. "You're completely nuts, aren't you? I mean, you've really lost it."

He shrugged. "Maybe. Maybe not. But either way, I still say we can't just keep driving around forever."

"Okay. What do you suggest?"

"How about my place? If you get on the highway up here going north we can be there in less than an hour."

She chewed her lip in an incredibly engaging way for a few seconds and then turned toward the on ramp. They were halfway up it before she spoke again.

"It was *Goldfinger.*"

"What?"

"The ejector seat. It wasn't *Dr. No.* It was *Goldfinger.*"

41

"My turn!" Kali squealed, jumping up and nearly managing to snatch the remote from Matt Egan's hand.

"Shhhhh!" he said, holding it out of reach and trying to see around her as she bounced on the sofa cushions.

"No more news!"

"Kali! Either sit and be quiet or go play. Daddy's watching now."

Recognizing defeat, she slinked off down the hall in search of an alternate mode of entertainment while

Egan climbed over the back of the couch. The hospital attack had gotten a little time on the local news, but Billy had done his job with characteristic efficiency and it was being treated as some addict looking for painkillers. The leading theory about Egan continued to be that he was just an armed bystander who didn't want to come forward because he didn't have a permit to carry. The rest of the program was dominated by Stephany Narwal, the latest victim in the Collector case, whose body was due to show up in a couple of days. So far, the murders had run like clockwork and the media was once again gearing up for the unhappy event.

He moved on to CNN after the local program went off the air and caught the tail end of a show on Special Forces operatives. The angle was that they were trained to be remorseless killers and when they left the military, they would almost inevitably become a danger to society. The guy doing the show seemed enamored with the phrase "ticking time bomb."

"Should I be worried?" Elise said, leaning her elbows on his shoulders from behind the sofa.

"Can you fucking—"

"Matt! Kali's just down the hall!"

He lowered his voice. "Can you fucking believe this? Like these guys' jobs aren't hard enough without everyone thinking they're a bunch of psychos. They put their lives on the line for this country."

"I know," she said, kneeling and sliding her arms around his neck. "It's just because of that al Fayed guy. They'll tone it down after he gets caught."

Egan didn't answer, instead going back to staring blankly at the television as an anchor came on and began to speculate as to whether a young woman named Elizabeth Henrich, who had recently been reported missing, was Stephany Narwal's replacement.

"Did you get a chance to look at the ceiling in the garage? It's getting worse . . . Matt? Hello? You really need to do something. The spare bedroom is right above it and when me and my lover were in bed up there, it almost fell through the floor."

"Careful you don't land on the car," he said finally and her arms tightened around his neck, choking him.

"You're a real ass, you know that?"

Kali, who had apparently been hiding just around the corner, saw her opportunity and dashed out, making another grab for the remote. He jerked it out of range, but didn't anticipate Elise grabbing it from behind.

"You're right, Kali. Your father's being selfish. It is your turn."

Egan sighed and stood, pulling Elise over the sofa and ending up with her legs wrapped around his waist.

"Are you sure you have to go?" she said, content to ride along on his back as he walked to his den.

It was already early evening—hours after he'd promised himself he'd be gone. Not that he was worried Fade would break their temporary truce. It was more a concern that his time there would pull him back into his role of husband and father, completely fragmenting what little focus he'd managed to construct.

"I've already missed a full day of seminars, Elise. You want to get me fired?"

She made a noncommittal grunt as he leaned over to examine a note stuck to his lamp.

"You know," she said, still stuck firmly to his back. "I've been thinking. I've got a couple of free days. Why don't Kali and I drive up with you? I got an e-mail from one of the guys in Neutral Milk Hotel and he said they're doing an acoustic set at a bar there tomorrow."

Egan froze for a moment and then pretended to concentrate on the note as he ran through plausible reasons she shouldn't go to New York.

"Doesn't Kali have school? And I don't think they let girls her age in bars."

A fairly pathetic effort.

"They'd let mine in. And besides, it's not every day you have a free place to stay in New York. She's never been there."

"So, let me be clear on this. Your suggestion is that we pull our daughter out of kindergarten to take her to a New York bar to see a subversive alternative band."

"My God, I married Tipper Gore," she groaned, tightening her grip on him. "What subversive? It's an acoustic set. And then I could take her to the Museum of Modern Art and maybe to the symphony. I think that's a hell of a lot more educational than playing with blocks at Mistress Martha's House of Middle Class Values."

"Oh, please. You like Martha and you know it. You agreed to that school."

"No point in overdoing it."

"Maybe while we're there we could get her a nice tattoo . . ."

"I was going to wait and surprise her for her birthday."

He flipped through his Rolodex and stuck one of the cards from it in her hand.

"What's this?"

"The number of the plumber you're going to meet here tomorrow so he can fix the pipe in our ceiling before the guest bed really does fall through the floor."

"Couldn't we just—"

"Why don't we do New York this fall when I have some time, Elise? The three of us."

She planted a chin on his shoulder as he started back toward the kitchen. "You promise?"

He was ready this time and lied seamlessly. "I promise."

Elise finally slid off his back when he leaned over to kiss his daughter on the head. "Gotta go, kid. Can you tear yourself away from the tube long enough to walk me to my car?"

Egan eased out of the driveway, trying to steer, wave, and dial his cell phone at the same time.

"What's going on, Billy?" he said, narrowly

avoiding sideswiping a parked car.

"Matt! Have you talked to Hillel? He's going nuts trying to reach you."

"I know. I've got about twenty messages from him on my phone."

"You might want to think about calling him back. Word is, he met with Crenshaw and that Crenshaw's hot to talk to you."

"Uh-huh."

"Look, Matt . . . Take it from a political hack—you should be involved in this stuff with the director. There's no way of knowing what Hillel's saying to him."

"I don't know. I'm not sure I trust your political advice anymore."

"Thanks, man," Fraiser said, taking Egan's statement as the compliment it was intended to be.

"Did you get anything from Lauren?"

"Yeah, but it wasn't easy. You want the good news or the bad news first?"

"Good."

"I don't think she's screwing with me—I think she's given me everything."

"Let me guess. The bad news is that it isn't much."

" 'Fraid so. You've got all of it except the fact that al Fayed's called Karen Manning a few times."

"Karen Manning? Really?"

"Yeah, seems like he might be kind of into her. The cops have her tapped, but they aren't focusing too hard on her because they still figure al Fayed's long gone. Hillel's got some guy named Roy Buckner watching her."

Egan frowned and put his wheels into the gravel shoulder to get around an RV. He'd managed to spend the entire day avoiding the question "what now," hoping that Billy would find something useful. But now it was time to face the fact that the only thing he could do is wait around for Fade to make his next move. And in the interim, he was going to have to figure out how to control the latest variable in all this: General Crenshaw.

"I assume we've still got nothing on the place he took Manning to."

"Not yet."

"Great," Egan said, and then fell silent for a few moments. There were just no good choices.

"Okay, Billy. Here's the deal. When I get off the road, I'm going to e-mail you the identities Fade's been using and the passwords you need to watch the credit cards he had issued under those names—"

"You're kidding me! You have that stuff?"

"Yeah, I have it and I need you to see what you can do with it. But if you find anything, I want you to call me first. Then we'll talk about whether we want to bring Hillel in on it. Agreed?"

"Absolutely. Agreed."

"Okay. Give me Karen Manning's address."

"You think there's something there?"

"Probably not, but I don't have anything better to do."

"What about Crenshaw?"

"I'm going to think about that."

42

"This is it?" Karen Manning said, coaxing the Cadillac into a small garage. When they were fully inside, Fade reached for the remote and the metal door began to grind noisily down behind them.

"All the hollowed out volcanoes were taken," he said, getting out of the car and limping through an open door near the front bumper. He turned on the sink, waited a few seconds for the water to run clear, and then filled a couple of glasses. When he turned around to offer one to Karen, he found her frozen in the doorway staring at the duct tape still clinging to the chair centered in the room.

"What would you have done?" she said. "What would you have done to me if you hadn't turned on the TV and found out I was a cop?"

He spun the chair around and sat, flexing his right leg experimentally. It was working better than it had an hour ago, but the improvement was minimal. It seemed likely that some of the damage done by Buckner's kick was permanent.

"I'd have scared the hell out of you and then I'd have let you go."

She apparently wasn't convinced enough to actually step across the threshold.

"Come on, Karen, don't look at me like that. I'm a soldier, not an animal."

"Did you really say it?"

"What?"

" 'Oops.' When you killed that family."

He looked down at his ankle and absently rolled his foot in circles. "Is our relationship already that far along?"

"What do you mean?"

"Is it time for me to act out one of those bad movie scenes where the guy says how he killed one too many people and he was suddenly filled with remorse?"

"I don't know. Is that what happened?"

"Yeah," he said, pushing himself out of the chair. "That's exactly what happened."

She surprised him by moving out of the doorway and not stopping until their faces were only a few inches apart. "No. That's not good enough. I want to know the truth."

"The truth, huh."

She nodded, though there was a hint of uncertainty in the movement.

"You know what pisses me off, Karen? That a navy pilot can push a button and shred a thousand women and children and no one has anything to say about it. But a guy like me kills a tiny fraction of that number—damn near every one a sadistic wack job who had it coming—and everybody thinks I'm creepy. The answer you're looking for is no. I don't feel bad about killing. You think we can just go negotiate with these people? You might as well try reasoning with a wounded civet cat. I did what I did because I believed it was right. That I was making the world a better place."

"And now?"

It took him a few moments to answer. "And now I think maybe that was never even the point. Maybe I was out there just so a bunch of pasty bureaucrats could feel tough and provide voters with the illusion they're being protected. Or worse, maybe the politicians were just using me to stir up trouble so they could scare the American people into giving them more power. At best, my life didn't mean anything at all. At worst . . ." His voice trailed off and he took a sip from his glass. "Well, no point in dwelling on the worst, right?"

Karen didn't seem to have a response, instead she just stood there staring at him. On the bright side, she didn't look like she was afraid anymore. He was starting to get tired of people being afraid.

"We should get rid of the car," she said finally.

"What?"

"If I were Strand, I'd be calling the police with a description and telling them you're a terrorism suspect and that if anyone sees you, they should tail you and get on the phone to Homeland Security. The Cadillac's not exactly subtle."

"Not a chance. That car's the one bright spot in my life right now. I'll die in it before I get rid of it."

"Jesus Christ!" she shouted, surprising him enough

to actually make him take a step back. "Maybe you could work with me a little, here! You know, my life isn't all that hot right now either. A few weeks ago, I was doing just fine. Sure, some of the guys on the force were chauvinistic assholes, but I was good at my job and all their complaining just looked pathetic. I was going to make captain one day, almost guaranteed. Hell, I might have even found a guy secure enough to marry me and have a few kids. But all that's gone now. These days, I need a PR firm working full time just to keep me from looking like a complete jerk-off! And on top of all that, now I'm running from killers hired by the government. It's been nice meeting you, asshole!"

For a moment, Fade thought she might take a swing at him, but she actually looked like she felt a little better after her outburst.

She was right, of course. He really had screwed her over. It was hard to dwell on that, though, in light of how fun his day had been. He'd killed Roy Buckner with an ejector seat, shot blanks at Hillel Strand's men with a trunk-mounted machine gun, and secured a temporary ally who was beautiful, smart, and tough as nails. It was by far the best day he'd had in years.

"Yeah, you're right, Karen. I'm sorry—"

"Shut up! I'm not finished!" she said, jabbing a finger in the air toward him. "What gives you the right to go around trying to kill people who piss you off? That's not the way people resolve disputes, Fade."

"Actually, it is. In fact, it's what I used to do for a living . . ."

A frustrated scream erupted from her throat and she turned away, walking toward his makeshift bedroom. "Just . . . just leave me alone. I need to think. Okay?"

"Hey, I understand. It's been a tough day. We're both a little tense. You know what always makes me feel better in situations like this? A quickie."

She stopped suddenly enough to make it look like she'd run into an invisible wall. "What did you say?"

"You know, a little roll in the hay. Admit it. It always helps put a new perspective on things."

"Are you . . . are you crazy? I just killed a man and you're . . . you're . . ."

It appeared that she was now so angry that she couldn't even finish her own sentences. On the other hand, she hadn't actually said no. Fade felt his mood improve even more. "No point reliving ancient history, Karen."

"It was a couple of hours ago!" Her habit of talking through a clenched jaw when she was angry had kind of a seductive quality to it.

"An hour. A year. A decade. No one ever got anywhere constantly dredging up the past. Well, except historians . . ."

Another frustrated squeal and then she stalked through the door, slamming it hard enough to knock a piece off the jamb.

"And paleontologists," he called. "I guess paleontologists probably do okay."

"Shut up!" came her muffled answer through the door.

He grinned and found a more or less comfortable place on the floor where he lay down and closed his eyes. For the first time he could remember, he actually felt like he could sleep. Not just lie there, drifting in and out of half-realized dreams, but actually sleep.

Things were looking up.

Fade jerked awake, not sure where he was. It took a few seconds for him to shake off his uncharacteristic grogginess and when he did, he half expected to be surrounded by cops with shotguns or piano wire–wielding government agents. The room was empty, though, and the only sound was from the television filtering through the closed door to his bedroom.

He pushed himself to his feet and stretched, yawning wildly. The improvement in his right leg had ground to a depressing halt and he couldn't bring himself to look down at it. There was nothing he could do, so there was no point thinking about it. He'd always known this was coming and now it was real—not just some ghost waiting to jump out at him when he let his guard down.

He concentrated on steadying his gait as he made his way over to the closed door and poked his head inside. Karen was sitting on a futon that took up most of the floor, transfixed by the little black-and-white television in front of her.

"Are we on TV?"

She held a hand out for silence. "They found her."

"Who?"

"Stephany Narwal."

"Who's that?" he said, moving around so he could better see the screen.

"The missing woman. They found her body."

"Oh, right. I forgot. You were working on that case."

"It's always the same," she said, more to herself than to him. "The naked body always shows up lying in a wooded area of Virginia exactly sixteen days after the woman disappeared . . ."

"So?"

"So this is fourteen days. And she was found hanging from a tree, burned." Karen looked up at him. "These guys just don't change the way they do things. They have a program . . ."

"You want a beer? They're war—"

"Do you have a phone?"

He tossed her his, then watched her jab at the keypad.

"John! What the hell's going on?"

Fade wandered back into the other room and dug a beer from under the sink, half listening to her side of the conversation.

"You've got to be kidding me. A note? Are you going to be able to get anything from it? Uh huh. But you're sure it's him . . . Come on, that's not funny. You're serious. Christ. Me? No, everything's great. Why wouldn't it be? Uh huh. All right. Get him, okay?"

Fade leaned against the doorjamb and watched her drop the phone on the bed next to her.

"You're not going to believe this," she said.

"What?"

"You know why he changed his MO?"

Fade shook his head.

"He's jealous."

"Of?"

"You."

"I don't get it."

She repositioned herself so she could look up at him more easily. "You've got to understand that this guy lives for media attention. In his mind, he's famous, powerful . . . the most feared man in America. And then you come along and all of a sudden, you're all over the TV being portrayed as this incredibly dangerous psychopath—a man who can kill an entire SWAT team without even breaking a sweat. Suddenly, he looks kind of pathetic . . ."

"You've got to be kidding."

"I'm not. So now he's upping the ante—trying to upstage you. Do you know what that means?"

"Not really."

"Everything he's done so far has been planned down to the last detail. But now he's deviating from that plan. He could make a mistake."

Fade popped the top off his beer, holding it away from him in case it sprayed. "Well, good luck to him. I *don't* live for media attention. The crazier he gets the less scrutiny I have to deal with."

She suddenly looked like he'd shot her cat. "What?"

"They think he's already got his new girl, right—the one who disappeared a few days ago? With the media all fired up and the new leads, the cops are going to throw everything they have at finding him before he kills her. It'll take some pressure off. Hell, if the cops saw me on the street, they'd probably just let me go. How would it look if they caught me now? They'd get crucified for using manpower to get revenge on someone who killed their friends while some girl is dying a horrible death." He took a pull from his beer. "Now I can keep my car for sure."

"Your car? *Your car?* What about that girl? What about what she's going through? And what about the girl who's next?"

Fade shrugged "Women die every day all over the world, Karen, and they do it in ways so terrifying this guy can't even imagine it. Why aren't we crying for them?"

43

"I just wanted to remind you that I'm still out here, Hillel. And I'm coming for you."

Strand slammed the phone down, the sound of cracking plastic amplifying the throbbing in his head, and then deleted the message. He had all his calls coming through Lauren and when she'd told him al

Fayed was on the phone, he'd refused to take it. Why the fuck would she put him into voice mail?

He reached for the phone again, preparing to dial Matt Egan for what must have been the hundredth time, but instead stood and turned toward the window and tried to slow his breathing.

The situation had gone from being virtually solved to deteriorating almost beyond hope. Buckner's corpse and car had been removed and would never be found, but Strand couldn't put the description of the ex-soldier's body out of his mind. Buckner hadn't been shot, or even efficiently knifed. He appeared to have been beaten to death with some sort of heavy, blunt instrument. During Banes's report, it had been impossible not to picture al Fayed, spattered with blood and bone fragments, smashing a hammer against Buckner's skull while he fantasized about his real objective.

Strand folded his arms across his chest and leaned back on his desk, trying to concentrate on the view outside his window, but not really seeing it.

Karen Manning had completely disappeared, leaving only an empty vehicle behind. It seemed certain that she'd been told everything and had heard Buckner's side of their phone conversation. The fact that she hadn't resurfaced suggested that she was with al Fayed, perhaps seeing him a protector. Right now she would be confused and frightened, but her uncertainty wouldn't last forever. She was a highly recognizable former cop from a prominent family, making it unlikely that she would run. Her options at this point were the police, the press, or her father. He was covering all three.

Finally, Strand reached for the phone and dialed Egan's number again, and, again, got a recording prompting him to leave a message.

This couldn't be happening. Everything he'd worked for, everything he'd accomplished—all balancing on the actions of a psychotic navy grunt and a disgraced street cop.

Matt Egan walked silently through the long grass separating two small houses and came out onto the sidewalk. Karen Manning's home was directly across the street, still completely dark except for a dim lamp next to the door.

He'd been scouring the neighborhood thoroughly enough that he was starting to worry that someone would notice and call the police. So far nothing. It seemed likely that Manning had gone out and that Roy Buckner had followed. Which left him with nothing to do but wait. Pointlessly, probably. He seriously doubted Fade was going to show up there and if he did it wouldn't be to find Manning, it would be to find him.

Egan was beginning to wonder how much longer was he going to be able to play this game. His day at home, instead of helping his stress level, had done the exact opposite. He wasn't sure how much waiting he was going to be able to stand before he just called

Fade to suggest a meeting place. Somewhere to finish this thing.

His phone began vibrating in his pocket and he retrieved it, glancing at the number before answering.

"Hey, Billy. Tell me you've got some good news."

"I wish. Look, man, you've got to call Hillel."

"Not now."

"Please, Matt. He's going nuts. I can't keep him out of my office and with him hanging over my shoulder I can't help you."

Egan let out a long breath. "Fine. Patch me through."

"I owe you one."

There was a click on the line and then Strand's voice, sounding uncharacteristically weak.

"Matt, we've got to talk."

"Go ahead."

"Not over the phone. In person. I want you to come in."

"No."

"Look, we've got to get on the same page here. This is getting way too dangerous for us not to be working together. I know I've made some mistakes, but there are some developments that you need to be aware of."

Egan considered that for a moment. He'd never trusted Strand, but he was right that the feud they'd developed wasn't exactly productive. "Fine. Meet me in the parking lot of the Tyson's Corner mall in front of Nordstrom in two hours."

"You know I can't do that, Matt. Al Fayed could

be—" To his credit, he shut up when he remembered that Egan had been on the street since this thing started.

"Your call, Hillel. Good-bye."

"Wait! Wait . . . You win. I'll be there."

44

"Could you just put me into his voice mail?" Karen Manning said into Fade's phone.

"Your father's in his office, Karen. He'll want to talk to you . . ."

"No, I just want to leave a message. I'm . . . I'm about to walk into a meeting and I don't have time to talk right now."

She watched Fade tape off the Cadillac's chrome bumper while her father's secretary silently fretted. His limp seemed to be getting a little less noticeable and his mood continued to improve. Or maybe it would be more accurate to say it was on a very delicate upswing.

"Okay, Karen. I'll put you straight into it, but you insisted, right?"

"I insisted."

She waited for the beep and then began speaking in a calculatedly cheerful voice. "Daddy? I'm afraid I'm going to be tied up for the next couple of days and I'm not going to be able to do any more appearances. Could you tell your PR people to try to carry on without me and that I'll call them as soon as I can? And maybe we could get together this weekend for dinner? Anyway, I'll chat with you in a couple of days . . ."

She turned off the phone, hoping she'd been convincing, and then went back to watching Fade. She still wasn't sure who he was or where she stood with him. He wasn't a psychopath—of that she was certain. A sociopath? Maybe, but after hearing his story, it was easy to see where his rage and lack of conventional morality came from. Was a person who killed legally at the whim of politicians any less a murderer than someone who killed for revenge or personal gain? Had he been completely reasonable in assuming that she and her team were a mortal danger to him? And if so, had he been justified in protecting himself? What would she have done in his place?

She shook her head and forced herself to clear it of anything that didn't directly relate to getting herself out of this mess.

"I think the green was a mistake," he said, glancing up at her. "What about pink with a big skull and crossbones on the hood?"

"So, kind of a Mary Kay saleswoman from hell feel?"

"Buy this lipstick or your family gets it."

"Can we talk for a minute?"

He ignored her question, instead concentrating on staying away from the front gun mounts while taping off the headlights.

"Fade?"

"Have you ever had a fun conversation that started with 'can we talk for a minute?'"

"I guess not," she conceded. "Look. You seem like an all-right guy for a mass murderer—"

"Thanks."

"But you understand that I'm not looking to be half of Bonnie and Clyde."

He moved on to the gleaming chrome of the front grill. "You were the one driving, Karen. You could have pointed the car anywhere you wanted. I wasn't stopping you."

"I'm not saying you were. I mean, I'm in a little bit of a bind here and I'm not sure who to turn to. It seems likely that Strand is covering the press and the police . . ."

"FBI?" he said, refusing to look at her.

"I thought about that, but let's face it, the lines between Homeland Security and the FBI are pretty blurry these days."

"What about your dad? Isn't he Bill Gates or something?"

"There's no way I'm getting him involved in this. No way."

He smiled. "Sounds like you're stuck with me then."

"Fade . . ."

Finally, he stood and turned toward her. "Look, Karen, we have the same problem: Hillel Strand. You're a good investigator, right? And let's face it, I'm a good killer. Why not put those abilities together and solve the problem?"

"Because I'm not a murderer. And even if I was, we wouldn't have a snowball's chance in hell of getting him. He's got all the resources in the world and we've got nothing."

Fade nodded, disappointed but obviously not surprised. "I assume this is leading to some kind of point?"

"More like an observation. The only reason Hillel Strand wants me dead is to keep all this quiet."

"So?"

"So we need to get it out into the open."

Fade turned and started wrapping tape around the car's antenna. "You said it yourself, Karen. They're going to be watching the media and they're going to threaten them with all kinds of Patriot Act bullshit to keep this quiet."

"I agree. We've got to get around the mainstream press."

"*The National Enquirer*? Salam al Fayed is the father of my alien love child?"

She frowned deeply. "The Internet."

Fade stopped taping. "No."

"Why not?"

"Why not? Because as much as secrecy helps Hillel, it helps me, too. If this all goes public, it's going to be impossible for me to get anywhere near him or Matt. They'll end up transferred to Antarctica or put in the witness protection program or something. No way. Shining a light on this thing just makes my job harder."

"Your job? What job is that, Fade? Shooting them? I don't care about your stupid revenge. This is my life!"

His limp seemed to get worse again as he moved around to the other side of the car, reminding her of the paralysis that was slowly spreading from his injured spine.

"I'm . . . I'm sorry Fade. I can't even imagine how I'd feel if I was in your position. I'd probably be doing the same thing. But as an outsider looking in, I can tell you that killing them isn't going to undo what's been done. What about this? What if I promise you that we'll put those assholes in jail? How would that be?"

Fade didn't seem impressed. "I never wanted any of this to happen to you, Karen. I know it's my fault. But . . ." his voice trailed off.

"I know."

She kept wracking her brain, trying to find a way out for Fade. No matter how she twisted the problem, though, she always came to a dead end. The fact that he'd killed a bunch of cops, half poisoned an entire division of Homeland Security, and then tried to shoot up a hospital was inescapable. But what if, by some miracle, he managed to beat those charges? By the time he made his way through the courts, would he be strapped into a mechanical wheelchair unable to move or speak? She tried to look into his face, but then just turned away and stared at a cracked brick wall.

"Okay," he said, finally breaking the silence

between them. "Hypothetically speaking, what are we talking about?"

45

Egan turned off his headlights, navigating entirely by the glow coming off the closed shopping mall. When he coasted up behind a lone car parked at the far edge of the lot, three men stepped out.

Hillel Strand was careful to stay safely between Banes and Despain, moving his head in jerky, birdlike movements as they approached the passenger-side door that Egan had thrown open. Strand slid silently into the seat, but when Banes grabbed the handle to the back door he found it locked.

"Just you," Egan said.

Strand seemed uncertain for a moment, though it was hard to read his expression through the semi-darkness and the lingering effects of Fade's birthday surprise. Finally he nodded and Egan pressed the accelerator, aiming the car at the road that circled the mall. He kept his eyes on the rearview mirror, but Banes and Despain just disappeared back into their car and stayed there.

"So what's important enough to make you crawl out from under your desk to tell me?"

Strand ignored the insult. "We need to put our differences behind us, Matt. We aren't going to get through this otherwise."

"I'm listening."

"Have you spoken to the director yet?"

Egan shook his head.

"After the attacks on us at our office and the hospital, his staff's all over me. You made a mistake going in there and throwing the haz-mat people out—"

Egan started to laugh and Strand held his hand out in an uncharacteristically submissive call for silence. "I'm not trying to allocate blame here, Matt. All I'm trying to say is that it's a situation we're going to have to deal with. Crenshaw wants to know how you knew it wasn't a biological attack. We're moving forward with the story that you spoke to the doctors when you were at the hospital and they told you it was chemical. Obviously, I've made serious mistakes, too . . ."

There was something in his tone that suggested he wasn't talking about his general stupidity for getting them into this situation but something more specific and recent.

"After you shook Roy Buckner loose, I put him on Karen Manning," Strand continued. "It was kind of a wild hunch but I thought al Fayed might try to contact her."

Egan frowned but caught himself before it became deep enough for Strand to see it in the intermittent light. He didn't know that Lauren had spilled the beans about the censuring of the police files and he wasn't going to mention the fact that his "wild hunch" was based on a number of taped phone conversations between Manning and Fade. Hardly a good start to trying to bring the trust back to their relationship.

"And?"

"The hunch paid off. Buckner called me and told me he had Fade in custody at a trailhead outside D.C. He also told me that he had been too late to save Karen Manning. That al Fayed had killed her."

Egan tightened his grip on the wheel in an effort not to wrap them around Strand's neck. There was no way in hell Fade had gone after Karen Manning.

"If that woman's dead, Hillel, I swear to God I'm go—"

"She's not dead!" Strand said, some of the anger Egan was accustomed to creeping into his voice. "Let me finish! When I talked to Buckner, he sounded . . . strange. You were right about him. He was unstable . . ."

"Jesus Christ, Hillel. Get to the point. What happened?"

Strand avoided the question, staying with a narrative that sounded a bit overrehearsed. "He told me where he was and I sent Banes and Despain right away. When they got there, al Fayed and Manning were driving up the road. They got away."

Egan let out a long, slow breath. "And Buckner?"

"Dead."

Strand settled back in the seat, apparently finished, and let Egan try to absorb what he'd been told.

Of course it was all bullshit. Hillel had been concerned that Fade had told Manning his story and he'd realized that he was in a position to kill them both—a tidy little murder/suicide that wouldn't generate too many questions. Except Buckner had fucked it up. So now Strand had the director's staff starting to dig, Fade still breathing down his neck, and Karen Manning wondering what to do about the fact that she had government contractors trying to kill her. Lovely.

Egan's phone rang and he grabbed it off the dash. "What?"

"Matt! Thank God." Bill Fraiser's voice.

"Hang on." He put in his earpiece as Strand looked on. "What's up?"

"First of all, Hillel seems to be gone and so are his goons. I don't know where, but according to my sources he actually left the building. Watch your back—it would take something major to get him out of here."

"I got it covered, thanks—"

"Wait! Are you still there?"

"Yeah."

"Are you sitting down?"

"Uh huh."

"He used one of his credit cards."

Egan felt a weak jolt of adrenaline—probably all he had left—but kept his voice passive. "Go on."

"He must be running low on cash. We've got a charge from Computer City and from a store that sells auto paint."

"Details?"

"A couple hundred bucks at the Computer City, but I'm having some trouble getting a list of the items he bought. On the brighter side, the guy at the auto store remembered him. He's apparently going for burgundy."

"Where?"

"It's up near Baltimore, but I may be able to do better. There was another charge—from an Internet service provider. They're closed right now but I'm trying to get the owner at home. If al Fayed signed up for access he'd have to give his physical address."

"Hang on a second," Egan said, leaning over and throwing open the passenger-side door. A hard shove, combined with a sharp left turn, sent Strand flying out onto the pavement. Egan watched him tumble to a stop in the rearview mirror and aimed the car at the mall exit.

"Sorry, Billy. Now what were you saying?"

46

Karen Manning leaned back against the futon and tapped a few more sentences into Fade's laptop. A couple years ago, she'd taken an adult education class on Web programming—a horrible ordeal that she'd stuck with solely because of the mild crush she'd developed on the instructor. And while things hadn't worked out with him, she had managed to create a rather pathetic but more or less functional Web site that earned her the only C she'd ever received. Particularly humiliating in light of the fact that she was sleeping with the professor when the final grades were posted. If she'd known that her life might someday depend on her programming skills, she'd have spent less time messing around and more time studying.

Glancing out the open door, she saw Fade in the same position he'd been in for the last hour: sitting on the floor with his back wedged into a corner staring blankly at the wall. He'd finally agreed to her plan and then plunged with startling speed into a semicatatonic depression that she knew she was responsible for. He saw what she was doing as the end of any chance he might have had to get the men who had destroyed his life and she couldn't help feeling a pang of irrational guilt at putting a stop to his spree. Insanity, it seemed, was contagious.

"What were the dates you worked for that CIA front company, Fade? And who exactly did you report to?"

He adjusted his gaze from the wall to her but didn't answer.

"Fade? Can you focus for a minute?"

"You're going to piss a lot of people off with this stuff, Karen. Everything you're writing about is heavily classified. Why don't we just kill them?"

"We're not killing anyone, Fade. So just let it go, okay? Come on, this is a great piece of revenge. Not only is it going to completely screw Hillel Strand, but it's going to get your story out there for everyone to see. But if we don't tell the whole story—completely straight—those assholes will use every inaccuracy and omission to destroy our credibility."

He pushed himself to his feet and crossed the room, disappearing from her line of sight. A moment later she heard the television go on.

"Fade, turn off the TV and come in here. I can't do this on my own."

Again, no answer.

She laid the laptop down next to an open copy of *Building a Web Site for Dummies* and walked to the doorway, flipping the light switch that controlled a bare bulb hanging from the ceiling. "Fade?"

He pointed at the television and she walked up behind him, leaning over his shoulder to see.

"We now have confirmation that the man depicted here is Harold Logner, a suspect in the Collector case," a disembodied voice said as a shaky video that looked like it had been shot from a helicopter began to play. It followed three police cruisers chasing a blue minivan with heavily tinted windows. One of the tires blew as the van swerved onto a freeway off ramp and a moment later the driver was on foot, running to the edge of the road and trying to climb down a concrete barrier wall. He'd only made it about five feet when he lost his footing and pitched over backward, falling a good twenty more before landing hard in a grassy median. The police were on foot now, too, with all but one running back along the road to find a safe place to get down. The remaining cop was standing at the rail where Logner had gone over, watching his motionless body below. When Logner began to move again and then managed to get to his feet, the cop just jumped over the rail. He fell almost thirty feet before landing directly on top of the suspect, leaving both unconscious.

"Shit," Fade said, walking over to the sink and filling a pot with water. "You should have had that guy on your SWAT team."

The tape ended rather suddenly and the small screen filled with the face of the news anchor. "I understand that we have a live feed at the hospital where the suspect was taken."

The scene cut again and, instead of a reporter, the camera focused on a small man with neat hair and a meticulously groomed mustache lying in a hospital bed. His hands and left leg were covered with a blanket, but it was still obvious that they were secured to the metal rails along each side. His right leg was in a cast and was suspended above the mattress with a cable.

He was squinting a bit against the lights being shined on him by what looked like every news crew in town, but otherwise appeared to be in good spirits.

"Oh my God," Karen said quietly. "That's him? Fade, come and look!"

He seemed more interested in watching his water boil.

"As you can see," Logner said in a slightly effeminate voice, "the police were a bit heavy-handed in apprehending me and I suffered a severely broken hip and leg as well as a hairline fracture to my collarbone. That kind of violence by the government against its

335

citizens is absolutely unacceptable and I'm looking into legal remedies."

"Since when do the cops let people like that do interviews?" Fade said.

Karen kept her eyes glued to the television. It was a good question.

"I know what you are all wondering," Logner continued. "And the answer is yes on both counts. I have Elizabeth Henrich and she's very much alive. Of course I'm not currently at liberty to disclose her location . . ."

"He's not even denying it," Karen said. "Jesus. It's really him. They got him . . ."

Fade dumped a box of mac and cheese into the water and moved to a position where he could see the screen.

"Ms. Henrich—a lovely young lady, by the way—has enough water to survive for another few days. Though I suppose it's conceivable that she could live longer if she's careful . . ."

"What is it you're asking in return for information on her whereabouts?" a reporter asked.

"I think it should be obvious. I want to be released and put on a plane to Brazil. When I get there and I've settled in, I'll happily make her location public."

"You've got to be kidding!" Karen shouted, jumping to her feet suddenly enough to almost catch Fade under his chin with the top of her head. "I'm going to go down there and choke the life out of that son of a bitch. Ten minutes and I'd wipe that condescending smile right off his face!"

"You seem kind of tense," Fade observed.

She spun, jerking to a stop with their noses about six inches apart. "What?"

"This is a good thing, Karen. Right? They caught him. Even if this Henrich girl dies, there won't be a next one."

"What, were you an accountant in a previous life? This isn't lost money or spoiled produce, Fade. It's a girl's life!"

"Why don't we forget the mac and cheese," he suggested. "Go out. Have a few beers and a decent dinner. Get your mind off things."

"There's a woman slowly dying in some horrible prison that this freak built for her and that makes you want to go out to eat?"

He shrugged. "A thousand people starve to death or die of thirst every day, Karen. I never let it keep me out of restaurants before."

She moved forward a little bit until their noses were almost touching. "Is your point that I'm a hypocrite? Is that your point?"

He took a step back. "I don't have a point. No point at all."

She wanted to shout at him, to take a swing at him, to make him care about that girl. But nothing she said was going to change the things he'd seen and done and suffered.

"I do what I can, Fade. There's only so much . . ."

He walked back to his corner and sat, fixing his eyes

on the wall across from him again. "I know. I did, too."

She just stood there, watching him sink into himself and trying to untangle the flood of sensations washing over her. Exhaustion, fear, anger, elation, guilt . . .

"I'm not really crazy, you know," he said, as though he was talking to the wall. "I'm just hopelessly, irretrievably fucked. It's not crazy to want to enjoy the time I have left."

She walked back into the bedroom, unable to look at him any longer. It was like his life, what made him who he was, was just leaking away. And there was nothing she or anyone else could do about it.

Pulling the computer back onto her lap, she tried to concentrate on the screen but could barely see it. She'd be dead if it weren't for him. Of course, it was his fault that she was involved at all but still, she couldn't shake a nagging sense of obligation.

"I'll tell you what," she said, leaning to the side far enough to see him through the door. "Why don't you sit down with me and help me finish writing the content for the Web site and then maybe we can have a few drinks and something decent to eat. Here, though, okay? I think it makes sense to stay under cover as much as we can."

47

Most of the spotlights bolted to the decaying brick buildings were broken, adding to the post-Armageddon atmosphere and making it difficult not to trip over the debris littering the ground. Egan continued carefully forward, getting close enough to read the building number on an old machine shop and confirming that he was still moving in the right direction.

The road came to a T and he took a deep breath before running across an exposed thirty-foot stretch and slipping behind a Dumpster. His heart was pounding harder than could be justified by the brief burst of speed and he stayed there for a moment, willing it to slow. The buildings lining either side of the street gave the impression of bunkerlike mini storage units. There were no windows and no conventional doors in any of them—just a single metal garage-type door centered in each facade.

Egan leaned around the Dumpster and squinted at another number, then ducked back under cover. Billy had called him an hour ago with the address obtained from the Internet service provider Fade had signed up with. It was less than thirty feet away.

His heart rate rose again and he cursed silently to himself. This had just never been his thing. Fade used to say that combat focused him—made him forget all the bullshit the modern world crowded into his mind. As far as Egan was concerned, though, combat was all about being cold, wet, and scared while people tried to kill you. And all for less than you could make working at a gas station.

He rolled onto his stomach and focused on the second door on his right. It was closed and there was no light bleeding around it, but that didn't necessarily mean anything. Were Fade and Karen Manning inside? Or was it a trap? Fade might have recognized the hopelessness of his situation and used his credit card to bring his enemies to him. In fact, he might be standing on the building across the street with one of those stock hunting rifles he'd used to such effect all over the world.

Despite the darkness and unseasonably cool temperatures, Egan could feel the sweat beginning to run down his back. Realistically, he had two options. He could wait there and hope Fade showed his face before morning, when people would undoubtedly be curious as to why there was a guy with a gun behind their Dumpster. Or he could go get his car and use it as a battering ram against the garage door in hope that he could surprise his old friend.

After careful consideration, Egan came to the conclusion that, while both plans sucked, the first sucked slightly less.

His shoulders were beginning to ache and he lay out flat, resting his cheek on the hand not wrapped around his gun. A little bit of luck. That's all he needed. Just a little bit of luck.

After about half an hour of complete silence, his

phone began vibrating. He checked the incoming number nervously, expecting it to be Fade informing him that he had his scope all lined up and was about to put a bullet through his skull, but it turned out just to be Billy.

"What?" Egan whispered.

"Al Fayed used his card again! About twenty minutes ago. A grocery store a couple miles from you."

Egan relaxed a bit at the realization that Fade probably wasn't within rifle range.

"What did he buy?"

"Dunno. Damn store closed right after he used it. But he spent fifty-eight bucks."

"Okay. Thanks."

"Hillel just got back to the office—he looks like he got beat up or something, but he's not talking so I have no idea what happened . . . Anyway, his goons are here too and they look available. You want me to send them out to back you up?"

Egan let out a quiet breath. In theory it would have been nice to have a couple of talented operators on the rooftops, but based on his last meeting with Strand, it seemed likely that he would accept nothing less than the deaths of both Fade and Karen Manning. It might have also occurred to him that it would be fairly convenient if Egan ended up shot, too. He knew a little more than Strand would be comfortable with and would make a more compliant scapegoat if he were a corpse.

No, the worst case scenario for him would be getting

341

killed alongside Fade. If he was destined to die here tonight, he wanted to go out knowing that Fade would continue to chase Hillel around until one of them dropped. Vindictive? Sure. But he had a right.

"No. I'll deal with this myself."

"Are you sure, Matt? I mean, I know you did okay at the hospital but last time this guy had a home field advantage an entire SWAT team ended up dead."

"Thanks for reminding me, Billy. I feel a lot better now. Really."

"I just don't want anything to happen to you, man."

"Look, I'll give you a call in an hour to check in. If you don't hear from me . . . well, you're probably not going to."

He turned off the phone and inched to his right a bit, replacing his view of Fade's building with a view of the only street leading up to it.

Another half hour passed before a high-pitched metallic rattle became audible. The sound continued to get louder as whatever was making it moved closer, and Egan concentrated on keeping his breathing even and his family out of his head.

The dark shape that began to emerge from around the corner was initially unidentifiable but the sound it made was strangely familiar. A shopping cart. His educated guess was confirmed when the light from the machine shop glinted off it.

The man pushing it was wearing a baseball cap that shaded his face and a formless jacket that effectively hid his build. He seemed to be leaning a little harder on the cart than he should have been and still his limp was plainly evident. Egan had noticed Fade favoring his right leg at Elise's show. Was it him?

He pulled back, pressing himself against the Dumpster and watching in his peripheral vision as the man passed by. The disguise and poor light weren't enough to obscure the face that had been so prominent in Egan's mind for the past two weeks. Fade.

His back was turned as he wrestled the heavy cart up onto the curb and Egan silently aimed his pistol. It was the smart move—a little pressure on the trigger and Fade would never know what hit him. The great Salam al Fayed would crumple to the ground behind his shopping cart, shot in the back by his best friend.

He was fishing in his pocket now, finally coming up with a garage door opener. *Shoot,* Egan told himself. His finger wouldn't move. The door began to grind upward and Fade took a position behind the cart again.

Most of the road between them was covered with gravel that would make a hell of a lot of noise if Egan tried to run up from behind. He could just aim over the Dumpster and yell, but with the distance and weird light it seemed likely that Fade could safely dive for cover and start shooting back. Not really ideal.

The door was about halfway up when it began to start jerking against its rusted rails, the sound of screeching metal filling the air. It was loud, but was it loud enough?

Egan broke from cover, opting for speed over stealth

and made it to within ten feet before Fade spun and found himself staring into the barrel of a gun. His hand had stopped mere inches from the pistol grip sticking out of his waistband.

"Matt, you sneaky son of a bitch. It was the credit cards, wasn't it? That pot smoking, Hawaiian-shirt-wearing asshole Syd gave me up."

Egan concentrated on keeping his gun steady as he moved sideways, maintaining a marginally safe distance.

"Where's your backup?"

"Just me," Egan said.

"I'm insulted."

"Let's have the gun, Fade. Really slow. Seriously."

He lifted the 9mm with his thumb and forefinger and tossed it on the ground.

"Where's your girlfriend?"

"Karen? Actually, I don't think she likes me all that much."

"Where is she, Fade?"

"You sent that freak Roy Buckner after me and ordered Karen dead. I don't think I'm going to tell you shit about where she is."

"Yeah, Fade. I got involved with fucking Roy Buckner. Look around. It's just you and me here. I could have come with an army. I could have shot you in the back when you walked by. I could shoot you now."

It may have been just a subtle shift in the light but Fade's face suddenly seemed to lose all expression. "Do it, then."

"Put your hands on top of your head and turn around."

He did as he was told and Egan inched forward, giving the shopping cart a quick glance as he passed by. A couple of steaks, two potatoes, a hibachi, a bottle of wine, and a bag of what looked like women's clothes.

"Having a party?"

"They say you should live every day like it's your last. Particularly good advice in my case, don't you think?"

Egan waved him inside and followed a few feet behind.

"Nice car," he said as they skirted around an old Cadillac that had been taped off but not painted. There was an open door at the back of the bay that led to a grimy little room with an uneven wood floor and bare brick walls. The only furniture was a chair and an old footlocker with a small television on it. There was a single door to their right, but it was closed.

"Hello?" Egan called as Fade stopped in the middle of the room. "Ms. Manning?"

He moved toward the door, keeping his gun trained on Fade, and took a position along the wall next to it. He wasn't sure what to expect from Karen Manning. Based on her experience with Buckner, she was probably a little suspicious of men with guns.

He reached for the knob and threw the door open, withdrawing his hand as quickly as he could. Nothing.

"Ms. Manning?"

Still nothing.

He allowed himself a cautious peek around the jamb and was surprised to see her sitting motionless on a mattress. Her back was pressed up against a pipe that ran from floor to ceiling and her hands were cranked behind it. There was a piece of duct tape stuck over her mouth.

"What's up with this?" Egan said, backing slowly into the room with his gun still trained on Fade. Maybe his old friend really was losing it. The thought of him keeping Karen Manning tied to a pipe didn't really jibe with the Fade he'd known.

Egan moved back a few more steps and began running his hand blindly along the wall, searching for the pipe Karen was secured to. A moment later, he felt the unmistakable sensation of a gun barrel being pressed to the back of his head.

"If I've learned anything in life," Fade said, lowering his hands, "it's that women can be treacherous creatures."

"Ms. Manning," Egan said as he listened to her stand up on the mattress and rip the tape from her mouth. "I know this is going to be hard to believe, but I'm one of the good guys."

"I know all about you, Matt. And about Hillel Strand and Roy Buckner. Now I'd appreciate it if you'd drop your gun."

"That thing with Roy . . . I had nothing to do with it. Hell, ask Fade. Ask him if he really believes that I'd get involved with Buckner."

"Don't look at me," Fade said, stepping into the doorway and looking down at the gun Egan still had aimed at his chest. "I have no power of persuasion over this woman. I've been trying to get her in the sack since I met her. Nada."

"I'm going to tell you one more time, Mr. Egan. Drop your gun or I'm going to kill you like I killed your friend."

"He wasn't my friend!" Egan said emphatically. "And I've got to tell you, I'm a little reluctant to drop my gun. Fade's made his intentions pretty clear where I'm concerned."

Again, his options were less than stellar. He could definitely shoot Fade, but that would almost certainly end with the back of his head being blown off. Or he could drop the gun, which Fade would probably then pick up and use to blow off the front of his head. Any way he looked at it, his skull ended up in more than one piece.

"I'm going to count to three, Mr. Egan. And then you're dead. One . . ."

"Okay! Fine. I'm putting it down." He crouched and set the gun on the floor, then slowly stood again, raising his arms in the air.

The pressure of the gun disappeared and Karen stepped cautiously away from him, then began gathering up a laptop and the papers strewn around it. She kept the gun aimed in his general direction but didn't seem terribly worried about him now that he was unarmed and Fade was advancing toward him.

"So what do you have to say for yourself, Matt?"

"I don't know. What do you want to hear?"

"You should have killed me when you had the chance. Another bad decision in a lifetime of them, huh?"

Egan shrugged. "What, am I supposed to start begging now? Fuck you."

Fade took another step forward and Egan glanced over at Karen to see that she seemed to have everything she wanted cradled in her left arm while she used the right to once again aim directly at him.

So there wasn't a lot he could do other than double over and try not to throw up when Fade slammed a fist into his stomach.

"Stop it!" he heard her shout. Based on her tone, he decided that she wouldn't mind if he dodged the blow about to come down on the back of his head. A quick shift of his weight and Fade's hand sped harmlessly past his ear. The momentum caused Fade's normally flawless balance to fail him and he pitched forward just in time for Egan to straighten and catch him under the chin with the back of his head.

"Damn it!" Karen shouted. "I said—"

Egan ignored her and rammed Fade back into the wall. With his right leg barely able to support his weight, Fade wasn't anywhere near as fast or powerful as he used to be, giving Egan an even chance at actually winning this fight. And while it probably wouldn't save him, at least he'd go down swinging.

The impact with the wall didn't produce the effect

that he had hoped for and less than a second later, Fade brought both hands down on his shoulders with enough force to drive him to his knees.

Egan managed to catch Fade's right arm before he could land another blow and he jerked down on it. The maneuver worked and Fade's bad leg crumpled beneath him, spinning him around before he could catch himself and leaving Egan with a clear shot at his lower back. He cocked a fist, concentrating on the place in Fade's spine where he knew the bullet was lodged, and then hesitated. He didn't see the elbow coming until it connected with his temple.

A moment later he found himself on his back, blinking hard and trying to focus as Fade straddled his torso and landed a hard right cross against his cheek.

"How's that beautiful, brilliant wife of yours, Matt?"

Egan raised his arms and managed to partially deflect Fade's second punch.

"After her concert, did you go back with her to your great house and kiss your daughter good night? *Did you?*"

He reached out to grab Fade's shirt, but didn't have the strength left to grip it. The third blow got him in the other cheek and he realized it didn't even hurt anymore.

"Fade!" he heard Karen shout again. "I said stop!"

There was a strange shimmer on Fade's face and Egan squinted, trying to focus. Tears. They were tears.

A moment later Karen Manning appeared behind

Fade and swung the butt of her gun into the side of his head. Not hard, but hard enough to tip him over onto the floor and leave him too dazed to get up.

"I just don't need this crap today," she said, shoving the gun into her waistband and grabbing him by the collar. Egan tried to stay conscious as she dragged Fade from the room, but his peripheral vision had already gone dark. Finally, he just laid his head on the floor and drifted off.

48

"Geez . . . What the hell did you do that for?" Fade said, rubbing the back of his head with a distended pout on his face.

Karen tore the brown paper off the side view mirror and accelerated out of the industrial park, matching the speed limit exactly as she headed for the highway. The car had been conspicuous before, but now taped for painting, it was like a neon sign flashing "Call the police!" Thank God it was dark.

"Oh stop. I barely even touched you."

"Barely touched me? I think I may have a concussion."

"Are all SEALS this whiny?"

"Damnit, Karen! I had him!"

When she glanced over, he started rubbing his head again in an obvious attempt to make her feel guilty. "Had him? You had him? Give me a break. What exactly was it you were you going to do?"

"You know what I was going to do!" he shouted loud enough to briefly drown out the sound of the wind blowing through the convertible. His anger seemed a little forced. "I haven't made a secret out of my plans. If you want to interfere, maybe you ought to just pull the car over and get the hell out."

She changed lanes, examining the rearview mirror as she did so. There was no one at all on the road behind them. "Who are you trying to convince here, Fade? Me or yourself? You weren't going to kill him."

"Was too."

"Don't make me use the ejector seat."

He crossed his arms and sulked with such self-conscious intensity that it actually made her smile. Who would have thought anything could do that tonight?

"Okay," he said finally. "So it was a little harder than I thought. But I was going to get around to it."

"Uh-huh. You know why you won that fight?"

"What do you mean?"

"What I mean is that when your leg gave out he had a clear shot at your spine and he didn't take it. Did you ever think maybe it's time for you two to have an adult conversation? I want to help you, Fade. I really do. But who am I? An unemployed former cop. Based on what you've told me about Egan, he's heavily connected and I think when push comes to shove, he's going to come down on your side of this thing."

Fade remained silent for almost a minute. "All right.

Fine. I'll agree to temporarily put Matt on the back burner. But Strand's still a dead man."

Fade tried to ignore the feeling of Karen's eyes boring into him as he got out of the car. Despite doing everything he could to try to move naturally, there was no obscuring the fact that the simple act of standing was taking all his concentration. The numbness had spread upward and while he'd gotten pretty good at working around the leg, there wasn't much he could do to compensate for his sudden inability to fully control the muscles in his back. Even with Egan's apparent self-restraint, their fight had done enough damage that at least some of it would never heal. Maybe tomorrow would be the day. Maybe tomorrow he'd wake up to the start of an endless life of staring up at the ceiling, motionless and alone.

He finally managed to pull himself to his feet and he moved awkwardly around the car to where Karen was waiting. The windows of the townhouse they were parked in front of were dark, as was the rest of the neighborhood. Karen put an arm around his shoulders, subtly helping to steady him as they moved toward the front door. When they arrived on the porch, she raised her hand but didn't knock.

"What's wrong?" Fade said quietly.

"I . . . I think maybe this was a mistake. I got freaked out and wasn't thinking straight. We just need to find somewhere I can get a couple quiet days to work . . ."

"Knock on the door, Karen."

"What are you talking about? You've been against this from the beginning."

He rang the doorbell, grabbing her arm as she tried to back away. A light upstairs went on, partially illuminating her face. Oddly, it was as close to panic as he'd seen.

"No. We've got to go," she said when the porch light came on. He increased his grip, but if she really wanted to break free, it wouldn't have been difficult.

"Fade . . ."

"Let's just talk with him, Karen. Then, if you want, we can leave."

The door opened a crack and Fade saw half a face peering around it. A moment later it was thrown wide open to reveal a man who didn't much look like the computer wizard Karen said he was. Instead of being four foot two, he was at least six-two, wearing cutoff camo shorts and a tank top over a tanned, fit body. Where were the polyester pants and *Star Trek* T-shirt?

"Karen? Jesus Christ! What are you doing here?"

"Nothing, Jeff. Actually, I was just leaving."

"What are you talking about? Get in here."

She hesitated again, but then stepped across the threshold and gave him a long, exhausted hug. According to her, Jeff had been an instructor at a computer class she'd taken and they'd dated for a while before a friendly break-up. Fade felt a pointless pang of jealousy that was probably weaker than it should have been. The truth was, Jeff looked like an all right guy. And even if he wasn't, there was a good chance he was an improvement over a half-crippled mass murderer.

"I'm Jeff Grant," he said, reaching around Karen.

Fade shook his hand and stepped inside, trying to ignore the fact that his grip strength was noticeably off. He'd never really had problems with his hands before.

"What the hell's going on, Karen?" Grant said as he led them into a spotless kitchen. "Are you all right? I can't believe what happened to you. I tried to call . . ."

"I got your message. Thanks. It's been a little hectic . . ."

"A little hectic? Yeah, I guess so." He redirected his gaze toward Fade. "I don't think I caught your name."

Fade remained silent while Karen chewed her lip. "That," she said finally, "is Salam al Fayed."

Predictably, Jeff's eyes widened and he took a step back. Actually, it looked like he was going to try to back right out of the house, but Karen grabbed his hand. "It's okay, Jeff. His reputation's a little bit exaggerated."

"So . . . he didn't wipe out your entire SWAT team?"

"No, he did. But it was an accident."

"An accident," he repeated.

Fade looked down at the floor. It seemed likely that this conversation was going nowhere as long as he was standing there. Grant seemed to be looking for a window to jump out of.

"Hey, Jeff. Do you mind if I pull my car into your garage?"

He shook his head a little too energetically. "Do whatever you want."

Fade tore a long strip of paper from the Cadillac's bumper and tossed it in a pile of trash growing in the middle of the floor. He'd left the door leading into the house open so he could hear, but so far there had been mostly silence. About halfway through the process of scraping the remaining tape off his windshield, Jeff's voice finally drifted in.

"Shit, Karen. Is all this true?"

Fade lay down on the still-warm hood and stared blankly at the garage door opener suspended from the ceiling.

"Yeah. It's true."

"Jesus . . ."

"Will you do it, Jeff? I'm having a lot of trouble with the programming and the fact that I have to constantly look over my shoulder isn't helping."

Silence.

"Jeff?"

"Man . . . Karen . . . I mean we're friends and all, but a lot of this stuff has to be classified." He lowered his voice but the acoustics of the house conspired against him.

"And he's . . . Well, he killed a bunch of cops, Karen! Do you know what you're asking me to get involved in?"

There was a rustling of papers. "Yeah, I'm sorry. I knew this was a mistake. It was totally unfair for me to—"

"Hey, I didn't say I wouldn't do it. I'm just trying to think it through, okay? I mean, they already tried to kill you, so they might do the same thing to me. And I'm not some SWAT chick with the Grim Reaper for a bodyguard."

"It's not a big deal, Jeff. I—"

"Okay," he said, cutting her off. "Fine. I'll do it."

"What? Really?"

"Yeah. But I've got to make sure I set it up in a way that it can't be traced back to me. And then we've got to assume that the government is going to try to shut it down the second it goes online . . ." His voice trailed off.

"How long before people can actually access it?"

"Programming will only take a couple hours, but getting it up will take longer. And then we'll have to send anonymous messages to the media and all the conspiracy theory boards pointing to it. . . ."

Fade tried to motivate himself to get up and finish cleaning off the car, but he couldn't find the energy. The truth was, he had missed his only chance at Hillel Strand. Even if he managed to concoct a brilliant plan to find him before Karen's Web site went live, he couldn't move fast enough or shoot straight enough anymore to do anything but get himself killed. And then there was Matt. It was time to just admit that there was no way he was ever going to pull the trigger on the best friend he'd ever had.

In a few hours, Karen would be safe and she

wouldn't need him anymore. She'd go back to her family and try to straighten out the problems he'd caused her. So by midafternoon tomorrow, every reason he had to keep breathing would have disappeared.

49

Matt Egan filled a pillowcase from the ice machine, ignoring the stares of a couple of kids dragging their suitcase down the stairs. He went back to his room and fell onto the bed, pressing the wet pillowcase against his face.

And so ended yet another unsuccessful run in with the now infamous Salam al Fayed. He wondered if he'd still be breathing if it hadn't been for Karen Manning's intervention. Not worth thinking about.

After a few minutes, he rolled off the bed and walked into the bathroom, filling his mouth with water and then letting it run red back into the sink. What now? Karen Manning was clearly exerting a fair amount of influence over Fade at this point. What was her plan? To use her considerable investigative skills to help Fade get Strand? Unlikely. To go to the press? She'd have to know that the media was being covered. Her father? Maybe. He had juice, but he'd be covered, too, and Egan had a feeling that she would be hesitant to get her family involved.

But eventually, she'd be compelled to make a move.

She didn't seem the type to run or to just hide forever in Fade's skirts.

He walked out of the bathroom, careful not to look at his swollen face in the mirror, and crawled back onto the bed. It turned out that lying on a floor unconscious wasn't a great substitute for a good night's sleep and he was just too tired to think about this right now.

He reached for the light switch but then changed his mind and began dialing his phone instead. He was way past due calling in and Billy undoubtedly thought his boss was dead.

"Hello?"

"Hey, Billy. Guess who?"

"Matt! Oh my God! Are you all right?"

The connection wasn't very good and Egan winced in pain when he had to press the phone harder to his ear. "I've been better, but I'm gonna make it. Where are you? I can barely hear."

"I'm on the highway headed toward al Fayed's place to look for you."

"Really?" Egan said, genuinely surprised that his assistant would take that kind of risk for him.

"Yeah."

"Thanks, Billy. Seriously."

"Don't thank me. I figured anywhere would be better than the office. The atmosphere's getting a little oppressive."

"Yeah, my day hasn't been all that hot either."

"So I gather. Good thing Karen Manning was there

to save your ass, huh?"

Egan moved the ice pack off his cheek. "What? What did you say?"

"I'm afraid I've got a little bad news for you, Matt." He paused uncomfortably. "Can you connect to the Internet where you are?"

50

Matt Egan narrowly avoided skidding into the back of his wife's van and jumped from the car. As he ran toward the house, he tried to calm himself down by picturing her sitting in the basement with her earphones on, oblivious to the world. If he could just get lucky this one time . . .

When he burst through the front door, the first thing he saw was a startling shock of green hair. Of course.

The woman spun and spread her arms so that her hands touched either side of the hallway. "She doesn't want to talk to you."

"Out of the way, Amy."

"Didn't you hear me? You're not welcome here!" She was able to contain the grin trying to break through the carefully constructed rage on her face. It was probably the greatest day of her life—she got to be involved in sticking it to her least favorite person in the world and had undoubtedly deluded herself into thinking that Elise would see the error of her ways and run right into her arms.

He had to hand it to Fade—or, more likely, Karen Manning. The Web site was a work of art. It was all there in teeth-grinding accuracy and detail: Fade's SEAL training, his transfer to a CIA front company, narratives on his more interesting missions abroad including exhaustive accounts of Egan's involvement in them, his injury, Hillel, the SWAT team, Buckner. His entire adult life laid out in lively prose and wrapped in a well-designed package that featured a picture of him and Karen holding yesterday's newspaper. And then there was the name. That was the best part. SWATKILLER.COM.

"Last warning, Amy."

She stood her ground and stared at him with eyes that were probably pretty but that he'd always thought of as beady.

"I assume you looked at Fade's Web site," he said. "Was there anything in there about me that suggested it would be a good idea to get between me and my wife?"

Her expression turned uncertain and by the time he reached her, she'd retracted her arms to let him pass.

He found Elise in Kali's room, pulling things from the closet and stuffing them into a tiny Powerpuff Girls suitcase. She didn't acknowledge him at all but his daughter did, silently moving her wide eyes from her mother to him.

"Why don't you go play with Amy for a few minutes, honey?"

She screwed up her face.

"I know. But do it for me, okay? Just for a few minutes."

She gave him a nervous hug as she passed, glancing back at her mother as though she was going to get in trouble for it. Then she disappeared through the door.

"Hello, Elise."

She didn't turn, instead shooting a furtive glance into the mirror above Kali's dresser. She didn't seem surprised at his swollen face—but then, why would she be? It was covered in gory detail on SWAT-KILLER.

"Amy called me about it this morning," she said finally. "When I first looked at it, I thought it wasn't true. But truth has a funny quality—a sound and feel all its own."

Everything he'd planned to say suddenly left his mind and he stood there in silence as she started packing again. After another thirty seconds or so, she suddenly stopped.

"Come on, Matt. Deny it. Say something."

In what was undoubtedly a very carefully crafted "fuck you," everything Fade had written about him was factual and more or less fair. The son of a bitch had done it on purpose—left him with no room to spin at all.

"It's all true," Egan said finally. "Every word."

She put a hand on her forehead and stared down into the open suitcase without really seeing it. "Oh, Christ . . ." Her voice was barely a whisper.

"Elise, I—"

"Why didn't you tell me, Matt? How could you lie to me like this? What else have you lied about? What—"

"How could I? How could I drag you into all this?"

"So you're saying you did this for me? Is that a joke?"

"That's not what I meant," he said, finding it impossible to meet her eye. "The truth is, I didn't want my past to be . . . well, to be in quite that sharp of focus."

"So you just didn't say anything? You put me and Kali in danger without saying a word? How could you do that? What about my right to make my own decisions and decisions for our daughter? How could you just take that away from me?"

"Look, I understand how much I've hurt you, Elise, but I want you to listen very carefully. You and Kali were never in any danger. Never."

"How can you be sure, Matt? You know what that man is capable of. He's killed children before. You . . . you sent him to do it."

It would have been nice if that bastard could have omitted a few of the more lurid mission details from his descriptions. What could Egan say? *Gee, honey, we didn't actually set out to kill children, but you can't make an omelet without breaking a few eggs.*

"People call you the baby killer behind my back. They didn't think I knew, but I did. I didn't care. Hell, I used to laugh about it. Just more of my naïveté, huh, Matt? Maybe when you think one thing and everyone

362

else thinks something else, you should be wondering if they're right."

"I don't know, Elise. Maybe they are. But I'll tell you something that I honestly believe: The world needs people like you to make it worth living in. But it also needs people like me to make it possible to live in."

"By killing people. By going to another country and doing things to people we would never do to our own citizens. How has that helped the world, Matt? How has that created peace?"

It was a good question—one that almost everyone in his position had asked once or twice.

"How many people have you killed, Matt?"

"Come on, Elise. The things Fade—"

"Forget Fade. I don't want to hear about how many people you've ordered dead or contributed to the deaths of. I want to know how many people you've *personally* killed."

He leaned back against the wall and stared down at the floor. "No. You really don't."

Then the tears came. She slammed the suitcase shut and ran past him into the hall. He didn't bother to follow.

Elise and Kali had been gone for an hour, but the house felt like it had been empty forever. Egan reached for the bottle of vodka on the desk but instead picked up the phone and dialed a number from memory.

It rang a few times and then a recorded message began to play. "You've reached the phone of Salam al Fayed. I'm on a tristate killing spree now, but if you leave a message after the beep I'll try to get back to you as soon as possible."

"You'll be happy to know that Elise left me. She thinks I was risking her and Kali's lives by not telling her about you. Oh, and after all these years of marriage, she finally asked me how many people I'd killed. Thanks for that, Fade. Tell you what. I'm at my house. Why don't you stop by. We'll have a drink and then we'll finish this thing once and for all."

51

"Sir, I—"

"Shut the fuck up and sit down," Darren Crenshaw said, not bothering to hide his disgust and anger. "You know what woke me up this morning, Hillel? A phone call telling me that the entire life story of one of our CIA assassins is plastered all over the Internet. Can you guess what I said to that?"

Strand remained silent, resisting the urge to crane his neck around as Crenshaw moved behind him.

"I said, 'well, get it off the damn Internet.' And you know what they told me then? That we can't. That in addition to SWATKILLER.COM, there's also SWATKILLER.IR in Iran and a SWATKILLER.SY in Syria. It won't surprise you to know that based on the content of that Web site, neither of those countries are feeling terribly cooperative right now."

Strand knew this already. He'd discovered the existence of the site hours before Crenshaw had and tried himself to shut it down.

"Now here's what we're going to do, Hillel. We're going to forget all the bullshit you fed me at our last meeting and we're going to start over."

"Sir . . ." Strand said, but then had to pause when he realized that his mouth was too dry to speak clearly.

"Be careful," Crenshaw warned, walking around him and starting a recorder sitting on the desk. "Keep in mind that I've read every word on SWAT-KILLER—just like everyone else in the goddamn world—and I've got ten people researching its accuracy."

"Yes, sir. I understand."

"You're aware you're being recorded?"

"Yes."

"Talk."

Strand took a deep breath, trying to control the panic that had been getting hold of him over the last few hours. Walking away from this thing unscathed was no longer a possibility. Damage control was all that he could hope for and even that would have to be done very carefully. Al Fayed and that bitch Karen Manning had ended his career in the government and any political aspirations he might have had. The only question now was whether or not he could avoid prosecution.

"Salam al Fayed was highly qualified for our . . . project. The most qualified candidate we had, in fact. I wanted him for the job and when he turned us down, I had my people do some research on him to see if there was anything we could do to change his mind."

"But Matt thought you should just let it go."

Apparently, the researchers he had working for him were doing more than just looking into the allegations in SWATKILLER.

"That's correct, sir. But I disagreed. I felt we needed men like al Fayed and that we should do everything possible to get him."

"So I gather."

Strand ignored the sarcasm and continued on with the story he'd been crafting since he'd discovered the site.

"My people turned up the fact that al Fayed had gone to work for the cartels and . . ." He feigned discomfort. "And that Matt had covered up those activities. We also had some admittedly circumstantial evidence that al Fayed might have been involved in the recent deaths of the Ramirez brothers. So what started as a relatively straightforward situation became very complicated. We now had information that al Fayed had been employed as an enforcer for the Colombians and might now be working in that capacity inside the U.S. Based on that, we obviously didn't want him anymore, and the question became what do we do with our information? Obviously, it wasn't a Homeland Security matter. In the end, I decided to inform the police. Anonymously, so as not to get us involved. Then we'd just let them run with it or not as they saw fit."

"Al Fayed gives a rather detailed list of all the people he's killed," Crenshaw said. "Interesting how the Ramirez brothers aren't on it. In fact, no one in the U.S. is except for those cops."

"Yes, sir. As I said, our information on that point wasn't concrete. It may be that he wasn't involved in their deaths or he may have omitted those killings from the Web site to increase public sympathy for him."

"Public sympathy," Crenshaw repeated. "Right. Go on."

"The police sent an entire SWAT team because of al Fayed's military background and . . . well, you know what happened."

"And then you covered up your involvement."

"My involvement was pretty much nonexistent, sir. There was nothing to cover up. I gave the police information about a criminal. That's all."

"Well, if you're such a good citizen, Hillel, why did you walk in here a few days ago and lie through your teeth to me?"

"I made a mistake. I thought I was protecting my career. While I don't believe I did anything wrong, I did provide the police with information that got a bunch of their men killed. Someone's going to be blamed for that and I didn't want it to be me. I felt that we could handle the situation quickly and quietly."

"And by 'handle the situation,' you mean execute al Fayed and dump his body on the steps of the nearest police precinct."

Strand glanced down at the recorder. "As you know, he had threatened my life and Matt's. It wasn't our intention to execute him, but we wanted to put an end to the threat he posed—to us, to the public, to the police, to the government . . ."

There was no question that Crenshaw would have to take decisive action on this issue and Strand knew that action would take one of two forms: The director could defend his organization and deny wrongdoing, or he could admit to an abuse of power and very publicly punish anyone involved. Strand had to make sure Crenshaw had a reasonable enough explanation for what had happened to make the first option the more attractive.

"And to do that," Crenshaw said, "you withheld information from the police. You knew that al Fayed was still in town because you knew he was after you. Hell, you had the cops put out an APB on him and told them not to approach."

"I didn't want any more of them killed—"

Crenshaw actually laughed at that. "Goddamn, Hillel. I'll give you one thing. You're the master of spin. And on such short notice, too. My compliments."

"It's all true, sir."

"So is everything on al Fayed's site as near as I can tell. I suppose that brings us to Roy Buckner."

"What he wrote about Buckner is *not* true, sir."

"Ah, so we've found the one thing he lied about. How convenient. Entertain me with your take on that one, Hillel."

"Al Fayed began calling Karen Manning and we thought he might try to contact her in person. So we put someone on her."

"Roy Buckner. I've read his record."

"Yes, sir. A reasonably good man who has history with al Fayed."

"A negative history. I gather that they didn't like each other. I also gather that Buckner is unstable. According to your own records, Matt vetoed him for your program."

"That's correct."

"And you didn't think that was a problem."

"Honestly, sir, I thought that the Karen Manning angle was a long shot and that Buckner would follow his orders."

Crenshaw nodded wearily. "Go on."

"Buckner called me and told me he had al Fayed. He also told me that he'd arrived too late to save Karen Manning."

"Was this the call you received while you were in my office lying to me?"

Strand had assumed that Crenshaw would have pulled those phone records, but hadn't been able to come up with a graceful way to deal with the subject.

"Yes, sir. He called when I was in your office. And then I called him back and told him to bring al Fayed in. He agreed and asked me to send someone out to get his car."

"But he told you that al Fayed had killed Karen Manning."

"Yes sir."

"Well, there's a fairly detailed transcript of Buckner's side of his conversation with you that includes him telling you specifically that Karen Manning was alive and you ordering her dead. How do you explain that?"

"I don't know, sir. It's possible that he was saying those things into a dead phone—either before I answered or after I hung up. Or, I suppose she could have become infatuated with al Fayed and now she's trying to justify staying with him—"

"So your best explanations are that either Buckner went to great lengths to provide disinformation to a woman he was about to kill, or that a former cop with an excellent record, who was working like a dog to clear her name, decided to ride off into the sunset with a doomed former SEAL."

"I really can't say what happened for sure at this point, sir."

Crenshaw finally sat down behind his desk. "Where's Matt?"

"We don't know. He isn't returning calls."

52

"Dad!" Karen shouted into the phone. "Calm down! I told you, I'm fine."

"He's holding you, isn't he? He's making you say this. Is he listening? Tell him I can get him anything he wants. Money, a private jet, the best lawyers in the country. Anything."

She looked across the hotel room at Fade, who was lying like a corpse in front of the television. She'd barely managed to get him out of the car and up the stairs, though his injuries shouldn't have prevented him from doing it himself. He seemed to be slipping away.

"Listen to me, Dad. First of all, he's not on the phone. Second of all, I'm perfectly fine. And third, he's not holding me here. In fact, if it weren't for him, I'd be dead."

"What was your first dog's name?"

"Huh?"

"Tell me the truth if you're really okay and lie if you're not."

"Scruffy, Dad."

He let the air out of his lungs in a loud rush that sounded like static over the phone. "I've had government agents here trying to find you—for all I know, they have this phone tapped."

"I can almost guarantee it."

"They made some threats about you being involved in disseminating classified information . . ."

"I'm so sorry I got you involved in this, Dad."

"Don't be silly, honey. I've already talked to the governor and gone through this with my legal team. If they come after you I'll crucify them."

The silent commercial playing on the TV was replaced with the director of Homeland Security standing in front of a podium bristling with microphones. Karen jumped on the bed and grabbed the remote, tapping the volume button and then using it to jab Fade in the ribs. He opened his eyes for a moment and then rolled away from her and closed them again.

"Honey? Are you still there?"

"Yeah, I'm here."

"We've been flooded with requests for interviews. We're talking about—"

"I think it's time for me to shut up for a little while, Dad." She leaned against the headboard and watched Crenshaw shuffle the papers in front of him. "We said what we had to say on the Web site and now it's time to let this thing settle a little bit."

"I understand, but—"

"I've got to go, Dad."

"Karen—"

"I'm going to see you soon, though, okay?"

She turned off the phone and put a hand on Fade's side. He didn't move.

"First," Crenshaw started, "let me say that I only became aware of the al Fayed situation yesterday when everyone else did. Since then, I've initiated an investigation into the allegations and statements made on the Web site and I'm personally overseeing that investigation. But it's going to take some time to sort through everything."

He paused for a moment and then looked directly into the camera. "My top priority at Homeland Security is to ensure the safety of America's citizens. But a very close second to that is protecting what this country stands for. Americans have given their government a great deal of power to fight terrorism and I believe that's a sacred trust. I take any abuse of that trust very seriously and I will deal with it as harshly as the law will allow."

A number of hands shot up in the audience, but he just waved them off.

"To anticipate your questions, we do not know where Karen Manning and Salam al Fayed are at this time. We also have no way of knowing Ms. Manning's status—by that I mean whether or not she's being held against her will. We are, however, doing everything we can to find them and to ensure Ms. Manning's safety. Hillel Strand and Matt Egan have both been suspended pending an investigation and both are cooperating fully. That's it."

He gathered up his things and walked off the stage, ignoring the shouts of the reporters. Karen rose to her knees on the mattress and pulled Fade onto his back. "Wake up," she said, running a hand through his hair. "Fade? Can you hear me?"

He opened his eyes but she wasn't sure he really saw her.

"I'm going to ask you again to come with me, Fade. I'll do everything I can to help you. Who knows? We might even get you off the hook."

He smiled almost imperceptibly and she had to swipe a hand across her face to keep a tear from falling on him.

"Fade . . ."

But there was no hope for him. They both knew it. He'd go to jail and most likely die there, paralyzed in an infirmary bed. He didn't deserve that. He didn't deserve any of it.

"What can I do to help you?" she said, wiping at her face again. "Tell me."

He just closed his eyes, the slight smile still playing at his lips. He didn't seem to be aware of it when she leaned down and kissed him.

Karen took a few breaths, trying to steady her voice and then slid off the bed, taking the pistol lying on the nightstand and tucking it into the back of her pants. "I have to go now. I'm going to turn myself in to the police and that means I'm going to have to tell them where this hotel is. I can stall for a little while, but you have to be gone by morning. Did you hear me, Fade? By morning."

53

The phone rang, but Egan didn't bother to reach for it. The machine in the kitchen picked up and the voice shouting over it echoed down the hall. "Matt! This is Darren Crenshaw. I'm about to come through your front door and I'd appreciate it if you didn't shoot me."

Egan poured himself another drink, listening to the creak of hinges followed by footsteps in the entryway.

"So, how's your day going?" Crenshaw said as he dropped into the chair in front of Egan's desk. He pointed to the bottle of vodka on it and when Egan nodded, grabbed a glass and poured himself some.

"You wouldn't believe how many people I had working on finding you before someone thought to look here. I swear to God sometimes I wonder if I'm just wasting my time."

Egan remained silent.

"Is Elise gone?"

He nodded and Crenshaw leaned back in his chair, sipping thoughtfully at the drink in his hand.

"Quite a predicament Hillel's gotten us into," he said finally. "Did you hear that Pakistan's already lodged a formal complaint with the UN and we're expecting at least four more countries that al Fayed mentioned in his Web site to follow suit. Apparently, the Saudis are so mad they don't know what to do with themselves."

"With all due respect, sir, fuck the Saudis."

Crenshaw laughed. "I couldn't agree more, though you'll never hear me say that outside this room . . . So my people are telling me that everything they've looked at on that site is exactly true. I've talked to

Hillel and . . . well, let's just say that man has a real future in politics."

"If he lives that long."

Crenshaw shrugged and took another drink. "Why don't you tell me your side of the story, Matt?"

"A little late for that, isn't it, sir?"

"You don't have anything better to do."

Egan tipped the vodka bottle into his glass and then topped off Crenshaw's. "Everything on SWAT-KILLER that relates to Fade's missions is absolutely true. He risked his ass over and over again to fix our problems and then he got hurt and we turned our backs on him. I tried to get the money for the surgery he wanted, but I couldn't get it done."

"You can't make the bureaucracy do something it doesn't want to do, Matt. What I'm hearing is that it was a bad call on the part of the government but that you did everything humanly possible to help the guy."

"Someone once told me that if you fail at something it's either because you weren't smart enough or you didn't try hard enough."

Crenshaw smiled. "I admire that philosophy, Matt, but we both know that it's bullshit. Anyway, it sounds like al Fayed figured out a way to get the money himself. He went to Colombia to work for Castel Vela."

"And I knew all about it," Egan admitted. "But I buried the reports from DEA."

"Apparently not deep enough."

"No, not deep enough. Hillel had a hard-on for Fade—for good reason, I suppose . . ."

"You can't deny that he has some desirable qualities."

Egan nodded. "We went to see him at his house and
he told us to fuck off. Hillel was pretty pissed and he
wouldn't let it go."

"So you told him about the Colombians?"

"No. Lauren found that. I kept my mouth shut."

"And the Ramirez brothers?"

"Complete nonsense. Hillel needed something local
to get the cops interested."

"So the plan was to frame al Fayed, get him arrested,
and then get him off the hook."

"For a price."

"And how did you feel about all this?"

"I didn't know anything about it. And if I had been
involved, you can be damn sure I wouldn't have sent
a bunch of cops in there to arrest him. It wasn't hard
to predict how he'd react. No, as far as I was concerned, Fade had done his fair share for his country
and, frankly, wasn't physically or mentally stable
enough for the job anyway."

"And that brings us to Karen Manning."

"Does it?"

"What do you know about that?"

"Same as everyone else: Hillel had Buckner
watching her and he caught them out in the woods
somewhere."

"The site says Strand ordered her dead. But he tells
a different story. He says that Buckner told him al
Fayed had already killed her . . ."

"I couldn't say, sir."

"Speculate."

"I don't see what I can tell—"

"Come on, Matt. Humor me."

Egan took another sip of his drink and looked toward the curtains covering the window next to him. Was Fade out there? Waiting?

"Matt?"

He looked back at the general and shrugged. "Hillel had every reason to want her dead. He couldn't be sure what Fade had told her and it would have been simple to make it look like he'd killed her. Is Manning telling the truth when she says that Hillel gave the order? Sure. But, as usual, he left himself some wiggling room. Buckner has a history of being a loose cannon and he'll use that."

"Thin," Crenshaw said.

"Not if you back him up, sir. He's counting on that. He knows the media and the Democrats have you under a microscope, just waiting for a story about Homeland Security turning into the new Gestapo. Hillel's been careful to leave you with enough ammunition to make it safer for you to defend him than to use him as a whipping boy. And even better, he's given you me—a man who looked the other way while one of our operatives helped destroy our youth with cocaine. A nice little diversion, if you play it right."

"So, you end up in jail and Hillel gets a medal for doing his civic duty."

"If I live that long."

Crenshaw scooted his chair around so he could tilt it back and lean against the wall. "You know what pisses me off, Matt? I'll tell you. It's when people assume that because I was career military I'm some sort of fascist jerk-off who wants to declare martial law and start shooting Arabs on sight. Every morning, when I turn on my computer, a quote by Ben Franklin comes up on the screen. You know what it says? It says 'Anyone who would give up liberty for safety deserves neither.' I've got a bunch of politicians running around the world scaring and pissing off everybody they can and then looking to me to protect them from all those pissed-off and scared people. And I've got Americans a little too willing to let the government play games with their rights in return for some bullshit promise that we'll keep them out of harm's way."

"Then why do you do it?"

"Why do you?"

"Because I'm good at it? Because somebody's got to? Sometimes I'm not sure."

Crenshaw fell silent for a few minutes and finished his drink. Finally, he set his empty glass on the windowsill and leaned forward, dropping the front legs of his chair to the floor with a loud crack. "You fucked up here, Matt. I have to say I'm disappointed in you. I don't mean about the Colombian thing—I understand that sometimes you just have to stand behind your men. I'm disappointed that you didn't come to me on this."

"What would you have done, sir? You'd have put together a team that wouldn't make the same mistakes as the police. They'd have either executed Fade or buried him in a brig somewhere for what's left of his life. He deserved better."

"Yeah, he did. But you weren't going to be able to give him better. And now, on top of everything else, I've got SWATKILLER.COM to deal with."

"Yes, sir."

"So now Strand thinks I've got no choice but to stand behind him and all his bullshit about the Ramirez brothers and Roy Buckner. To let him walk away after perverting the authority the American people have so unwisely given us."

"As much as I hate to say it, sir, it seems like your best option."

"And sacrifice you up as a diversion, right?"

"Yes, sir."

Crenshaw stood and walked around the den, examining the record industry memorabilia on the walls. "What would you say if I told you that Hillel had sent Roy Buckner a number of encrypted e-mails and that some of them are extremely incriminating?"

Egan didn't respond immediately, trying to work through what he'd just heard. "I'm sorry, sir, I don't think I understand."

"What's to understand? We have a whole trail of communications between the two from Buckner's laptop—all definitely sent from Strand's computer with his encryption signature."

"Uh . . ."

"Cat got your tongue?"

"Well, sir, encrypted e-mail is a good way to communicate—I use it myself sometimes. But it sort of presupposes that the person you're sending the mail to is smart enough to delete it. I can't imagine Hillel would make an obvious mistake like that. In fact, I'm finding it hard to believe that Buckner even owned a computer."

Crenshaw turned away from a particularly glowing review of Elise's last CD and faced him. "You're right. He didn't. The whole thing's a complete fabrication."

"Sir?"

"You know Strand's assistant, Lauren? Bright girl. Ambitious. Helped us create the whole thing."

"I'm sorry, sir. You've lost me."

"I have no interest in spending the next five years of my life in hearings over this thing. Besides, I've been wanting to make a clear statement regarding how I feel about us overstepping our bounds—that it won't be tolerated."

Egan wasn't sure what to say.

"Are you shocked, Matt?"

"I guess I am. And a little confused."

"Understandable, I suppose."

Crenshaw started for the door, but then paused. "So are you going to just sit here in your house getting drunk and waiting for al Fayed to get around to killing you?"

"I honestly don't know."

"You should have shot him in Baltimore, Matt. It was a stupid mistake." He tapped a picture of Kali on the wall. "You have a lot of responsibilities."

"I wanted to. But it turned out to be harder than I thought."

Crenshaw nodded. "I understand that your wife and daughter are at her mother's house. Why don't you get on the phone and convince her you're going to make this up to her? Then take a nice trip. I had that doctor who was going to do the surgery on al Fayed look at SWATKILLER. Assuming Fade's being honest about the numbness and paralysis he's experiencing, the doc says that it'll be one week, maybe two at the outside before he's in a wheelchair. Or worse."

Egan let out a long breath and stared down at the glass in his hand.

"I'm going to do what I can to protect you," Crenshaw said, starting down the hall. "Talented people are damn near impossible to find these days."

54

How long had Karen been gone? He didn't really know—the drone of the television just seemed endless and the heavy curtains were pulled closed, leaving nothing but unwavering artificial light. Fade let his head loll to the left and looked for the gun that had been on the nightstand. Gone. Clever girl. She'd forced him into a decision: either get up and do something or lie there and wait for the cops to drag him away.

His eyes wanted to close again but he wouldn't let them, instead trying to focus on the slow collapse of the ceiling above. At first he just felt like he was drowning, but the more he concentrated, the more he seemed to come back to life.

He'd finally reached the dead end that had been coming for so long. Karen would give the police the address of this hotel and a detailed description of his car. Matt would have to give up his aliases and credit cards. Nearly everyone in the world knew what he looked like from the photograph on the Web site. And his hundred-yard dash was now measured in minutes, not seconds.

Fade swung his feet to the floor and tried to stand but his right leg collapsed, sending his knee into the sharp edge of the nightstand. No sensation at all. He rammed it against the unyielding wood again, even harder, and listened to the dull, empty thud it made. A moment later, he found himself hammering his knee repeatedly into the small table, trying to force himself to feel something that would prove he was still alive.

Finally, he fell back on the bed, trying to focus on his labored breathing and not the numbness that was inching its way through his body.

The volume of the television suddenly increased and he looked over at the screen as the newscaster was replaced by a woman in her fifties speaking through intermittent sobs.

"We just want our daughter home safe," she got out before being forced to use a crinkled hanky to wipe her nose. "She's such a wonderful girl. She has so many people who love her. She's studying nursing . . . All she ever wanted to do was help people . . ."

Fade found himself mesmerized by the woman's unwavering intensity as she told stories of Elizabeth Henrich's childhood, her love of animals, the plans she'd had for her life. Why couldn't he turn away?

Finally, the scene changed and the camera focused on a reporter standing outside a sprawling building surrounded with people shouting and pumping their fists in the air. He recognized it as the hospital where he'd almost put an end to Hillel Strand.

"Harold Logner, known widely as the Collector, is still a patient of the orthopedic ward of this hospital. He's still refusing to give the whereabouts of Elizabeth Henrich and continues to insist on being provided sanctuary in Brazil. A spokesman for the Brazilian embassy has publicly stated that his country will agree to take Mr. Logner if they're requested to do so. So far, no reaction at all from the American authorities."

"Are we expecting one soon?" came the disembodied voice of the anchor. "My understanding is that we are running out of time."

"That's absolutely correct. By Mr. Logner's own estimate, Elizabeth Henrich can only survive for another few days. Having said that, the sense here is that he's just playing a game—that he knows it's unlikely that the Brazilians would refuse extradition after Ms. Henrich is found."

"And the protestors behind you? What's your sense of their mood?"

"Confusion, really. I've talked with quite a few of them and there seems to be no consensus about what should be done. It's more a venting of frustration and anger than anything else."

Fade listened for a while longer, then reached for the phone lying next to him and retrieved his messages. Nothing at all from Karen, just the normal mob of reporters, crazies, and cops. There were a few exceptions toward the end, though. General Crenshaw had personally called and guaranteed his safety if he were to turn himself in and Matt Egan had left a message saying that his wife had left and inviting him to come by his house and finish things.

He dropped the phone back on the bed and returned his attention to the gory history of the Collector murders. He and Harold Logner had a lot in common. All they did was cause pain. The world would be a better place if neither of them had ever been born.

Fade finally pushed himself off the bed again and hobbled to the closet, digging through one of the drawers inside and coming up with a small sewing kit. He took both that and his laptop to a desk in the corner of the room and after a few near misses, managed to use the hotel's data line to get onto the Internet.

His research skills had been steadily improving and it took him a little less than two hours to find a phone number that most nine-year-olds could have turned up in a few minutes. He stood again, using his chair as a crutch, and crawled back onto the bed. There was a half-full water glass on the nightstand and he smashed it against the headboard as he dialed his phone.

"Hello?" An older woman's voice, understandably suspicious sounding.

"May I speak to Elise, please," Fade said, using one of the larger pieces of broken glass to cut his right pant leg off just above the knee.

"She isn't here. Who is this?"

"Salam al Fayed."

She hung up and he hit redial.

"I'm going to call the police," the woman said when she picked up again. "What are you thinking, call—"

"Ma'am! Please! I really am Salam al Fayed. Look, I wrote on my Web site that I met Elise at her concert a few days ago. What I didn't say is that I was wearing a white shirt with a mandarin collar, jeans, and a pair of glasses with blue lenses. Could you tell her that, please?"

Another brief silence. "I'm not saying she's here, you understand. But hold on."

Fade examined his knee while he waited. It had already started to swell and turn yellow from his tantrum earlier and he used his index finger to poke at his kneecap, trying to determine if it was broken. Not that it really mattered.

"Hello?" The voice was uncharacteristically timid, but still unmistakable.

"Hi, Elise."

"How did you get this number?" she said, obviously realizing that if he had the phone number, he probably had the address, too.

"Well, first, I asked myself where would a woman in your situation go. Back to her folks, right? So I pulled up your bio on your record company's site and found out where you were from originally. Then I pulled up copies of your CD jackets and enlarged them enough that I could see the names of the people you thanked. And there were your parents' names, right near the top. Then all I had to do was—"

"What do you want?"

He held the piece of glass in his hand like a pencil and used it to cut a deep arc in the side of his knee. It was strange not to be able to feel anything. Kind of like slicing into a piece of fruit.

"I heard one of your songs on the radio yesterday. And today there was concert footage of you on the news . . ."

"My record company says they're printing another twenty-five thousand of my CDs. They tell me my last one's ranked number ten on Amazon. It's amazing what a murderous psychopath can do for your career."

"I'm not really a psychopath, you know."

"I was referring to my husband."

"Oh. Right."

He probably should have threaded the damn needle

before he'd sliced through his knee. The blood was running down his shin in sheets and he hadn't even gotten close to hitting the eye yet. It wasn't going to get any easier if he started getting light-headed.

"I heard you left him."

"What do you want, Mr. al Fayed?"

"I guess I want a chance to explain some things that might be hard for you to understand."

She didn't respond, but she didn't hang up either.

"First of all, you and your daughter were never in any danger. Never. Matt knew that for certain. In fact, not only were you not in danger, he and I agreed that nothing would happen to him in front of either you or your daughter. I would never, under any circumstances, break my word on that."

He finally succeeded with the thread and tied a knot in the end before he started carefully sewing his knee back together. "But I'm guessing you already knew that."

Again, no response.

"Come on, Elise. I have all your CDs. If there's one thing that defines you, it's that you're committed to what you believe is the truth. You don't look away from it."

"I know he wouldn't put us in danger," she admitted finally.

"So then you left him because he's killed people. But you knew that before, too."

"Matt's my one blind spot. He's my concession to hypocrisy."

"Everyone should be lucky enough to have that, don't you think? Something or someone that has the power to make you lie to yourself?" He bent the needle against the desk, making it slightly better adapted to the work. Not entirely sanitary, but infection wasn't an overriding concern at this point.

"Let me tell you a little bit about the world Matt and I live in. It's a place where governments punish a man for adultery by making him watch his sister being gang-raped. A place where a father cuts his children's arms off to put in a stew because some witch doctor told him it would make him invincible in battle. I've seen people partially skinned and covered in battery acid because of a difference in opinion on political systems that neither person really understood. I've met people who would kill every man, woman, and child on earth without a second thought because they think God wants them to. It's a world where there are no good guys—the people the press portrays as innocent victims really aren't. They're just poorly armed. If they had the firepower, they'd be out there doing the exact same thing being done to them."

He paused for a moment to bite off the end of the thread. "What Matt and I have done might not have been right. And it might have done more harm than good. But we were trying to help. It sounds kind of stupid when I say it out loud, but we were."

The silence following his speech stretched out a long time.

"How's your relationship to the truth, Mr. al Fayed?"

"What?"

"You say Matt didn't stand behind you when you were hurt. Even with my blind spots, I know that's not who he is."

Fade smiled weakly. "I think maybe I needed someone to blame and he was the only person with the strength to take it. Matt did what he could for me."

"You have no right to kill my husband, Mr. al Fayed."

"I was never really going to. I was so angry about . . . well, about everything. I wonder now if, in the back of my mind, I didn't want it to come out the other way. If I didn't want him to kill me. To have to live with that for the rest of his life."

"And now?"

"And now I'm tired. Of being angry. Of being scared. Of wondering what might have been if everything hadn't gotten so fucked up."

He leaned forward and ran a finger over the stitches in his knee. Not overly artistic, but the effect was pretty convincing. "You're going to go back to him, right, Elise?"

For a few seconds he didn't think she was going to answer. Finally, "Like I said, he's my one blind spot."

55

The activity in the office had become increasingly feverish over the past few hours and now encompassed everyone. The birth of SWATKILLER.COM had changed everything. The entire staff was now fully aware of what was happening and were reporting directly to Darren Crenshaw's office. An outside team of investigators was working desperately to confirm the facts on al Fayed's Web site while Bill Fraiser and Lauren McCall had been moved to a group charged with finding him.

Hillel Strand was the only person with no role at all. He had no idea where Matt Egan was or what progress the various task forces had made. He was still living at the office but, for all intents and purposes, was completely isolated. When he stepped through his door, the people in the hallway went silent, staring at him as he walked stiffly to the copy room or the bathroom or wherever, and not speaking again until he was back behind closed doors.

Worse than the silence from his staff was the silence from the rest of the establishment. His friends and political allies had stopped returning his calls and the upper management at Homeland Security was acting as though he didn't exist. No reprimands, no debriefings, no comments to the press. Nothing.

Strand sat and reached for his coffee mug, one of the only things left on his desk. His file cabinets, his computer, his disks—even his notepad and calendar—had been gathered up and hauled away. It wouldn't do them any good, though. He'd written nothing down that would contradict the story he'd created. He told himself over and over that he'd played this thing the best it could be played, though it didn't seem to be doing anything to ease the pain of the ulcer he could feel forming.

There was no way Crenshaw could possibly win this fight. The strain of trying to break through the reasonable doubt Strand had blanketed himself in would crack the very foundations of the organization. He would have no choice but to do everything he could to make this thing go away. Well, one choice. He could try to coerce a confession by firing Strand and putting him out on the same streets traveled by Salam al Fayed. The lawyer Strand had hired didn't seem concerned about that, though. It would be so obvious a ploy as to make any admissions completely retractable.

The bottom line was that he was going to be all right. It would take some time for all this to pass, and his career in the government was over, but he was going to be all right. Strand closed his eyes for a moment, letting his mind go blank and his muscles slack. He was going to be all right.

A moment later, his door was thrown open and he jumped to his feet as Darren Crenshaw strode in, followed by two men Strand didn't recognize. Both were dressed in inexpensive suits and one was overweight enough to be breathing hard from having to chase Crenshaw at the half-run that was his normal pace.

"What can I do for you, sir?" Strand said, as Crenshaw took a position by the wall and the men with him planted themselves in the center of the room.

"Hillel Strand?" one of them said, digging into his pocket.

"Yes."

He produced a badge, holding it out so that Strand could see. It identified him as a cop. Just a plain cop.

"Sir, you're under arrest for obstruction of justice and the attempted murder of Karen Manning and Salam al Fayed."

"What? What the hell are you talk—"

"Sir, if you could step out from behind the desk, please."

Strand looked over at Crenshaw. "What the hell is going on?"

"We found the e-mails you sent to Roy Buckner, Hillel. He didn't delete them."

"What are you talking about? I never sent e-mails to Buckner!"

Crenshaw just shook his head disappointedly as one of the cops came around and grabbed Strand by the arm. He pulled back and a moment later found himself pinned to his desk with his hands held firmly behind him. Then there was the cold metal against his wrists and the unmistakable ratcheting of handcuffs. When he was jerked back upright again, Crenshaw had already turned to leave.

"I know things that could be very damaging," Strand shouted after him, beginning to panic. "You can't just turn me over to the goddamn police."

Crenshaw stopped in the doorway but didn't look back. "What do you know, Hillel? What do you know that isn't already plastered all over the fucking Internet?"

56

In light of the growing mob outside and Fade's own recent antics, security at the hospital was understandably tight. Metal detectors that had sprung up at the entrance precluded bringing any meaningful weapons and everyone seemed to be hyperaware of what was going on around them. Fade kept his head down, trying to get used to moving on the crutches he'd bought, and avoiding eye contact with the cops and security guards wandering the halls. He was wearing a Lakers baseball hat that, combined with a pair of lightly tinted sunglasses, gave him the generic look of a thirty-something with a self-destructive penchant for pickup games. The key to the rather lame disguise, though, was his knee. Black and blue, swollen and stitched, it was clearly visible beneath his cutoff pants and drew the eye of nearly all the nonmedical personnel that passed by.

He stopped with his back to a security camera and traced a finger along a color-coded map of the hospital, locating the orthopedics ward and starting off down the hall again.

"Sorry," he mumbled as he hopped into a crowded elevator on one leg, whacking no fewer than three people with his backpack as he did so. His normal MO would have been to rappel down the side of the building, or have a helicopter drop him in, or at the very least, slink up the back stairs. In his current condition, though, riding the elevator was about as athletic as he wanted to get. It was a frontal assault or nothing.

Not surprisingly, when the elevator doors slid open and Fade nearly fell out into the orthopedics ward, there was a cop watching.

"Who are you here to see?"

"Dr. Pritchard." He'd gotten the name off the hospital's Web site.

"Do you have an appointment?" the cop asked, tearing his gaze away from Fade's bulbous knee and looking down at the clipboard in his hand.

"I don't know. I just talked to him about a half an hour ago and told him what my knee looked like and he said to meet him here. He thinks I might have an infection."

"Looks nasty."

"You have no idea."

"Okay. Go ahead."

Fade started down the hall, but then paused and craned his neck around. "Hey. Is this where you guys are keeping that Collector freak? There's like a thousand people outside . . ."

The cop just frowned and sat down in the folding chair facing the elevator.

The layout turned out to be almost ideal for his purposes. There was really only one way to go and the hall had enough twists and turns to put the various security people out of sight of one another. He finally came around the last corner and headed toward a set of solid-looking double doors with a beefy, short-necked cop sitting next to them. He stood as Fade crutched forward, focusing predictably on his damaged knee.

"Can I help you?"

"I'm supposed to be meeting Dr. Pritchard. But honestly, I'm not sure I'm in the right place."

"I can guarantee you're not. You need to go back to the desk you passed and talk to the nurse."

Fade had briefly toyed with the idea of having Isidro convert his new crutches into twelve-gauge shotguns. The incredibly high cool factor, though, hadn't quite outweighed the obvious impracticalities. So instead, he'd spent some time experimenting with his right leg, determining exactly what it would and would not do. He figured he had about 40 percent power and 30 percent maneuverability, but only for short bursts. It was just enough to give his utterly inelegant plan a remote chance of succeeding.

As he turned around, Fade pretended to lose his balance, dropping one of his crutches in a maneuver he'd rehearsed in the full-length mirror at his hotel. When the cop bent to pick it up, Fade swung the other one into the back of his head. He went down hard, letting out a grunt that seemed impossibly loud in the empty hallway. Fade tensed and looked back down the corridor but no one materialized. His good karma for this type of thing continued to hold.

Leaning over with a little difficulty, he took the cop's gun and stuffed it into his waistband, grabbed his crutch, and then pushed through the doors.

The hall he entered wasn't as long as he expected, extending about forty feet before it dead-ended into a window that looked out over the Virginia suburbs. This time there were two cops, both of whom jerked from their positions guarding the last door on the right and started immediately toward him.

"Hi," Fade said, actually having to raise his voice a bit to be heard over the drone of the protestors outside. "I'm here to meet Dr. Pritchard. He's supposed to examine my knee."

They both stopped and Fade continued forward until he was within a normal conversational distance. "Do you know which room I'm supposed to wait in?"

They both seemed a bit confused and one of them called to their now unconscious companion. "Hey, Andy? What's up with this?"

Fade reached behind him and pulled the gun from his waistband before it became obvious that their colleague wasn't answering. One cop wisely raised his hands but the other stared malevolently, swinging his arm to within inches of his holster.

"You don't want to be fucking around here, boy," he said. "You're gonna get yourself hurt."

"We'll see," Fade said, pushing off his hat and glasses. "You guys have probably heard of me. My name's Salam al Fayed."

The recognition was clear in both their faces and the man who'd threatened him suddenly lost some of his resolve.

"Now, I don't particularly want to kill either one of you, but then I'm not really dead set against it, either." He pointed to the man on the left. "Why don't we start with you? Take your gun out, nice and easy, and lay it on the floor."

He didn't move and Fade nodded toward the door they'd been guarding. "I admire your courage and your sense of duty, but I want you to think hard about this. Do you want to die for him?"

A few moments later, both men's guns were on the ground and they were facing the wall with their hands laced on top of their heads. Fade took his backpack off, dropped their guns inside, and pulled out a doorstop with carpet tape on the bottom.

Keeping a close eye on his two prisoners, he moved next to the door they'd been guarding and took a few deep breaths. It looked thick enough to be fairly soundproof, but that certainly wasn't guaranteed. The bottom line was that there was only one way to know what was waiting for him on the other side. He threw the door open and jumped inside as gracefully as he could, slamming it closed behind him and crouching low to stay out of the line of the window at the far side of the room.

"Who the hell are you?" Harold Logner said from the bed he was secured to. Fade ignored the question, panning the room with his gun stretched out in front of him and confirming that there was no one else there. How convenient.

When he was satisfied that they were alone, he peeled the paper off the carpet tape on the doorstop and shoved it under the door. A quick test confirmed that it was completely jammed.

"Who the hell are you?" Logner repeated as Fade skirted the wall and pulled the curtains closed, leaving the room in a deep gloom. There was a narrow ledge outside that someone could probably use to approach the window but they'd have to be more or less suicidal.

"What are you doing?"

Fade turned, confirming that Logner's arms and unbroken leg were secured to the bed with heavy leather straps, and pulled a roll of duct tape from his pack. He ran a strip along the bottom of the door and then went to work on the air vents. The ceiling was solid—not drop panel—so he wouldn't have to worry about that.

Finally, he used his crutch to smash a video camera bolted to the wall and then pushed the bed against the opposite wall while Logner tugged halfheartedly at his bonds.

Fade was reasonably certain he'd left no cracks that

the police could get fiber optic cameras through, but it still made sense to stay out from in front of the window.

"You can't do this," Logner said. "I'm severely injured! I demand to talk to Captain Pickering. Do you hear me? Right now!"

Fade scanned the room silently, trying to find anything he'd missed. By the time he decided the area was as secure as it was going to get, his eyes had fully adjusted to the semidarkness.

"Did you hear me? I want to talk to Captain Pickering! This is not part of our agreement!"

"No, Harold. I guess it's not."

Fade had met more than his share of psychos in his life—Serb mass murderers, African strongmen, Arab terrorists—and they all had one thing in common: They were surprisingly unimpressive.

This guy took the cake, though. He was wearing appropriately bloodred silk pajamas that seemed unwilling to conform to his thin, angular body and that gave his head a turtlelike quality. His hair was meticulously trimmed and his nails appeared to have been recently manicured. Apparently, he was milking his position for all it was worth.

"Who are you?"

His voice had risen to almost a screech and his eyebrows had crinkled in a way that made Fade think of a child gearing up for a tantrum. A little disappointing, really. Karen had been right. Just a pathetic little man who liked to sneak up behind women.

"I'm the guy who's been stealing all your publicity. My name's Salam al Fayed. But why don't you call me Fade."

Logner watched him carefully as he grabbed a stool and limped up alongside the bed.

"You're the one who killed all those police. The one with the Web site . . ."

"That's me," Fade said as the phone started ringing. He pushed himself off the stool again and crawled across the floor until he could get hold of the cord.

"What are you doing here?" Logner whined as Fade pulled the phone off a small nightstand, catching it just before it hit the floor.

"Hello? Hello? You still there?" Fade said, rolling onto his back.

"This is Captain Seymore Pickering. Who am I speaking to?"

"You already know the answer to that question, don't you, Seymore?"

"I suppose I do. Tell me what's happening in there, Mr. Fayed."

"It's *al* Fay— Oh, never mind. The truth is, I feel bad about killing your guys and I figured I'd try to make it up to you."

"We don't want anyone to get hurt, Mr. al Fayed. What can we do to disarm this situation?"

"I'm glad you asked that. I want you to find Karen Manning and Matt Egan and send them up here. Let's start there."

"What are you going to give me in return? I need

some kind of gesture . . ."

Logner was straining forward as far as his bonds would allow, craning his neck to see. Fade flipped him off.

"Well, the way I figure it, you want two things: to save Elizabeth Henrich and kill me. Not necessarily in that order. Let's just say I'm willing to work with you on both of those."

He hung up and crawled back to the stool, dragging the phone along with him.

"What do you want?" Logner said again, jerking his right arm uselessly against the strap holding it.

"You repeat yourself a lot, don't you, Harold? Here's the deal. I want to know where the girl is."

"What? What do you care? You're a cop killer. I read all about you. The government abandoned you . . . What's Elizabeth Henrich to you?"

"She's not really anything to me. But I've decided to go out on a positive note. Maybe you should consider doing the same. They say confession's good for the soul, you know? Now would be a good time to find out if they're right."

Logner stared directly into Fade's eyes for a long time, his jaw clenched tightly shut, and then, suddenly, he relaxed. Easing back into his pillow, he smiled serenely at the ceiling. "I guess you're not as tough as everyone says you are, eh, Mr. Salam al Fayed? They got you, didn't they? This is all a trick. They're going to give you a break on your sentence and all you have to do is scare me into giving up the girl. Good try. Now why don't you run along and get me a nice cup of hot milk. It's time for my nap."

Fade grinned. "I admire your optimism, Harold, but what are the chances that I'd let a bunch of cops take me alive? Or that they'd even want to?"

The phone at his feet rang again and he picked up. "Yeah?"

"We've talked to both Egan and Karen Manning. They're on their way."

"Great work, Captain. Send them up when they get here. Don't do anything stupid, though, okay? If you just keep cool and sit on your hands for a couple of hours this is going to turn out to be the best day of your life. You have my word."

He replaced the handset and looked down at Logner again. "Now where were we? The girl, right?"

"Fuck you. Get out of my room."

Fade shrugged and pulled a plastic Bic from his pocket. "The lighter or the girl. You've got three seconds to decide. One . . ."

Logner seemed uncertain for a moment and then just looked away, making a show of ignoring Fade, apparently prepared to bet a fair amount that this was all an elaborate plot dreamed up by the police.

"Two . . . Three."

His scream was incredibly piercing—like a little girl's. He thrashed wildly on the bed, arching his back and swinging his broken leg violently back and forth on the cable holding it. Fade stuck a hand over his right ear to block out the noise and used the other to keep the flame against Logner's wrist. When he finally withdrew the lighter, Logner's screams degenerated into choking sobs.

"You should count yourself lucky that I couldn't get a set of pliers through the metal detectors," Fade said, ignoring the phone that had started ringing again. "Now let's try one more time. Where's the girl? Count of three. One . . ."

Logner's eyes shot open. "Stop!"

"Two . . ."

"Wait! She's—"

This time the screams were even louder. He should have brought some cotton balls or something—the guy could shatter glass.

"Okay," Fade said, pulling the lighter away again. "You know the question. One . . ."

"I'll tell you! I'll tell you! Please! You have to stop."

The phone was still ringing and Fade picked up. "Captain?"

"What's happening in there? We heard screams. Is everyone all right?"

"Mr. Logner has something he wants to talk to you about." Fade held the phone up to the man's ear and he whimpered an address in it.

"Did you get that?" Fade said. "You should find the girl there. I've got a TV in here and I'm going to turn it on. When I see her, I'll give myself up."

"I need a doctor," Logner said weakly. "Please, get me a doctor."

Fade covered the phone's mouthpiece. "Shut up."

"We're sending someone right now, Mr. al Fayed. I want you to just calm down and relax. Is there anything I can do for you?"

"Nope. Just get the girl on TV." He reached over and grabbed the fly to Logner's pajamas, ripping it open and holding the lighter beneath his scrotum. "Because if I don't see her in an hour, it's going to get really ugly in here." He watched Logner, who was breathing like a woman in Lamaze class, and began to slowly replace the handset.

"Wait!" Logner shouted.

"Is there something on your mind, Harold? Maybe you got that address confused? Because you should make sure you're remembering it right. It's probably the most important thing you'll ever do."

Logner flailed back and forth for a moment, venting his frustration and pain, then looked over at the phone in Fade's hand. "Let me . . . let me talk to him again."

57

It was quite an operation. At the far end of the corridor, there were two SWAT men crouched behind a steel barrier, rifles trained on a closed door. The one window had been covered with blankets, undoubtedly to keep the press from filming through it and broadcasting what they saw on the television Fade had access to.

The two men having a hushed conversation in the

middle of the hallway didn't seem to notice Egan until he spoke.

"Would one of you be Captain Pickering? I'm Matt." The younger of the two men melted away as the other stuck out his hand.

"Thank you for coming so quickly, Mr. Egan."

"What's going—"

The sound of swinging doors being thrown open drowned him out and he turned to watch Karen Manning burst through them. Her pace faltered a bit when she recognized him.

"I never had a chance to thank you for intervening on my part," Egan said when she got close enough.

"He wasn't going to kill you. He was . . . he was just angry."

Egan nodded and she focused on Pickering. "What's the situation, Captain?"

"You tell me."

"Pardon?"

"Are you going to stand there and say that you didn't put al Fayed up to this?"

She looked down at the floor for a moment, giving the appearance of perfect calm, then suddenly lunged.

While Pickering did seem like kind of an asshole, Egan hadn't been expecting a physical attack and he barely managed to get between them before Karen's hands made contact with the man's throat. She was a hell of a lot stronger than she looked and almost managed to get around Egan before he could drive her back.

406

"If I ever hear even a *hint* in the press that I had something to do with this, my family will do whatever it has to to make sure that you're out of a job and spending your entire life savings fighting lawsuits. Do you understand me, you officious little prick? *Do you?*"

She tried to get by Egan again and he maneuvered behind her, getting his arms around her waist and leaning into her ear. "Relax, Karen. He isn't going to do shit. You've beaten him. You beat all of us."

She seemed to calm down a bit and Egan released her. Pickering was visibly shaken.

"Well, Captain, I think it's safe to say that Karen doesn't have any information on the subject. Maybe you could help us out."

He didn't answer immediately, obviously trying to calculate a way to regain the upper hand, but finally resigned himself to the fact that his momentum was irretrievably stalled. "Al Fayed stormed in here a couple hours ago, gave one of my men a concussion, pulled a gun on two more, then locked himself in Harold Logner's room."

"Why?" Karen said.

"He's torturing him to get information on Elizabeth Henrich's whereabouts."

"What?" she said, looking down the hall at the heavily guarded door. "Why would he do that?"

"We have no idea."

"Is it working?" Egan asked. Pickering glared at him but it seemed like a relevant question.

407

"We've been given an address and we're in the process of following up. No word yet."

Egan let out a long breath and then looked over at Karen. "Are you up for this?"

She nodded.

"Okay, Captain. Call him and tell him we're coming in. And get those men away from the door. I've got enough problems without getting caught in a cross-fire."

"Are you armed?"

"Huh?"

"We don't need anyone taking weapons in there that al Fayed could get his hands on."

Egan laughed. "I'm guessing he's already got your men's guns. But the answer to your question is no. I'm not. Karen?"

"No."

Pickering motioned toward two bulletproof vests lying on the floor.

Egan shook his head. "I'll pass."

"Okay, Fade! Truce, right? If you want to start shooting, I need to go back and get a gun," Egan yelled as the door swung open. The curtains had been pulled and it was dark enough inside that it was hard to make out detail.

"I just don't know how I'd live with myself if I shot your ass," came the answer. Predictably, Fade was up against the wall behind the open door.

Karen pushed by and went in first, obviously not

worried. Egan followed, but a little more cautiously. When he was fully inside, the door slammed closed and Fade shoved a doorstop beneath it.

"You've got to help me," a weak voice behind Egan pleaded. "I've been badly burned. I'm in horrible . . . pain."

"Take a fucking aspirin," Karen said, eyeing Fade's knee as he limped over to a stool and lowered himself carefully onto it.

"What the hell's going on?" she said, nodding toward the quietly sobbing man strapped to the bed. "You told me you didn't care about him or those women. What are you doing here?"

He shrugged. "I got to thinking that maybe I was wrong."

"Please," Logner moaned. "You have to help me . . ."

The unmistakable stench of burned hair and flesh was hanging in the air and Egan walked over to the bed, squinting through the gloom to find a small circle of charred skin on Logner's wrist. "That's it? That's what you're whining about? I've gotten worse making pasta."

"Low threshold for pain," Fade said. "Which is going to turn into a real problem for him if the address he gave the cops is bogus."

"So you're going to just sit here and light parts of him on fire until they find the girl?" Karen said.

"Pretty much. Yeah."

"And after that?"

"I haven't really thought that far ahead. So, how are

things with your wife, Matt?"

Egan sat down in a vinyl easy chair near the base of the bed. "She called me from the road. She and Kali are coming home."

A wide grin spread across Fade's face. "That's great, man. Congratulations."

"Well, we have some things to work out, but I think we'll be okay. I'm not sure yet how living with everything out in the open like this is going to work. Who knew it would be possible for our relationship to get any more complicated?"

"Complicated's okay. And besides, now you're rich. I hear the stores can't keep her records on the shelves."

Egan let out a quiet snort. "We haven't really talked about it, but I can pretty much guarantee that she sees this as blood money and it's all going to go to save some endangered African snail or something."

"Can I make a suggestion?"

"Go ahead."

"You probably shouldn't point out that all that money just ends up in the pockets of gun dealers and Swiss bankers."

"Don't worry. I've learned my lesson."

"Uh, excuse me," Karen interrupted. "Could we focus for a minute on the fact that you've barricaded yourself in a fifteen-by-fifteen room surrounded by a bunch of very motivated police snipers."

Fade shook his head slowly. "She's so practical. And kind of a badass. How can you not love her?"

"Fade, I'm serious . . ."

"And what about you, Karen?" he said. "Has Daddy managed to make everything all better?"

She frowned at his wording but then just shrugged. "Yeah, I guess he has. It turns out that there's almost nothing an army of lawyers, publicity people, and politicians can't accomplish. I'm going to be on Larry King tomorrow night." Her voice seemed to lose its strength and she looked down at the floor. "You should watch it."

"Maybe I will."

The silence that ensued lasted almost a minute.

"Jesus," Fade said finally, standing and hobbling around the room. "I brought you two here because you're my only real friends in the world. This was supposed to be fun."

"Hillel wanted to send a cake," Egan said.

Fade laughed. "And how is that piece of shit? I gotta tell you, I really regret not having an opportunity to put a bullet through his skull."

"Doesn't really matter. He's fucked. Actually, he's in jail right now. If you play your cards right, maybe you two could be cellmates."

"Yeah, right. Somehow I don't think they're looking to put me in one of those country club places."

"It's not a country club, Fade. Just plain old jail. Crenshaw blew a gasket when all this came out. He says he's going to personally make sure Strand ends up in a maximum-security prison for the rest of his life. And you know the general. What he wants, he gets."

Fade nodded and kept limping around the room for no apparent reason, seeming to become more detached and distant with every awkward movement. Finally, he dug into a backpack and pulled out a large Ziploc full of neatly bundled hundred-dollar bills.

"The rest of my money," he said, tossing it to Karen. "It's not much, but why don't you split it up between the families of those guys I killed. There's also a disk in there—the very last installment of SWATKILLER. Maybe you could post it for me."

"Fade. I . . ."

"And I want you to go by my shop. That hope chest is still there waiting for you. Fill it up for when you find that guy who's secure enough to marry you."

She didn't answer and it was too dark for Egan to make out her expression clearly, but he could see her wipe a sleeve across both cheeks.

"These are for Elise," Fade said, tossing Egan a set of car keys. "A woman like that shouldn't have to drive around in a minivan. You might want to take it to a mechanic and have a little work done before you give it to her, though . . ."

Egan opened his mouth to speak, but was interrupted by the ringing of the phone. Fade limped excitedly toward it and picked up. "Hello?"

He jabbed a finger toward the TV and Karen turned it on, flipping channels until she landed on one depicting a young woman wrapped in a blanket and surrounded by police. One of the cops stepped aside, allowing the camera to focus on her face.

Fade covered the phone's mouthpiece. "Is that her?"

Karen rose to her tiptoes, examined the screen for a moment and then nodded.

"Now you have her!" Logner screamed. "I need a doctor! Get me a doctor!"

"I thought I told you to shut up," Fade said, replacing the handset and pulling a gun from his waistband. Karen jumped for his hand, making contact a split second after a bullet slammed into Logner's chest. Egan didn't move as she shoved Fade back hard enough to nearly topple him.

"What the hell was that?" she shouted, running up to the bed and looking down at the bleeding hole in Logner's breast bone. Egan pushed himself up on the arms of his chair to get a better angle, but then settled back into the cushion when it became clear that Logner hadn't survived.

Karen came to the same conclusion a moment later and turned back toward Fade just as the phone started ringing. "What were you thinking? You just killed a helpless man tied to a bed! Are you crazy? How is this going to help your case?"

He shrugged, the simple motion seeming to take nearly all his strength. "Not the worst thing I've ever done, huh, Matt?"

Egan didn't answer, instead, concentrating on Fade as he wandered across the room and stopped in front of the window.

"Kind of dreary in here," he said, reaching for the

closed curtains and throwing them open. "Maybe a little light . . ."

Even with everything he knew about her, Egan still underestimated how quickly Karen could react. He threw himself out of the chair and barely managed to get hold of her and drag her to the floor.

She was still thrashing wildly when the first round hit Fade between his chest and right shoulder. Egan pressed his face into her back and forced her head down as the air filled with shattered glass. A thick-sounding thud that seemed to shake the room marked the impact of the second round. When Egan looked up again, Fade was falling backward, eyes closed and arms spread wide.

Karen managed to swing an elbow at Egan's head and he was forced to release her in order to dodge it. She crawled forward, ignoring the glass cutting her knees, and dragged Fade from the snipers' line of fire. For a moment she tried to stop the bleeding, but then just fell back against the wall.

Egan went back to his chair and put his head in his hands, taking deep, measured breaths. When he finally looked up again, Karen was staring at him with eyes full of tears and accusation.

He shook his head meaninglessly. "How did you want him to die?"

EPILOGUE

...nal Entry

Looking back, I think a lot of the things I've done were wrong. I hope the fact that I believed in them— that I believed I was helping—will make people remember me more fondly than maybe I deserve.

I wish there had been time to balance the scales. But there just wasn't.

—Salam al Fayed

Center Point Publishing

600 Brooks Road • PO Box 1
Thorndike ME 04986-0001 USA

(207) 568-3717

US & Canada:
1 800 929-9108

SV

Fi